CHAOS OF THE GODS

DONOVAN COOK

First paperback edition September 2022

Cover design by Rafael Andres

ISBN 978-1-8383008-4-5 (paperback)
ISBN 978-1-8383008-5-2 (eBook)

www.donovancook.net

To my parents,
who have always supported all of my ventures,
no matter how bizarre.

CONTENTS

CHAPTER 1

The gods were angry. Ulf didn't need to see the dark clouds forming in the sky to know. Neither did he need to see the birds disappearing over the horizon. He didn't need to hear the rumbling of Thor's displeasure or feel the rocking of the ship as Ran's fury came to the surface. Ulf felt it in the air. He knew what was about to happen before the first raindrop fell from the sky. The gods were angry, and they were going to pay for it.

"It's the Kraken!" the shrill voice screamed over the roaring wind.

Ulf turned to the sound of the voice, his blood frozen in his veins at the thought of seeing the giant squid-like monster from the deep. Lightning flashed, illuminating everything around him. Ulf didn't see the Kraken, but what he saw wasn't much better. Rain lashed down as enormous waves crashed over them. The black-and-white striped sail of the Sae-Ulfr strained in the wind, pulling the ship through the billowing waves. Thunder rolled through the sky as more lightning flashed nearby, so close, Ulf could reach out and touch it. The men of the Sae-Ulfr were tossed across the deck as a gigantic wave threw the ship into the air. Ulf lost grip of the rope he had been holding on to as the ship came crashing down. His shoulder screamed as he fell between two chests. Ulf was sure the deep cut he had received from the fight in Rouen was bleeding again. Another wave crashed over Ulf, choking him with the salty water.

"The sail!" Snorri roared, trying hard to be heard over the storm. His long light-coloured hair, usually kept tidy and braided, was plastered to his face. Men rushed past the huge slumping form of Drumbr as they grabbed hold of the ropes tied to the sail. They grit their teeth and strained as they struggled to reef the sail, the strong winds overpowering them. Ulf tried to get up, wanting to help, but another wave struck the side of the ship. It sent him rolling across the deck and crashing into a chest on the other side.

"Hold on tight, you bastard!" Thorbjorn screamed as he grabbed hold of Ulf's brynja. The short warrior hunkered down by his chest, using his stocky frame to keep him in place. Ulf nodded and saw his friend smile through his bushy beard. "That mad bastard will drown us all one day!" Thorbjorn pointed towards Rolf Tree-Foot at the stern of the ship. The greybeard with his wooden leg was standing by the rudder, laughing into the wind as he kept the Sae-Ulfr under control. But as Ulf and Thorbjorn watched, a giant wave swept over Rolf, plucking him from the ship like a giant hand. "Ran's tits!" Thorbjorn's eyes were as wide as Ulf's. No one else seemed aware that their steersman was gone, and Ulf thought he could hear the gods laughing in the storm. Snorri was too busy helping with the sail, while the others were sheltering from the storm. Drumbr was still sitting by the mast, holding on to the body of his brother who had been sent to Valhalla. Drumbr was taller than all but Oddi and was almost as round as he was tall. His name was Brak, like his brother and his father, but everyone called him Drumbr, which meant fat.

Ulf jumped to his feet and rushed towards the rear of the ship. Another wave crashed over him, sending him into the men struggling to pull up the sail.

"Careful!" One of them turned, ready to push him out of the way until he realised it was Ulf. The man shook his head and grabbed hold of the rope as Ulf struggled to his feet, his body hurting all over. He wasn't sure if it was from the battle at Rouen or from Ran venting the gods' anger at them. They had fled from a battle, the mighty Norse warriors running away from a fight with their tails between their legs. Ulf pushed the thoughts from his head as he reached the stern and grabbed hold of the rudder. He grit his teeth against the pain in his shoulder and pulled the rudder, trying to control the Sae-Ulfr. But Snorri's ship was not ready yet for a new master. She still mourned the loss of Rolf and refused to obey Ulf as she crashed through the white-capped waves, sending men and chests rolling across her deck. Ulf screamed as he pulled harder, not sure of what to do or why he grabbed the rudder. He was no sailor, he had no experience with these things, but the men who did were too busy to understand the danger they were in. Ulf thought he heard the cry of an eagle over the thunder. He looked up and saw nothing but dark clouds and lightning above him. There was no way an eagle would be flying in this storm, unless... Odin. Ulf scanned the sky as he struggled to control the ship, worried by the presence of the All-Father. He didn't notice the giant wave in front of them until the Sae-Ulfr was thrown into the air once more. As she crashed down into the sea, the rudder jerked in his hands and struck him in the cut he received in his side from Ubba. Bile rose from Ulf's stomach as the pain shot through his body. Ulf collapsed, clutching his side and forgetting about the rudder. Men screamed as the ship rolled, bringing Ulf back to his senses. He tried to get up, but lost his balance as another wave washed over him. Lightning flashed as he grabbed hold of the rudder again and struggled to his feet. But before Ulf could manage, a wave hit the side of the ship. The Sae-Ulfr turned with it, and before Ulf knew what was happening, the rudder twisted out of his grip and struck him in the head. The screams of the crew faded, and the last thing Ulf heard was the cry of an eagle before everything went black.

*

"Think he's still alive?" The voice dragged Ulf out of the darkness. That and something kicking his leg. Ulf groaned, wishing that whoever it was would leave him alone. Alone in the darkness where he didn't feel the pain.

"Aye, he is still alive." Ulf recognised the voice and knew it spoke the truth. He was still alive. "The gods aren't ready to kill him yet."

"I wish they would." Ulf groaned as the voices laughed at him. Waves broke against the side of the ship, their rhythm in line with the pounding in his head, although Ulf didn't understand why it hurt so much. He understood the pain in his shoulder, the fire from it burning into his chest and the sting in his side. But the pain in his head was a mystery to him. Ulf prodded his skull with his fingers and felt the cut above his left eye where Griml had struck him and the lump above it. The lump was new and probably explained why his head hurt so much.

Heavy footsteps came towards him, the vibrations from the deck not helping his head. "The pup's still alive?" Ulf recognised Ragnar Nine-Finger, the champion of Snorri's father and one of the fiercest warriors in Norway. Ragnar was half a head taller than Ulf, broad-shouldered and thick-limbed. He had a barrel-like chest and narrow waist and liked to keep his red hair loose. As his byname suggested, Ragnar only had nine fingers. The little finger on his left hand was missing, and Ulf had heard many different stories about how that had happened.

"Aye, he is," Snorri responded, kicking Ulf's leg again as if he was making sure. He was as tall as Ulf but broader at the chest and shoulders, having lived a life of luxury and constant warfare. His light-coloured beard, with a thick braid in the centre, came down to the bottom of his neck.

"What was he doing with the rudder, anyway?" Ragnar asked with a sneer. Although Ulf didn't care, he just wanted to go back to the darkness. There was no pain in the darkness. Only the sounds of the waves and the gods laughing at him.

"A wave took Rolf," Thorbjorn explained. He was shorter than most men, something his friends always made fun of, but was one of the fiercest warriors Ulf knew. Thorbjorn had a neck thicker than his head and a barrel-like frame with thick limbs. The sides of his head were shaved and tattooed with a bear on the right and a wolf on the left, leaving only the long hair on the top, which he always kept braided and tied. Violent eyes sat over a large nose and his face was heavily scarred.

"Aye, I guess Ran wanted her old lover back," Snorri said, the sadness in his voice clear to all. There was silence for a while, the only noises being the waves and the birds flying above them, mocking them with their cries.

"The old bastard is back with his mistress. There's no point crying over it," Ragnar said and walked away.

Snorri kicked Ulf again. "Come on, we have a lot to do." Ulf tried to turn onto his back, but as he pushed himself over with his left arm, his shoulder gave way, sending more pain into his chest. Ulf cried out before collapsing.

"Steady now." Thorbjorn helped him onto his back.

Ulf squinted in the blinding sunlight. He was only eighteen winters old, but was taller than most men, his body more athletic than muscular. Ulf had long, light-coloured hair, with three thin braids on top of his head, and a short beard. Three thin scar lines ran down the right side of his face, from his eye to his mouth, given to him by an enormous bear he fought the previous summer. Although his face was not disfigured, he was still uncomfortable to look at. The left side of his face was still swollen from his fight with Griml, but his right eye was slowly adjusting to the world around him. The first thing he saw was the rudder above his head, the sight of it sending bile into his throat. He looked away, not wanting to see the cause of his pain. Ulf's heart sank at the devastation around him. The Sae-Ulfr was stranded on the beach, broken.

She was tilting to her side, not enough to fall over but enough to make it awkward for the men. Her mast was broken, the splintered stump reminding Ulf of the spear that had stuck in his side so long ago. Sea chests were scattered all over the deck, some knocked over and their contents spilt. To one side, men leaned against her hull, some of them nursing injuries while others walked around, trying to clear the mess from the storm. Oddi limped around as he directed men, his brother sitting with the injured, his face as white as the few clouds above them. Oddi was taller than them all, had narrow shoulders, but a muscular frame and long arms. He had light red hair and a thin beard which reached his chest. Thorbjorn knelt beside Ulf and handed him a flask with water. Ulf took it and started drinking carefully before gulping it all down.

Snorri stood above them, surveying the land. The beach they were stranded on was flat, the waves shallow as they lapped over the pale sand. Sand dunes topped with grass met the beach and obscured the land in the distance. Only the gods knew what lay beyond the dunes. A wide river made its way to the sea not far from where the Sae-Ulfr lay, a source of fresh water which hinted that there might be villages nearby.

"Where are we?" Ulf managed after another cup of water. "And where's Tormod?" There was no sign of the king's man, sent to watch them, or his ship.

"Odin knows, I wish I knew where we are or where Tormod is." Snorri looked down at him with knitted brows. "That storm could have taken us anywhere."

"Came out of nowhere." Thorbjorn shook his head. "Thought we'd all be on our way to Ran's Hall."

Snorri nodded his agreement. "Aye, I pray to Odin that is not where Tormod is with his crew."

"The gods send that storm," Ulf said before he could stop himself. He saw the alarm on the faces of his friends.

"Why do you say that?" Snorri asked.

There was no point in staying quiet now. "They're angry with us."

"Because we ran from the fight?"

Ulf only shrugged. The gods were difficult to understand. Perhaps they just wanted to amuse themselves.

"Doesn't matter now," Snorri responded, his voice breaking as he looked at the Sae-Ulfr. "We need to find out where we are and fix my ship." With that, he turned and walked away.

Ulf tried to get up, groaning from the pain.

"You sure?" Thorbjorn offered a hand. Ulf nodded and accepted Thorbjorn's help, but regretted it as soon as he got to his knees. The world around Ulf spun violently, and the bile rushed up from his stomach before he could do anything about it. "My boots!" Thorbjorn complained before Ulf slipped back into the darkness.

*

The men stood strong as they glared at the enemy from over the rims of their shields. Sword and axes ready, they waited for the attack they knew would come. Faces grim, they prepared to face their fate. These men knew they were not in

8

control of their destinies. The three sisters who dwelled beneath the tree of life were. The Norns. And for a reason these men did not understand, the Norns had brought them here. But they did not care about that. Their leader, a tall warrior with light-coloured hair, stepped forward, raising his sword to the sky and calling to the All-Father as he summoned the courage of his men.

Wild creatures erupted from the hills, charging at the men as they cried their own war cry. These men did not understand the words shouted, but they did not care. All they cared about was protecting what was theirs. Soaring above the warriors, he watched as they locked their shields together. He wanted to be there with them. That was his place. But no matter how hard he tried, he could not get there. Instead, all he could do was watch as the wild creatures crashed against the shield wall of his brothers. The men called to the gods, the wild creatures cried to their own. Sword and axe struck their shields as the men grunted, determined not to be pushed back. Blood sprayed through the air as limbs were chopped off and skulls were crushed. Men and wild creatures roared to summon their strength or cried in pain as they begged to die. And still, all he could do was watch.

But there was a new presence, one he didn't feel before. One closer to him than the others. He turned his head and saw the giant wolf lying on the beach as it nursed its wound. On its back, he saw another man, a young warrior with a scarred face. One he knew better than the rest. And rushing at this warrior was a wild creature. It must have slipped past the shield wall. He knew he had to help, but still could not go down. All he could do was soar above them, helpless. But he wasn't. There was still one thing he could do. He sucked air deep into his chest as he turned towards the stricken warrior and screamed as loud as he could.

Ulf woke to the sounds of men screaming and weapons striking shields. He tried to pull himself up into a sitting position, his vision still blurry. His back was stiff, which meant he must have been out for a while. Ulf wondered at the sounds of fighting when he heard an eagle cry above him. Its piercing scream brought his eyes into focus in time to see a shadow standing above him, spear in hand. He rolled out of the way as the spear stuck into the deck of the Sae-Ulfr. But before he could do anything else, rough hands grabbed him and pulled him to his feet. Ulf's world spun like a whirlwind, the bile threatening to rise again. He lost his balance and tried to grab hold of the gunwale, but missed and collapsed, dragging whoever was holding him with. They fell over the side of the ship, landing in the shallow water of the beach. Ulf's attacker responded first and was on top of him in a blink, and forced his head under the water. Seawater burnt Ulf's throat and nostrils as he choked on it. Thrashing wildly, he tried to free himself, but the man was too heavy. The hand around his neck pulled his face out of the water, and as Ulf sucked in the air, he was punched. Blinding pain shot through his skull, and before Ulf could do anything about it, his head was shoved under again. He choked on more seawater, unable to stop himself from swallowing it. Desperate to find a way out, Ulf prayed to his ancestors for help. But the voices in his head remained quiet, and Ulf panicked until his hand fell on the sax-knife in his belt. Ulf pulled it out of its scabbard and stabbed up. The blade caught on a rib, but he was too weak to force it past. Another punch landed on his face, the water taking some of the force out of it, but it still hurt him. He pulled the sax-knife back and stabbed again, this time aiming lower. The body on top of him shuddered as the blade slid in under his ribs and into his gut. Ulf twisted the blade before he pulled it out and stabbed, again and again, as the body on top of him grew heavier. He stabbed one more time and felt the body tense before it collapsed on top of him. Summoning the last of his strength, Ulf rolled the body off him and sat up, sucking in mouthfuls of air as he vomited up seawater.

Ulf frowned at the chaos around him as he struggled to his feet. Before he could make sense of what was going on, another man rushed at him with an axe held high and screaming in a language Ulf did not understand. Ulf swayed out of the way of the strike, but his attacker crashed into him, sending Ulf back into the water. Ulf rolled over immediately and ended on top of his attacker. He palmed the man's face down and stabbed him in the throat. Blood mixed with the seawater as his attacker squirmed underneath him. Ulf pulled the sax-knife free and was about to stab down again when someone grabbed hold of his long hair and pulled his head back. Ulf had no strength left to fight what he knew was coming. His limbs were suddenly heavy, his breath ragged as he closed his eyes and waited for the killing blow. Warm blood sprayed over his face and, surprised at not feeling any pain, Ulf opened his eyes, only to see Ragnar in front of him, his sword dripping with blood.

"Don't look so surprised, pup." Ragnar sneered as he spat into the water. "We need all the men we have, so you have no time to die now." Before Ulf could respond, Ragnar turned and ran back towards the fight. The shield wall had broken up, and most of the men were fighting in small groups. Ragnar was running towards Snorri and his hirdmen, decapitating one of their attackers on the way. To Ulf's surprise, Magni was also there, fighting beside his younger brother. None of the Norsemen wore any helmets, and a few were without armour, which told Ulf they had been caught by surprise. Ulf looked around him and spotted the axe of the man he had just killed lying in the surf. Nausea hit him as he bent over to pick it up, but Ulf ignored it. The men of the Sae-Ulfr were fighting for their lives, and he wasn't going to sit around. He picked up the axe and stumbled to his friends, swaying as he struggled through the shallow water. But before Ulf got there, he heard a new noise. One that pierced the sounds of the fighting. Ulf looked in the direction the noise was coming from and almost dropped the axe. More men rushed over the sand dunes. The new attackers were dressed similarly to the ones they were fighting, and Ulf thought they must have been reinforcements. He saw the Norsemen thought the same. Shoulders sagged as many realised they would die this day. Some men rubbed the Mjöllnir pendants around their necks, no doubt praying to the gods, while others turned and faced the new threat. His friends did the same and were about to rush to them when something unexpected happened.

The men they were fighting turned and fled.

CHAPTER 2

Snorri turned towards the newcomers and watched them through the strands of his light-coloured hair as sweat stung his eyes. He sucked in huge gulps of air, exhausted like the men who formed up around him, but he was not ready to give up. Gripping his sword tightly, Snorri raised his shield in front of him and waited for the new force to attack. But instead of charging at them, they turned and ran after the scavengers who fled over the dunes.

"What in Odin's name…?" Thorbjorn asked, the sides of his shaved head glistening with sweat.

Snorri shrugged. He did not understand either, but was glad for the respite. It gave him a chance to assess his men. His hirdmen stood around him. Thorbjorn, with his short stocky frame to his right. Oddi was to his left, his red hair plastered over his face. Asbjorn was there as well, gripping his sword as he sucked in deep breaths, and beside him stood Drumbr, his eyes red. Snorri knew it was because of the death of his brother, Brak, who had been one of Snorri's hirdmen for more winters than he could count. Snorri had not yet had the time to feel that loss. Or the pain of betrayal from a man he had thought a friend. Ubba the White. A man who had welcomed them with open arms when they had joined his fleet to raid Francia at the behest of King Halfdan the Black. That raid had been a disaster for Snorri and the men of Thorgilsstad. Constant ambushes had left the Norsemen not knowing who to trust. Ubba had come to them as a friend, offering to help them find those responsible. But as they attacked Rouen, a large city on the west coast of Francia, Ubba revealed himself to be the treacherous snake behind everything. Snorri's biggest regret from that was that he wasn't the one who got to kill Ubba. That pleasure went to Ulf.

Snorri looked around and saw that his friend was not amongst his hirdmen. Ragnar Nine-Finger was there, his dark eyes glaring at the dunes from under his flame-red hair. Magni, Oddi's older and taller brother, was there as well. Magni's father had sent him with them, wanting his oldest to learn how to raid after spending most of his life in luxury, drinking ale and sleeping with thralls. But Magni had proven that he was a capable warrior and had survived where some of Snorri's best men had fallen. "Where's Ulf?"

His men shrugged, and Snorri felt the dread creeping up his spine.

"The pup is fine." Ragnar thumbed over his shoulder towards Snorri's broken ship where Ulf was hobbling towards them, his face pale and bruised.

"Snorri," Thorbjorn called, pointing at the dunes as the second group of attackers returned.

"Skjaldborg!" Snorri ordered out of instinct and felt the satisfaction as his men reacted instantly. Snorri studied the group as they came closer. They outnumbered his men, but most of the newcomers were greybeards and the rest were boys barely old enough to grow beards. They wore no armour, not even helmets, and most of the weapons looked as old as the men holding them. All the men wore drab-coloured tunics and trousers that only went to their knees. Their lower legs were covered with strips of cloth which were tied together with leather laces. "Francia," Snorri said, remembering the clothing worn by the men of Hammaburg and Rouen.

"Aye, the storm must have blown us back onto her shore," Oddi responded.

The Franks stopped a short distance away from the Norse shield wall, their spears wavering. Snorri saw the uncertainty in their eyes and the way the young men bit their lower lips. He knew then that if it came to a fight, then his men would win. But Snorri would lose more men, of that he was certain. He grit his teeth, his men around him waiting silently for his order. A commotion amongst the Franks caught Snorri's attention, and he raised an eyebrow when a broad-shouldered Frank limped forward and stopped a few paces away from them with a lobsided smile on his scarred face. He held his sword, its sharp edge glinting in the sun, like he was born with it in his hand. Snorri recognised a warrior when he saw one, but the man's limp and grey hair showed he had not fought a battle in many winters.

The Frankish warrior stood there, as calm as the water behind them, and studied the Norsemen growling in front of him as if he was admiring a stud bull. He said something to the men behind him and they responded with nervous laughter.

"Let me kill the bastard." Ragnar was about to take a step forward when Snorri stopped him.

"No, I think he wants to talk." Snorri was taken aback by the audacity of the Frank who showed no fear of them, unlike the men behind him who were trembling. He lowered his shield and walked towards the man. Behind him, there was a rattling and a thunk as his men closed the gap in the shield wall. Snorri stopped in front of the Frank, close enough to see the sharpness and amusement in his brown eyes. There was a deep scar in his moustache which ran from his lip to his cheek. Waves lapped on the beach and seabirds cried out above them as the two men stared at each other, their companions silent. The Frank smiled broadly, revealing a mouth with a few broken teeth and one missing below the scar, before sheathing his sword. Snorri raised an eyebrow as he tried to understand what this Frank was up to. He glanced at the men behind him, their nervousness in stark contrast to their leader. Snorri saw no threat from them, but he was still uncertain. Francia had proven to be a treacherous place for them so far, and Snorri couldn't help but wonder if this was another trap. He glanced at the dunes, but saw no sign of the men who had attacked them. He wanted to look at his men behind him, but didn't want to seem weak in front of the Franks. The Frank in front of him waited patiently, still smiling as if he was talking to a long-time friend. In the end, Snorri decided to take a chance. *Trust the Norns*, he looked at his sword, Tyr's Fury. She was covered in blood, so he did not want to sheathe her. Instead, he stuck her into the sand by his feet. The men behind the Frank seemed to relax a little and the old warrior's smile grew bigger. Behind him, Snorri heard his men hiss, the uncertainty of the situation making them nervous.

The Frank asked Snorri a question in his language and then laughed when Snorri frowned. Again, he said something to the men behind him, who laughed more freely now. The Frank shrugged and walked back to his men, turning his back on the Norsemen without a thought.

Snorri couldn't help but smile as Thorbjorn commented behind him, "Must have balls as big as Thor's, that man."

"He doesn't follow Thor, so they'll be as big as his own god's," Oddi responded, unable to help himself.

"Well, I don't know how big their god's balls are!" Thorbjorn retorted.

"But you know how big Thor's are?" Ragnar asked, which made some men laugh.

"Quiet!" Snorri glanced at his men and noticed Thorbjorn's red face from behind his shield. Turning his attention back to the Franks, he saw the old warrior say something to a young man, who nodded before sprinting off in the direction they came from.

"What are they doing?" Magni asked. Unlike before, Snorri's men didn't mock him. Magni had earned his right to be amongst them.

"Only the Norns will know." Snorri watched as the Frankish warrior sat down on the beach and pulled an apple from his pouch. He rubbed it on his tunic and took a bite, the crunching sound echoing around them. The Frank looked at Snorri and offered him the apple. Snorri shook his head before pulling his sword out of the sand and walking back to his men. He fought the urge to tense his shoulders as he walked with his back to his enemy, but if the Frank could do it, then so would he.

"Well, they're not going to tell us." Ragnar glared at the Franks, almost like he wanted them to attack.

"Aye, so we'll just have to wait." Snorri scanned the dunes. He grabbed one of his men. "Sven, watch those dunes. Blow your horn if you see anything." Sven nodded and walked off to find a spot that would give him a good view of the sand dunes. "Geir," Snorri called the young warrior who was always trying hard to become one of Snorri's hirdmen, "watch those bastards. Let me know if they do anything." Snorri nodded towards the Franks, most of whom had sat down, their old legs not able to stand much longer. Geir nodded and made himself comfortable as Snorri walked towards his broken ship.

"I'll see to the injured men," Oddi offered, and left without Snorri having to respond.

Ragnar caught up to Snorri. "What do we do now?"

"We wait."

*

Ulf grunted as he sat down, his legs too weak to support his body for much longer. The pounding in his skull made him want to close his eyes and block out the bright sunlight, while his throat and nose burnt from the seawater. But Ulf knew he couldn't close his eyes and sleep. Not when the threat of another attack was still there. He just survived the last one and if it hadn't been for Ragnar, he might not have done.

Ulf had watched with uncertainty as Snorri stepped out of the shield wall and faced the old warrior, the silence between them even reaching him. He wanted to get to the wall to stand with his shield brothers, but his body could not get him there. He bit his lip as the two of them stared at each other. But then the old warrior walked back to his men and started chewing on an apple. With relief, he dropped the axe and sat down where he was, watching as Snorri spoke to his men. Oddi broke off from the group and came towards him, pointing at the other men as he gave them orders.

"What's going on?" Ulf asked as Oddi reached him.

"We're waiting." Oddi studied the cut above Ulf's left eye and then prodded Ulf's head where the tiller had struck him. Ulf winced at the pain. "Don't think it cracked your skull, but wearing a helmet will be uncomfortable for a while." Oddi looked at the broken links of Ulf's brynja on his shoulder as Ulf watched Drumbr walking back to the Sae-Ulfr, his head hanging low.

"I should go talk to him," Ulf said, trying to get up.

Oddi stopped him by putting a hand on his shoulder. "Why?"

Ulf swallowed, not wanting to say the words, but he knew he had to. "Brak died because of me."

"Brak died because a spear went through him."

"But…"

"Did you throw the spear, Ulf?" Oddi's eyes bore into him.

Ulf squirmed. "If it wasn't for me, then we would not have been in Francia and Brak would still have been alive." Ulf winced as Oddi pulled his brynja off to get a better look at the cut on his shoulder.

"If it wasn't for you, then Brak would have died somewhere else." Oddi sighed when he saw the shock on Ulf's face. "Ulf, we are warriors and like all warriors, Brak would not have wanted to die an old man in his bed. We all accept that there will be a day when the Norns decide it is our time to join Odin's Einherjar."

"Oddi's right," Snorri said as he sat down beside Ulf, surprising them both. Snorri found a flask lying in the sand and, after picking it up, opened it and sniffed the contents. He swilled his mouth and spat out the fluid before gulping most of it down. Snorri smacked his lips and offered the flask to Ulf and Oddi, both declining. "The Norns decided it was time for Brak to go to Valhalla, so if we weren't here, then he would have died in some other battle." Ulf saw the moistness in Snorri's eyes. "I've known both brothers since I was a child and they've fought beside me for many winters. Losing Brak hurts more than I can describe, but right now, we cannot dwell on that." Ulf frowned, and so Snorri tried a different tactic. "Look around you, Ulf." Snorri swept his arm over the beach, where the Norsemen were scattered. Some were collecting the bodies that had washed ashore with the ship, men who had died during the storm, and those who died fighting the scavengers. Seabirds and ravens filled the sky above them, screaming at the men as if telling them to hurry so they could feast. Other men were collecting their belongings strewn all over the sand and carrying them to a pile near the Sae-Ulfr. Ragnar and Thorbjorn stood over the pile, arms crossed and faces stern, while Magni sat and spoke to the few men his father had sent with him. Few of them had survived, and Ulf wondered how Oddi and Magni's father would feel about it. He was a minor jarl whose hall was across the bay from Thorgilsstad and a kinsman of Snorri's father. Other men sat on the sand, nursing their wounds or those of their friends, much like Oddi was doing with Ulf. "Most of these men will never grow grey beards. They'll either die here in Francia," Ulf scowled - he had not realised they were still in Francia, "or in some other land." Snorri's shoulders slumped as he said this. Snorri cared for his men and, to admit that most of them would die, could not have been easy for him. "And I need to get them home, so we cannot sit and grieve for Brak. Not yet."

Ulf nodded. He guessed he understood and thanked the gods he was not in Snorri's position.

"Aye, we're not all protected by Odin like you," Oddi said as he took the flask from Snorri and poured its contents over Ulf's shoulder wound. Ulf grit his teeth as it stung, but he did not respond. He had made an oath to Odin that he would avenge his family and until that oath was fulfilled, Odin would not let him die. He looked at Drumbr, who sat on the Sae-Ulfr, his body slumped and remembered what the Volva had told him in Ubba's tent before she had freed him.

You belong to the gods.

21

CHAPTER 3

"Something's happening," Thorbjorn said.

Ulf opened his eyes and saw the Franks were stirring. He had fallen asleep while they waited, and when Ulf glanced at the sun, he realised it had moved quite a bit since the fight. The tide had also moved out, leaving the Sae-Ulfr stranded on the sand, with Drumbr hunched over on her deck. The rest of Snorri's hirdmen sat around Ulf, with Ragnar and Magni also there.

"Must be someone important," Ragnar said as Ulf turned back to the Franks. They parted as a young man led a horse-drawn cart down the dune. On top of the cart sat another man, a cloak wrapped around his body, even though it was still warm.

Snorri got to his feet, sheathing Tyr's Fury which he had been cleaning. "Let's find out." He walked towards the Franks as the rest of the Norsemen got to their feet. Oddi turned to Ulf as he tried to get up.

"You need to rest."

"I've had enough rest." Ulf held his hand up for help.

Thorbjorn pulled Ulf to his feet. "The Bear-Slayer's fine."

Ulf swayed a bit and caught the skewed glance from Oddi, but soon steadied himself. His shoulder was numb from the cut and his stomach smarted. But at least his headache was better. With a deep breath, Ulf followed Snorri's hirdmen, eager to see who this newcomer was.

He arrived as the young Frank helped the man off the cart. It was an old man, not much older than the warrior Snorri spoke to before, but certainly softer. Whoever he was, he led a comfortable life. His hair was grey under his cap, and his moustache long. The man looked around, running his dull eyes over the Norse warriors. He frowned as he asked the old warrior a question. The warrior responded by pointing at Snorri. Around Ulf, the Norsemen muttered to each other, all of them curious about what was happening, but Snorri's hirdmen kept quiet and so did Ulf. Drumbr appeared from behind them, his face tear-streaked and grim. The old Frank glanced at him before approaching Snorri.

"You…" the Frank scowled as he thought of the word, "… jarl?" He smiled a merchant smile. The same one Ulf had seen the merchants in Suðrikaupstefna use.

Snorri glanced at Ragnar, who shrugged, before responding, "No, not a jarl, but I am the leader of these men."

"Leader?" The old Frank struggled with the word. He glanced at the old warrior beside him, but the man said nothing. From what Snorri had told Ulf, this man did not speak Norse.

Snorri waved his arm over his men. "These are my men," he pointed to the broken Sae-Ulfr and hesitated for a heartbeat, "that is my ship."

The old Frank nodded as if he understood and then stared at Snorri's ship. "Ship break."

"Aye, ship break," Snorri said with a sigh. The old Frank scrutinised Snorri some more while glancing at the ship and the bodies of Snorri's men lying next to it. Seabirds and ravens flocked over the bodies while a few of Snorri's younger men shouted at the birds as they tried to keep them at bay.

"Should just kill the bastards and be done with it," Ragnar growled, his frustration threatening to bowl over.

"Aye," Thorbjorn agreed with a curled lip.

But Snorri did not respond as he stared at the Frank. The Frankish men were getting restless. One of them said something that none of the Norsemen understood, but from his tone, it did not sound friendly. Others agreed with him and soon most of the greybeards were talking, all of them shouting at the old man who stood in front of Snorri. The Norse warriors felt uneasy, most of them grabbing the hilts of their weapons. The sudden tension in the air chased the seabirds away and Ulf felt his headache getting worse again. But the old man paid them no attention, and it was a shout from the old warrior that quietened the Frankish men. Ulf saw they were unhappy and couldn't help but glance at Snorri's men. Most of them had injuries, like him, while the rest looked tired.

"We trade," the old frank said at last, smiling his merchant smile again.

"Trade?" Snorri raised an eyebrow.

"Yes, trade."

Snorri glanced at his men, all of them shrugging. "Trade what?"

The old Frank pointed at Snorri's ship and then at Snorri and his men. Snorri frowned, and Ulf felt his headache beating in his head as he tried to understand what was going on. He hoped that whatever the Franks wanted, they would get to it soon because his legs were starting to weaken and he had to fight the urge to sit down.

"You're not taking my ship," Snorri growled and if by some hidden signal, his men took a step forward, their hands on their weapons still. Ulf's hand went to his side, but then he realised he didn't have either of his weapons with him. He prayed to Odin they were still on the ship.

The old Frank raised his hands as he took a step back, the rest of the Franks trembling behind him. "Not want ship," he blurted. "Want help you."

"Help us how?" Ragnar growled, his nostrils flared. The old man paled and glanced at the old warrior beside him.

"Ragnar," Snorri said, his voice as calm as the water lapping on the beach behind them. Ragnar glanced at Snorri, but said nothing. "Help us how?" Snorri repeated the question.

The old Frank glanced at the warrior beside him again. "Fix ship. We plenty wood. We help fix ship." He pointed at the Sae-Ulfr again as she lay on the beach with her mast broken and a few of the side planks shattered in her hull.

"They want to help fix the Sae-Ulfr," Oddi said, stroking his beard.

"We understood, Oddi Viss." Thorbjorn looked at Oddi as if he wanted to smack him, but decided his friend was too tall. The Franks glanced at each other, trying to understand what the two Norse warriors were saying.

Snorri ignored his men and studied the old Frank. "In return for what?" The old Frank scowled and so Snorri tried again. "Why fix my ship?"

The man pointed at Snorri and his men and smiled.

"He wants us to be his thralls?" Magni's face paled, no doubt thinking about the way he treated the thralls back in his father's hall.

"I will not be any man's thrall!" Thorbjorn stepped forward and pulled his sword, Bloodthirst, out of her scabbard. The rest of the Norse men agreed and followed Thorbjorn's example. "I'll kill any bastard who tries to make me his thrall." The Franks paled, the men cowering behind their spears and rusted swords while the old warrior put himself between the old man and the Norse.

"Enough!" Snorri bellowed, looking at his men over his shoulder. "Nobody wants you ugly bastards as thralls!" He faced the Frankish warrior in front of him and made a calming motion with his hands. The Norsemen sheathed their weapons and Thorbjorn looked sheepish after his outburst. "What do you want from us?"

The old Frank pointed at the dunes the scavengers had come from.

"Your friends?" Snorri asked, understanding what the old man meant.

"Friends? No friends." The old Frank scowled as he shook his head. "Was friend. Now attack home. They take animals, women. Kill men." He spat to the side. "Friends no more."

"So attack them back!" Thorbjorn waved his arm towards the dunes. "That's what we do. A man must defend his home."

The Frank looked lost as he struggled to understand what Thorbjorn was saying.

"You attack them?" Snorri asked, trying to keep it simple.

The old Frank glanced at the warrior beside him before slumping his shoulders. "They bigger, stronger." He pointed to the men behind him. "This our army."

"Why do they attack you?" Oddi asked.

"What does it matter?" Thorbjorn turned to his friend, always ready to argue with him.

Oddi shrugged. "Just curious."

"I agree with Thorbjorn. What does it matter?" Ragnar growled.

"Might give us a better idea of what we are getting ourselves into," Snorri said, scratching his cheek.

The old Frankish trader tried to follow the conversation, but the frown on his face showed he couldn't. He glanced at the warrior beside him, who looked bored. The old warrior reminded Ulf of most of the fighting men he had met so far. Ulf wondered if all warriors, no matter where they came from, were the same.

Snorri turned back to the trader. "Why are you not friends anymore?"

The old Frank paused for a short while and then, "When king dead, sons take land. We follow one son, they," he pointed to the dunes, "follow other son. So now we fight."

"The civil war," Ulf growled.

Thorbjorn scowled at him. "Between the brothers?"

"Aye," Oddi responded. "It seems old Louis made a mistake when he thought he could divide his kingdom into three and give each of his sons a part to rule."

"And now they're fighting over it like three cocks over a hen," Snorri said.

Thorbjorn shook his head. "Worse than Fafnir and his gold, those greedy bastards."

The old Frank frowned as he nodded. "War, yes."

"What's this got to do with us?" Ragnar asked.

The old Frank looked at Snorri, who nodded, and then pointed at the Sae-Ulfr. "We help fix ship. You," he pointed to Snorri and his men, "help fight."

Ulf saw the grim stare on Snorri's face and knew his friend had expected this. He should have seen this as well.

"No," Ragnar said through grit teeth. He stared at Snorri. "This is not our fight."

"I agree," Ulf said, surprising everyone, even Ragnar.

Snorri ignored them and spoke to the Frank. "I'll talk to my men, and we will decide."

The Frank scowled. "You not leader?"

"I am," Snorri smiled, "but I want to have all my men behind me when I fight."

The Frank did not understand, but nodded anyway. He scowled as Snorri led his men away.

"I don't see how we have a choice," Oddi said, glancing at the dunes as if he expected the raiders to come back.

"Of course, we have a choice," Thorbjorn almost shouted. "We can just attack them instead and take the wood they have. Look at them. Only one of them looks like a warrior."

Magni puffed his chest out. "Thorbjorn is right. We should attack them now. Slaughter all of them!" Oddi shook his head, while Thorbjorn glared at Magni, not liking that he agreed with him.

Snorri ran his fingers through his light-coloured hair, usually neatly tied and braided, but not at that moment. "We kill them now and then what? We don't know where their village is, and look around you." He pointed at all his men. "The men are tired and injured."

"There are also the scavengers," Oddi added. "We don't know where they are or how many of them there are. They could attack the ship while we try to find their village." He pointed to the waiting Franks. Ulf looked at them and saw the trader and the warrior were also in discussion. The trader looked nervous, while the warrior looked bored. Again, he reminded Ulf of all the warriors around him. The Norsemen started arguing with each other, some men agreeing with Oddi, while others agreed with Thorbjorn. Ulf kept quiet. He was too tired. His body ached, and he felt weak. Ulf knew that if the men decided to fight now, then he wouldn't be able to do much. All he wanted to do was lie down and rest. His tired mind drifted, and he thought of Hulda, Lady Ingibjorg's strange thrall who he had slept with. He remembered how they would sneak away and find a quiet spot where she would climb on top of him and ride him until his troubles went away. But that thought led to another, and he remembered being tied up in a tent, a woman of the forest smiling a blackened smile at him. Ulf shivered and realised the men had gone quiet. Snorri stared at him before turning back to his men. Ulf wondered if he had said something aloud.

"Attacking them is too much of a risk, and we've lost too much on this raid already." Most of the men glanced at Drumbr, who stood there silently.

"But how do we know we can trust these Franks?" one of the men asked.

"Aye, what's stopping them from leading us into another trap?" another added.

The men started up again, but Snorri silenced them by raising his hands. "I understand, Odin knows I have the same concerns."

Ulf had the sudden urge to glance at the sky and when he did, he saw two ravens circling above them. Odin was watching, and Ulf knew that whatever choice Snorri made, Odin would use it to his advantage.

Snorri also spotted the ravens and smiled. "We trust the gods."

"Aye, they've been very helpful so far," Ragnar muttered as the men followed Snorri back to the Franks.

"How do you speak our language?" Snorri asked.

"I trade Hedeby many years. Learn some words." The Frank smiled as he stood there, his hands folded in front of him, but looked unsure about the question.

"What's Hedeby?" Ulf asked. He had never heard of it before.

"It's a market town like Suðrikaupstefna, just bigger," Oddi responded. The old Frank must have recognised the name of Suðrikaupstefna because he nodded.

Snorri looked at the old trader. "You help us fix my ship, and we will help you with your friends."

The old Frank smiled broadly, but there was no joy in the smile as he translated Snorri's words to the warrior beside him. The Franks muttered to each other, some of them shaking their heads, while others made the sign of a cross on their chests. The old Frankish warrior stepped forward and held his hand out for Snorri. "Friends," he said in a bad accent.

Snorri smiled and gripped the man's arm. "Friends."

Ulf heard the ravens scream above him and when he looked up, saw the large black birds fly north. He rubbed the Mjöllnir around his neck as he wondered what plans Odin had for them.

*

"By the gods, they ask us to help them, but then they treat us like animals," Thorbjorn complained again as they sat around their fire outside the village. Ulf glanced up from his axe and understood Thorbjorn's frustration. They all did. It had been a few days since they washed up on the beach. After Snorri and the old trader, Humbert, agreed on their deal, the unhappy Franks had led them back to their village. The men lashed ropes to the Sae-Ulfr's hull and pulled her along the river, which led to the village. Snorri had the men put all the heavy stuff at the stern of the ship, so her nose was pointed up and the damaged hull was above the water. It had been a laborious task, as most of the men were injured, but none of them complained. Many of the men had sailed on the Sae-Ulfr for many winters, and none wanted to abandon her. They had also placed the dead on the ship, so they could get a proper funeral. The men had looked forward to reaching the village of their new hosts, but they were all disappointed when they arrived. The village was bigger than Thorgilsstad, but smaller than most of the other villages and towns they had seen in Francia. It was built in a circle and in the centre were two large houses. One looked like a jarl's hall and belonged to the old warrior. His name was Ansovald, and this was his village. He was the one who wanted them to help. Opposite Ansovald's house was a church, its tall tower sticking out above the houses like a beacon. On top of the tower was a cross, much like the ones Ulf had seen on top of other churches. The church was also the only building in the village built out of stone and did not look as impressive as the others he had seen. Another sign that there was not much wealth in this village.

Even the people were not what the Norsemen had expected. They had all gathered outside their village as their men returned with the feared invaders. Ansovald had waved to his people and wore a large grin on his face. But he had been the only one pleased. A group of priests stood with the villagers, shouting and chanting at the Norse warriors. The women looked sullen and afraid, and Ulf saw a few cross themselves. A handful of children were braver and had run towards them while ignoring the shouts of their mothers. But as soon as they came close to the Norsemen, they screamed and ran back. The Frankish men had joined their women, some of them shaking their heads. It was not the warm welcome they had expected, but the Norsemen did not care. They had pulled the ship out of the water and spent the first night preparing their tents and funeral pyres for their dead. The priests were angry about this, but Ansovald had chased them away. After that, the villagers kept to themselves and Snorri had forbidden his men to go near the village.

"You are an animal." Ragnar chewed on a piece of bread. Ansovald provided them with some bread, cheese and ale, but the men had to hunt for themselves. Luckily, it was still summer and there was plenty of game in the forest near the village.

"At least I smell better than them. These Franks don't wash often, do they?" Thorbjorn waved his hand in front of his nose. The men laughed and started complaining about the Franks and their habits, but Ulf was not paying attention.

His gaze was fixed on the handle of his axe as he tried to understand the meaning of his name being carved on it. Drumbr sat beside him, quietly chewing on cheese and drinking ale. He still mourned the loss of his brother, but was returning to himself now. Ulf still hadn't spoken to him about Brak, but Oddi had told him not to, and Ulf took his friend's advice. He didn't know what to say to Drumbr, anyway. Ulf remembered the awkward conversation he had with Lady Ingibjorg after Hulda, her thrall and Ulf's lover, had been killed. He pictured Hulda's face, her smile which soothed his anger, almost making him smile, but then, as before, he saw *her* face. The dirt trapped in the pores and the blackened teeth grinning at him. Ulf gripped the handle of Olaf's axe so tight, he thought he might break it. The axe had belonged to his uncle Olaf. Ulf had sworn his oath on it, and it was the weapon he would use to kill Griml. If it lasts that long, he thought as he thumbed the cut in the handle. It had happened during his fight with Ubba, the treacherous Danish jarl who had pretended to be their friend. Ulf had used the axe to block one of Ubba's strikes and the sword bit deep into the handle, just below where he had carved the names of his family. Brak's name had been added as well, even if his friends told him that Brak's death was not his fault. Ulf still felt it was. His vengeance was killing everyone around him and not for the first time, Ulf wondered if he was as bad as the man who had slaughtered his family. He sighed as he tried to take his mind away from that. His headaches were gone and the cuts on his shoulder and stomach were healing. But with the lack of pain, Ulf's frustration and anger were returning.

"What's his problem now?" Ragnar sounded bored, and Ulf looked up, seeing the red-headed warrior glaring at him.

"Probably the same thing as always. I want to kill Griml, not sit here and suck on my thumb," Asbjorn mocked Ulf with a whiny imitation of his voice.

Ulf, caught out by the sudden shift of attention to him, was speechless. But he felt the flames come to life inside him.

"Tell me, Ulf." Asbjorn waved a finger at him. "How many more of us must die before you finally kill Griml?"

"Asbjorn, enough." Snorri tried to calm them down.

Asbjorn jumped to his feet, his face turning red. "No! I'm sick of it. Odin knows Ulf has been nothing but bad luck since he joined us. Since you," he jabbed a finger at Snorri, "let him join us!" The men gasped, shocked at Asbjorn's outburst. Even those sitting by the other fires stopped what they were doing.

"Asbjorn," Oddi tried in a gentler tone.

But Asbjorn waved him away. "By Thor, don't Asbjorn me. You all know it's true. First the battle, then the sea storms. And look at the men we lost. Rolf! Brak! Half your crew, Snorri!"

Snorri kept his face calm, but Ulf was sure his friend was furious, just as he was. Ulf put the axe down, remembering the last time he had been insulted like this and had the axe in his hand. He had almost killed Thorvald, Snorri's younger brother. Although, that might have been a good thing. "Asbjorn, we are warriors. Brak was a warrior. And our fate is to die in battle."

Drumbr stopped eating at the mention of his brother, but he remained silent. Ulf glanced at him and saw the large warrior just staring into the fire, his eyes tearing up.

"But ask yourself this. How many men have you lost on previous raids? How many of your hirdmen had died in battle until now?"

Snorri couldn't answer, and Ulf knew Asbjorn was right. He grit his teeth as he glanced at the others, wanting to see their reactions.

"Asbjorn has a point, Snorri," Ragnar said, sounding calm. The words came like a punch in the gut to Ulf, almost killing the flames inside him.

"See!" Asbjorn pointed at Ragnar. "Thor's balls, Snorri. If Ragnar can see it, then why can't you?" He glared at Ulf again. "We lost good men because of you!"

Ulf, still gritting his teeth, refused to respond. The voices of his ancestors started whispering in his ears, telling him to kill Asbjorn. To cut his tongue out and to strangle him with it, but Ulf ignored them. He did not like Asbjorn, but he was one of Snorri's men.

"All you complain about is getting your revenge, but twice, twice!" Asbjorn held up two fingers. "You had the chance to kill him. But you couldn't. And do you know why?" Asbjorn leaned forward to stare at Ulf across the fire, his face lit up red by the flames. "Because you can't! Because you are not good enough! And because of that, Brak is dead!"

Ulf lost it. The voices in his head took over and Ulf launched himself at Asbjorn, roaring as he leapt over the fire. The flames licked his trousers before he crashed into the man who had been taunting him ever since he joined Snorri's crew. Ulf landed on top of Asbjorn, who had been too stunned by Ulf's sudden attack to move out of the way, and started punching him. His knuckles crunched as they connected with

Asbjorn's head. Asbjorn ignored the punches and grabbed Ulf's tunic, rolling them over so that he was on top. Before Ulf could respond, Asbjorn punched him. None of Snorri's men moved to stop them. Even Snorri stayed out of the way as the two men traded blows on the ground. Ulf brought his knee up and caught Asbjorn between his legs. Asbjorn's eyes almost popped out of his head, and it gave Ulf a chance to throw Asbjorn off him and jump to his feet. Asbjorn somehow ignored the pain, his many years as a warrior teaching him to fight through it, and blocked Ulf's punch. He kicked at Ulf, but Ulf, fuelled by the voices in his head, moved out of the way and hit Asbjorn in the chest. As Asbjorn staggered back, his face creased in pain and anger, Ulf charged at him. Asbjorn turned and avoided Ulf before punching him below the ear. Ulf's world spun as he stumbled to the side, the voices telling him to drop to his knees. Ulf obeyed and felt Asbjorn's fist fly over his head. Still on his knees, Ulf turned to punch Asbjorn in the stomach, but before he could get a chance, large hands grabbed him and pulled him away. Oddi and Thorbjorn grabbed hold of Asbjorn; the warrior struggling to free himself, his face red. Ulf wondered who grabbed him when someone struck him hard in the stomach. The hands let go of him and Ulf collapsed to the ground, gasping for air. Clutching his stomach, Ulf looked up in time to see Snorri punch Asbjorn in the face, knocking him to the ground.

"This stops now! Or, as Odin is my witness, I'll kill you both!" Snorri's face was red, his fists clenched by his side.

Asbjorn looked up, his face bloody. "Only the Norns know why you keep protecting him."

Snorri stared at Ulf, who could not read the thoughts that must have been running through Snorri's head. "He saved my life."

Asbjorn spat blood into the flames. "So you say, Snorri. But you really want us to believe that you could not have killed that bear?"

Ulf saw from the looks of the men around that many of them felt the same. He remembered the giant brown bear they came across in the clearing when he and Snorri had first met. Ulf had thought he would die that day, but the scars on his face were a reminder that Odin held Ulf to his oath. Snorri was staring at Ulf, studying the three lines on the right side of his face that started a finger away from his eye and ran to the tip of his mouth. They rarely bothered Ulf, but when the weather got cold, the skin on the right side of his face always felt tight.

Snorri turned to face Asbjorn again, his shoulders tense. "He saved my life." His harsh tone showing that the conversation was over.

Oddi helped Ulf to his feet and Ulf caught the glance from Drumbr, who turned away as soon as he spotted Ulf looking at him. The men sat down again. They quickly forgot about the fight and got back to their own conversations, but those sitting around the fire with Snorri and Ulf remained silent.

"It is strange how Griml keeps appearing everywhere we go," Oddi said after a while, rubbing his bearded chin and catching Ulf by surprise. The image of the troll came to Ulf, but like before, he saw his own face on the huge shoulders of the beast.

"Who is this Griml everybody keeps going on about?" Magni scratched his head.

"He killed my family," Ulf whispered through clenched teeth, struggling to get the words out as the memory of that day came to him. "He raped my aunt and burnt their farm down." His hands, already bruising from his fight with Asbjorn, started hurting, and Ulf realised he had been clenching them.

Magni was about to say something, but his brother stopped him.

"But why is Griml in Francia?" Thorbjorn asked.

Ulf looked up from the fire and realised everyone was watching him, including Asbjorn, who was wiping the blood off his face.

"And what's Hulda's mother got to do with it?" Thorbjorn added before Ulf could answer.

Tyr knows, I wish I knew. "I don't know how Griml keeps showing up." Ulf felt his hands shake, so he crossed his arms to hide it from everyone. "But I feel like she is behind it all."

"Hulda's mother?" Drumbr asked with a cocked head.

Ulf nodded, still remembering how she smiled at him with a knife in her hand while he was tied up on the ground.

"Hulda had a mother?" Thorbjorn looked at Snorri, who only shrugged. "Ragnar, do you know about this?" Ragnar was the oldest one around and had been with Snorri's father for more winters than some of the crew had been alive.

But Ragnar shook his head. "No, the Jarl and Lady Ingibjorg just showed up with her one day. I don't know where she came from."

"You didn't ask?" Oddi frowned at the red-headed warrior.

"I don't question the jarl." Ragnar's hard eyes bore into Oddi, who held his hand up in an apology, but Ulf felt like he was hiding something.

"So Hulda had a mother, and now she is doing what?" Snorri scratched his neck as he tried to make sense of what he was hearing.

"Ulf said she wanted revenge," Oddi responded, remembering what Ulf had told them on the ship as they fled Rouen. All the men looked at Ulf, waiting for him to explain.

"Revenge for what?" Thorbjorn asked.

"Hulda, perhaps." Oddi looked at Ulf, questioning him with a raised eyebrow.

"By Odin! This is rubbish!" Asbjorn jumped to his feet, the men around tensing as if they expected him to attack Ulf again. But Asbjorn stood where he was and glared at Ulf. "Again, all we have are his words. Have any of you actually seen this woman?" He looked at his friends, who all shook their heads. "Exactly! Ulf could have made her up!"

"She's real," Ulf growled and held up his arm to show where she had cut him with her knife.

"You could have got that during the battle." Asbjorn dismissed the cut.

"Asbjorn is right," Ragnar said, exasperated. "We don't know if this woman is real, or just another story by Ulf."

"But Griml is real. We all saw him," Oddi defended Ulf.

"Oddi has a point. Griml is real, and Odin knows a man that ugly can't be very smart. So someone must be controlling him." Snorri looked at Ulf, his grey eyes telling Ulf he believed him.

"You really think that someone like Griml can be controlled?" Thorbjorn asked.

Ulf stared at his friends as they pondered at what Thorbjorn had just said when he remembered something else from the tent. "Griml is afraid of her."

"Afraid of her!" Snorri raised his eyebrows. A sudden breeze flew over the flames, causing them to flutter. The men went quiet, all of them staring at the fire as it came back to life. One by one, they grabbed the Mjöllnir pendants around their necks, some of them even muttering prayers to the gods. Like them, Ulf knew that had been an omen from the gods. And like them, he knew it was not a good one.

CHAPTER 4

Ulf grunted as he lifted his shield arm. The injury protested, but he managed to raise the heavy shield. Whether he could block a powerful strike was another question. Many of the men were red-faced as the sun glinted off of their armour in the heat. Sweat poured down Ulf's body, his tunic clinging to him like a wet rag. In his right hand, Ulf had a borrowed axe. He had wrapped the handle of Olaf's axe with a leather rope, but did not want to use her now. She was still needed, and with the sun out, Ormstunga had to stay in her scabbard.

Thorbjorn faced Ulf, the short squat warrior grinning at him as he held his sword ready, his brynja almost blinding Ulf. Thorbjorn's helmet did not have an eye guard like Ulf's and the rest of Snorri's hirdmen. Drumbr was the only other one without an eye guard as well, but Thorbjorn's at least had a nose guard.

After the previous night, Snorri had decided that his men had rested enough and ordered them to train. He wanted to keep them busy and tired, so no more fights broke out. Oddi faced Drumbr, while Asbjorn was fighting against Geir. As always,

Geir was happy when Snorri had told him to fight against one of his hirdmen. From the way he had been fighting all morning, it looked like Geir was trying to prove that he could take Brak's place in Snorri's hirdmen. But so far, Asbjorn had gotten the better of him every time. Snorri was fighting against Ragnar, the two warriors like gods of war, as they stabbed and cut at each other, but neither able to land any blows.

"Wake up, Ulf," Thorbjorn warned before attacking. He stabbed at Ulf, who just had enough time to turn out of the way. Ulf swung his axe at Thorbjorn's head, but the short warrior easily took the blow on his shield. Thorbjorn took a few quick steps forward and shoulder barged Ulf in the chest. Ulf grunted as he staggered backwards, but stayed on his feet. Not that it made any difference, as Thorbjorn did not give him time to recover. He chopped down with his sword, forcing Ulf to lift his shield to block the strike. Ulf's shoulder protested, but he got the shield up in time. He groaned as his shoulder gave in and his arm dropped. Thorbjorn smiled as both men knew Ulf would be on his way to Valhalla now if this had been a proper fight. He stepped into Ulf and punched out with his shield. This time, Ulf fell onto his back and before he could roll to his feet, Thorbjorn was on top of him, his sword aiming for Ulf's neck. Ulf had a flashback of his father's sword coming towards his neck while the man who had slaughtered his family laughed. He froze, unable to do anything as fear gripped his body and held him in place.

Thorbjorn must have noticed something was wrong and pulled his sword away. "You're not paying attention," he admonished Ulf as he offered him a hand, deciding not to mention Ulf's reaction. Ulf took his hand and Thorbjorn helped him to his feet. Next to them, Geir was also on the ground, with a grimace on his face as he rubbed his leg. Not far from them, a small group of children from the village watched, cheering every time one of the Norse warriors fell.

"Doesn't like making it easy." Thorbjorn laughed as Geir struggled back to his feet. Asbjorn struck at him with his shield, which only caused Geir to fall down again and the children to cheer near the village.

"Thought that was the idea." Ulf understood how Geir felt. He often ended sparring sessions against Asbjorn with bruises.

"Aye, but I think that bastard just enjoys hurting people."

"Especially me."

Thorbjorn glanced at Ulf, his eyebrow raised. "Asbjorn has always been a miserable bastard. Maybe his mother's milk had gone sour, I don't know." Thorbjorn wiped his sword clean on his trousers and put her back in her scabbard. "Been like that since the day he arrived in Thorgilsstad."

"He's not from there?" Ulf took his helmet off and rubbed his hand through his wet hair. His thumb grazed over the groove left behind on his helmet by Ubba's sword, and Ulf had another flashback of a sword coming towards his face. Ubba should have killed him, but Ulf's foot had slipped on the bloody mud and he fell to one knee. The movement taking his head out of the way of Ubba's blade. Odin had come to his aid that day. That was the only reason he was still alive.

"No, he came from somewhere else, although never told us where. He always had to prove he was better than us and I think for a while he resented me and the brothers. We grew up on the farms around Thorgilsstad, so we all knew each other. He was an outsider, and I think he felt that."

Ulf looked at Asbjorn as he stomped away from Geir, spitting to the side. "So what has he got against me?"

Thorbjorn scratched his thick neck. "Don't know. Once Snorri accepted him into his hirdmen, Asbjorn found a place where he felt happy. I think you threaten that, especially after everything that has been happening since you arrived."

Ulf studied his helmet, taking in the two open-mouthed wolves as they faced each other on his eye guard. It was like they were trying to attack each other, much like the constant conflict Ulf felt inside him. "You think this is all because of me?"

To his surprise, Thorbjorn laughed. "Course not! You think too much of yourself. The gods are bored, and so they are using you to entertain themselves. We just do what they want us to do."

Follow me to your deaths, Ulf thought, but did not say. He heard a raven somewhere, its cawing sounding like it was agreeing with him. Ulf looked up and spotted something in the distance which sent a shiver of fear down his spine.

"What, in Odin's name, is happening now?"

The Norsemen stopped what they were doing as Ansovald walked towards them. He was surrounded by many others, including the old trader, all of them protesting against something.

"This will be interesting," Asbjorn said as he stood next to them. His face was heavily bruised from his fight with Ulf, but it didn't seem to bother him. Ulf wondered what his own face looked like.

As the old Frank came closer, Ulf saw he was wearing an old leather jerkin. On his head, he had a helmet that shone brightly in the sunlight, despite its age. The group stopped a few paces away from the Norse warriors and Ansovald silenced the people around him. Ulf glanced over his shoulder as Snorri and Ragnar stopped their fight. With a frown, Snorri walked towards the Franks, Tyr's Fury still in his hand. Some of the older men cowered behind their leader as he approached, his brynja blinding in the sun and his helmet fierce, with its golden fish-scaled eye and cheek guards. Snorri's arms were covered in scars and gold and silver arm rings, all of them showing that he was a warrior of renown. He took his helmet off as he reached Ulf, clapping his friend on the shoulder before turning his attention to the Franks.

The old trader stepped forward and glanced at Ansovald, who nodded. "Ansovald want ask something."

Snorri looked at the old warrior with a raised eyebrow. Just like on the beach, Ansovald stood with his hands on his hips and wore a relaxed smile. "What does he want to ask?"

Humbert swallowed nervously as he glanced at the old warrior again. "When you fight friends, he also fight."

"What?" Thorbjorn asked, frowning. He took his helmet off and the shaved sides of his head glistened in the sun from the sweat.

"He wants to join us when we attack their enemy," Oddi responded in a helpful tone.

"I know what he wants, Viss!"

"Then why ask?"

"Enough!" Ragnar silenced them before Thorbjorn could respond, much to the delight of the men. "Snorri, I don't think that's a good idea."

"Why not?" Snorri had an amused smile on his face.

"He's old," Magni said, unable to stop himself from getting involved.

"And a Frank," Ragnar added.

Ansovald frowned as he watched the conversation between the Norsemen. He glanced at Humbert, who only shrugged.

Snorri looked at Ansovald. "Why does he want to fight?"

"He chief," Humbert responded. "He protect village."

Snorri stroked his beard as he thought of the answer, but to Ulf, it made sense. Snorri had told him many times that a jarl's duty was to protect those in his hall. That was one reason Snorri was angry at his father. Before they had left for Francia, Thorgilsstad was attacked by men who had served a jarl Snorri had killed. Jarl Thorgils had stayed in his house, unwilling to protect his people.

Ansovald said something to Humbert, who looked at him before shaking his head. The other Franks surrounding the old warrior started complaining, all of them chirping away like angry birds as they waved their arms in the air. A priest held his wooden cross up to the sky and started praying. Ulf glanced up and saw no sign that their god was listening. But Ansovald seemed unconcerned by them. He held up his hand, and they all went silent.

"Bet Snorri wishes he can control Gunnhildr like that," Thorbjorn said, which caused the men to laugh. Snorri glanced at them and shook his head, but Ulf saw no anger at Thorbjorn's words. Probably because they were true.

"He fight good," Humbert said, feeling the need to defend his leader.

"I'm sure he can." Snorri shrugged. "But can he run?" He pointed to Ansovald's leg. They had all seen him limping as he walked.

Ansovald saw what Snorri was pointing at and said something to the trader. There was a brief exchange between the two before Humbert turned back to Snorri. "Why run? You no run. You fight."

Snorri smiled. "We fight, but we fight fast."

"I fight good. I show!" Ansovald said with a thick accent which was hard to understand. He stepped forward, separating himself from the men around him, and drew his sword. It was not a sword that belonged to a rich man. Her hilt was plain and so was her blade, but she looked sharp and well looked after.

"Snorri, don't." Oddi saw the smile on his friend's face and, like the rest of them, knew what Snorri was thinking.

But Snorri ignored his taller cousin. "Give the old man a shield. Let's see what he can do." The Norse cheered, and the Franks paled. They might not have understood the words, but they knew what was about to happen. Ulf glanced up, trying to see if Odin's ravens were nearby. He saw neither and blew out a breath of relief. If Odin's ravens weren't watching, then it meant nothing bad was going to happen. But that didn't stop Ulf's hand from going to where Olaf's axe would usually be. When his hand felt nothing, he remembered he didn't have his axe with him and rubbed the Mjöllnir around his neck instead. Thorbjorn handed his shield to the old Frank, who nodded his thanks, before pushing the men back so that Snorri and Ansovald had room to fight.

"Just don't kill the bastard," Ragnar growled. "Not until after we fix your ship."

Snorri smiled his wolf grin as he put his helmet back on. Everyone went silent as Snorri and Ansovald got into position, both men crouched behind their shields and swords ready.

"This'll be interesting," Thorbjorn said as Snorri lunged at Ansovald.

The old Frank took the blow on his shield but did not retaliate. Instead, he stepped back and invited Snorri to attack again. Snorri rushed in and swung his sword high, forcing Ansovald to lift his shield to block it. Ansovald stepped back again.

"Why is he not attacking?" one of the young warriors asked.

"Because he is afraid of Snorri. Odin knows Snorri will gut him," Geir said, a vicious grin on his face.

"He's learning. Something you idiots should do," Ragnar said as Snorri attacked again, this time with a backhanded swing of Tyr's Fury. Ansovald stood rooted to the spot and had to lift his sword to block the strike. Before the swords connected, Snorri stopped and pulled out of the swing, not wanting to damage his blade. Ulf realised that Snorri's side was exposed and knew that Ansovald saw it as well. A well-aimed strike with his shield could have broken a rib, but Ansovald did nothing. This was not a proper fight. This was two warriors getting to know each other.

"Could have had Snorri there." Asbjorn must have seen the same thing, but Ulf kept quiet, not wanting to show that he agreed.

"Only because Snorri didn't follow through with his attack," Oddi said, and Ulf wondered if that was true.

Snorri stabbed at Ansovald, who blocked with his shield, but instead of taking a step back as he did before, swung his sword at Snorri. Snorri reacted late, but got his shield up in time to block the blow. The two men smiled at each other.

This time, Ansovald attacked first, chopping down with his sword. Snorri twisted out of the way, but before he could strike, Ansovald turned and lifted his shield, ready for any attack from Snorri. Snorri stabbed at the shield, the force of the blow pushing Ansovald back. His weaker leg was now in front and unprotected. Ulf saw Snorri glance at it and knew that if this had been an actual fight, he would have attacked the leg. But instead, Snorri punched with his shield, forcing Ansovald back. Ansovald swung his sword at Snorri's head, who ducked under the blade. The villagers gasped as they crept closer, all of them wanting to watch their leader fight the Norseman. Snorri stabbed his sword at Ansovald's exposed side and before the blade connected, he turned it away.

"Thank Odin, the bastard is thinking," Ragnar said as they all knew the fight could have been over.

Ansovald saw the same thing, his face red at his own foolishness. With a roar, he charged at Snorri. Ulf guessed he wanted to show his people that he was still a capable fighter. But he was fighting one of the best warriors in all of Norway, if not Midgard. Snorri lifted his shield, but twisted out of the way just before Ansovald's sword connected. The move caught Ansovald by surprise and there was nothing he could do as Snorri's sword came for his weak leg. Ansovald's eyes bulged as he saw this, but Snorri turned Tyr's Fury and slapped Ansovald's leg with the flat of the blade. Ansovald grimaced as he took the blow, but then smiled at Snorri as he stepped back.

"The fight's over?" someone asked as Snorri and Ansovald stood facing each other.

Before anyone could respond, Ansovald and Snorri charged at each other again. Snorri stabbed high, forcing Ansovald to duck low. Ansovald punched with the rim of his shield, Snorri blocking it with his before bringing his sword down hilt first. Somehow, Ansovald anticipated this and twisted out of the way. The old man was still supple, despite his age. He stabbed at Snorri, who danced out of the way, and before Snorri could attack, turned the stab into a backhanded swing. Snorri blocked the blow with his shield before stabbing at Ansovald's front leg. Ansovald could not get his shield down in time to block it, so was forced to pull his leg back. This left him standing on his weak leg, which could not hold his weight, and Ansovald collapsed. A woman cried from the crowd as Snorri rushed in and kicked Ansovald's shield away.

"Bastard," Ragnar muttered as Snorri stood over Ansovald with his sword raised. Even Ulf wondered if his friend would kill the Frankish leader. Snorri could be cruel when he needed to be and despite the agreement between them, Ansovald was still a Frank. He was still an enemy.

But Snorri had no intention of killing the old warrior. He sheathed Tyr's Fury and offered Ansovald a hand. There was silence as everybody waited to see what Ansovald would do, even the birds watched quietly. In the end, the old warrior laughed and took Snorri's hand. Snorri pulled him to his feet, and Ansovald sheathed his sword and spoke to his people. A few of them smiled, but most looked worried.

"What's he telling them?" Ulf asked.

"Probably not to worry. If we decide to attack, their deaths would be quick because none of them can fight." Asbjorn sneered at Ulf. "Apart from the women, we might keep them alive a bit longer."

Ulf grit his teeth as he fought to stop the flames from igniting in his stomach. But as he glared at Asbjorn, he spotted something in the distance behind him. "What's that?"

"He's been standing there the whole time Snorri and Ansovald fought." Oddi glanced at the hill in the distance where a man stood watching them. "Most likely from the village we are supposed to attack." Ulf nodded, relieved he was not the only one to notice the man. It would not be the first time he had seen someone the others hadn't.

"Should we get him?" Geir asked, always eager to do something for Snorri and his hirdmen.

"No, by the time you get there, he'll be long gone. Besides, there are probably more of them around watching."

"Unless you can run as fast as Ratatoskr," Thorbjorn mocked.

They turned their attention away from the man on the hill as Ansovald approached Snorri, with Humbert behind him. "Ansovald say you great warrior, he happy fight with you."

Snorri smiled and held out his hand, which Ansovald took in a forearm grip. "It'll be an honour to fight with you as well."

"Well, Thor fuck me, we're fighting with the Franks now." Ragnar turned and walked away as the men laughed.

CHAPTER 5

Snorri scratched his beard with its thick braid in the middle, which was itchy because he hadn't bathed for a few days. They stood on a hill and watched the village from a distance. Most of his hirdmen were with him, apart from Oddi and Drumbr. Oddi stayed behind to lead the men in his absence, and Drumbr was too heavy for the horses they had borrowed from the Franks. Snorri glanced at Ulf, seeing how his scarred friend sat uncomfortably on his horse, his cheek still bruised from his fight with Asbjorn. Ulf had almost fallen off a few times on their trek to this village. Snorri was sure Ulf's determination not to make a fool of himself kept him on the horse. Then there was Ragnar. But his problem was that he was too big for horses. The red-headed warrior's feet almost touching the ground as they rode along. Snorri had wanted him to stay behind, but, as always, his father's champion refused.

Ansovald was also with them and a young man who was their guide. The Frank sat comfortably on his horse, like he spent most of his time on it, his face relaxed as always. Snorri was intrigued by the man. He seemed to possess no fear of them. If anything, the man seemed amused by the Norsemen. They had spoken deep into the night about the town they were supposed to attack, as Snorri wanted as much information as possible. He had lost too many men on this cursed raid and didn't want to lose anymore. But it had been difficult. Ansovald spoke only a few words of Norse and Humbert not enough to understand what Snorri wanted. So, Snorri had come to see the town for himself. They left as soon as the sun was up and it was the middle of the afternoon by the time they reached the neighbouring town. There was no direct route for them to take. They travelled south first, through the forest to a point where the wide river between the two towns was shallow enough for them to cross. Then they had to go northwest to find the town.

"It's bigger," Ragnar said as he stood beside his horse. He got off it as soon as they reached their destination, the horse looking relieved, as most horses did when the large warrior climbed off them.

Snorri turned his attention back to the town. "Aye. More men too." Like their host village, this town was round. In the centre stood a large building that Snorri knew was a church — a common feature in all villages in Francia. In front of the church was a large square, most likely where the market would be on market days or where they would punish criminals. *The Christian god has many rules, and he expects his followers to follow them.* The voice of the old godi he had met near Rouen came to him. Snorri wondered if the old man was still in that forest, or if he fled after their encounter. Opposite the church was a large house where Snorri guessed the leader of the village lived. Two main roads crisscrossed by the church, with many smaller streets branching off and leading to the many houses within the wooden palisade. There were four entrances, all of them linked to the large roads, with one gate sitting by a small river that ran alongside the village.

"More than who? Us or Ansovald's village?" Thorbjorn asked, looking like a bearded child on his horse.

"Both." Snorri watched as the people of the town went about their daily lives, oblivious to the wolves on the hill. The wooden palisade was lightly manned. Just like Ansovald's village, all the fighting men were supposed to have left to fight in the war between the brothers. But Snorri was sure that this village had not sent all of her men. From what Humbert had told him, it seemed the leader of this place saw an opportunity to rid himself of his neighbours and perhaps increase his lands. Snorri remembered the men who attacked them on the beach. Those men might not have been warriors, but they were of fighting age and they had outnumbered his men. That was why Ansovald could not stop them from raiding his village, and why he had made a deal with the enemy.

"But they're not fighting men, not if what we saw on the beach is anything to go by," Asbjorn said. Snorri looked at his bruised face, wondering what would have happened if they hadn't stopped the fight.

"Aye, but they're still more than us." Thorbjorn spat, the sound frightening the horse, who suddenly stepped to the side and almost threw Thorbjorn off. "Thor's arse!"

The men laughed as Ansovald just frowned at them.

"What do you think, Snorri?" Ragnar ignored what was going on around them as Thorbjorn threatened to kill and eat the horse, which only made the men laugh more. Apart from Ulf, who just sat on his horse scowling.

Snorri sighed. "I'm thinking I don't want to lose more men."

"Then you shouldn't have agreed to fight the Frank's battles for him."

Snorri knew Ragnar was right. "The gods—"

"If you say the gods brought us here for a reason, then I'll gut you before Thorbjorn kills his horse," Ragnar threatened him.

Snorri smiled, but looked to the sky for any sign of the gods. The clouded sky was empty. No eagles or ravens, just the occasional small bird which chirped as it flew over their heads. The light breeze offered nothing, either. The gods were silent. Perhaps that was a sign. "We need his help to fix the Sae-Ulfr. And besides, like Asbjorn said, these men are no warriors."

"So we are going to kill more farmers then?" Ulf's harsh voice surprised both of them.

"What's your problem now?" Ragnar scowled at the fair-haired warrior. Snorri closed his eyes, hoping he would not have to break up another fight.

"I didn't come here to kill farmers."

"Those farmers almost killed you." Ragnar hawked and spat. "Should have let them. The gods know it would be more peaceful."

"Odin wouldn't have let that happen. He wants Ulf alive," Thorbjorn said, winking at Ulf.

"Odin didn't save the bastard. I did."

"Perhaps it was Odin who sent you to do it?" Thorbjorn scratched his head.

"You're sounding like Oddi now," Asbjorn mocked.

"No, I don't." Thorbjorn went red in the face. Snorri smiled at his friends and wished he could go back to being like them. The Norns chose their paths and all his hirdmen cared about were ale, women and fighting. But this raid made Snorri question everything he thought about the gods. *Have I offended you, Odin?* Deciding that he had seen enough, Snorri turned his horse around and headed back to Ansovald's village, with the others behind him.

Later that day, Snorri was brooding by their fire. His men sat with him, chewing on the venison given to them by Ansovald while they waited for Snorri. The flames danced away in the summer breeze, reminding Snorri of Jarl Arnfinni. He used to be an ally of Thorgilsstad and the father of Snorri's wife. He was also the reason they were in Francia. At first, Snorri had thought this raid was a gift from the gods. A chance to become one of the richest men in Norway and earn more fame than ever before. But now, as he pictured the burning hall in the flames, he wondered if this was not in fact a punishment for killing the jarl.

"So what do we do?" Oddi asked. Snorri had explained to him what they had seen, and like the rest of the men, Oddi understood the danger they faced.

"What can we do?" Thorbjorn asked. "Unlike this village," he thumbed over his shoulder, "they have a wall."

"Not to mention more men. Odin knows, this might be one of the worst situations you've ever gotten us in." Ragnar's eyes bored into Snorri.

Snorri looked up from the flames and stared at his father's champion, but said nothing. He had always gotten his men out of difficult situations, and he knew they trusted him to do so now. But this time, Snorri wasn't sure how.

"We need wood for the ship. Snorri had no choice," Magni defended him, surprising everyone. Thorbjorn almost choked on the meat he was chewing on, while Oddi stared at his brother with raised eyebrows.

"Shouldn't have been here in the first place. The gods were against this from the beginning," Ulf complained, much to the frustration of Asbjorn and Ragnar.

"Don't start this again, pup. You wanted to chase Griml, and you found him here. Not our fault you couldn't kill him," Ragnar growled.

Snorri thought his friend would explode again. But this time, Ulf kept quiet, his eyes fixed on Ragnar as he curled his lip. Snorri saw something in them that surprised him. He thought his friend's fire was returning. It had seemed so the other day. But now, that flame, while there, did not seem to burn so brightly. Ulf jumped to his feet, his fists clenched, and Snorri thought he had been wrong, that Ulf might attack Ragnar. Ragnar tensed his shoulders, also expecting the young warrior to attack. But Ulf did not. After glaring at Ragnar for a few heartbeats, he turned and walked towards his tent.

"Too afraid to fight," Asbjorn mocked, which Snorri thought was strange, considering his face was covered in the bruises from his fight with Ulf.

"Ulf is not afraid," Thorbjorn defended their young friend, "and you know it. As brave as Thor, that bastard." Asbjorn held his hand up. He knew the truth about Ulf.

"He blames himself. Thinks this is all because of him," Oddi said, glancing at Drumbr.

"Brak didn't die because of Ulf," Drumbr said, a sad smile on his face. "I'm sure when Ulf sees him in Valhalla, Brak will tell him the same."

"Aye, he will." Snorri watched as his friend disappeared into his tent and sighed. "But it's not just that. Like Asbjorn and Ragnar said, twice he fought Griml, and both times he failed to kill him. Only the gods will know what that is doing to him."

"That Volva probably cast a spell on Ulf, so he couldn't kill Griml." Thorbjorn rubbed the shaved side of his head.

"Perhaps." Snorri scratched his beard. "But we've all seen that troll. It must be like fighting a mountain. Tyr knows it'll be hard even for us to kill that bastard." The men fell silent after that. They all saw the truth in his words.

"Perhaps I should go talk to him," Oddi offered, but Snorri shook his head.

"No, leave him. He needs to face his own demons."

"You think the gods were really against this raid?" Geir asked, the slight quiver in his voice distracting the men from their conversation.

"Why would the gods be against this raid?" one of the men asked.

"You remember the storm on the way to Suðrikaupstefna!" Geir said, his eyes wide. They all did. The storm had come out of nowhere and sunk the second ship Snorri had taken with him, the War Bear. And sent half her crew to Ran's Hall at the bottom of the sea.

"That storm had nothing to do with the gods." Ragnar spat into the flames, but they all saw him rub his Mjöllnir pendant.

"How can you be so sure?" Geir asked.

"Why would the gods care about this raid?" Ragnar responded.

"How else can you explain everything that has happened to us on this raid?" Oddi stroked his beard and adopted his wise look.

Snorri stared at his friend, frowning as the same question as before came to him. *Have I offended you, Odin?* He threw the bone he had been holding for a while into the fire and stood up. "It doesn't matter whether or not the gods are against us." Snorri saw his men grab the Mjöllnir pendants around their necks. He resisted the urge to do the same. "What matters now is that we need to get home. We have no way of knowing if King Halfdan had kept his word, and the longer we stay here, the longer Thorgilsstad sits without her best warriors." Halfdan was the king of Vestfold, a region in the south of Norway. Thorgilsstad was in Vestfold and Snorri's father was one of the king's strongest jarls, or at least had been until Thorvald betrayed them. Jarl Thorgils had not been the same man since, and Snorri feared the king might want to replace him with another jarl.

"The king swore he would protect Thorgilsstad," Magni protested. He would be concerned about this as well as his father's village was across the bay from Thorgilsstad and relied on Snorri's father for protection.

"The king swore to protect Thorgilsstad, but said nothing about her people." Ragnar understood what Snorri was saying.

"Exactly. Odin knows I don't like this situation we're in, but we need to get home and the only way to do that is to repair the Sae-Ulfr. Leaving her on the beach was not an option. Those scavenging worms would have stripped her bare and

Ansovald has promised us wood to fix her mast and to replace the broken sideboards."

"But for that, we must kill his enemy," Asbjorn said. "Who has more men than we do and a large wall protecting their town."

"Aye." Snorri stared at his men as Asbjorn's words set in. He sat back down again and rubbed his face. "What would my father do?"

"Your father?" Ragnar asked, surprised by Snorri's question.

"Can't we just attack them like we did Hammaburg?" Geir asked. "It worked then, and that was a big city."

"No." Snorri had spent the entire trip back trying to solve that problem. "We don't have enough men for that, and I'm not losing the few I have left." His face darkened. "My father is one of the smartest warriors there is," he turned to Ragnar, "so how would he attack this town?"

Ragnar stared at Snorri for a while, the only sounds in the silence being the flames as they chewed through the wood and some men eating. "I don't know what your father would do. There's a reason he's the jarl and not me."

"Perhaps the question is not what the jarl would do." Oddi stroked his beard.

"By Odin, here we go again." Thorbjorn shook his head.

Oddi ignored him and continued when he saw he had everyone's attention. "Perhaps we should ask what Loki would do?" He saw the shocked expressions on their faces and smiled.

"Oddi Viss might be right," Asbjorn said. "It'll take Loki magic to take that village and not lose any more men."

The men were silent as they contemplated what Oddi had said. Snorri looked around the fire, surprised by what he saw. His friends would normally be laughing and joking around the flames, regardless of the dangers they faced, but not tonight. He took a deep breath and looked at the stars to see if there were any signs from the gods. "Oddi's right. We'll need Loki magic to take that village. We'll also need more men."

"And where are we going to get them from? Ask Odin to send us his Einherjar?" Thorbjorn shook his head. Some men smiled at that, which pleased Snorri.

"Doubt Odin will do that, but hopefully Ansovald will lend us some of his men."

"What men?" Ragnar asked, staring at the village.

"Aye, greybeards and no beards, that's all they've got," Magni agreed. Snorri raised an eyebrow at Magni. The man was speaking more like a proper warrior every day. Perhaps they would turn him into one by the time they make it home.

"There's a reason the Frankish bastard needs our help. He has no men to fight his own battles," Asbjorn said.

Snorri smiled as part of a plan started forming in his head. "They don't need to fight. They just need to look like they're there to fight."

"By Odin, Snorri. Might as well also ask for their women." Ragnar rubbed his eyes.

"Aye, there's more of them than men." Thorbjorn laughed.

Snorri stared at the village not far from them. It was late evening, so not much was happening. The men had finished their work in the fields and the boys were bringing the cattle in. Women would be busy preparing their evening meals in their houses as the church bells were ringing. Snorri never understood why the Christians wanted to make so much noise. They must have realised by now that all those bells did was attract raiders like him and his men. Some women were walking around, all of them making sure they kept their distance from the Norsemen. But Thorbjorn was right. There were more women than men and many of the women had to take over the roles of the men in the village. He had seen how they repaired the roofs and worked in the fields. "You know what? That might just be a good idea." Snorri laughed at the stunned expressions on their faces.

Thorbjorn glanced at those around him, all of them shrugging in return. "Perhaps that Loki magic has worked its way into him."

CHAPTER 6

Ulf stalked through the trees, spear in hand, as he searched for his prey. He had lost track of how long he'd been pursuing it, but his prey kept eluding him, only to appear when he least expected it. The forest was quiet. No birds were singing from the tree branches, no leaves rustling in the wind. In front of him was a large tree, bigger than the others, its enormous trunk blocking his view of what was behind it. Ulf approached the tree and gripped his spear tighter, certain his prey was hiding behind it. His heart started beating faster in his chest as sweat ran down his face, stinging his eyes. The spear started trembling in his hands. *Could it be the prey?* Ulf stopped again and lowered his spear. *What am I hunting?* He could not remember. He scanned the trees around him, hoping they would offer some clues, but the trees remained silent. *Where am I?* He could not remember how he got here, either. Looking up, he tried to get his bearings, but there was no moon in the night sky, nor were there any stars. Fear crept up his spine again as he gripped the spear and faced the large tree in front of him. Ulf wasn't sure why, but he knew he had to go past it. As he took a step forward, a loud laugh came from behind. Ulf turned to the sound, spear levelled, but there was nothing. All he saw were the dark trees, casting their shadows over him. The spear trembled again as his fear took hold of him. He turned back to the tree and took a deep breath, surprised at how cold the air was. Suddenly things started feeling familiar and Ulf turned around, expecting to find his prey there. But still, there was nothing.

"Tyr, give me strength," Ulf whispered, forcing himself to walk towards the large tree. The loud laughter boomed again and Ulf froze. He stood still for a few heartbeats and then slowly rounded the tree. He wasn't sure why, but he felt that his prey was hiding behind it, waiting to ambush him like it had done so many times before. But this time, Ulf would be ready. He raised his spear, fighting hard to keep it steady and to slow his heartbeat. His breathing became laboured, and each step became heavier and heavier. The air around him went cold and no matter how hard he tried, he could not stop the spear from quivering in his hands. Knowing there was nothing else he could do, Ulf summoned his courage and jumped around the tree with a scream. It was not a battle roar, but the scream of a man who was trying to overcome his fear.

Ulf stood there, feet planted wide and spear pointing at nothing. There was no threatening presence or large shadow looming over him. All he saw was a small campfire in the middle of a clearing. Ulf frowned. The air was still cold, and Ulf still felt the familiar fear in the pit of his stomach, but the small fire seemed to calm him. It was like the flames were calling to him and before Ulf understood what he was doing, he started walking towards it. He scanned the trees around, trying to find someone hiding amongst them, and saw nothing but dark shadows. There were a few logs placed around the fire, just like the ones they would normally sit on when they prepared a camp for the night.

Sit, the voice came to him. Not the deep male voice he normally heard, but a soft, feminine voice that hissed in his ears. Ulf sat down on one of the logs. As he stared at the fire, he realised the flames were not burning through the wood, but merely sat on top. Movement caught his eye and as Ulf turned towards it, a viper slithered away into the shadows. Ulf wanted to follow it, but he couldn't. He was stuck to the log, held there by some force he could not see. Ulf struggled to free himself, the fear returning to him as an enormous shadow appeared from behind. He reached for his spear, but it was not there anymore. He tried to reach for the logs in the fire, but couldn't either, as the fire had moved away from him. Laughter rang out behind him, and Ulf turned, determined to face his prey, who had yet again snuck upon him. But the face staring at him was not the ugly troll who had haunted his dreams since the day his family had been killed. The face staring at him, laughing at his fear, was his own.

*

Ulf woke up in his tent, soaked in sweat, and his hand on the hilt of Ormstunga. His heart was beating hard in his chest as he sat there, taking deep breaths to calm himself. He hated these dreams. The gods were speaking to him; he was sure of it. But he wondered why they couldn't do it in a nicer way. He peered through the opening in his tent and saw that the sun had risen. Outside, the men were already up and about. Some went down to the river to clean themselves, while others prepared fires for their dagmál. Ulf wiped the sweat from his face and crawled out of his tent.

"Porridge for the dagmál, although I think there might still be some venison left." Drumbr was stirring a small pot over a fire between their tents.

Ulf nodded his thanks, his mind still foggy from his dream. He grabbed his flask and drank some of the warm water before pouring the rest over his head, hoping it would clear his mind.

The rest of his friends joined them. Thorbjorn's hair was still wet, the tattoos on the shaved sides of his head glistening in the morning sun, as the short warrior sat by the fire. He started combing his hair as Magni joined them, looking as immaculate as ever. Apart from being covered in blood after battle, Ulf had never seen the man looking rough. They called him the Cockerel because, like the bird, he was always flamboyant. His red hair was neatly braided, as well as his beard, which was also covered in rings. It was something he had picked up from the men, as many of them liked to tie the finger rings of their enemies into their beards. Ulf stroked his own beard, feeling the knots and tangles. He needed a clean, so he stood up and walked towards the river.

Many of the men were there already. Something the Franks did not seem happy about, as they all stood to one side, glaring at the Norsemen as they bathed and played in the water. Although, Ulf caught a few admiring glances from some of the Frankish women, which only seemed to annoy their men even more. He removed his stained clothes and waded into the chilly water, shivering as it touched his skin. After wetting his hair, Ulf used his fine bone comb to brush the tangles out of his hair and beard.

"Thought I'd find you here." Ulf turned and saw Snorri standing there, apple in hand, as he smiled at Ulf. "Feeling better?"

Ulf shrugged. He was still embarrassed about walking away from the fire after what Ragnar had said. But Ulf had struggled to contain his anger and did not want to get into another fight with one of Snorri's men, especially not Ragnar. Ulf had fought him before, when they had first met. He had let his anger get the better of him then and attacked Ragnar. But Ragnar had no problem dealing with him, and if it hadn't been for Lady Ingibjorg, Ulf might not have been here on this raid. So, he had gone to his tent and sharpened his axe until he fell asleep. He thought of the dream again, seeing his face on the troll's body laughing at him. It reminded him of the dream he had after the ambush at the farmstead. *You are me*, the voice rumbled in his head.

"Ulf?"

"The pup's lost it again," Ragnar's voice brought Ulf back. He saw the red-headed warrior standing next to Snorri. Like most of the men, he wore no tunic and his hair was wet. It was as if some signal had been given and the Norsemen had all decided they needed to bathe today.

"I…" Ulf started and realised he had nothing to say.

"Leave him, Ragnar." Snorri took a bite of his apple and threw the rest of it into the water. "Hurry up." He turned to Ulf. "We're going to see Ansovald today."

Ulf frowned at Snorri. "And you want me to go with?"

"I want all my hirdmen with. Those Franks are dangerous." He smiled before walking away. Ragnar glared at Ulf before turning to follow Snorri.

Ulf tried not to pay attention to the nine-fingered warrior. The jarl's champion had never liked him, something Ulf could never understand. He finished his bath and pulled his trousers on. The fabric stuck to his wet legs, but Ulf didn't mind. The sun would dry them soon enough. He rushed back to his tent and saw all of Snorri's hirdmen were there, all of them wearing their brynjas.

"We expecting a fight?" he asked as he took a loaf of bread offered to him by Oddi.

Snorri smiled. "No, but we should still look the part." Ulf nodded and went into his tent to grab his war gear. As he crawled out, Geir arrived wearing his leather jerkin. Ulf guessed Snorri had asked him to come with.

"Where are you going?" Ragnar growled at the light-haired warrior who was about Ulf's age.

"I thought I'd come with." Geir stood tall and squared his shoulders. Thorbjorn rolled his eyes while Oddi sniggered.

"Sorry Geir, but I'm only taking my hirdmen," Snorri responded with a smile. They all knew that Geir wanted to be part of Snorri's hirdmen, and Snorri tried not to upset the young warrior.

"I know, but Odin knows I'm ready to be one of them." Geir puffed out his chest.

"Well, Odin doesn't decide who becomes one of Snorri's hirdmen." Thorbjorn jumped to his feet and faced Geir.

Geir stood his ground and looked at Snorri. "With Brak dead, I thought—"

"You thought what?" Drumbr stood up and towered over the young warrior, whose head only came to his chest, his face turning red. Geir paled, realising he might have gone too far. "You thought what? That you could just take my brother's place?" Geir took a step back as the men around stopped what they were doing and looked at them. "You think it's that easy to just become a hirdman for Snorri?"

Geir looked to Snorri for help, but Snorri stayed out of it. Ulf knew that Snorri never got involved in these things. It was the same when Thorbjorn had accused Ulf of killing his own family. Ulf had also looked to Snorri for help, but had received none. Not even when the two of them had fought. Ulf guessed Snorri used these moments to test his men. "Snorri…"

"Enough," Snorri said when Drumbr's hand went to his large two-handed axe. The huge warrior glanced at Snorri and, with a nod, sat down and got back to eating his porridge. Snorri walked up to Geir and put his hand on his shoulder. "Geir, I know you want to be part of my hirdmen, and Odin knows that one day you will. But not now."

"But…"

"No, I'm not looking to replace Brak yet, and besides, you still have to prove yourself," Snorri spoke in a fatherly voice, trying to let Geir down gently.

But Geir did not go for it. "So Ulf can just walk up and join your hirdmen, but I have to prove myself." He stabbed a finger at Ulf, who frowned. Ulf had always thought that Geir liked him.

"Ulf didn't just walk into my hirdmen," Snorri growled as he lost his patience. "He saved my life." Snorri held up one finger. "He attacked Griml's army alone, and he killed Ubba." Three fingers were held up in Geir's face. Geir's shoulders sagged as Snorri glared at him.

"And don't forget," Thorbjorn said. "He's a descendant of Tyr!" Everyone looked at Thorbjorn, who only shrugged. "What? It's true."

Ulf shook his head and pulled his brynja over his head. He felt its weight as it dropped on his shoulders. The links on the shoulder were still broken, as were the ones by his stomach from his fight with Ubba. There was no smith in this village and Ulf did not have the tools or know-how to fix the links.

Geir still stood there, staring at them all. He opened his mouth to say something, but the glares he got from Snorri and Drumbr kept him quiet. "Forgive me, Snorri," he said after a while.

Snorri smiled as if nothing had happened and clapped Geir on the shoulder. "One day you will be part of my hirdmen. The gods know it, and so does everyone here. But you need to wait. When the Norns decide you are ready, then it'll happen." Geir nodded and walked away without saying anything.

"You're losing control of your men." Ragnar shook his head.

"No, I'm not."

Ragnar scowled at Snorri. "First you have the pup and Asbjorn throwing punches at each other and now you have Geir arguing with you."

Snorri watched as Geir walked away. "Let's go talk to Ansovald."

Ulf tightened his belt around his waist so it would take the weight of the brynja and followed his friends, while making sure he had his sword with him. He caught the backward glance from Geir and felt sorry for him. Geir was a good warrior, probably better than him, but his dream, like Ulf's, remained elusive.

They reached the village and saw a young man run towards the large house opposite the church. Silent whispers surrounded them as the villagers watched them walk past their houses. Women grabbed hold of their children and held them close while the men scowled at them. Some crossed themselves as if to ward off the evil the Norsemen presented. A few of them paled as Ulf scowled at them, the scars on his face frightening them.

"I think they like us." Thorbjorn waved to one child. The young boy turned and hid his face in his mother's skirt, which only made Thorbjorn laugh. For Ulf, though, it brought a memory from the day his journey started. His aunt standing by their longhouse, her two daughters holding on to her as Griml killed their father. Ulf's face darkened at the memory and for a reason he could not understand, he was angry at the Franks.

There was a loud crashing noise as they walked past one house and a man came flying out of the door, landing by their feet. All of them were stunned as a large woman stormed out of the house, the sleeves of her dress rolled up. She grabbed the man by his tunic and lifted him as if he weighed nothing and shook him, all the while shouting at him in their language. Ulf glanced at his friends and saw their raised eyebrows. Before any of them could say anything, the woman pulled her arm back and punched the man in the face. He flew through the air and landed hard, his face beaten and bloody.

"We should get her to stand in our shield wall," Asbjorn said, a hint of sarcasm in his voice.

"Aye, she'll frighten Thor with that arm of hers." Drumbr rubbed the back of his neck.

The woman realised they were staring at her. She glared at them before shouting something. None of the men understood what she was saying, but Ulf was sure she was threatening them.

Snorri held his hands up to show they meant no harm, but that only made the large woman shout even more. She was almost as tall as Snorri and as round as Drumbr and Ulf wondered if she would attack them.

"Theoda!" Ansovald shouted at the woman. He stood on the road, his face flushed as he must have rushed out to come and meet the Norse warriors. Humbert was with him, also flushed and sweaty, while a few priests gathered behind the village leader, glaring at Ulf and his friends. Theoda turned to Ansovald and, ignoring everyone else, started shouting back while waving her arms at the man on the ground, still out cold. Snorri and his men stood amused as Ansovald and the woman argued before she hitched up her skirt and stormed back to her house. Ansovald puffed out his cheeks, while the priest looked stunned by what they had just witnessed. One of them grabbed the cross around his neck and muttered to himself.

"By Freya, have you ever seen anyone more beautiful than that?"

They all turned to Thorbjorn, who was staring at the woman's house, his eyes wide.

CHAPTER 7

Griml growled, the deep rumbling noise that came out of his throat startling those around. The Danes glanced at him, but none were willing to stare into his empty eyes. Even Asgeir, the Danish leader of the Rouen raid, avoided him. But it was not just Griml they were avoiding, or feared. Griml thought about the woman who was in the tent he was guarding as if he was her servant. Another growl escaped from his throat. The men moved away, aware of what would happen if he lost his temper again. After the scarred warrior and his friends fled from a battle they should have lost, Griml took his axe and chopped Ubba's body into tiny pieces. Ubba's men had tried to stop him, saying that Ubba would not be able to go to Valhalla. Griml had been furious. He killed another six Danes before she told him to stop. The Danes were weak, just like the pathetic Swedes who were supposed to help him raid Francia. Their leader had been a spineless runt and after Griml took over his men, he kept the young jarl chained to the chair in his new hall. And then there was the girl he was supposed to marry. Griml grit his teeth at the thought of the skinny Swedish girl. Her father had thought himself a mighty jarl when all he had was a tiny village on a hill. Griml needed his men, though, and had to put up with the old bastard's boasting and the bitch's constant whining. Perhaps the Bear-Slayer did him a favour by killing the old fool and kidnapping his daughter. But that was what led to his demise and him into the arms of the only woman to ever frighten him. Griml's mind drifted to when he first met her.

It was after the battle by some large stone that looked like a giant's toe. Griml had fled, his arm mangled and a feeling he had never felt before eating him from the inside. Fear. Griml still did not understand what had happened that day. He was so sure that Odin would grant him his victory. But the All-Father had abandoned him. He remembered the young boy, the son of the jarl. "It was his fault," Griml growled. The men glanced at him again, a few muttering to each other. Griml ignored them. After the battle by the giant toe-shaped stone, the jarls' boy tried to flee with him. Griml still remembered the stench of fear and piss on him. But Griml refused. He had chased the boy away and ran north. He didn't know why. There was nothing there for him, not after he had killed his jarl and slaughtered his family. But that was the only place Griml really knew, so he ran north. After a few days, Griml found himself in a cave, his arm infected and his stomach empty. He had no strength left and no desire to live anymore, but he had been too weak to even kill himself. So he lay there, waiting for the Norns to decide it was his time. That was when she showed up.

Thunder flashed outside, its sound echoing through the cave. Griml flinched, too weak to do anything else. "Odin, why did you abandon me?" he complained again. "I should have won. I gave you a sacrifice!" he shouted, which only made him cough. His throat was dry. He had not eaten or drunk anything for days. Griml could hear water running down the walls of the cave, but he didn't have the strength or desire to crawl to the entrance. He did not care about his life anymore. The gods had abandoned him and his reputation was ruined. "I was going to be rich. Francia was ripe, the bastards too busy fighting each other to think about us attacking them." Griml coughed again. He raised his arm to wipe his mouth and regretted it as flaming hot pain tore through him. At first, he had thought he was lucky the boy did not have enough strength to chop his arm off. But now he wondered if that would not have been better.

"You really think that? To lose your arm, Griml Jotun?" A woman's voice echoed through the cave.

Griml froze, his eyes darting around but seeing nothing.

The voice laughed in the darkness, a shrill sound that ripped right through him. "My my, the mighty Griml. Is that fear I can smell in the air?"

Griml tried to summon his courage, but fear was not something he was used to. He did not know how to deal with it.

"How disappointing. The gods had much faith in you, so did I. Perhaps we were wrong." Lightning flashed, briefly illuminating the cave. Griml saw something near the entrance and grabbed a stone with his left hand. He flung it towards where he had seen the shadow and heard the stone clatter against the cave walls.

"Pathetic." The voice was closer now. Griml strained to see in the darkness, praying that Thor would send another flash of lighting. "And what would you do then?" The voice was next to him. If Griml had enough strength left, he would have jumped away from the pungent odour which suddenly assaulted his

nostrils. There was a spark and a flame burst to life near his face. Griml shut his eyes as the light blinded him and when he opened them up, he shuddered. Staring at him were two mismatched eyes, one green and one blue. A mouth filled with rotten teeth and black gums smiled, the stench of her breath making him gag. Her hair, what he could see of it, was filled with twigs and bones, tiny insects crawling all over her, but she did not seem to mind. Griml had never known fear like this before and as he breathed in to scream, she blew something into his face. He inhaled the sweet powder, and that was the last thing he remembered of that cave.

When Griml woke again, he was surrounded by trees. Birds flew above him, singing, while the scent of a cooking fire filled his nostrils. Griml tried to sit up but was too weak. He looked at his arm and saw it had been bandaged. The colour had returned to his fingers, which he could move for the first time in days. Looking around him, he saw the woman sitting by the fire and stirring something in a small pot.

"You are awake," she said to him without looking up. Griml grunted. The woman spooned something from the pot into a bowl and brought it to him. Griml gagged at her stench. She smelt like a dead animal left out in the sun for too long. "Drink this." She handed him the bowl.

Griml sniffed at the brown liquid and turned his nose away. "Not drinking this shit."

The woman shrugged. "Then you die." She walked back to the fire, not paying any more attention to him.

"Woman, I'll rip you apart with my bare hands."

She smiled a wicked smile that made him shiver. "Not if you don't drink that."

Griml looked at the bowl again, his aggression gone. "What is it?"

"It's what saved your arm."

Griml scowled at her. She wore an old hide dress, her black hair all tangled up, with twigs and bones tied in. Around her neck, she wore dried snakeskin, much like he wore a Mjöllnir around his neck. Her feet were brown with dirt, but her hands were painted green. She looked and smelt like she had not bathed for many winters. "Why are you helping me?"

The woman looked up and gave him a cruel smile. "The gods are not done with you yet."

Griml stared at the large city of Rouen just beyond the Danish camp, seeing the dark smoke drifting up from behind the stone walls. The attack had been successful and Asgeir was now a very rich man. Not only from the loot they plundered but also from the many captives, more than Griml could count. The captives were kept in a makeshift pen near to where he was sitting, their cries enough to irritate the gods. The Danes had been in good spirits since they captured the city, boasting and laughing about their great victory. A victory that should have been his. Griml would have burnt the entire city to the ground, with all her people locked inside as an offering to the gods so they would return to these lands. But Asgeir had other plans. Griml had heard some of the Danes say that the leader of the raid wanted to sell the priests back to the Franks. Griml would rather tie them up to the trees and make them hang there, just like Odin had done. But Asgeir was more interested in plunder than the gods of Asgard. Perhaps that was why the Danes were so weak.

Griml got to his feet and walked into the large tent behind him, ducking to fit through the opening. The tent had belonged to Ubba, but since the bastard got himself killed, the volva had taken it over. None of the Danes complained, though. They feared her more than him. He shivered as he saw her bent over a small fire, stirring something in a small pot, just like she had done in the forest.

"We're wasting time." He scowled.

The volva looked up from the pot, her different-coloured eyes focused on something far away. For a while, she did not respond, but slowly her eyes came into focus and she smiled at him. Griml tried to suppress another shiver. She did this often, but he still did not understand what she was doing. "Are we?"

Griml growled. "You should have let me kill that young shit."

The volva smiled, revealing her blackened teeth and gums, but she did not respond. Instead, she turned her attention back to the pot she was stirring.

"He needs to die!"

"Why?" she asked without looking at him. "Because he scarred your pretty face?"

Griml knew she was mocking him and took a step forward before he felt the air go cold around him. He froze and swallowed nervously. "N... no. Because he humiliated me in front of my army."

The volva stopped stirring but did not look up. Griml could smell the contents from the pot, an odour he could describe no other way except that it stank. He grimaced at the stench and fought the urge to turn his head away from its source. But she had fed it to him and it healed his arm. "He did not humiliate you." She looked at him now, her eyes tearing through him and making it hard for him to breathe. "Odin punished you for being stupid!"

"I… I gave him a sacrifice."

"Did you?" Her glare made him feel smaller than a dog, something Griml did not know how to deal with. He wanted to run, but his legs would not obey him.

"I… I…"

"You killed the boy with a cursed sword." The volva looked back at the pot she was stirring. "That was why you lost. Not because of the young wolf." Griml growled. He hated that she called him that. "But don't worry, soon the time will come for you to meet him again."

Griml smiled for the first time in days. "Good, I'm tired of being surrounded by the filthy Danes." He looked around the tent. They had left it untouched, and it was still filled with Ubba's belongings. Griml had watched the fight between Ubba and the boy from a distance. He thought Ubba was going to kill Ulf. The boy was not a natural warrior, that Griml had learnt. *But then why does he always win?*

"Because the gods are with him," the volva responded and Griml's blood froze in his veins. The volva looked up and smiled. Griml saw an insect crawl out from her hair and crawl over her face before making its way back. The volva did not seem to notice.

"Is that why I can't kill him?"

"No, you can't kill him because the gods are not done with him." She went back to the pot. Griml wondered what she was doing. She spent most of her time stirring it and staring at its bubbling contents.

"Still don't understand what you want with him?"

The volva stopped stirring as her face went dark. Griml was sure he could hear people screaming in agony in the distance at the same moment. "I have my own deal with the gods."

There was silence for a while as the volva turned her attention back to the pot, her gaze transfixed on it. Griml just stood there like a statue, studying the tent again. Ubba had liked his comforts. That was why he died. He had gone soft, just like his old man. That both of them died at the hands of the scarred boy amused Griml, although he wasn't sure why. Rich furs lay in a pile on one side of the tent while a large chest sat nearby — filled with fine clothing and fancy swords.

The volva looked up from her pot; her smile catching Griml off guard. "Get ready. It's time to go."

Griml frowned. "Go where?"

"For your final meeting with the young wolf."

"I don't have a ship or men."

"Take Ubba's. He doesn't need them anymore."

"I'm not fighting with Danes."

The volva glared at him. "You fight with who the gods tell you to fight with."

Griml swallowed his fear back down. "Fine, but the gods know that getting to their village is not easy. I need someone who knows the way."

The volva smiled again. "They are not in Norway."

Griml raised his eyebrows at this. "Then where are they?"

"In Francia still."

"How do you know?" He scratched his head, feeling the stubble growing.

"Because I saw him." Her face was serious. Griml wasn't sure how she saw him. She never left the tent, but he knew better than to ask. "One ship should be enough. There aren't many of them left, but take more if you need."

Griml sensed the criticism in her words but didn't respond. Instead, he asked, "Where in Francia?"

"Sail along the coast and keep your eyes on the shore. You will see a sign." The volva went back to stirring the contents in the pot.

"So I finally get to kill the runt?"

The volva smiled without looking up. Griml waited for a few heartbeats and realised the conversation was over. With a grunt, he turned and left the tent. Outside, he scanned the ships along the river until he spotted Ubba's and then made his way towards them. Men were on board, repairing ropes and carrying their share of the plunder onto the ships. As he approached, a man stepped in front of him. He was big, reaching Griml's chest, which meant he was taller than most men. He wore a fine brynja and his arms were covered in arm rings. The signs of a great warrior.

"Where do you think you are going, Norseman?" The Dane crossed his arms in front of his chest and glared at Griml.

"You the new leader of Ubba's men?" Griml asked. The man nodded and before he could say anything, Griml grabbed him by the throat. The Dane's eyes bulged as Griml squeezed hard, the man's throat crushing in his hands. Around them, the Danish warriors could only watch, none of them brave enough to stop him. Griml smiled as he lifted the man and threw him to the ground. The Dane landed hard and held a hand up as he coughed up blood, his eyes pleading for mercy. But Griml only sneered at him before stomping down on his head. The noise of the Dane's head cracking open silenced all those within earshot. They all stared at Griml, eyes wide and hands trembling. "Ubba's ships are mine, and so are you. Prepare this ship. We are leaving."

One man, braver than the rest, stepped forward, his hands folded together. "Where are we going?"

"To kill the Bear-Slayer."

CHAPTER 8

"Odin knows this is one of your dumbest ideas yet, Snorri."
Ragnar shook his head as the mix of young beardless men and
greybeards stood in a ragged line before them. All had sour
expressions on their faces and none made any eye contact with
the Norsemen. The only one smiling was Ansovald. He was
also the only one who wore armour and had a weapon with him.
The rest of the Frankish men only had tunics and trousers on,
some were even barefoot.

Humbert was also there to translate. He wore a fine tunic,
longer than the ones worn by the other men, with a silk trim.
Around his waist was a thick leather belt which matched the
leather boots he wore. His hair was neatly combed, as was his
beard and moustache. He did not look like a man who was
planning to spend his day on the training field. Ulf glanced at
the women scurrying around the village and wondered if it had
anything to do with that. Since sunrise, the women had been
busy. They rushed past the Norse camp, all of them turning
their heads away from the Norse warriors, and pretended not to
hear the whistles and comments directed their way. Young girls

were running around the field, collecting flowers while their mothers were down by the river, washing clothing and large sheets. Inside the village, those men who were not required to come to the fields were butchering livestock, while others were collecting vegetables. The priests walked amongst the busy people, their arms behind their backs as they commented on the ongoings. They had avoided the Norsemen, even when Snorri went into the village to talk to Ansovald. The priests didn't want them there, and Ulf was sure they prayed every day for their god to chase them off. But none of that happened. Instead, it looked like they were here to stay and as much as Ulf wanted to get away from this land, he knew he could not. Not only because Snorri had agreed to help the Franks, but also because Griml was still here. And despite losing their last fight, Ulf was still determined to get his revenge. He grit his teeth as the dark memories of their fight in Rouen came to his mind. Ulf had spent the last few days reliving that battle, trying to find a way to kill the troll. But he could not. Griml was faster than any man Ulf had ever fought, faster than even him. Ulf was starting to doubt if he could ever defeat Griml and get his vengeance.

"Must be some feast happening." Drumbr's comment saved Ulf from his dark thoughts. So did the rumbling of his large friend's stomach.

"I believe they have some holy day coming soon," Oddi said, eyeing the church in the distance. Every morning, the church bells would ring, waking them all up. The men constantly complained about it and even threatened to burn the church down.

"A holy day?" Ulf scratched his ear.

"Aye, on holy days, they remember some saint or event or something like that." Oddi shrugged. Ulf was sure Oddi knew more, but didn't want to seem too interested in the faith of their enemy, not with Thorbjorn standing beside him.

"What's a saint?" Ulf had never heard of this before. "Are they like Valkyries?"

Oddi looked at him, his eyebrow raised, before answering. "They are people who performed magic in the past, usually to help others."

"Like a godi or volva?" Ulf thought of Hulda's mother and had to fight to stop the shiver running down his spine.

"Godar and volvas don't help people." Thorbjorn hawked and spat. "They only cause trouble." The men around agreed with Thorbjorn, and again Ulf thought of Hulda's mother. He still couldn't understand what she wanted from him.

"Odin knows it's all nonsense." Asbjorn scowled at Ulf. "Their magic isn't real."

"How do you know?" one of the young warriors asked. He had been creeping closer to them, trying to listen in on their conversation.

Asbjorn turned to the young warrior, his face turning red. "Because I have seen none of their priests use magic to protect themselves from us."

"Asbjorn's right. If I had magic powers, I'd use them." Thorbjorn nodded.

"To make yourself taller, no doubt," Drumbr said, which caused the men to laugh.

Snorri and Ragnar turned from their conversation to see what the men were laughing at.

"At least they are having a great time," Ragnar growled, which killed the laughter.

"Relax," Snorri patted him on the back. "The Franks don't need to fight, they only need to look like they will. Loki knows this plan will work."

"Aye, that's what worries me. We're depending on Loki and the trickster is the ficklest of the gods." Ragnar ran his hand through his red hair while glancing at the sky.

Humbert cleared his throat, the old trader looking uncomfortable when all the Norsemen suddenly looked at him. "We... we be long?" Snorri frowned at him, so Humbert tried again, this time speaking louder. "We be long?" He pointed to the field they were standing in.

"You have somewhere else to be?" Ragnar took a step towards him. Humbert paled and shook his head. He glanced at Ansovald, hoping his leader would protect him, but Ansovald only smiled.

"Why?" Snorri placed a hand on Ragnar's chest, stopping the nine-fingered warrior in his tracks.

Humbert blew out a breath of relief. "Tomorrow, day of St Eoaldus of Vienne. Special day," he said and pointed at the church in the village. "Much to do. Men needed."

"Who?" Ulf glanced at his friends, who only shrugged.

Snorri looked at the church and then at his men, his wolf grin spreading on his face, and they all knew a plan was forming in his mind. But before anyone could ask Snorri about it, a scream pierced the air. All the men, Norse and Frank, turned towards the sound as the girls in the fields fled to the village, their baskets of flowers flying through the air behind them. The women by the river looked up and spotted the same threat their daughters had. They added their screams to the noise as they dropped the clothing they had been washing and fled.

"What in Odin's name?" Thorbjorn frowned, but they soon saw what had caused the panic as the church bells started ringing frantically. Birds took flight from the church's roof as dogs barked in excitement. Men appeared from the forest, weapons in the air, their war cries lost in the ringing of the church bells and the screams of the fleeing women.

"Fucking cowards!" Asbjorn waved his fist in the air as the Frankish men turned and fled back to their village. Only Ansovald stood his ground, his sword already in his hand, as he glared at the men attacking his village. Humbert tried to keep up with the fleeing men, but his longer tunic and old age meant he soon fell behind. He cried out as he tripped and fell flat on the ground. Ulf thought the old man had died, but then he covered his head with his hands.

Ansovald was shouting something at Snorri, which none of them understood, but the sword pointed at the oncoming attackers gave them all an idea of what he wanted.

"Danes?" Thorbjorn asked as the Norse warriors stood patiently and waited for an order from Snorri, something which frustrated Ansovald even more as his shouts became louder. He looked like he was about to charge at the men attacking his home himself when Snorri spoke.

"No, Franks. The very ones we are supposed to be attacking." Snorri smiled, then glanced to the sky as he had been constantly doing since they got here — looking for a sign from the gods. They wanted their chaos, and this fight looked like just that.

"Aye, they're wearing the same clothing as the bastards who attacked us on the beach," Oddi said, and the men nodded, some of them gritting their teeth.

"What do we do, Snorri?" Asbjorn asked, his sword already in his hand.

Snorri pulled Tyr's Fury from her scabbard and punched her into the air. "Men of Thorgilsstad! Protect that village as if it was our home!"

"Odin! Thor!" the Norse warriors roared and charged at the attacking men.

It was a race to get to the village first. The Norsemen, all dressed in their war gear, sped to intercept the attacking Franks before they could reach the village. The church bells were still ringing as men and women grabbed their children and ran for their houses. All the preparations for the feast were forgotten, some of it trampled on as people thought of nothing but their safety.

"Fucking cowards!" Asbjorn shouted again.

The Frankish attackers paused when they saw the Norsemen storming towards them, their war cries drowning out the church bells. For a moment, they were stunned, but they quickly recovered and charged at the Norsemen.

"What are they doing?" Magni asked between gasping breaths. He kept pace with the rest of them, even though Ulf was sure Oddi's taller brother could outrun them all.

"They outnumber us!" Oddi responded. "The gods love chaos!" He laughed as they reached their attackers.

There was no call for a shield wall from Snorri. The Franks might have outnumbered them, but the Norse all wore armour and had better weapons.

Ulf gripped Olaf's axe tighter as the sounds of the church bells disappeared behind him. All his focus was on the man charging at him, his sword high in the air and his eyes wide. The man looked about the same age as Ulf, but was smaller and thinner. Ulf ducked behind his shield and sped up. Before the Frank could chop down with his sword, Ulf rammed into him, his shield catching the man in the chest. He grunted from the collision, but his bigger size and strength meant the Frank was sent flying back. Ulf stopped and stared at the young man as he lay on the ground, clutching his chest. His eyes filled with fear as he struggled to breathe. Growling in frustration, Ulf stepped over the man and punched down with the rim of his shield. The crack echoed around him as he caved the man's face in, killing him. As Ulf straightened up, he heard laughter in his mind. It was not the voices of his ancestors which usually came to him during a battle. They knew he did not need them for this. It was the deep rumbling laugh from before, and it sent a shiver down his spine as he pictured the troll in his mind's eye.

Ulf shook his head to clear the laughter from it. Because of this, he almost saw the next attack too late. The Frank, older than the one Ulf had just killed, swung his rusty sword at Ulf's chest. Ulf had no time to bring his shield to block the sword and didn't want to use his axe. Olaf's axe was the weapon he needed to kill Griml and with her handle already damaged, he had to be careful. So instead, Ulf tried to twist out of the way. The sword cut across his chest, but his movement and the Frank's lack of strength meant the blade did not break the links of Ulf's brynja. Still, the blow hurt, and Ulf had to stop himself from bending over and exposing his neck to his attacker. The man jumped back before Ulf could retaliate. Keeping his shield in front of him, Ulf took a step back, glancing around him to see how the rest of his friends were doing.

Snorri and Ansovald were fighting a group of men together. Their warrior instincts meant they did not get in each other's way as they fended off blows and killed the men facing them. Asbjorn was dancing around his opponent, stabbing and cutting at the man until the Frank could not stand anymore and collapsed. But instead of killing him, Asbjorn moved on and left the Frank to die a slow death. The rest of Ulf's friends were behind him, and he did not want to take his eyes off the Frank facing him. He turned his attention back to that man and was about to charge when a new scream tore through the battle noise. Ulf and his opponent turned towards the village, both men expecting to see the attackers burning the houses. But instead, the large woman Ulf had seen a few days before stormed towards the battle with a large rolling pin in her hand. Her face red and her wild hair streaming behind her, she lifted her skirt and charged at the men threatening her village.

"By Freya, isn't she amazing?" Thorbjorn said from behind Ulf.

Ulf's opponent laughed at the sight of the large woman and shouted something to his comrades. But he was quickly silenced as Ulf launched himself at the man. Before the Frank could react, Ulf punched him in the face with the rim of his shield and sliced his throat open with Olaf's axe. Blood sprayed through the air as the Frank collapsed, his face a bloody mess and the blood gushing from his neck like fresh meltwater in the spring heat.

"Leave her alone, you fucking bastards!" Thorbjorn shouted as two Franks attacked the woman. He quickly dispatched the man he was fighting by ducking under his spear and stabbing him in the chest. He then ran towards Theoda. But he wasn't needed.

The woman faced the two men, shouting something before one of them lunged at her. She used her skirt to deflect the sword before hitting the man on the head with her rolling pin. Even over the battle noise, they heard the man's skull cracking before he slumped to the ground. Her other attacker hesitated long enough for her to kick him in the chest with her large leg. The man was sent flying backwards and when he landed on the ground, Thorbjorn was there to stab him through the neck. Blood squirted up into the air as Thorbjorn freed his sword and smiled at the woman. For a few heartbeats, Theoda stared at him as if she wanted to crack his head open as well. Thorbjorn lowered his sword and just stood there, facing her.

The battle noise suddenly stopped, surprising Ulf. He turned away from the woman and his friend and saw their attackers fleeing.

"Run, you worms! Flee from the mighty Magni the Cockerel!" The men laughed as Magni stood on the battleground, his arms spread wide and his face covered in blood.

"Just when you think the bastard is normal, he does something like that," Snorri said, walking up to Ulf. Ulf looked at his axe and was glad the handle was still in one piece. He licked his lips and tasted the saltiness of his enemy's blood. Snorri smiled at him, the battle lust still in his eyes. "That was something not even the gods ever expected." Snorri pointed a bloody Tyr's Fury at Thorbjorn. Ulf turned and saw the woman was walking back to the village, her head held high and the rolling pin still in her hand. Thorbjorn stood there and stared after the woman like a lovesick child, which only made Snorri laugh.

"Aye, the Norns must have been drinking too much mead today." Oddi appeared, wiping his sword clean with a cloth before putting her in the scabbard.

"The Norns drink mead?" Ulf scratched his cheek. He had always thought the Norns would be too busy weaving the fates of men to be drinking.

"I think so. All that weaving must be thirsty work." Oddi turned to Snorri as Ulf thought about his answer. "Doesn't look like we lost anyone."

Snorri scanned the battleground and didn't see any of his men amongst the fallen. "Aye, Odin smiled on us today, in more ways than one."

"How do you figure that?" Ragnar asked as he approached them.

Snorri smiled at his father's champion. "I've been trying to come up with a plan to attack their town, and Odin sent them to us instead."

"Well, at least now we know how bad your plan was," Ragnar said, leaning on his axe. Snorri frowned at him. "None of those cowards stayed to fight for their home."

"Aye, it's no wonder they need us to protect them," Asbjorn agreed.

"Perhaps we should get the women to fight."

The men looked at Ulf with raised eyebrows, not used to him saying anything other than complaining about his revenge, before Snorri laughed.

"Aye, Freya would be proud of her." They all looked back at the village and saw Thorbjorn following the woman. He was saying something to her, although he was too far away for any of them to hear what. Theoda got to her house, the same one they saw her throwing the man out of. She turned and glared at Thorbjorn, who looked like he was about to kiss her. The woman took a step back and slapped Thorbjorn hard in the face. They all laughed as Thorbjorn fell to the ground.

"By Odin, someone has finally bested Thorbjorn," Snorri joked.

"A woman, no less," Drumbr added, tears streaming down his cheeks.

Ulf looked around him, studying the battleground. The Norsemen were walking through the bodies of the dead, looking for anything valuable, when the priests came running out of the village. They berated the warriors while trying to chase them away, but the men of Thorgilsstad ignored them.

"Nothing worth taking anyway," one of the men said as he glared at the red-faced priests in front of him.

Ansovald shouted at the priests as he wiped the blood from his scared face. The priests went quiet and, after a few heartbeats of staring at the village leader, turned and walked away. Ansovald shook his head and looked their way before he, too, turned and walked back to his village.

"Fought well, the old man," Snorri said.

"Aye, it's a pity none of the other men are as eager as him," Asbjorn said.

Oddi scratched his beard. "He did say most of his warriors were fighting in the civil war."

"But most of the men we faced today were fighting men," Ulf said, remembering the man he had fought.

With the danger gone, the villagers left their houses and picked their way through the ruined preparations for the holy day. Humbert appeared from somewhere, his fine tunic and face covered in mud. "This bad! This bad!"

"Why?" Snorri frowned and glanced at his men, who shrugged. "We won. They ran away."

Humbert shook his head, his eyes welling up. "Day of St Eoaldus of Vienne ruined. Very important, but now we can not."

Snorri looked at his men again, who were as confused as he was. Ulf didn't understand himself. Their village was safe, but all the trader cared about was some celebration.

"Well then," Snorri looked in the direction their attackers had run, his wolf grin on his face again, "it's only fair that we go spoil their celebration as well."

CHAPTER 9

Heavy clouds filled the dark sky as the Norsemen approached their prey. A town larger than the one they had been staying in and surrounded by wooden walls taller than Magni. There were no watchtowers, not like some of the other towns and cities they have attacked in Francia. The men knew, though, there would be a platform behind the wall where defenders could keep a vigilant eye out for attacks. But in the morning darkness, they saw no torches on the wall.

It was the day after the attack on Ansovald's village, the day of St Eoaldus of Vienne, and the Norsemen came to finish the job so they could go home. After the attack the previous day, Snorri had told Ansovald that they had to attack today. It was their best chance. Not only would their enemy not expect them to attack so soon, but they would be weaker and tired after their failed attempt. The village elders, Humbert included, had protested. Today was a holy day. It was a day of their god and the old men did not want to anger him. The priests had admonished the Norse pagans in their language. Humbert did his best to translate their words for Snorri and his men, as if he believed they would have any effect. But Snorri had not been paying any attention to them. He had been watching Ansovald who was sitting on his seat, his brow creased and face red as he listened to everything the elders had to say. At that moment, he had reminded Snorri so much of his father that Snorri felt angry with the Frankish chief. Jarl Thorgils would sit on his chair, his face stern as he listened to all his trusted men give their opinions before he would speak. Snorri wondered if his father was still hiding away in his longhouse, or if his mother had convinced him to come out and lead his people. After the old men and priests ran out of air and their voices went silent, Ansovald finally spoke. Snorri did not understand the words that came from the old warrior's scarred lips, but he understood the meaning. Ansovald was angry that their neighbours had attacked before a holy day. He wanted them to pay. In the dark hall, the Frankish chief looked Snorri in the eyes and Snorri saw the fire burning in them, a fire he knew well, and agreed to attack. The old men complained, and the priests wailed, waving their arms in the air and imploring Ansovald not to attack on the day of their God. But Ansovald had turned his back on them and walked away.

Snorri glanced over his shoulder and saw the figure of Ansovald in the dim light. Humbert had explained that the old warrior was furious that the men of his village had fled, instead of defending their home. He had been embarrassed because he had to ask Norse pagans to protect them. Humbert had explained to Snorri that Ansovald worried his God would punish him for what they were about to do. But Ansovald wanted to protect his village and to do that, he had to make a deal with the very men who came to rape and pillage his lands.

Snorri kissed the Mjöllnir hanging around his neck, glad that his gods did not run away from violence. Today would be a holy day, but not the holy day the Christians wanted. It would be a day of blood and death, a holy day for Odin and the gods of Asgard.

"It's almost time," Ragnar said beside him, his voice low as if he was concerned he might warn the town in the distance. Church bells started ringing as the horizon lit up, but the Norsemen weren't concerned. They knew the bells were not because of them.

"Aye." Snorri gripped the hilt of his sword. The day would be dark as heavy clouds filled the sky. Thunder sounded in the distance, giving Snorri confidence that the gods, or at least Thor, were with them. But then, the red-headed god always loved a fight. "Let's go," Snorri ordered, his wolf grin on his face. Around him, his men got to their feet, their armour jingling in the quiet of the morning. Humbert had told him that the gates of the village would be open today because people would travel from the surrounding farmsteads to attend the church service. Only about thirty men remained of the two crews he took with him when he left for Francia, the rest either drowned or killed. But he knew these thirty men would be enough, as they had killed many of the Franks who attacked them the day before.

Humbert muttered something behind Snorri. Ansovald had tried to learn some of their words, but he found it difficult, so he had ordered the old trader to come with them. Snorri didn't understand why. They were here to kill and burn, not to talk. But Ansovald and Humbert were the only Franks with them, apart from Theoda. After the attack on their village, Snorri had decided against using the Frankish men. They were farmers, not warriors, and he was sure they would just run again. He did not want their enemy to see men running from his army. It would give them the courage to fight back. The large woman, though, insisted on coming with. There had been a heated debate which she won. The Norse warriors had grumbled, apart from Thorbjorn, who beamed like a virgin boy seeing a woman naked for the first time. Thorbjorn was standing next to the woman now, barely taking his eyes off her. Snorri prayed to Freya that his friend would not die today because he was too busy staring at Theoda to fight.

Like wolves, they approached the village from the west, staying low and using the dim morning light to conceal themselves. This way, they could hide in the shadows for longer and also avoid the gate by the river on the other side of the town. Ansovald was next to Snorri, the Frankish chief wanting to be near the front of the attack. Snorri didn't mind, though. He knew there would be no shield wall today. The old chief's face was hard as he gripped his sword, but he kept up with the Norsemen, despite his limp. As they got close, Snorri held his hand up. His men stopped and crouched in the shadows. The sun was slowly climbing into the sky, but the heavy clouds hid it from them. Snorri glanced at Ulf, seeing his hand on the hilt of his sword. At least Ulf could use his sword today. Snorri had given him another axe, knowing that Ulf did not want to use his, but that axe would not be needed. Perhaps another sign that the gods were with them.

Out of sight, they waited for the right moment to attack as the people from the nearby farms arrived. Snorri needed the guards by the gates to be distracted by the people coming in. That way, his men could get into the town.

Again, Humbert muttered something and Ansovald shushed the old man. Ragnar growled beside Snorri — if the trader didn't keep his mouth shut, Ragnar would cut his tongue out. But the old trader went quiet as the first of the farmers reached the gates. Snorri watched as they walked in groups, some pulling carts while others carried baskets. Men greeted each other loudly as women started chattering, no doubt sharing gossip. The gates swung open; the guards greeting the newcomers warmly, calling out the names of those they knew. Snorri felt his men tense behind him. He glanced at Ansovald, but the old warrior only stared at the gate with hard eyes. A small dog followed a cart pulled by a single ox. As it got close to their position, it stopped and sniffed the air. Snorri felt his blood go cold as it looked in their direction and he sent a silent prayer to the gods that the dog would not start barking. But then, as if the gods were with them, the dog's owner called and it ran after the cart, quickly forgetting about them.

Snorri waited until enough of the farmers had entered the gates, wanting to cause as much chaos as possible. Thunder rolled through the clouds again and through the eye guards of his helmet, Snorri saw those still outside the village look up and shake their heads. They worried that rain might ruin the day's festivities, but Snorri knew they were unaware of the real threat as he kissed the Mjöllnir around his neck for luck. Gripping Tyr's Fury tightly, he shouted, "Odin!"

Thunder ripped through the clouds as the Norsemen broke from cover and charged at the gates, their battle cry loud enough to wake the gods. Snorri had told his men to make as much noise as possible. He wanted the people to be as frightened as children at the sound of thunder in the middle of the night. And they were. The Franks turned at the noise, many staring at the oncoming Norseman with their mouths agape, unable to make sense of what they were seeing. A woman screamed, snapping the villagers out of their shocked state and, like startled birds, they scattered. It was exactly what Snorri wanted as he reached them, with Ragnar to his left and Ansovald to his right, the old warrior somehow keeping up. Some farmers fled away from the town gates, but most rushed into the town, preventing the guards from closing the gates. The noise was deafening, even if it was muffled by his helmet, as his men roared and the people screamed. The Frankish guards stood frozen by the gates, uncertain of what they needed to do. These men had never been in this situation before and were caught between protecting the town and those trying to find safety. In the end, it made no difference.

Snorri used his shield to barge the farmers out of his way, while Ragnar swung his mighty two-handed axe in a wide arc, killing man, woman and child. Oddi jumped over one cart and stabbed a guard through the neck before punching another in the face with his shield. There was a sickening crunch as the rest of the Norsemen collided with those still trying to get into the town. Those who couldn't get out of the way were slaughtered. Blood sprayed through the air, drenching Snorri and his men, but soon they were through the gates and into the town.

The church bells rang more frantically as word of the attack spread. Men burst out of their houses and stared at the invaders in shock before ushering the women and children towards the church in the centre of the village.

"Stay together!" Snorri ordered his men. There were a lot of smaller streets in this town and he did not want to lose his men amongst them. His men spread out and fought against those brave enough to defend their homes. A tall Frank charged at Snorri, his arm covered in a bandage. Snorri raised his shield to block the man's sword strike. He turned his shield and deflected the blow, leaving his opponent open. Before the man could react, Snorri buried Tyr's Fury in his chest. The Frank grunted, his eyes wide, as Snorri pulled his sword free. He muttered something before dropping dead. "Kill only the men!" Snorri shouted. That was the only condition made by Ansovald. Not to kill or rape any of the women and children. The men were unhappy about it and Snorri hoped they would obey him, but he understood his men and the world they lived in. Most of them did not care who stood in front of them when they gave in to their blood lust. That was clear by the bodies of the women and children who lay dead on the ground, slaughtered as his men forced their way through the gates. A man ran past Snorri. He had no weapon that Snorri could see, but Snorri cut him down. For all he knew, the man was running to his house to get one.

A roar caught his attention and Snorri saw a heavyset man, most likely the town's smith, judging by the large hammer he carried and his muscular arms and shoulders. The man bellowed before charging at him, his hammer swinging above his head. Snorri smiled his wolf grin as the smith brought the hammer down, intent on crushing Snorri's helmet and skull. He jumped to the side and cut the back of the smith's leg with his sword. The smith cried out in pain as he dropped to his knee. Snorri stepped back, grinning savagely as he gave the smith a chance to get to his feet. Near him, Ansovald killed a man, the old

Frank roaring in anger as he finally got to avenge his village. With a grunt, the smith got back to his feet and glared at Snorri while holding his hammer in both hands. With another roar, he charged. Ignoring the pain in his leg, the Frank swung his hammer at Snorri's head. This time Snorri ducked underneath it and, as the smith moved past him, cut the back of the man's other leg. Again, the smith cried out in pain as he dropped to his knees. Snorri knew the large Frank would not get to his feet again, but stayed wary of the hammer. He walked around to face the smith, seeing the hatred in his creased face and smiled. The smith tried one last attack, but this time, Snorri cut his arm and the smith dropped the hammer. Snorri stepped back again, not paying attention to the battle around him as he stared at the smith through the eye guards of his helmet. The smith glared at him while muttering something, but Snorri wasn't listening to him. He looked to the sky, searching for a sign from the gods in the dark clouds. "Odin!" he roared before he lunged forward and rammed Tyr's Fury in the smith's throat. He pushed the sword all the way through until the hilt reached the smith's neck, all the while staring into the man's eyes and seeing the defiance turn to fear. Again, Snorri looked to the sky. "Odin!" He pulled his sword free, covering himself in a spray of blood. For a few heartbeats, the smith sat on his knees, staring at Snorri with wide eyes as the blood squirted out of his throat before he collapsed to the ground.

"Was that really necessary?" Ragnar asked.

Snorri turned to his father's champion, seeing him covered in blood, and nodded. "Making sure Odin sees what we are doing." The fight looked like it was almost over. There weren't many defenders in the town left after the attack the day before, but a few of the men still stood their ground and tried to protect their families. Most of the women and children had fled to the church, whose bells were still ringing. Snorri wondered who they thought would come to help them. From what Humbert had explained, their village was the closest to this town.

"Perhaps they think their god will come down and fight us." Ragnar grinned as if he liked the idea of fighting the Christian god.

Snorri looked around and saw Theoda swing her rolling pin above her head as she charged at a man with a spear. Thorbjorn ran beside her, cutting a man down who tried to attack the woman. Snorri almost laughed as she batted the spear out of the way before crushing the man's skull with the rolling pin. Blood sprayed over her, but Theoda did not seem to care as she searched for another man to fight, her eyes wild.

"By Odin, that woman is dangerous," Ragnar said. "It's a good thing the men don't fight like her."

"Aye, let's just hope the rest of their women don't decide to fight us." They both laughed, which sounded strange amongst the carnage and death around them.

They heard a scream and turned in time to see a Frankish man stab a pitchfork at Ulf. Ulf twisted out of the way, his speed no match for the young farmer, but refused to strike back.

"He's no warrior." Ragnar shook his head. "Not like his father."

Snorri watched as the farmer turned and swung the pitchfork at Ulf. This time, Ulf blocked it with his shield before stepping in and stabbing the farmer through the stomach with Ormstunga. The farmer spat blood into Ulf's face and collapsed to the ground after Ulf freed his sword. "No, he is a warrior.

The gods know it, otherwise, they wouldn't have chosen him for whatever they are planning. He's just not..." Snorri paused as he tried to find the right word.

"A killer." Ragnar had been around long enough to understand what Snorri was saying.

"Aye. Ulf is not a killer. Not like us."

"Or his father."

Snorri nodded. Ulf's father had always been good to him, always making time to train Snorri. Ragnar took over when Bjørn had died protecting his father in a battle many winters ago.

"Where's he going?" Asbjorn asked, freeing Snorri from his thoughts. Snorri looked to where Asbjorn was pointing and saw Ansovald limping towards the church.

"Let's find out. Oddi, protect the gate!" he shouted to his tall hirdman. "And someone, go find that trader!"

"On my way." One of his men ran to where Humbert was hiding outside the gate.

"Expected Geir to be grovelling up to you again," Ragnar said.

"Aye, me too. Perhaps he's still angry at me."

Ragnar shook his head. "You're too soft on your men."

"I am what I need to be to my men," Snorri responded. "Odin knows that's all I can do." He watched as Oddi grabbed a few men to guard the gate, and then turned back to Ansovald, who was already halfway to the church. "Now, let's see what he is up to. To the church!"

CHAPTER 10

Ulf stared at the farmer he had just killed as a deep laugh rumbled in his head. *You are me*, the voice echoed in his ears, and Ulf thought of his uncle. A farmer who died trying to protect his family, just like the man Ulf had skewered with his sword. Ulf tilted Ormstunga in his hand, seeing how the blood ran down her blade. Although Ulf could only see out of one eye. He tried to wipe the blood away by sticking his finger through his eye guard.

"To the church!" He heard Snorri shout. Ulf looked around and saw the fight by the gate was over. Dead bodies lay everywhere, men, women and children, all of them slaughtered so they could get back home. Ulf looked at the blade of Ormstunga again, wondering whose blood mixed with the farmer's. When Snorri had given the order, he charged alongside his friends. They had to get through those gates, so like the others, Ulf had stabbed and cut his way through those who crowded the entrance to the town. His hands shook at the thought. *Frigg, please don't let me turn into the monster I mean to kill.* The deep laughter rang in his ears again. Ulf turned away from the bodies, desperately trying to push the laughter out of his head, when he spotted something that chilled him to the bone. A movement so quick, he almost missed it. But he still caught the deer hide dress and thick black hair disappearing behind one of the houses. Open-mouthed, he took his helmet off and rubbed his eyes, hoping that he was just seeing things because of the blood in his eyes. He wanted to run to the house to make sure. But the last time he had done that, he came face to face with the man whose laugh he couldn't get out of his head. And Ulf was not sure if he was ready to face the troll again.

"Ulf, you coming?" Drumbr called to him. He turned to the large warrior and saw him leaning on his large two-handed axe, Shield Breaker. The axe's blade was covered in blood, just like Drumbr. The spark which disappeared after the death of Brak had returned as Drumbr smiled at him. "Snorri will gut you if you run off again."

"Aye, he will," Ulf said, putting his helmet back on. After a quick glance at the house, he followed Drumbr and the rest of Snorri's men as they walked to the church.

The Norse warriors stayed wary, their weapons still in their hands as they scanned the smaller streets which branched off the main road. They had learnt to be extra vigilant on this raid. Ulf gripped Ormstunga's hilt tightly in hand, his eyes darting between the houses. He was sure the volva could not be here. It was impossible. But the hairs on the back of his neck stood on end, and Ulf felt like he was being watched.

They reached the church without any problems, as most of the defenders were either dead or had fled. Ravens and other scavenging birds circled above their heads, a few of them landing on the roofs of the houses, their cries deafening in the silence. Some men were eyeing up the doors, a few of them with dangerous glints in their eyes. They all knew there would be women hiding in the houses. But Snorri had told them there would be no raping women or killing them. They already failed at one of these, and Ulf wondered if they would obey the raping part.

"Would you look at that," Thorbjorn said as they got to the church. He was still next to the large woman from Ansovald's village, her face and rolling pin covered in blood.

The church was simple, nothing as elaborate as the one they found after they had attacked Hammaburg. It had a tall tower at the front, its bell finally silent. Its windows were plain, not colourful like the other church, and this one was smaller. But that's not what was interesting. Standing in front of the church was a handful of men who looked like warriors. They wore the same conical helmets as the other Frankish warriors Ulf had seen, as they stood behind their round shields. The men all had leather jerkins on and had spears pointed at the Norse invaders. Behind the warriors was a group of priests, all wearing habits like the priests in the church they had plundered. To Ulf, it looked more like a long brown dress. They all had the same hairstyle, the tops of their heads shaved clean and only a ring of hair left behind. The priests were screaming at the sky while waving their arms in the air. A few of them carried books while the other priests had empty hands, but all their faces were red.

Ansovald shouted at the church, ignoring the armed men and the priests. Ulf glanced at Snorri and saw the frown on his face.

"Let's kill the bastards," Magni said, licking his lips.

"No, I think this is something Ansovald wants to do." Snorri glanced at the Frankish chief.

"And why do we care about what he wants?" Thorbjorn adjusted his helmet.

"Because we still need his help to get home."

"That's if he helps us." Ragnar spat to the ground.

Snorri smiled. "If he doesn't, we kill all the men in his village and sell all the women after we burn his home to the ground." The men smiled at that, vicious smiles that had the Frankish warriors looking nervously at each other.

Ansovald shouted again, this time cupping his hands to his mouth. Ulf did not understand the words, but it sounded like a challenge. After a while, a man stepped out dressed in a fine tunic and carrying a beautiful sword on his hip. He looked similar to Ansovald, although he was younger and rounder at the waist.

"Who's he?" Drumbr scratched his forehead under his bowl helmet.

"Ansovald brother," Humbert said from behind them, giving some men a fright, as no one expected him to be there, with the man Snorri had sent to fetch him.

"Ansovald's brother?" Snorri frowned, his eyes studying the new man. Humbert nodded, his face pale at the sight of all the violence he passed to get to the church.

"They do look the same," Asbjorn said, before looking at Snorri. "Never told us we'd be fighting against his brother."

"I didn't know." Snorri grit his teeth, although Ulf was not sure if it was because of this new information or the way Asbjorn spoke to him.

"Does it really matter?" Ragnar sounded bored. "We are here to kill Franks. I don't care if they are related."

Ansovald's brother walked past his guards, scowling at them in disdain. He spoke to Ansovald in a mocking tone, and Ansovald responded with a retort as the Norsemen watched on.

"What are they saying?" Thorbjorn looked at Humbert.

Before the old trader could respond, Snorri said, "It doesn't matter." He glanced at Humbert, who tried to shrink away from Snorri's hard eyes. "We were asked to attack this town. It doesn't matter who their leader is."

"But still, he asked us to attack his own brother." Drumbr frowned at the thought.

"Sometimes brothers just want to kill each other." Snorri hawked and spat. "You can't always trust the treacherous worms." Ulf saw the hardness in Snorri's eyes and knew who he was thinking about. They all did. Snorri's brother had betrayed them all. It was because of him that Vidar had died, but Ulf knew that wasn't the real reason Snorri was angry with his brother. He was angry because when Thorvald had seen that the battle was lost, he ran.

"Not all brothers are like that," Drumbr retorted, his eyes red.

Snorri sighed. "I know Drumbr. The gods blessed you with Brak."

"Is this really the time and place for this?" Ragnar shook his head as if he was dealing with children. "I swear by Odin, Snorri, I sometimes wonder how you make it out of battles alive when you waste so much time talking." The men laughed and Snorri grinned, but Ragnar wasn't done yet. "We have a job to do. So let's do it and go home. Then you two can cry over your brothers."

"Aye, Ragnar. Let's do that." Snorri turned back to the two Frankish chiefs, who were still having a heated debate. "Think this'll take long?"

"If he's anything like you, then most likely," Ragnar responded.

Just then, Ansovald's brother shouted something, which made Humbert gasp, and drew his sword. The Norse warriors tensed, expecting the last few defenders to attack, but Ansovald held his hand up and said something without looking at them.

"He say no. It his fight," Humbert explained.

"He's going to fight all of them?" Thorbjorn asked, with a hint of admiration in his voice.

Humbert shook his head. "He fight brother."

The Norsemen took a step back, giving the two brothers more space to fight. Ansovald glanced over his shoulder and nodded.

"Should we be concerned?" Oddi asked. "If he dies, then we won't get the help he promised."

Snorri glanced to the sky, but saw nothing in the dark clouds. "Only the Norns will know that."

"You really think the Norns know about the lives of the Christians?" Ulf couldn't stop himself from asking.

"Perhaps not, but they know our fates and right now ours are tied with Ansovald's." Snorri looked at Ulf, who saw the concern his friend was trying to hide.

Ulf turned his attention back to the two Franks as they prepared to fight each other.

Ansovald's brother roared and charged, his face red from anger and effort, his sword held high in both hands. Ansovald stepped out of the way and avoided the blow. His brother stopped and turned, all the while glaring at Ansovald who only stood there. He suddenly realised he had his back to the Norsemen and couldn't stop the nervous glance over his shoulder. Thorbjorn smiled and waved his sword at the man. The fat Frankish chief quickly moved away so that he didn't have his back to them anymore. The Norsemen cheered at this, which made the Frankish defenders look more afraid than they already did. Their lives depended on this fight. Behind them, the priests were screaming into the sky, a few of them on their knees with their hands clasped together. Ulf guessed they were praying to their god and glanced up. He wasn't sure why, perhaps he was expecting their god to appear above the tower of the church.

"He's not coming." Thorbjorn must have seen Ulf. "Never has before, so I don't think he'll come."

Ulf nodded, but said nothing. Instead, he turned his attention back to the fight. Ansovald's brother was slowly circling around Ansovald, trying to get away from the Norsemen. Or perhaps he was trying to take advantage of Ansovald's weak leg. But Ansovald stood his ground and just followed his brother with his head, unconcerned about the defenders behind him. His brother attacked and the priests' screams increased in volume, as if to encourage him. It looked like he was trying to force Ansovald onto his weak leg, much like what Snorri had done when the two of them had fought. But Ansovald didn't move. Instead, he batted his brother's sword out of the way and punched him in the face. His brother's head snapped to the side, but the fat man stayed on his feet. Ansovald twisted around and swung his sword at the man's head. His brother somehow got his sword up in time to block the blow, but the force of it sent him staggering back. The priests went quiet as the Norsemen cheered. Ulf found it strange that they were supporting a Frank, but he himself hoped Ansovald would win. Ansovald's brother found his footing and attacked with a vicious chop, spit flying from his mouth as he screamed. Ansovald pivoted on his good leg and deflected the blow. As his brother's momentum took him past, Ansovald kicked him in the back with his weak leg. He grimaced, but the kick was enough to send his brother sprawling in the dirt. The Norsemen cheered again, and the priests wailed to the skies. Ansovald ignored all of that as he limped around his brother, staying out of the way of the sword he still held in his hand. His brother looked at his guards as he struggled to get up and shouted something to them.

"He's telling them to attack Ansovald. I'd bet my balls to Freya," Ragnar said, his hand twisting on the haft of his axe, like he was waiting for a reason to attack them.

"He is," Humbert said, and Ulf wondered how much of what Ragnar had said he understood.

Ansovald spoke to the guards, turning his back to his brother. The guards looked even more uncertain now. They glanced at the Norsemen who were glaring back, all of them covered in the blood of people they knew. Ansovald's brother tried to take advantage of the situation and attacked him from behind. But his scream gave him away, and as fast as an eagle striking, Ansovald turned and ducked underneath the attack. His brother's sword swung through empty air, the man's eyes wide in shock at missing his brother. Some of the Norsemen gasped as Ansovald defied his age and struck with his sword. But it was not the killing blow they had been hoping for. Instead, Ansovald cut his brother's sword arm, forcing him to drop his sword, and then kicked the back of the fat man's leg. His brother dropped to his knees while gripping his bloody arm. Ansovald grabbed his thick hair, pulled his head back, and placed the blade of his sword against his brother's exposed neck. He shouted at the defenders, who, after looking at each other, all dropped their weapons.

Snorri wasted no time. "Asbjorn, get their weapons." Asbjorn grabbed a handful of men and did what Snorri had asked.

"I think he was toying with you when the two of you fought," Thorbjorn mocked Snorri.

"No, he wasn't," Snorri responded, but Ulf saw the uncertainty in his eyes and smiled.

Ansovald's brother shouted at the defenders, his face red and spit dribbling down his fat chin, but they looked too afraid to do anything. Asbjorn squared up to one of the Franks, who only shrank away. The priests fell to their knees, wailing with tears streaming down their faces. Some of Snorri's men imitated them, which caused the others to laugh. The fight was over. They had taken the town.

But Ulf did not feel the same joy they did. The hairs on the back of his neck stood up again, and Ulf couldn't help but glance over his shoulder. He felt like someone was watching him, but there was no one there.

"Geir! Run to the gates and tell Oddi to come to the church," Snorri ordered, and frowned when there was no response. Ulf scanned the men, but could not see the fair-haired warrior.

"Perhaps he is at the gates with Oddi," Drumbr suggested with a shrug.

Snorri nodded. While they were looking for Geir, Ansovald stepped away from his brother, but still held the sword at his neck. Ansovald's brother glared at him, his eyes filled with venom, but his shoulders sank as he understood he had lost.

"Tell Ansovald to hurry and kill the bastard. We have a lot to do before sunset. And somebody go get Oddi!" Snorri walked towards the church, eager to see what was inside. One man ran down the street to fetch Oddi as Humbert responded, stopping Snorri in his tracks.

"He no kill brother."

Snorri turned to face Ansovald as he spoke, "Why, in Odin's name, not?"

"God say you not kill brother. You go to hell."

"Our gods say different." He glared at the fat man, who was still on his knees.

"This not land your gods. This land our God."

Some men bristled at this, a few even taking a step towards Humbert. Ragnar lifted his axe and turned to the trader, but Snorri stopped them. He turned to the old trader, who was quivering as he realised his mistake. "So it is. But tell Ansovald we must hurry."

Oddi arrived with the men he had with him at the gate as Humbert spoke to Ansovald.

"Is Geir with you?" Snorri asked.

Oddi frowned and looked at the few men he had brought with him. "No, I didn't use him at the gate."

"Perhaps the bastard died in the fight?" Ragnar suggested.

"No," Oddi responded. "We searched the dead while you were busy here. None of our men died, only Frankish bodies."

Snorri looked around at his men and then scanned the streets. "The bastard better not be in one of those houses." The other men grumbled at that. They had been told not to rape.

While this was going on, Theoda berated the guards and the priests who tried to stop her from going into the church. She waved her bloody rolling pin at them, but it was the glare from Thorbjorn, who was following her like a dog looking for food, that made them back off. As she reached the church doors, she stopped and looked like she was about to shout at Thorbjorn, but she just nodded at him.

"Looks like Thorbjorn is winning her over," Asbjorn said, grinning.

Snorri glanced at the church. His face creased in anger. "Aye, but where, in Odin's name, is that bastard Geir?"

CHAPTER 11

"I swear to Odin when I find that bastard, I'm going to cut his balls off and feed them to the fish!" Thorbjorn said as they left the town, his face creased. He was angry because Snorri had chosen him to lead the search for Geir, which meant he couldn't spend the rest of the day following Theoda around.

"Not sure Ran would like that offering," Ketil said, smiling. He was one of the five men, all known for their hunting skills, picked to search for Geir alongside Ulf and Thorbjorn. "She likes men, not boys." The men smiled, apart from Thorbjorn, but no one laughed.

After the fight, Snorri ordered his men to search all the houses to find Geir and any Franks who were hiding away. They kicked in doors, flushing women, children and sometimes men out of their hiding places, but by the time the sun was setting, there was still no sign of Geir. Snorri had been furious as he stood in front of the church, his arms crossed and face red. In the end, he decided Geir was not in the town anymore, something all of them found strange. So Snorri sent out hunting parties to search the lands and forest around the town. Asbjorn and Drumbr led the other party, which was searching north of the town. Thorbjorn and Ulf were to search the south.

"I don't understand where he could have gone," Arvid said. "He was next to me when we attacked."

"Perhaps Loki tricked you." Ketil glanced at Arvid. "Geir might never have been there."

"But why would Loki want to do that?" Torsten, a warrior a winter younger than Ulf, asked. He glanced nervously around as they approached the forest, almost as if he expected the trickster god to jump out of the trees.

"Because Loki likes to fuck with us!" Thorbjorn's face was red as he turned to the men behind them. The older warriors weren't too concerned. They all knew about Thorbjorn's short temper, and they knew he would never attack them. But Torsten did not and the young warrior paled as he took a step back.

"I... I...," he stammered.

Ulf shook his head and sighed. He was tired. He just wanted to find Geir and get back to their camp. "We're not gonna find Geir if we stand here and bicker all day long. The sun is setting and I don't want to be caught in the forest when it is dark."

Thorbjorn shivered at the thought, the movement so slight that Ulf doubted the others caught it. Most men feared the dark and none of them liked the idea of spending the night out in an unknown land.

"Aye, only the gods know what demons hide amongst these trees, ready to feast on us when the moon is out." Thorbjorn stared at the forest in front of them.

The men gulped as they nodded, and Ulf could only shake his head. He did not fear the night. He had spent many weeks living in the forest with the old godi and his silent companion.

After Griml had killed his family, the godi found him and nursed him back to life. It was in the old man's hut that Ulf had learnt there were darker things inside than outside in the middle of the night. The image of his young friend sitting next to the corpses of the godi and his large hound came to Ulf. That had been the start of their friendship. But Vidar was gone, slain by Griml to win Odin's favour, and there wasn't a day when Ulf didn't miss his friend. Especially when he walked into a forest. Vidar had loved the trees and the sounds of nature.

"Let's just get this over with," Thorbjorn growled, his hand clasped around the Mjöllnir pendant on his neck. "Going to gut that bastard." The men glanced at each other before following Thorbjorn.

Ulf looked back towards the town and saw the plumes of thick smoke drifting into the sky. Snorri was making sure this town would not threaten Ansovald's village again. But that was not the reason Ulf looked back. He still felt like he was being watched. The hair on the back of his neck stood on end and no matter how many times he looked over his shoulder or rubbed his neck, it would not go away. He was sure he knew who it was and the thought that she somehow was here filled him with more fear than anything in this forest could.

"Ulf! Stop wasting time. Odin knows I'll gut you too if some evil spirit kills me tonight!" Thorbjorn threatened.

Ulf gave one last glance over his shoulder and then followed his friends into the trees.

*

The flames of their campfire cast ominous shadows on the trees around them as they sat in the small clearing they had found. The men glanced around nervously and young Torsten chewed on his bottom lip as if they expected evil spirits to attack them from the trees. Thorbjorn, sitting next to Ulf on the ground, did his best to appear unafraid, but his hand never strayed far from his sword.

"We've searched all day, and no sign of that bastard," Thorbjorn said, his eyes fixed on the trees. "Ketil, you sure you didn't miss his tracks?"

Ketil raised his eyebrow at Thorbjorn. "I've been tracking and hunting for more winters than I can remember."

"Aye," Arvid responded with a grin, "but you missed that deer one time. Didn't see it until it crept up behind you and almost stuck its antler up your arse." Torsten laughed as Ketil glared at Arvid.

"If Vidar was with us, then we would have found that bastard by now. Odin knows I'm going to gut him when we do."

Ketil was about to retort when he saw Ulf's glare, the flicker of the flames making his scarred face even more frightening. Instead, Ketil turned his attention away and studied the trees.

"He might not even have come this way," Ulf said as he tried to get the image of Griml killing Vidar out of his head. "Frigg knows we're wasting our time."

"Well, you tell Snorri that—"

"What was that?" Ivor, a survivor of the War Bear, shouted, his face paler than his white hair.

"A draugr!" Torsten jumped to his feet, his axe in his hand as he scanned the trees.

Above their heads, Ulf heard the flap of wings as a white-faced owl landed on a branch and stared at them. "It's only an owl," he said, but could not keep the quiver of fear from his voice. The men laughed nervously at their own foolishness and made fun of Torsten, who sat down again, his face red with embarrassment. But Ulf ignored them as he watched the owl, its head tilted, and wondered if it was a sign from the gods.

After a while, the men settled down again, and Thorbjorn yawned. "Time to sleep. Tomorrow, we'll head back and see if Asbjorn and Drumbr found anything."

"Are you sure it's safe to sleep?" Torsten glanced around the trees again, his knuckles white as he gripped his axe.

"I'll keep watch," Ulf said, his eyes still on the owl.

"You sure?" Thorbjorn looked at him while making himself comfortable and placed his sword next to him. Ulf nodded. He didn't feel like sleeping. Every night, the same dream kept coming to him, and the clearing they were in looked a lot like the one from his dream.

As the men fell asleep, Ulf moved to a nearby tree and made himself comfortable, the owl never taking its eyes off of him. All around, the forest went quiet as it too seemed to fall asleep, leaving only Ulf and their campfire awake. The flames danced away, slowly losing their power as they chewed through the wood. Ulf set about getting some more to keep the fire going. He searched the trees, looking for a suitable branch, when something caught his eye. Ulf glanced up at the owl and saw it was gone. That must have been the flash of white he had seen. But when he looked at that tree again, he knew it wasn't.

Ulf struggled to breathe as he stared at the face he had not seen since the battle at The Giant's Toe. Sharp blue eyes stared back at him, and before Ulf could utter anything, they turned and disappeared. He jumped to his feet and followed, desperate not to lose his young friend amongst the trees. Ulf knew it was foolish. He knew Vidar was dead, but still, there was a part of him that hoped this might be real. Vidar moved fast, as he had always done, and Ulf struggled to keep up with him. The boy had been raised in the forest and understood it better than any man Ulf had ever met. As Ulf rushed to catch up with Vidar, he found himself in a small clearing similar to the one he had just left. For a moment, Ulf thought the boy had led him in a circle, but then saw that Thorbjorn wasn't there and neither were the other men. The fire in this clearing was burning strong and there was a small cauldron with a red base sitting on top of it. His heart skipped a beat as he recognised this clearing. It was the one from his dream. He cursed as he scanned the area, looking for Vidar, but as before, he was gone. Gripping the handle of Ormstunga, Ulf crept towards the fire. Just like in the dream, two logs were on either side of the flames, and Ulf tilted his head to look for the serpent he normally saw.

"Finally, you are here." The voice echoed from the shadows, chilling Ulf to his core. He recognised that voice. It was one he would never forget. Standing near the fire, he searched the trees to find the source of the voice when it came again. "Sit."

Ulf glanced at the log, its side worn smooth from constant use. Reluctantly, he sat down, his hand never leaving his sword, as he waited for what he was sure was going to happen next. But there was no looming shadow or monstrous laugh. Instead, from opposite the fire, *she* walked out of the trees. She seemed to move like the serpent Ulf had seen in his dreams, her eyes never leaving his as she strode to the log opposite him and sat down. Her black hair melted into the shadows behind her, while the flames made her face even paler and her mismatched eyes shine fiercely. She looked like the draugr Torsten had been frightened of, and Ulf couldn't stop the shiver running down his spine. They sat there, staring at each other for a long while, the only noise coming from the fire between them. In the end, Ulf could not take it anymore.

"Where is Vidar?" Ulf tried to keep his voice strong, but knew he had failed. He saw it in her smile.

"Dead. You should know that." Her words stung, even though they were true.

"But then...?" He looked at the trees behind the volva, almost as if he expected Vidar to walk out of them.

The volva looked at him, her smile never leaving her face. "I needed his help. You did not respond to the messages I sent you, so I had to resort to something more drastic."

Ulf frowned as he tried to understand what she was saying to him. "The dreams?" He looked around him, again struck by how this clearing looked just like the one in his dreams, even the small cauldron above the fire. The volva nodded, still smiling. Ulf saw glimpses of Hulda in that smile. "Why? What do you want from me?" He tried to add some steel to his voice but still couldn't overcome his fear. Ulf gripped the hilt of Ormstunga tighter, hoping she would give him some strength.

"You can let go of the sword." She leaned back, looking bored. "Griml is not here, not yet."

Ulf looked at her, his eyes wide. "What do you mean, not yet?" He still held on to Ormstunga. "Is he coming?" Ulf couldn't stop the concern from creeping into his voice. "How does he know where we are?" He struggled to make sense of everything. They didn't even know where they were. The storm had thrown them back onto the Frankish coast, but where on the coast, they didn't know.

"Because I told him where to find you." The volva smiled, her eyes filled with malice.

"You?" Ulf frowned. "How did you find me?"

The volva's smile turned cruel, revealing her blackened teeth. "The gods told me where to find you."

"The gods?" Ulf struggled to keep the fear out of his voice, which only amused the volva.

"You still have a part to play in their game."

"I don't want to be part of their games." Ulf scowled, but the volva only smiled as the contents in the cauldron boiled away.

"You were always part of their games, from the moment your mother pushed you out. And besides, you swore an oath to Odin, remember?"

Ulf did remember. It was the only reason he still lived. He was sure of it. Odin would not let him die until he avenged his family. But Ulf had failed twice to kill Griml and since their last fight, he had wondered if Odin would still stick to his part of the deal. He looked at the volva again, annoyed by her smile. "What about you? What's your part in all this?" Somewhere in the trees, an owl screeched and Ulf thought of the bird he had seen before.

The volva stared at Ulf for a while as the fire kept on dancing between them. "I also have my part to play."

Ulf frowned. "And what does it have to do with me?" He grit his teeth as a thought came to him. "You're here to make sure Griml kills me."

The volva laughed, surprising him. "No, I am not here to make sure Griml kills you. Your fight with him has nothing to do with me."

"Then why help him?" The contents of the cauldron reached his nostrils, and the stench of whatever she was cooking made his head swim. "You mean to kill me?" A chill ran down his spine at the thought. If she attacked him, would he be able to kill her? Not just because she was a woman, but she was also a volva, a wielder of magic who could speak to the gods. Surely the gods would punish a man for killing one of their servants.

The volva laughed and Ulf wondered if she had heard his thoughts. "If I wanted you dead, then I would have let Griml kill you." Ulf thought back to his fight with Griml in Rouen, and then in the tent after.

"In the tent, you said I belong to the gods."

"Aye, Tyr himself chose you." The volva pointed at his scars when she saw his frown.

Ulf rubbed the three rigid lines on his face. "Lady Ingibjorg suggested Tyr had sent the bear to test me."

"Ingibjorg is a wise woman."

Ulf studied her, seeing more similarities with Hulda. "They say she can speak to the gods."

The volva smiled, but said nothing. Ulf felt like she was toying with him and he tried to use that to ignite the flames of his anger, but nothing happened. He took a deep breath.

"I'm sorry about Hulda." Hulda had been Lady Ingibjorg's thrall, although Ulf wasn't sure if that was really true. The two of them had become lovers, although Ulf wasn't sure if that was true either. Hulda had used her body to temper his anger. At first, he had thought Lady Ingibjorg told her to, but Hulda had always insisted it was her own choice.

"You didn't kill my daughter." The smile faded as the volva's voice found the steel Ulf's couldn't. "Thorvald held the knife that cut her throat."

Ulf was slightly taken aback by her sudden anger. "B... but she died because of me."

The volva laughed, the sound of it echoing off the trees. "Men. You all think too much of yourselves." She sighed. "Hulda did not die because of you." Her face creased in anger, the light of the fire making it look even worse. "She died because of them!" Ulf was sure the fire grew bigger at that moment as the contents of the cauldron boiled even more. He had to fight the urge to grab the Mjöllnir around his neck.

"Them?"

"Thorgils and his coward son!" A strong breeze swept through the clearing, and for a brief instant, the volva looked frightened. Ulf thought he saw her nod, as if she had heard something. But it was over so quickly, he wondered if he had imagined it all.

"But the jarl and his wife had promised to protect her." That was what Snorri had told Ulf, although no one knew what from.

The volva jumped to her feet and pointed her finger towards the trees. Her face darkened, and the shadows seemed to creep in. "He took her from me!" Ulf almost fell off the log he was sitting on and fought hard not to run away from the volva's sudden fury. The volva stood rigid as she panted, her eyes glazed as she was no doubt remembering that day. Then, with a voice softer than Ulf had expected, she continued. "He took my baby from me." She slumped down, missing the log and landing on the ground. Ulf sat frozen on his log, held there by the invisible hands. "But not to protect her." The volva looked up, her mismatched eyes filled with a hatred so deep, Ulf felt it pierce his chest. "He took my baby to protect himself."

"But Lady Ingibjorg said —"

"Ingibjorg said what she needed to make herself feel better." The volva stood up and fixed her dress before sitting down on the log again as if nothing had happened. "Ingibjorg has always been weak."

Ulf scowled at the volva. That was not how he felt about Snorri's mother. To him, she was strong, intelligent and understood men better than they understood themselves.

"You disagree." The volva stared at Ulf over the flames of the fire. She shrugged when Ulf did not respond. "It doesn't matter."

They sat in silence for a while as the flames crackled away and the liquid boiled in the cauldron. The owl had gone quiet, and Ulf wondered if it had caught its meal. He shook his head to clear the dizziness caused by whatever was in the cauldron. The volva seemed to be in no rush to speak, so Ulf asked, "Why are you helping him?"

"Him?" She raised an eyebrow.

"Griml." Ulf knew she understood who he was talking about, but guessed she wanted him to say the name.

The volva smiled again. "The gods told me to help him."

"Why?" Ulf was starting to hate that answer. She was like Snorri, blaming everything on the gods.

"Like you, Griml also has a part to play."

"And what is his part?" Ulf grit his teeth as the memory came to him. "To slaughter my family for no reason?"

"Not for no reason. There is a reason for everything that happens, young wolf."

Ulf was stunned. "For what reason did my uncle, aunt and their daughters have to die?" He wanted to cry. He felt it build up in his chest. But since the death of Vidar, no tears would flow from his eyes. He knew it would not bring them back.

"Don't forget about your father, the mighty Bjørn Ulfson."

Ulf felt the thump in his chest as if he had been punched by the troll. "My father died in battle. His death has nothing to do with my oath to Odin."

The volva leaned forward, the light of the fire making her face even paler. "You swore to avenge the deaths of your family."

"But my father died in battle!" Ulf still remembered the last day he had seen his father. He had begged him not to go, but his father had been the jarl's champion.

"I have to go, my son. It is my duty to protect the jarl," his *father said as he stood over him like a giant.*

Ulf's young face was red with tears. "What about your duty to me?"

"I'll be back." Those were the last words his father had spoken to him.

Growing up, Ulf had always felt like his father had abandoned him, but since the deaths of the rest of his family,

Ulf understood his father better. The hatred was gone, but Ulf had sworn to be better than his father.

"Did he?" The volva's question brought him back. Ulf frowned, not sure how to respond. The volva reached behind her and Ulf tensed. He grabbed the hilt of Ormstunga, half expecting her to pull a blade from behind the log she was sitting on. But instead, she picked up a small wooden bowl and spoon. Without paying any attention to him, she stood up and walked to the cauldron. She stirred the contents before spooning some of it into the bowl. Ulf watched as she walked around the fire and handed it to him. Taking the bowl, he saw the thin brown liquid inside. "Drink it," she commanded, her smile gone.

Ulf sniffed the bowl and gagged at the pungent smell. "I'm not drinking this." He was about to throw the bowl and its contents at the fire when the volva said.

"Then you'll never learn the truth about your father."

He hesitated and saw the earnestness in the mismatched eyes. With a deep breath, he gulped down the contents. His stomach clenched as the liquid burnt its way down his throat, and Ulf thought he was going to vomit it all up. But before this could happen, Ulf felt dizzy. The surrounding trees spun so fast, they all melted into one. One large oak tree standing on its own and surrounded by nothing. Before Ulf could make sense of what he was seeing, he was swept up into the sky. From there, he could see all of Midgard, even the mountains in the north from his homeland. The wind blew in his face as the mountains came closer. He flew over the seas and forests, all the while travelling north. Towards the lands of his people. He flew over a valley where something caught his attention. Ulf stopped and hovered over the two wolf packs facing each other like two armies, one smaller than the other. But his attention was drawn to the smaller pack. Standing in the middle was a gigantic bear, its lips pulled back to reveal its fangs. Next to the bear stood a wolf, its coat shining brightly in the sun. As Ulf watched, this wolf lifted its head and howled. The two packs charged at each other, colliding like two shield walls coming together. The bear growled as it bit into the wolf facing it, its powerful jaw crushing the wolf's skull. Before this wolf died, the bear pounced on the next. It was too strong for the wolves and soon the smaller pack had the upper hand. But as Ulf watched, he saw a different wolf, this one younger than the rest and its coat tinged with red, sneaking up on the bear from behind. Ulf tried to warn it, but the bear wasn't paying any attention to his cries. There was nothing Ulf could do as the younger wolf prepared to attack the bear from behind. Just then, the wolf with the shiny coat suddenly collapsed, distracting the bear. As it turned to its companion, the young wolf attacked, sinking its teeth into the bear's back. The bear howled as those it had been fighting took advantage and ripped into it. One wolf grabbed one of its paws while another bit into its neck before ripping its throat out. The young wolf, its mouth covered in blood, stood over the fallen wolf with the shiny coat, protecting it from their enemies. But they were not interested in them. Ulf watched as the bear lay on the ground, drenched in its own blood, its mouth moving as it seemed to say something. He strained to hear the words when he suddenly heard the voice in his head.

Ulf

Ulf

CHAPTER 12

"What, in Odin's name, are we doing?" one of the Danish warriors complained. "We've been sailing up and down this coast for days now!" His face creased in frustration as he stared at the enormous back of Griml.

Griml ignored the man who stood near him, his focus fixed on the shoreline. He had been told to wait for a sign and so he was waiting for a sign. Not that he knew what that sign was.

"You don't know what you are doing, do you?" Griml curled his upper lip as the Dane carried on. The man turned to his companions, many of them lounging around, looking bored as the wind filled the sails of what used to be Ubba's ship. "Can you believe this Norseman? Takes over this ship, tells us we are his crew now, but he has no idea what is going on!" The Dane sneered at Griml. "All because that bitch told you to do it." He barked a laugh. "The mighty Griml Jotun running errands for a forest hag so ugly, my goat wouldn't even fuck her!" A few of the Danes behind him cheered, but the rest looked away, not wanting to be part of what was about to happen.

Griml turned before the cheers could reach their pitch and grabbed the Dane by the throat. The man's eyes bulged as Griml squeezed, at the same time lifting him off the deck. He growled at the Dane but said nothing. Instead, he crushed the man's throat with his huge hand and threw the dying Dane overboard. The man sank instantly as Griml glared at the rest of the crew. "Anyone else have anything to say about me and the forest hag?" His rough voice rumbled over the men as they shrank away from him.

One man at the stern slowly got to his feet, his hands trembling as he spoke. "We would just like to know what we are doing, that's all."

Griml stared at the man, seeing the grey in beard and hair, and wondered the same. "We are looking for the bastard that killed your jarl and stole my sword."

"Aye, we get that," the man responded, glancing nervously at those around him as they shuffled away. He gulped. "But as Sigmund said, we've been sailing up and down this coast for a few days now, not even being allowed to do some raiding." The Dane tensed, almost as if he expected Griml to launch himself across the deck of the ship and kill him.

But Griml wasn't paying attention to the man anymore. Instead, he turned to see what some of the crew were pointing at. In the distance, over the dunes on the coast, he saw a thick plume of smoke rising into the sky. *Is that the sign I am waiting for?* Griml did not like leading men but killing them, that was what he lived for. That was the reason Odin had put him on Midgard.

"Look!" One of the Danes pointed to the beach.

Griml looked at the beach and smiled. He felt the skin around the scar the young warrior had given him pull. The scar sometimes still itched, especially when he thought of the bastard who gave it to him. He stroked the Mjöllnir around his neck and thanked Odin, because Griml knew he would soon be killing Ulf Bear-Slayer.

"Make for the beach!" he ordered, and the man by the stern pulled on the tiller. Ubba's ship changed direction and headed towards the stranger waiting for them as Griml stood by the prow, ignoring the saltwater spray. He glanced at the seabirds flying above him, trying to find some sign from the gods in their movement. As they got nearer, Griml could make out the man on the beach. He was the height of most men, wore a leather jerkin that had seen more winters than the warrior and a bowl helmet on top of light-coloured hair. The man wore a sword on his hip and had a shield in his left hand. Griml saw the symbol on the shield. It was one he knew well. A black snarling wolf head on a white background. *The gods love their games,* Griml thought, because even though he did not recognise the warrior, he knew who the man fought for.

The ship ground to a halt on the beach, Griml barely moving while the Danes had to hold on to something to stop themselves from falling over. He glared at the young man who stood there looking smug, as if he was some elite warrior who had broken shield walls and sent armies running. Some of the Danes jumped overboard and secured their ship, while others waited for orders. Griml grunted and jumped onto the beach, his feet sinking into the sand because of his weight. He scanned the dunes behind the warrior, wanting to make sure this was not a trap. Although he doubted it would be. The volva would not betray him, of that Griml was sure. He was helping her kill the men who had killed her daughter. She had never spoken of it, but Griml had heard her talk in her sleep. He was sure she made a deal with Odin, and being a volva, Odin had listened to her and had given her the power to get her revenge.

The young warrior cleared his throat, but Griml made a point of ignoring him. He was not important, although Griml was curious about why he was here. The man fought for Snorri Thorgilsson. Griml had faced that shield enough times to recognise it. *The gods love their games.*

"Who are you?" Griml growled at the warrior after a while.

The young man straightened his back and put his free hand on his hip. "My name's Geir Hakonson." He looked like a bóndi who wanted to be a mighty warrior and although he had collected a few scars, he could not get rid of that dumb expression most bændr had. "I have faced you in battle before."

Griml smiled his vicious smile. "Boy, you would be in Valhalla now if you had faced me in battle, not standing here annoying me." The Danes near Griml laughed as the young warrior scowled.

"Perhaps, but I know of one man who faced you twice and still lives."

The smile on Griml's face disappeared as he clenched his fists. "Three times." He saw the confusion on the young warrior's face. "Three times the wolf bastard faced me, and three times I defeated him."

"But he still lives." The young warrior puffed his chest out.

"And yet you are here to betray him."

Geir's face darkened as he answered, "Ulf is nothing but bad luck. They say Odin is with him." He grit his teeth. "Odin keeps him alive, while all my sword brothers die around him."

"Nothing is free when the gods are involved," Griml responded, using words the volva had spoken to him before.

The young warrior nodded as if he understood, but Griml doubted he did. "Well, the price is too much. And not just for me."

Griml raised an eyebrow. He knew he wasn't very smart, but he understood the meaning of Geir's words. "How did you know to find me here?"

The young warrior hesitated a heartbeat before responding. "I was told to come here."

Griml now knew for certain that this was the sign the volva had told him to look for. Although he was surprised she would send someone who had fought with the Bear-Slayer. He glanced at the thick smoke plume as dark birds circled the sky around the smoke. Odin's messengers observing everything so they could tell the All-Father what was happening on Midgard. Griml never expected the Norse warriors to raid on their way home. "What do you want?" He turned his attention back to Geir, who was also watching the smoke in the distance.

Geir faced Griml, his face red as he grit his teeth. For a moment, Griml thought the young warrior might attack him, but then Geir said, "I want you to kill Ulf."

"Why?" Griml glanced at the smoke and the birds again.

"Because when the bastard is dead, then Odin will leave us in peace and we can get back to raiding like we used to."

Griml raised an eyebrow. "You really think Odin will just leave you alone?" He laughed, his deep voice rumbling over the beach and sending the nearby seabirds into the air. "The gods like to interfere in our lives."

Geir shrugged. "It's worth a try."

"Aye, that it is." Griml looked over the dunes again at the smoke plume. "Now, tell me where I can find the bastard and his friends."

"I'll show you." Geir was about to turn when Griml stopped him.

"The last time I trusted one of you, I almost lost my arm. Tell me first, and then we can go."

Geir looked at Griml and chewed on his lip before he nodded. "We are staying at a village southeast of that smoke."

Griml nodded. "How many men does Snorri have left? Can't be many."

"Less than a full crew, about half, I guess. We lost a lot of good men because of that bastard Ulf."

Griml did not respond to that. Instead, he launched himself at the unexpecting Geir. Before Geir could react, Griml punched him in the chest, the blow sending the young warrior flying through the air. The Danes went quiet behind Griml as he walked to where Geir lay, gasping for air. He stood over the young warrior and pulled Geir's sword from its scabbard. It was a plain sword but looked well made and well looked after. Griml appreciated good weapons, and he longed to hold Ormstunga again, despite what the volva had told him about the sword. Somewhere a raven screamed and Griml smiled at the fair-haired warrior, his face blue as he struggled to suck air into his crushed chest. "You will lose a lot more good men because of him." Griml stabbed down with Geir's sword. A fountain of blood sprayed through the air, soaking Griml's trousers and tunic, but he did not care. He turned and walked away, leaving the sword embedded in Geir's throat. "Leave a few men to protect the ship," he called to no one in particular, sure that they would respond. The Danes were too afraid not to. "The rest of you get ready. We are going wolf hunting."

The raven screamed again, and this time Griml saw it flying towards the smoke. Towards the bastard he was going to kill.

*

"Ulf! Ulf! Wake up, you bastard!"

Ulf murmured, refusing to open his eyes until the kick from Thorbjorn gave him no choice. He sat up with a start and saw the men staring at him, all of them looking confused, apart from Thorbjorn. Thorbjorn looked annoyed.

"You were supposed to be keeping guard, not sleeping." Thorbjorn's face was red, his large nose looking like a ripe apple.

"Aye, what if the forest spirits attacked us during the night?" Torsten nervously glanced at the trees.

Ulf was about to tell Thorbjorn of what had happened, but then realised that he wasn't in the clearing where he had spoken to the volva.

"Where are we?" Ulf asked, confused. He scanned the clearing in front of him as the sun beamed through the trees, lighting up the forest and casting shadows under the branches. It was smaller than the one from last night, and there were no tree stumps around the small campfire. The cauldron was missing as well.

"We're in the same place we were last night." Thorbjorn frowned. He must have seen the confusion on Ulf's face. "What's the matter?"

Ulf caught the glances the other men gave each other. "I…" he trailed off, unsure of what had happened last night. *Did I really speak to the volva?* It had felt so real, but then why was he back in the camp with Thorbjorn and the five men? The last thing he remembered was drinking that vile concoction the volva had given him. Could he have walked back here afterwards? There was some memory tugging at him, wanting him to remember something, but Ulf could not.

"Perhaps a forest spirit stole his wits?" Arvid suggested, and all five of them grabbed the Mjöllnir pendants around their necks.

Even Thorbjorn looked nervous, but he quickly recomposed himself. "No, Ulf was just more tired than he realised." He held out a hand, which Ulf took, and helped him to his feet. Around them, the forest was alive as birds flew above their heads and insects scurried around their feet. Flower pollen drifted lazily on the slight breeze. The morning air felt fresh and Ulf sucked in a deep breath, hoping it would clear his mind. "Come, we need to get back to Snorri." Thorbjorn turned, but Ulf saw the glance his friend gave him.

"But what about Geir?" Arvid asked, still holding on to the Mjöllnir around his neck. "We still haven't found him."

"Aye," Thorbjorn agreed, "but Odin knows, if we haven't found the bastard yet, then we won't now. We head back to

Snorri. He'll be waiting for us. Who knows, maybe Asbjorn and Drumbr found him already."

"There's another reason we need to get to Snorri, and fast," Ulf said, remembering something from his conversation with the volva. Thorbjorn frowned at him. "Griml is coming."

"How, in Odin's name, do you know that?" Ketil asked, his eyes wide as he scanned the trees.

"Odin's probably the one who told Ulf." Thorbjorn had been around Ulf long enough to understand his dreams and had learnt not to question some of the things he said. "Get our stuff. We need to move fast." Without waiting for a response from anyone, Thorbjorn went over to the embers of their small fire and scattered them with his boot. The other five glanced at Ulf, unsure of what to make of this, but then followed Thorbjorn.

Ulf stood where he was, staring at the trees as he tried to make sense of what had happened. His conversation with the volva had felt so real, but if he was here in this clearing with his friends, then it couldn't have been? It must have been a dream, but then this posed another question that Ulf struggled to make sense of. Was the dream a message from Odin, or was Hulda's mother toying with him? If Hulda's mother had been toying with him, then why warn him about Griml? At the same time, she was the one who told Griml where to find him. Ulf's head hurt as he struggled to make sense of last night. Then there was the strange taste in his mouth. He drank some water from his flask, wanting to wash it away as he followed the men. If last night had been a dream, then it was as cryptic as the rest of his dreams. He could not remember what had happened after he drank the stuff from the cauldron. Those memories were lost in the fog, and Ulf wasn't sure how to get them.

CHAPTER 13

They left the forest in silence, the men unnerved by what Ulf had said. Ulf's mood was as dark as the thick smoke, which still hung in the air from the day before. There had been no rain, so Ulf shouldn't have been surprised that some buildings were still burning. He still couldn't help but wonder if it was a sign of things to come. Ulf glanced over his shoulder. Even the forest seemed subdued. The birds were quiet, and they had seen no animals as they trekked back to the town. Although, Ulf had not been paying any attention to the trees or their occupants. Not in the same way he normally would.

"The sooner we get to the men, the better," Ketil said ahead of them, echoing Ulf's feelings. It was the first time anyone had spoken since they left the clearing.

"Aye," Arvid agreed, rubbing his arm. "This forest was making my skin crawl."

"The forest or your dream?" Thorbjorn muttered to Ulf as he walked beside him. "Must have taken them all day to burn that town," he said when Ulf didn't respond.

Ulf glanced at Thorbjorn. "What will happen to the people?"

Thorbjorn shrugged. "If it was up to Snorri, the men would be killed and the women and children sold as thralls."

"But it's not up to him." Ulf was glad about that. There was a dark side to his friend that scared him. "What do you think Ansovald will do? They are his people, after all."

Thorbjorn gave Ulf a sideways glance. "Does it really matter?" Ulf frowned at him. "They are his enemies, doesn't matter that they are all Franks. How many Norsemen have you killed?" Thorbjorn smiled when Ulf did not respond. "Exactly. But I think you are right. Ansovald will go soft on them, and when we leave, his brother will most likely take his village and kill him. Odin knows that's what I would do."

Ulf stared at the town they had attacked the day before. Much of the wooden walls remained, although there were sections where the fire had eaten through. The church tower was gone, its bell permanently silenced by the flames. The air was filled with the sweet, putrid stench of burnt bodies, mixed with the smell of burnt wood. It was a combination that made Ulf's stomach churn, and he was glad they had not eaten. The sky above the burning town was filled with dark birds, waiting for the flames to die away so they could feast on whatever the fire had left them. Ulf wondered if this was what Asgard would look like when Surtr finally destroyed it during Ragnarök.

"Does Ulf ever enjoy anything?" Arvid asked, frowning at Ulf's dark face.

"Aye, he does. But Ulf enjoys it on the inside. On the outside, he likes to look serious. Thinks it'll get him more women," Thorbjorn joked, clapping Ulf's shoulder. "Come on, they'll be waiting for us." He walked off towards the campsite next to the burning town. The other five laughed and followed Thorbjorn, while Ulf turned and looked at the forest they had just come from. *Are you there watching me, or was it all just a dream?* Ulf shook his head and rushed after the men, hoping that Snorri would listen to what he had to say.

"No sign of Geir then?" Asbjorn asked Thorbjorn as they reached the camp.

"No, the bastard wasn't in the forest. No sign he went that way. You?" Thorbjorn took a drinking flask from Asbjorn and drank from it. He handed it to Ulf, who smelt the ale and took a deep gulp.

"Geir didn't go north, or at least not that we could tell."

"So where is he?" Ulf frowned as he handed the flask back to Thorbjorn. Thorbjorn emptied it and then tossed the empty flask to one of the men.

"Only the gods will know," Asbjorn sneered at Ulf before walking away. Ulf did not react. He was used to this by now.

"Come, let's find Snorri. You need to tell him about your dream," Thorbjorn said, grabbing Ulf by the arm.

They found Snorri talking to the rest of his hirdmen in the centre of their camp. Ansovald was also there, with Humbert beside him. Ansovald's brother was on his knees, his hands tied behind his back, and kept away from his people. Not far from the Norse camp, Ulf saw the townspeople. They were sitting in groups, the women and children to one side and the men, tied up and guarded, to another. Heads hung low and shoulders sagged, while children cried as their mothers could not comfort them. Ulf felt the tightening in his chest and shook his head as he followed Thorbjorn.

Snorri looked up from his conversation with Ragnar and spotted them, the dark rings under his eyes showing he had not slept much. "You find him?"

"Sorry, Snorri. The bastard's gone," Thorbjorn responded while Ulf studied their camp.

"The men look nervous."

"Aye," Oddi said, glancing at the Norse warriors over his shoulder. "They're not sure what to make of Geir's disappearance."

"He's not in the houses?" Ulf looked at the town.

"You think we don't know how to search houses, pup?" Ragnar's eyes were as red as his face.

"Relax, Ragnar." Snorri held up his hand. "Ulf is right to ask. We searched all the houses twice before we started burning the town." Ulf nodded, but said no more.

"He must have run away," Magni said, his usually tidy hair dishevelled and his beard all over the place. Ulf had never seen the Cockerel like this before. Even Thorbjorn raised an eyebrow at Oddi's brother.

"No, Odin knows he's been trying hard to win Snorri's favour." Oddi scratched his neck. "He wouldn't run, not now when he might have a chance of becoming a hirdman." Oddi glanced at Drumbr, but the large warrior didn't react. He stood there, as tired as the rest of them, while leaning on his axe.

Ulf looked at Snorri. "You were considering him?"

"Aye, he's a good fighter. Was waiting until we got back home and gave Brak a proper farewell." The men nodded as Snorri said this.

"Then what could have happened to the bastard if he didn't run?" Thorbjorn asked.

"Perhaps someone took him, like what happened to Ulf," Drumbr suggested.

Everyone thought about this before Snorri responded, "Who could have taken him? There was no one in that town that could have beaten him in a fight."

"Griml?" Magni looked at the others. "He took Ulf."

"Griml isn't here. The big bastard is still in Rouen." Ragnar spat to the ground.

"No, he's not," Ulf said, and saw the confused expressions on the faces of his friends.

"What do you mean?" Snorri scowled as he stepped towards Ulf. "The troll is stuck in Rouen."

"Ulf had a dream," Thorbjorn responded, as Ulf tried to find the words to explain.

"Odin's arse! We're not doing this again!" Ragnar threw his arms up in the air and made to walk away, but stayed where he was.

Magni scratched his head as he frowned at Ulf. "What's so special about Ulf's dreams?"

"The gods speak to him," Oddi answered. Ulf wished he hadn't as Magni's eyes went wide. He still didn't understand his dreams. They were never clear, and he usually died at the end of them. Or at least, he would wake up before he died.

"I'm not sure if it was a dream." Ulf looked away from his friends, not wanting to see their reactions. Especially the scowls from Ragnar and Asbjorn.

"Then what was it?" Ragnar's sharp tone caught him off guard.

"I... I..." Ulf struggled to find the words. He took a deep breath as Thorbjorn nudged him. They needed to hear what he had to say, so Ulf forced himself to say the words. "I spoke to her last night."

"Spoke to who?" Snorri frowned.

"Hulda's mother."

Drumbr gasped as Ragnar and Snorri glanced at each other.

"What do you mean you spoke to her?" Asbjorn stepped towards Ulf, his fists clenched as if he was about to strike him.

Thorbjorn moved fast and placed himself between Ulf and Asbjorn. "It was just a dream. She isn't really here." He glanced over his shoulder at Ulf. "Isn't that right?"

"I don't know." Ulf saw Ragnar's face go redder than it was before.

"You don't know? Thor's balls, but you must have been dropped on your head as a babe."

"Enough!" Snorri yelled. Ansovald and Humbert were muttering things to each other while looking uncomfortably at the Norsemen. Ulf guessed Humbert was trying to translate what they were saying to his village leader, but it looked like he was struggling to keep up with them. "Ulf, was it a dream or not?"

"I'm not sure." Again, Ulf saw the frustration on their faces and tried to explain. "This felt too real to be a dream, but…" He struggled to find the words to describe it.

"I've had many dreams that feel real!" Asbjorn retorted. He turned to Snorri. "We are wasting our time here, Snorri."

Snorri held a hand up, signalling for Asbjorn to be quiet. "Let Ulf explain."

"In my dreams, I have no weapons with me."

"So?" Ragnar's arms were folded across his chest.

"Last night, I did. That's why I don't think it was a dream."

"But if it wasn't a dream, then how could she be here?" Oddi asked the question that Ulf had been struggling with since this morning.

"She followed us?" Drumbr scratched his head while looking at Snorri.

"She can't have done," Oddi said. "We're only here because of the storm. Until a few days ago, we didn't even know where here was."

"She's a volva, don't forget." Thorbjorn rubbed his Mjöllnir pendant.

"What does that have to do with anything?" Asbjorn asked.

"She could have used magic to get here." Drumbr grabbed the Mjöllnir around his neck, his face going pale as the words came out of his mouth. Ulf saw the rest of the men, even Ragnar, rubbing their Mjöllnir pendants or their weapons. Magic was something all men feared, and it was even worse when the person wielding the magic was a woman.

"But how?" Magni asked, for once not looking so cocky. "Turn herself into a bird and fly here?"

As Magni said the words, Ulf remembered the snakeskin Hulda's mother wore around her neck. It never made sense to him, but now he thought he understood. In his dreams, he always saw the serpent slithering away as he approached the fire and the volva had told him she'd been calling him through his dreams. "She wears a snakeskin around her neck."

Oddi understood before everyone else. "You think she turned herself into a snake and hid on our ship?"

"Bullocks!" Asbjorn shouted, but still looked uncertain. "She can't do that."

Snorri rubbed his beard before responding. "My mother used to tell me about shapeshifters. People who would wear the skins of animals and then turn into them."

"Aye, my mother told me the same. We all know of the shapeshifters. But they usually turn themselves into wolves and bears. Not snakes," Asbjorn said, still glaring at Ulf.

His aunt had told him the tales as well. "But why else would she be wearing a snakeskin around her neck?"

"To fool idiots like you." Asbjorn jabbed his finger in Ulf's face.

"I know what I saw!" Ulf grit his teeth as the fire of his anger ignited for the first time in days. It was good to feel its heat again as it coursed through his veins. If it wasn't for Thorbjorn still standing between them, then Ulf was sure he would have attacked Asbjorn again.

"But you said yourself. You don't know if it was a dream or not." Oddi's words killed the flames as quickly as they started.

Snorri rubbed his face, looking even more tired now. "That doesn't matter now. Ulf, what did she say?" The men went quiet. They had been so busy arguing that they had forgotten about that.

"Griml is on his way."

"This is ridiculous, Snorri!" Ragnar threw his arms up in the air.

"I agree," Asbjorn added. "Ulf just wants more attention. Doesn't like the fact that we are looking for Geir and not talking about him."

Ulf felt his body tense, but before he could say anything, Snorri shook his head. "No, I've learnt to trust his dreams."

Snorri turned to Ulf. "What exactly did Hulda's mother say to you?"

Ulf glanced at Thorbjorn, who nodded his encouragement. "That she told Griml where to find us, and that he will be here soon." He looked at his feet, not wanting to see their faces as he said the next part. "That the gods told her where to find us."

The men were silent. Those within earshot stopped what they were doing and stared at Snorri and his hirdmen.

"Odin knows I wish I killed you on the pier that day," Ragnar said before he turned and stormed away. He was talking about the first day they had met. Ulf had been in Thorgilsstad for a few weeks when the jarl returned from his raid. Jarl Thorgils had been angry that Ulf was there. He believed Ulf had killed his own family. The jarl had ordered Ragnar to kill him, and Ragnar would have done it if it had not been for Lady Ingibjorg.

Snorri watched as his father's champion walked away before he turned his attention back to Ulf. "Are you sure about this, Ulf?"

Ulf shrugged. "Like I said, I'm not sure if it was a dream or not. But I believe what she told me."

"The gods know that Ulf's dreams have an annoying habit of coming true," Oddi said.

"Aye, that's why the gods keep sending them to the bastard," Thorbjorn added with a scowl. He turned to Snorri. "What do we do?"

Snorri scanned the skies, the same way he had been doing since the Sae-Ulfr got wrecked on the beach. "Get the men ready," Snorri said at last. "We need to get back to our ship."

"What about Geir?" Asbjorn asked.

Snorri sighed. "Wherever he is, his fate is in the hands of the Norns."

"Good luck to the bastard then," Thorbjorn said. "Because the Norns are cruel bitches."

Snorri's hirdmen rushed off to get the men together, although no order needed to be given. They had all been following the conversation and understood what was expected of them. Even Ansovald understood what they were doing without being told. The old Frankish warrior grabbed his brother and pulled him to his feet, at the same time shouting something at the townspeople.

"What's happening?" Ulf asked when the Franks got to their feet. The men, their hands still tied behind their backs and guarded by the Norse warriors, struggled to get up, but the women weren't allowed near the men to help them. The Norse warriors guarding the Franks looked at Snorri, who only waved a hand at them.

"They're coming with." Snorri shook his head, clearly not keen on the idea.

"They'll slow us down," Thorbjorn said. "And Odin knows we have no idea where Griml is."

"We don't even know if Griml is coming." Asbjorn glared at Ulf.

"He's coming," Ulf responded, returning Asbjorn's glare.

"It doesn't matter. I spent all night arguing with Ansovald. Told him it's better to set the people loose, let them find their own way." Snorri took a deep breath. "But the old bastard refused. Said they were his people once and that he would look after them."

Ulf stared at the old Frankish warrior as he limped towards the Frankish people while dragging his brother behind him.

"He should at least kill his brother," Thorbjorn said, with a glance at Drumbr.

"Aye, told him the same, but their god doesn't allow it. Or so I'm told." Snorri turned and walked to his men, who were waiting to leave.

"Well, I wonder what their god will make of this war between the brothers then." Thorbjorn scratched his beard.

"As long as they don't kill each other, then I guess he'll be fine with it," Oddi said in his wise voice. "He only says not to kill your brother, nothing about other men's brother."

"And how would you know that, Oddi Viss?" Thorbjorn stared at his tall friend.

Oddi shrugged. "I don't, but why else would Ansovald be fine with killing other men, but not his own brother?"

CHAPTER 14

Snorri thought of his father as they marched back to Ansovald's village. It was something he had tried not to do since they arrived in Francia. But as the column of Norse warriors and Frankish people walked through the countryside, he could not help but wonder what his father would do in this situation. Jarl Thorgils believed in the gods as much as any other Norseman, but he was also a practical man. *Would you have listened to Ulf, father?*

That's what was bothering Snorri. He glanced over his shoulder, seeing how few of his men were left. Snorri had never lost more than a few men on his raids. It was the one thing he prided himself on. It was also one of the reasons he believed the gods blessed him. Something his father never agreed with, but his mother always encouraged.

"I always bring my men back alive!" Snorri remembered telling his father once. They were in the hall and Snorri had just returned from raiding in the north of Norway. Things had not gone to plan, but Snorri survived, and more importantly, so did most of his men.

"You got lucky!" his father's voice boomed around the hall, his heavily lined face creased in anger. He was sitting in his chair, a cup of ale in one hand and the other clenched in a fist.

Snorri laughed. "Lucky? The gods have blessed me, father. There is nothing I can't do."

Thorgils took a sip of his ale and glared at his wife, who was sitting next to him in her chair, her face as impassive as ever. "There are many men in Valhalla who said the same until the gods no longer paid any attention to them."

Lady Ingibjorg placed a hand on her husband's and smiled at him. "My husband, do not be so hard on our son. The gods watch over him."

"See, father." Snorri beamed. "One day, I'll be the greatest warrior in all of Norway."

"Only if your recklessness does not kill you first," the jarl retorted. "Or your men."

Snorri smiled a cocky smile. "Father. I always bring my men back alive."

His father sighed. "Until you don't."

Snorri stared at the sky again, but as always, there were no signs from the gods. Nothing to tell him what to do. Francia had been cruel to him. And not just to him. Many women and children will be without husbands and fathers. Thorgilsstad, his father's pride, the village he had built from nothing, will be without most of her warriors. And it was all because of him. All Snorri wanted to do now was to fix his ship and take what remained of his men home. But the gods were cruel, and they loved chaos. And if what Ulf had told him was true, then Snorri knew he was going to lose even more men.

Snorri glanced at Ulf, walking beside him. The three scars twisted like snakes as Ulf ground his teeth, clearly struggling with his own thoughts. "You really think he is coming?"

Ulf looked at him, frowning as if he had forgotten where he was. "Who?"

"Troll-Face."

Ulf took a deep breath, and, like Snorri had done so many times, looked at the sky. "That's what she told me."

"Maybe she lied?" Snorri knew this was wishful thinking, but still asked.

Ulf shook his head. "No, I don't think she did. Whether or not it was a dream, Griml is on his way and she is leading him to us."

"Why? What does she want?"

"I don't know. She claims to be doing what the gods tell her to do, but I feel like there is more to it."

They walked in silence for a while, the sound of the men talking and laughing washing over them. Snorri could hear women and children crying from the back of the column, and somewhere there was a dog barking. "Could it be because of Hulda?"

Ulf's sword-grey eyes lost focus as he stared into the distance, pursing his lips. "I think so. She wants revenge for her daughter, just like I want revenge for my family."

"Then why not just kill Snorri?" Thorbjorn asked. He was walking beside them, listening to their conversation. "If she can turn herself into a snake and appear out of thin air, then surely she could have killed him by now."

Snorri nodded. He dreaded that idea, but Thorbjorn spoke the truth. She was a volva, a woman of magic who belonged to the gods. If she wanted him dead, then he would be dead. "Perhaps she wants to make me suffer before she kills me."

"No," Ulf shook his head, "she is not after you. She doesn't blame me for Hulda's death, so I don't think she holds you responsible."

Snorri looked at Ulf, hoping that was true. He was not afraid of fighting men, no matter how big or fast, but he did not want to face a volva. Snorri gripped the hilt of Tyr's Fury, trying to chase away the fear creeping into his gut.

"She might decide to kill Snorri to punish his parents. They did swear to protect Hulda and failed," Thorbjorn said.

Ulf shook his head before he responded. "No, she would have killed him by now if that's what she wanted."

Snorri couldn't help but glance at Ragnar. He had been his father's champion since the death of Ulf's father. Something all the warriors had found strange because Ragnar was so young at the time. He had been there when Snorri's father brought Hulda to the village. Ragnar saw Snorri looking at him and nodded. Snorri nodded back and turned to Ulf and Thorbjorn. "Then what does she want?"

Ulf looked to the sky again before taking a deep breath. "She does what the gods want her to do. And the gods want her to sow chaos."

Thorbjorn shivered at those words as Snorri himself grabbed the Mjöllnir around his neck. *Until the day you don't,* his father's words echoed in his head again.

*

Griml and his Danes followed the smoke plume until they reached the burnt-out town. Not much remained. The walls were barely standing, and the town was now nothing more than a smoky skeleton. A sickly sweet smell filled the air, accompanied by the raucous noise of hundreds of ravens and crows. Griml glanced at the sky, seeing Odin's birds circling above, many of them diving to search for what food remained.

"What happened there?" one of the Danes asked. He was older than the others, his brown beard speckled with grey and his face scarred. Griml recognised him as the one who spoke to him on the ship. The man had been one of Ubba's captains, but Griml did not care to learn his name. Not that it mattered. He was not there to be their friend. He just needed them to kill the Norsemen so he could kill Ulf and get back to his life.

"Looked like we missed a lot of fun," another said.

Griml turned to the men behind him, growling at them. "We are not here to have fun! We are here to kill the bastard that did this to me." He pointed to the ugly scar on his cheek, the only scar on his face. In his many winters as a warrior, Griml had never been cut there. No one ever lived long enough. Not until a tall, skinny bastard on a shitty little farm got lucky. And he was still lucky. Three times Griml had the chance to kill him, and all three times he was stopped from doing so. But not anymore. Griml smiled. "His luck is about to run out."

The Danes behind Griml glanced at each other, not sure what Griml meant by that, but decided not to ask. Griml had killed two of them already for no reason, and all they wanted to do was to get back home alive.

"What do we do?" the brown-bearded Dane asked, making sure he was out of Griml's reach.

Griml noticed this and smiled. It would not help the bastard if Griml wanted to kill him, but he let the Dane think it would. "We find Snorri Thorgilsson and his men." He walked towards the burnout town, the Danes following him. As they neared, Griml sensed a familiar presence and knew she was here, watching him. "Once I kill the young bastard, I'll hack that bitch into pieces with that pretty sword," he muttered to himself. A gentle wind blew over him and for a reason Griml could not understand, he felt afraid.

"They're gone already," the Dane said, again, trying to keep his distance from Griml. At first, Griml found it amusing, but now it was annoying him. He wanted to grab the man and rip his head off just to show him he could, but decided against it. The man was a leader amongst the Danes, and Griml still needed him.

Griml stared at the field around the town, the churned-up ground that suggested a large number of people were here for a while. The boy on the beach had told him that Snorri was staying in a village southeast from here, but Griml didn't ask how far. He turned and took a step towards the Dane, taking pleasure in how much the man paled. "Send some men southeast from here," he ordered, his voice rough. "I don't want them back until they find Snorri and his bastard men." Griml turned to the others as the Dane ran off. "The rest of you swine, make a camp and find me some food!"

The men got busy setting up a camp and a group of them went back to the forest to hunt for some food. Griml ignored them and stared at the smouldering remains of the town. He wondered how many men Snorri had lost when he attacked the town. If he had fewer men, then Griml had a better chance of defeating him and killing Ulf. The scar on his face tingled, irritating Griml even more.

"There aren't any bodies anywhere," the brown-bearded Dane said. He had returned from his task and Griml saw a small group of men going southeast. He also saw that the older Dane was right. There were no bodies outside of the town. Griml grunted at that, not caring. "The fight must have happened inside," the Dane continued.

"I wonder how they got in." Another Dane joined them as Griml grit his teeth. "Those walls must have been quite high."

"Aye, and that town looks big, so they must have had a lot of men defending it," the brown-bearded warrior said.

"They went through the gates," Griml growled and walked away. He did not want to hear the Danish voices. They grated on his nerves and he resented the volva for making him use them. But then, how else would he be able to find and kill the young bastard who scarred his face?

*

Snorri watched as the Frankish people settled down outside of Ansovald's village, on the opposite side of where his camp was, and shook his head. The sun was setting and Snorri was exhausted. They spent the previous night searching through the town, looking for people and plunder, and Geir. To their disappointment, there had been little to plunder. The town was big, but not rich. And they had not found Geir. In his frustration, Snorri burnt the whole town down. Humbert had protested and Snorri guessed he wanted to move into the town, but Ansovald had agreed with Snorri. The town harassed his village for far too long. "I like the old man, but he is a fool."

"Aye, but that's not our problem." Ragnar stood with his hands on his hips. "The men need to be fed."

Snorri looked at his men. Most of them just collapsed when they reached their tents and fell asleep still wearing their armour. "That's not a problem for now, but in the morning, I will send a hunting party out. I doubt we can rely on the Franks to give us any food now."

"Not that we could rely on them before," Ragnar said, staying where he was, content just to watch the Franks.

Snorri glanced at him. "You were there when my father found Hulda."

Ragnar hesitated for a heartbeat before responding, "Aye, I was there."

"What happened when you found her?"

Again, Ragnar hesitated. "Your father never told you?"

"No, I guess I was too young." Snorri scratched his chin while glancing at Ragnar.

"Why is it important now?"

"Because Hulda's mother is hunting us."

"She's hunting Ulf."

Snorri turned to the nine-fingered warrior. "I don't know. There is more to it than that, and I think it has something to do with Hulda's death."

"Then we have nothing to worry about because Thorvald killed her and the snake is not with us." Ragnar turned and walked away.

Snorri watched him go, convinced there was more to it than that, but he wasn't going to fight his father's champion over it. It would just have to wait until they got home. *If we get home*, the voice whispered in his ear and Snorri shook his head. "We will get home. Tomorrow we start fixing the Sae-Ulfr and soon we'll be drinking ale in my father's hall," he said to himself.

"You really think so?" The voice came from behind him and Snorri jumped. He turned with his hand on his sword's hilt and saw Oddi smiling at him. "Sorry, I did not mean to frighten you."

"You did not frighten me." Snorri took calming breaths to slow his heart down.

Oddi laughed. "Of course not, cousin. Nothing frightens the mighty Snorri Thorgilsson."

"Aye," Snorri smiled. "Odin knows that's true." But Snorri wasn't so sure anymore.

"You really think we'll get home?" There was an uncertainty in Oddi's voice that Snorri had not heard before, and he frowned at his cousin.

"You don't?"

Oddi took a deep breath before answering, "From the beginning, this raid felt like it was cursed by the gods. First, the storm that took the War-Bear, and then the many ambushes and betrayals we've had to deal with. The gods are angry with us, Snorri, and we need to get them back on our side. Otherwise, we'll not be making it back to your father's hall."

Snorri looked at the sky. The clouds had given way while they marched back to the village, leaving the stars to watch over them. "At least you're not blaming Ulf for this."

Oddi laughed again. "People give him too much credit."

"You don't believe that Odin is watching him?"

"I do, but all our bad luck is not because of Ulf. Odin likes his games. We all know that, and Ulf is a part of it all, as are we. But I feel that what is happening is bigger than Ulf and his revenge."

Snorri nodded. He loved Ulf like a brother and saw the pain in his young friend's eyes every time someone blamed him for their situation. Perhaps Oddi was right. Perhaps the gods were angry with him for burning the hall of Jarl Arnfinni. Arnfinni had been an ally of his father and the father of his wife. But after the battle at The Giant's Toe, Snorri felt Arnfinni was planning to attack a weakened Thorgilsstad and become King Halfdan's strongest jarl. Snorri could not let that happen, so he had burnt the hall of the treacherous bastard and killed him with most of his warriors. The king had been furious with Snorri and demanded compensation. That was the reason they took part in this raid on Francia. The king had ordered them to, and Snorri was supposed to give two-thirds of the plunder to the king. Snorri knew many of his men thought the gods were angry about this raid. Many believed it was because they had left Thorgilsstad undefended, especially after the remaining men who had fought for Arnfinni attacked the village. He sighed. "How do we get the gods on our side again?"

Oddi shrugged. "A sacrifice should do the trick, but with everything that has gone against us, I feel it needs to be a powerful sacrifice."

Snorri scratched his cheek. He was afraid that Oddi would say that. Because it meant they would need a blood sacrifice. A human sacrifice. "You think Ansovald will let us sacrifice one of his people?"

Oddi rubbed his beard. "He doesn't need to know about it."

"True." Snorri studied the townspeople again as they started lighting their fires. The villagers brought out some supplies for them, most likely tents or sheets they could use as tents. He saw the large woman Thorbjorn had been fawning over and was surprised that Thorbjorn wasn't following her like a tail. They would be fed, and the villagers would forget it was the husbands, sons, and fathers of those people who had attacked them and took their children to be thralls. Those very children running into the arms of their parents now. "They share their food with the same people who spent months attacking their homes, but look down on the men who died protecting them." Snorri grit his teeth.

"Aye. Their god preaches forgiveness and love."

Snorri remembered what the strange old man in the forest had told him a few days before they attacked Rouen. *Their god has many rules, and he expects his people to follow them. Our gods are ruled by their emotions, by their love and their rage.* And now Snorri had to find a way of gaining the gods' love again. "Tomorrow we'll select a man to sacrifice to the gods."

CHAPTER 15

"Are you sure that'll work?" Thorbjorn asked as the men sat around their morning fire and ate flavourless porridge because there was no honey or berries to sweeten it.

"Nothing's more powerful than a human sacrifice," Oddi explained. "We all know that. If we really want to get the gods' attention, then that's our best chance."

"Aye, especially in this land." Snorri spooned more porridge into his mouth, grimacing as he chewed.

"It didn't work for Griml." Ulf remembered the day he lost Vidar.

"But that was because he drew Ormstunga in direct sunlight." Oddi adopted his wise smile. "Ormstunga's curse undid Odin's favour."

Ulf tilted his head to the side, frowning. "But would the All-Father's favour not be more powerful than a curse?"

Oddi opened his mouth to respond, but no words came out, which caused Thorbjorn to laugh.

"Not so smart now, Oddi Viss."

"It is a good question." Snorri put his bowl of half-eaten porridge to one side. "You'd think Odin would have the power to undo any curse, yet he didn't."

"Perhaps Ormstunga's curse is stronger than Odin?" Magni suggested.

"Stronger than the All-Father?" Thorbjorn scowled at Magni. "That's like saying the mouse is stronger than the snake."

"Well, Ormstunga came from a snake. A gigantic snake." Oddi stroked his beard.

"And not just any snake," Drumbr added, happily chewing on the porridge everyone else had given up on. "But Jörmungandr."

"So, Jörmungandr is stronger than Odin?" Thorbjorn scratched his head below the bear tattoo.

"Jörmungandr does kill Thor during Ragnarök, and Thor is the strongest of the gods." Oddi smiled, believing that explained everything. Ulf shook his head, amazed at how these men could lose themselves in trivial conversations with so much happening around them.

"Or perhaps, it was because Ulf is favoured by Odin and Griml isn't," Snorri said.

"Then we should sacrifice Ulf to Odin," Asbjorn mocked. "Perhaps then Odin will send us his horse Sleipnir to carry all of us home." The men laughed while Ulf ground his teeth.

"As much as I like the idea, that would only anger Odin," Ragnar said before turning to Snorri. "So, who do we sacrifice?"

Snorri looked at the camp of the refugees from the town they had attacked. "One of them should do."

"They are our enemy, and their god is the enemy of our gods," Oddi added. "That should really get Odin's attention."

They spent the rest of the morning discussing who they should sacrifice. Some suggested a warrior, a man who had fought in battles, while others thought a young woman, preferably a virgin, would be best. Ulf never realised it was this complicated, but he guessed his friends wanted to make it work. Then came the debate about when and where to do it. It had to be in the open so that the gods had a good view of the sacrifice from Asgard, but they had to make sure the Franks did not know about it. The Norsemen still needed their help to repair the Sae-Ulfr. Oddi thought that the best place to do it would be on the deck of the Sae-Ulfr so that the blood of the sacrifice could seep into the wood.

"We need the gods to provide us with safe passage across the seas. With Rolf gone, the voyage would be more difficult," Oddi explained. The men nodded as they agreed. The old sailor had a knack for getting their ship through the most dangerous storms. Most believed it was because he had been Ran's lover once, but now she had taken him back and the Sae-Ulfr had lost her steersman.

"Then we need to make the sacrifice after we fixed the Sae-Ulfr," Thorbjorn said, and the others agreed. The men discussed what they needed, and who in the crew had the relevant skills. The Sae-Ulfr's mast needed to be replaced as well as some sideboards which had broken when Snorri's ship came aground on the beach. Ulf struggled to keep up with what Snorri and his hirdmen were saying. Even Magni had fallen asleep, the tall warrior lying beside the men on his back, his arms stretched wide as he snored in the late morning sun. Ulf's mind drifted back to his meeting with Hulda's mother. He still wondered what she really wanted from all of this.

"We should hunt." Drumbr patted his stomach as the others looked at him in surprise. "Doubt we gonna get any more meat from them." He pointed towards the village. The men nodded, understanding what Drumbr meant. Many of the villagers were angry with the Norsemen and would spit at them when they walked past the Norse camp to go to the river. They had already forgotten it was their leader who asked the Norse warriors for help.

"Aye, Drumbr is correct." Snorri looked at his men. Most of them were lying about, some cleaning armour or sharpening weapons, others napping. Snorri had been so caught up in their discussion that he forgot to send men to hunt. He looked at Drumbr. "Grab a few men, see if the Franks left us any deer in the forest."

"I'll go with," Ulf said as Drumbr got to his feet. Drumbr nodded and went to get some spears while Ulf collected Ormstunga, glad to have a reason to get away. Snorri and his friends were talking about things he knew little about, and perhaps a hunt would distract his mind.

They left the camp, both content to be silent as they walked towards the forest. The men greeted them as they walked past, some offering to join the hunt, but Drumbr declined. Most were still tired after the last two days and were happy to let Snorri's two hirdmen go by themselves.

It didn't take them long to reach the forest, as it wasn't far from the village. "Not the best time of the day to go hunting," Ulf said as they walked past the first few trees. He took a deep breath, savouring the smells of the trees and the soil. He closed his eyes and listened to the wind as it rustled through the leaves and heard birds singing from the branches. Somewhere in the distance, Ulf heard a song louder than the rest, but he did not know what bird it was from. He had heard it plenty of times in Francia, but never in Norway.

"Aye." Drumbr glanced at the sun, now sitting at its peak. "The morning would have been best, but we had important things to discuss." The large warrior smiled. "Perhaps Ullr will be kind to us today and we'll get lucky." Ullr was the god of hunting and winter, although he preferred to hunt with a bow. All Ulf and Drumbr had were spears, and Ulf didn't even know how to shoot a bow. Ulf nodded and hoped his friend was correct. He had eaten little of the tasteless porridge and the thought of venison made his mouth water. Silently, they walked through the trees, both men scanning their surroundings, but neither expecting much.

Ulf listened to the birds singing from the branches and the rustling of the leaves as unseen creatures ran above them. The soil beneath their feet was damp, and the earthy aroma reminded Ulf of the forests in Norway.

"You ever wonder if Vidar would have liked these forests?" Drumbr's question caught Ulf by surprise.

Ulf looked around him, taking in the surrounding trees. Oak, pine, ash, and alder. The same trees that grew in the forests in Norway. "I often wonder the same." Ulf felt the familiar pang in his chest.

"He was a strange boy, that one. But I miss him."

Ulf smiled as he glanced at the large warrior. Vidar had been mute and his hands were too big for his body, but that was not what made him strange. It was his eyes, which looked like they had lived many lifetimes, even though Vidar had barely seen thirteen winters. Every time Vidar looked at him, it was like he knew what was going on in Ulf's head. "I sometimes wondered if the gods had not sent him, or perhaps he was one of the gods who came to aid me in the vengeance." Ulf felt his heart beating faster. He never liked talking about Vidar, but it felt good to say the words out loud.

"You think he is in Valhalla?" Drumbr asked. The two men stopped and Drumbr leaned against an ash tree.

"With Brak?"

Drumbr smiled. "Aye, my brother would be there. Feasting with our ancestors and probably doing his best to make sure there will be no mead for me when I get there. The bastard."

Ulf laughed. "I hope Vidar is in Valhalla. I would like to see him again." As Ulf said that, he remembered the vision of Vidar he had recently, the one used by the volva to lure Ulf away from his friends.

"Ulf?" Drumbr asked as Ulf's face grew serious.

Before Ulf could answer, he glimpsed a movement in the shadows. Thinking it was a deer, Ulf held his spear in front of him as he crouched. Drumbr frowned and Ulf pointed towards where he had seen the movement. The shadows were still, and Ulf wondered if he had imagined it. For a heartbeat, he thought it was the volva using Vidar's image again. Ulf opened his mouth to tell Drumbr it was a false alarm when he realised the trees had gone quiet. The birds were no longer singing and the rustling of the leaves had stopped. Behind him, he felt Drumbr tense, his warrior senses most likely warning him of danger. Neither spoke as they peered into the shadows, both men trying to see what was there. "Wolves?" Ulf whispered, but Drumbr said nothing. As Ulf glanced over his shoulder at the fat man, he saw his eyes were tight and his knuckles white as they gripped his spear. Drumbr's huge two-handed axe was back at the camp, but he had his small one-handed axe with him. Like Ulf, Drumbr also didn't have his brynja on and Ulf hoped that if it was wolves, there wouldn't be too many of them.

Drumbr took half a step forward, moving silently for someone that big when a man jumped out from behind the tree. He wore a leather jerkin and had a dull bowl helmet on his head. But it was the Mjöllnir around his neck that caught their attention. "A Dane!" Drumbr bellowed and launched himself at the man. The Dane tried to parry Drumbr's spear thrust with his axe, but Drumbr was faster and the spear pierced through his chest. The man gasped and blood sprayed from his mouth, as screaming birds took to the sky. Another man jumped out of the undergrowth, this one dressed the same as the one Drumbr had just killed, and took off running. "Get him!" Drumbr shouted as he freed his spear from the dead man's chest.

His words jolted Ulf into action, and he sped after the fleeing man. The Dane crashed through the forest like he was being chased by a pack of wolves, ducking beneath branches and jumping over roots. Ulf did everything he could to keep up, desperate not to let him get away. He launched his spear at the back of the Dane, who was about fifteen paces ahead of him. But the man twisted out of the way without glancing back and the spear missed. "Argh!" Ulf screamed as he pushed himself to go faster. The trees blurred past him, as leaves and branches stung his face and tugged on his tunic, but Ulf did not care. He was gaining on the Dane. When Ulf was within five paces, he tripped over a root and was sent flying through the air. He landed hard on the ground and felt a stone digging into his chest, but Ulf ignored that as he rolled back to his feet and continued the chase. The Dane had gained some ground, but Ulf's longer legs gave him an advantage and he was soon closing the gap again. The man glanced over his shoulder and Ulf saw the whites in his eyes as he twisted past a tree in an attempt to lose him. But Ulf had sensed the movement and followed only a few paces behind. As soon as he was within reach, Ulf launched himself at the man. He landed on the Dane's back, sending both men tumbling to the ground. Ulf tried to roll the Dane over, but the man struck him on the side of the head with the back of his elbow. Slightly dazed, Ulf fell off him, but managed to grab hold of the man's trousers and trip him up as the Dane tried to get away. The Dane kicked at Ulf, who got his head out of the way, but the Dane's boot caught him on the shoulder. Ulf grit his teeth at the pain, but held on to the man's leg. The Dane kicked at him again. This time, Ulf let go of his leg and jumped up to his feet. He rushed at the Dane before the man could react and punched him in the face. Just as Ulf thought he was getting the upper hand, another Dane appeared out of nowhere and tackled him off the man. Ulf landed on the ground, the new Dane on top of him. He twisted away and avoided the first punch aimed at his head, but not the second. Fists and elbows were flying as Ulf and the Dane wrestled on the forest floor. Ulf tried to get to Ormstunga, but the man was lying on top of her. Another punch came at Ulf, and he twisted his head out of the way as the Dane screamed, spraying spittle all over his face. The other Dane struggled to his feet and, when he saw what was happening, tried to stomp on Ulf's head. Ulf braced himself as the leather boot came, knowing he could not get his arms up to protect his head. Not while the other Dane was pinning them down. But before the boot landed, there was a roar as Drumbr crashed through the trees and punched the standing Dane in the face. The man's head snapped back and his limp body collapsed on the ground beside Ulf and the Dane he was fighting. The Dane on top of Ulf froze, and Ulf used the opportunity to roll them over so that he was now on top. He grabbed the man's head with both his hands and screamed as he smashed his head into the ground. The Dane's body tensed, juddered, and then went limp as blood started flowing out of his head. Confused, Ulf rolled the dead Dane over and saw the bloody stone sticking out of the ground. Over the rush of the blood in his ears and his heart thumping in his chest, Ulf heard the familiar noise of the raven croaking and then the flap of wings as it flew away, most likely to inform Odin of what it had just witnessed. Ulf looked at Drumbr, his tunic drenched in sweat, as he stood there with his hands on his knees and panting heavily.

"We might not have found any deer, but at least we found the perfect offering to Odin." Drumbr pointed to the unconscious Dane he had punched. But Ulf did not share Drumbr's smile. He knew the Danes could mean only one thing.

Griml was here.

CHAPTER 16

"There were no deer then?" Thorbjorn raised an eyebrow at Ulf and Drumbr as they walked back into the camp. The unconscious Dane slumped over Drumbr's shoulder.

"No deer." Drumbr dropped the Dane to the ground. "Found this bastard and a few of his friends in the forest, though."

Snorri squatted down and inspected the unconscious man. "What happened to his friends?"

"Both dead," Ulf said, rubbing his shoulder where the other Dane had kicked him. The men stared at him, seeing the dirt on his face and in his hair, as well as the light bruise on the side of his head.

"This was after they gave you a good beating?" Ragnar smiled, enjoying the discomfort on Ulf's face. Ulf glared at Ragnar and let go of his shoulder, determined not to show any more weakness in front of the red-headed warrior.

"The first one we spotted I killed, the second made a run for it, and Ulf chased after him," Drumbr explained. "By the time I caught up, Ulf was fighting two of them on the ground." He kicked at the Dane on the ground with his boot. "Ulf killed the other one, but this one we managed to keep alive. Thought he could be useful."

"Danes?" Oddi asked, and Snorri nodded. "You know what this means?" He looked at Ulf and Drumbr. Both men nodded.

"You sure there were no others?" Ragnar asked as Snorri studied the Dane, his face rigid.

"We saw no others." Drumbr looked at Ulf, who shrugged. "Only the three of them."

"Doesn't mean there weren't others." Thorbjorn hawked and spat. "Fucking Danes."

Magni frowned as he glanced from one man to the next. "I don't understand what you are all so worried about. It's only a few Danes."

"Where there are a few Danes, there are usually more." Snorri stood up and looked towards the forest, his eyebrows drawn together.

"Might not be him," Asbjorn said, glancing at Ulf. "Could be a raiding party."

Ulf shook his head, ignoring the sneer from Asbjorn. "It's Griml."

"Because your dream told you," Asbjorn retorted.

Ulf glared at Asbjorn, who turned to face him. Thorbjorn moved between the two warriors before they came to blows again.

"We'll find out soon enough. Wake the bastard up." Snorri's face was hard and Ulf shuddered when he thought of what might happen to this man.

The rest of the crew had gathered around them as Thorbjorn poured a bucket of water over the Dane. The man sat up, spitting water from his mouth and shaking his head, but his face soon paled when he realised where he was. But that only lasted for a few moments as the Dane squared his shoulders and hardened his face.

Ragnar squatted down in front of the man and punched him in the face. The Dane fell onto his back, blood gushing out of his already broken nose. Thorbjorn helped the Dane up, only for Ragnar to punch him again. To the Dane's credit, he just grit his teeth and glared at them as Ragnar stepped away so that Snorri could speak to the Dane.

"Why are you here?"

"To fuck your mother!" The Dane spat blood in Snorri's face. Snorri smiled as he wiped the blood off with the back of his hand and stood up. Before the Dane could react, Snorri kicked him hard in the face, knocking the man out again.

"That didn't help," Thorbjorn said, and was about to fetch another bucket of water.

"No, leave it," Snorri said, looking in the village's direction. "We have company."

Ulf turned and saw Ansovald and Humbert coming towards them with Theoda, carrying a large basket in her hands, and two men Ulf did not recognise. Both looked old, like most of the men in the village, their tunics old and frayed, but they were carrying woodworking tools, which made the rest of the Norsemen smile.

Asbjorn and Thorbjorn grabbed the Dane and tied his hands and legs, while the rest of them greeted the Franks.

Ansovald glanced at the Dane lying prone, while Humbert and the two other men looked on nervously. The village leader said something to them, pointing at the tied-up man.

"Who he?" Humbert translated, unable the hide the quiver from his voice at seeing the bloody Dane.

"A friend." Snorri smiled.

"Why he tied? And blood?"

"We were talking to him."

Humbert translated Snorri's words to Ansovald, who just stared at Snorri. He said something to Humbert, who translated, "Friend, trouble us?"

Snorri glanced at the unconscious Dane and smiled. "No, no trouble." Snorri's hirdmen smirked behind him, and Ulf wondered why he was not telling Ansovald the truth. If it really was Griml, then Ansovald's village was in danger. They did not know how many men Griml had. Perhaps Snorri was concerned that if he told them the truth, then Ansovald might not help them fix the Sae-Ulfr. Ulf looked at the village, seeing the people carry on with their daily lives, content now that they knew there would be no more attacks from their neighbours. None of those Franks cared about the Norse warriors who had risked their lives to protect them. Even the two men Ansovald had brought with him looked like they didn't want to be there. Ulf knew the priests had been spewing hatred of them every morning since they had arrived. The priests would stand at the edge of the village with most of the villagers gathered behind them and chant. Snorri's men amused themselves by watching and making jokes about what the priests were chanting. Some even made crude comments about the staff one priest was waving in the air and the women behind them. But they all knew what the priests were doing. Even after their neighbours attacked before a holy day and Snorri and his men repelled the attackers, the priests and villagers still treated them like the enemy. So if they did not care about Ulf and his friends, then why should he care about them? Let Griml come and slaughter them, and while the troll fucking bastard was distracted, Ulf would kill him and finally avenge his family. The deep rumbling laugh echoed in Ulf's head as the thought came to him. *You are me.* Ulf shook his head to chase the words away. "No, I'm not." Oddi looked at him with a raised eyebrow, but Ulf turned his attention back to the Franks as Humbert spoke again.

"These men. They help fix boat."

"Ship," Snorri said, which caused Humbert to frown. "The Sae-Ulfr is a ship, not a boat." Humbert only shrugged, making it obvious that it did not matter to him. "Thank you," Snorri said.

The two men were reluctant to step forward until Ansovald growled something at them.

"Do they know how to build ships?" Oddi asked.

"Build no," Humbert responded with a smile. "They build houses. Know trees very well."

"Great, more idiots who'll be trying to talk to the trees," Asbjorn muttered while glancing at Ulf.

"Thank you," Snorri said again. "Their tools and help will be very useful." He smiled at Ansovald, who beamed back.

Humbert was about to turn around and walk back to the village when Theoda blocked his path and scowled at him. The Norsemen could not help but smile at how Humbert squirmed and then turned to face them again.

"Theoda bring food. Say you be hungry."

With that, she walked forward, barging Humbert out of the way, and handed the basket to Thorbjorn. Ulf caught the glint in her eye and the shy smile from the short warrior.

"By Freya, but Thorbjorn's trapped now," Asbjorn joked, elbowing Thorbjorn in the side, as the Franks turned and walked back to their village, leaving only the two woodcutters. The men looked frightened, especially when the Norsemen started laughing at Thorbjorn's red face.

"Fuck off, all of you goat fuckers," Thorbjorn said.

"Aye, looks like I'll have to find a hirdman to replace Thorbjorn as well." Snorri stroked his beard as if he was serious. "Thorbjorn's going to grow old here in this village with Theoda's bosom to keep him warm."

"Better than putting up with you twits."

The men laughed and got back to their tents and fires as Thorbjorn put the basket by Snorri's tent.

"What about him?" He pointed to the Dane who was coming around.

Snorri looked at the Dane with his wolf smile on his face. "Oh, almost forgot about our friend. It's time to make the bastard talk."

"And them?" Oddi pointed at the two Franks.

"Send some men with them to the forest. Make sure they find the right tree for the mast and we need some planks for the side."

Oddi nodded and called to some men before leading them and the woodcutters to the forest. Ulf turned to follow him, preferring to go back to the forest than stay here and watch them torture the Dane.

"Where do you think you're going?" Ragnar asked him, his arms crossed. "Every time you go in the forest, bad things happen."

Snorri walked up to Ulf and clapped him on the shoulder. "Don't be so dramatic, Ragnar. Bad things happen everywhere." Ulf winced, and not just because Snorri hit him on his sore shoulder. "The gods love chaos. We all know that."

"Aye, and thanks to the pup, we're in the middle of the fucking chaos." Ragnar glared at Ulf while Snorri laughed.

"You wouldn't want it any other way."

To Ulf's surprise, he saw a small smile on Ragnar's lips, almost hidden by his red beard. But it disappeared quickly, and the glare was back. Snorri turned to the forest, his face serious as well. "What?" Ragnar asked him.

"We should send some men to the forest, make sure there are no more Danes trying to find us."

"How did they find us?" Asbjorn asked while sharpening his sax-knife. Ulf tried not to think of the reason he was doing that. "It's not like we planned on being here."

"Must have seen the smoke from the town Snorri burnt to the ground," Ragnar responded. "From there, it's just a case of following our tracks."

"Or the volva told them," Snorri said. Ulf wasn't sure if his friend had believed him or if he just didn't want to be the one responsible for leading Griml and the Danes to them.

"Doesn't matter." Ragnar hawked and spat. "They're here and we need to prepare."

"Aye. We'll send more hunting parties out, see if we can find any more scouts. We just need to keep them off our trail until the Sae-Ulfr is fixed." Snorri looked at the three of them and they all nodded. "Now, let's see what our new friend knows."

The Dane was sitting on a stool with Thorbjorn and Drumbr on either side of him. This was something they had done before, and Ulf realised he was about to see a new side to his friends. The Dane was awake and breathing through his mouth because of his broken nose while glaring at them. He had been stripped of his armour and tunic and his boots were also removed. Ulf glanced at the boots and wondered if they would fit him. He needed a new pair, but chastised himself for thinking like that when a man was about to be tortured. *Perhaps I am turning into him.* The rumbling voice echoed in his head again.

Asbjorn handed the sax-knife to Snorri, who walked towards the Dane, his wolf grin on his face. "You know what's going to happen now," Snorri said to the Dane, who only glared back. "Who is your leader?"

The Dane said nothing as Snorri pulled up a stool and sat in front of him.

"You better answer him, you goat turd." Thorbjorn slapped the Dane on the back of the head, but the Dane remained silent. He glared at Ulf, but Ulf kept his face hard to match those of his friends. He might not like what they were about to do, but he needed the know if the volva had been right. If Griml was really here.

Snorri placed the tip of the sax-knife on the Dane's leg, just above the knee. The Dane stared at the knife and then looked up at Snorri again as a single sweat bead ran down his face.

"Do what you want. Odin knows your days are numbered. When he gets here, there'll be nothing left of you to go to Valhalla." He was about to spit into Snorri's face, like he did before, but then Snorri slowly pushed the sax-knife into his leg. The Dane's eyes bulged and he grit his teeth against the pain. Ulf turned away as the blood seeped out of the wound.

"When who gets here?" Snorri twisted the knife still embedded in the Dane's leg. The man shook his head as tears streamed down his cheeks, but he kept his mouth shut. Snorri slowly pushed the knife in deeper. Ragnar grunted, and Ulf saw the smile on his face.

"Griml! That ugly giant of a Norse bastard!" the Dane finally cried. Ulf felt his hands shake at the mention of the troll as the voices of his ancestors started whispering in his ears. The volva had been right, Griml was here. Ulf caught the glances from Thorbjorn and Drumbr, but he tried to ignore them as he focused on the Dane.

Snorri kept the knife where it was, about two fingers-width inside of the Dane's leg. The Dane glared at him with grit teeth and red eyes. "How many men has he got?" Snorri asked. Around them, Snorri's crew stopped what they were doing and watched as Snorri interrogated the Dane. Some men were making bets on how long the Dane would last, others on whether Snorri would kill the man. Ulf even heard one man make a bet on whether he would kill the Dane. With the voices of his ancestors getting louder in his ears, Ulf himself wondered if he would. He clenched his fist to stop them from shaking.

The Dane shook his head as he screwed his eyes shut against the pain and refused to answer. To Ulf's surprise, this only made the voices in his ears go louder. *Can you kill him?* The question came to him, silencing the voices of his ancestors. Ulf looked at the forest behind him, as if he was trying to see where Griml was. *Can I kill him?*

Snorri thrust the knife in hard, burying it hilt-deep into the Dane's leg. The man's eyes shot open as he screamed. He tried to lunge at Snorri, but Thorbjorn and Drumbr grabbed hold of him. "How many men?" Snorri screamed.

"Enough to slaughter all of you Norse pigs!" Tears streamed down the man's face, his cheeks red as Snorri pulled the knife out. Blood seeped from the wound and rolled down his leg like a waterfall. Ulf saw some villagers look their way and realised they must have heard the Dane scream.

Snorri smiled at the Dane and placed the tip of the knife on his other leg. The man went white, but he grit his teeth and tried his best to keep his face hard. Ulf almost admired his courage. "How many men?" Snorri asked again, slowly pushing the knife into the man's leg. The Dane threw his head back and bit his lip, determined not to answer.

"You're losing your touch, Snorri," Ragnar said.

Snorri glanced at Ragnar and then looked back at the Dane. The man was glaring at him again, his lip bloody. "How many men?" The knife went deeper, Snorri forcing it in slowly until the hilt stopped on the Dane's leg.

The Dane started laughing. A crazed laugh brought on by the pain. "It doesn't matter. He will slaughter you all!" His eyes darted from man to man until they settled on Ulf. "He wants you more than anyone. Oh yes, he keeps talking about you. Keeps telling us how he wants to make you scream, just like your aunt screamed when he fucked her over the body of her dead husband." The Dane shook his head as he laughed.

Before Ulf knew what was happening, the voices of his ancestors erupted in his ears, all of them howling at him. The flames in the pit of his stomach exploded to life, sending the heat of his fury coursing through his veins. Ulf roared and launched himself at the Dane. Ragnar tried to grab him, but Ulf was too fast, and Snorri simply moved out of the way as Drumbr and Thorbjorn let go of the Dane. Ulf tackled the Dane and landed on top of him. He punched the man in the face, again and again, while screaming at him. Nothing else existed to Ulf at this point other than him and the Dane on the ground. "Where is he?" Ulf roared. "Where is the troll fucking bastard? Tell me!" He kept punching the Dane, not feeling the man's jaw break or face being crushed. Ulf grabbed the knife, still stuck in the Dane's leg and was about to ram it in the man's throat when he was grabbed from behind and pulled away. "I'll fucking kill him! Odin knows I'll kill the bastard!" he roared as he was dragged away from the unconscious body. "You tell the troll I am coming for him!"

Drumbr and Ragnar threw Ulf to the ground, and Snorri moved quickly to grab the knife from his hand. "That bastard isn't going to tell anyone anything now," Ragnar growled. Ulf slowly came to his senses as the words reached him and saw the Dane lying there, his face bloody and swollen. Snorri's men all looked at Ulf, each of them with a tinge of fear on their faces. Apart from one man, who was smiling.

"Told you Ulf will kill him," he said to the man next to him. "Now pay up."

Ulf saw Thorbjorn check if the Dane was still alive as the voices of his ancestors were replaced by the deep, rumbling laugh. *You are me.*

CHAPTER 17

"Come, Bjørnson. Come and see."

Ulf opened his eyes at the sound of the voice. It sounded familiar, but unfamiliar at the same time. That was what had woken him, not the words. It was a voice he was sure he had heard before, but at the same time, had never heard.

"Come, Bjørnson. Come and see." The voice came again, further away this time. Ulf looked around but saw nothing. It was dark, but not the middle of the night dark. This darkness was different, and it was one Ulf knew too well. He groaned as his hand searched for Ormstunga and was not surprised when she was gone. So were his friends and the men of Thorgilsstad. The familiar fear started creeping into his stomach. "Come and see, Bjørnson." The voice repeated, uncaring of Ulf's trepidation.

Ulf took a deep breath and got to his feet. The old man would not wait for him. But Ulf did not know where he needed to go, or what he needed to see. He shivered at the icy darkness which surrounded him. At least the ground was dry. The last time this cloaked man came to Ulf in his dreams, he found himself in a marsh of blood and bone. "Where are you?" Ulf shouted, trying to fight the fear creeping into his limbs.

"Come and see, Bjørnson." The voice came from his left. Ulf turned and ran to it, fearing that he might lose the old man again.

"I can't see anything," he said when he felt the figure beside him. The old man stood as straight as an oak tree and wore a cloak that hid his face. An ancient hand, its skin stretched thin over the bones and mottled with age, held on to the long staff the cloaked figure carried but never leaned on.

"Come and see," the old voice drifted over him.

"See what?" As if in answer, a light appeared in the distance. It wavered in a wind that Ulf could not feel, and he was sure it was a fire. Ulf strained his eyes, trying to find the other figure that always came to him in his dreams. The giant mountain troll.

"Look," the figure said, and Ulf imagined he was pointing at the fire as it grew.

Ulf squinted as he noticed something inside the flames. At first, it looked like a house, and Ulf wondered if it was Arnfinni's hall. But as the fire grew bigger, Ulf could make out more houses. A noise reached his ears, one he did not recognise at first until the scream of a woman made him understand what he was looking at. It was a village. A village much like Ansovald's. Flames danced from the rooftops as they chewed through the straw roofs and crept down the wooden walls. People ran out of the buildings, women clutching their children, their hair and dresses ablaze. Men stumbled as the flames tore through them. The church, with the large cross on the tower, was engulfed in flames which leapt high into the darkness. The priests, who this very day were berating the Norsemen from the safety of the village, were running around like chickens, screaming and waving their arms in the air as the fire showed them no mercy. Ulf expected to feel the heat of the blaze as it grew and enveloped more of the houses. But all he felt was the cold of the fear spreading through his limbs and rooting his feet to the ground. The sounds of the villagers screaming drowned out the noise of the flames and only made Ulf shiver more. "Odin, what is this?"

A deep rumbling laugh echoed over the fire and screams as the flames jumped to something new. A ship. And not just any ship as Ulf recognised the long, sleek shape he loved and the proud beast head, a wolf with its teeth bared as it snarled and growled at all those who stood against her. The Sae-Ulfr.

"No!" Ulf cried, but the deep rumbling laugh continued. Ulf trembled when he recognised it. It was the same one that had been haunting him since they first came to Francia. He tore his eyes away from the Sae-Ulfr as the flames ran up her mast and chewed through the sails, searching for the source of the laugh. Beside him, the cloaked figure stood like a silent guardian, yet Ulf did not feel safe. Especially not when he saw the giant frame of the troll standing in front of the burning village, its feet wide apart and clutching its stomach as it threw back its head and laughed. Ulf shivered when the troll stopped laughing and stared at him. A movement by the troll's feet caught Ulf's eye and when he glanced down, he thought he spotted a snake slithering between the troll's legs. But before he could be sure, the troll roared and charged at him. In its hands, the troll held a huge two-handed axe which it lifted above its

head. Ulf turned to the cloaked figure beside him, seeing the long grey beard flowing out of the hood of the cloak. "Odin, what is this?"

The troll was now close enough for Ulf to see its face and, as he had expected, Griml's dark eyes sat above an enormous nose. But what Ulf didn't want to see were the three scar lines, just like his, running down the troll's face. The cloaked figure started laughing beside Ulf, as the troll was almost on top of him.

"This is chaos!"

Ulf woke with a start. He jumped to his feet and grabbed Ormstunga from where she was lying beside his sleeping mat before rushing out of his tent. His eyes took a few heartbeats to focus on his surroundings, but when they did, he saw the sun climbing above the horizon. In the morning light, the smoke from the village was slowly rising from the rooftops. But the smoke was not from flames burning the houses. It was from the morning fires inside as the villagers prepared the morning meals. Ulf stared at the village, taking all this in as the day slowly brightened. The Sae-Ulfr was still sitting beside their camp on the wooden logs they used to keep her keel off the ground. Just like the village, she was not in flames and neither was her mast and beast head. Instead of the sounds of fire and people screaming, there were birds singing their morning songs and men yawning and groaning as they woke with the sun. He also heard the raven as it flew away.

"Ulf, what, in Odin's name, are you doing?" Thorbjorn asked. Ulf looked around him and saw his friends frowning at him and glancing at each other.

"I…" He looked at the village again, unable to get the images from his dream out of his head.

"Put the sword down!" Ragnar growled. "You look like a fucking fool!"

Ulf looked at Ormstunga in his hand, almost confused as to how she got there. He did not have the sword with him in his dream. Especially not when the troll charged at him. Ulf shivered at the thought and just sat down. He looked at his friends as they all still stared at him, waiting for him to explain. But Ulf did not know how to explain. He struggled to make sense of what he had seen.

"Another dream?" Snorri asked, his eyebrows drawn together. Ulf looked at him and nodded.

"You going to tell us what it was about?" Asbjorn sneered.

"Leave him be." Thorbjorn took his comb from his pouch and ran it through his beard. "He'll tell us when he's ready." Asbjorn waved a hand at Thorbjorn as he got to his feet and walked away while untying his trousers. "Aye, I need a piss as well." Thorbjorn got up and rushed after Asbjorn while putting his comb away.

"Must have been a bad one for you to react like that," Oddi said, stretching as he sat up.

"I don't understand. What is it with his dreams?" Magni asked, flattening his morning hair.

"I told you—" Oddi started.

"Aye, I know what you said. The gods speak to Ulf in his dreams," Magni imitated his brother's voice. "But it never seems to do you any good."

Ulf looked at Magni, unsure of how to respond to that. None of the men did. Ragnar got to his feet and rubbed his neck.

"Aye, that's why it's better he keeps them to himself. Life was a lot simpler before Ulf joined us, and if you say I should have been a bóndi again, then I'll kick you in the face," Ragnar said to Snorri, who was just about to say something.

Snorri shook his head and smiled, before looking at Ulf. "Anything we should worry about?"

Ulf glanced at the village again, seeing how some people were leaving their houses. Women were emptying their night buckets while greeting each other as men left to start their morning jobs. The church bells were ringing and the image of the tower on fire came to Ulf. "I don't know." Ulf never understood these dreams. And he hated the fear he always felt in them.

"Well, no point dwelling on that. We have plenty to do today." Snorri got up and sniffed his armpit. The grimace on his face showed it was time for a wash.

Ulf stank as well, but he was too tired to do anything about it. And not just because of his dream.

It had been a week since they found the Danish scouts and the Norsemen had been hard at work ever since. Every day, Snorri sent out three groups, each commanded by one of his hirdmen, but never Ulf. Two of the groups would be armed with swords and axes. Their job would be to find and kill any other scouts that Griml might send. So far, they had found two more scouting parties, most of who they killed, but they always tried to keep at least one man alive to question. They had three Danish captives now, including the one Ulf had beaten. The man had survived, although his jaw was broken and his wits gone. His face was swollen to the point that the man could not open his eyes. So they needed other men to question and sacrifice to Odin. Oddi didn't believe that Odin would be happy with a broken Dane.

"Trust Ulf to beat a good sacrifice to the point he is useless," Asbjorn complained that day.

"Aye, doesn't want to attack a village because he doesn't want to kill the farmers, but happily tries to kill a man with his hands tied behind his back," Ragnar added.

Ulf growled, the flames of his anger still coursing through him. "He is a warrior, not a farmer or woman."

The third group went out with the Frankish woodsmen to find wood for the Sae-Ulfr. This proved to be more difficult than finding the Danish scouts, and Snorri could only send Oddi with this group. He was the only one calm enough to deal with the stubborn Franks who wanted to cut down the first tree they found. Ulf did not know how Oddi dealt with them, but both Frankish men came back alive after each day.

It had taken them a few days to find the right tree for the mast. Ulf was not sure how they knew which tree to choose. He remembered how the men had cheered when the tree was dragged into the campsite. Even some villagers had wandered closer to find out what all the excitement was, and Ansovald had sent over a cask of Frankish ale. It wasn't as nice as the ale in Norway, but the men still drank it after offering some of the ale to the spirits of the forest to thank them for the tree. The priests had complained about this, and Humbert asked Snorri to stop, but they were all ignored. That was also the first night Thorbjorn slipped away, only to return the next morning, grinning from ear to ear. The men knew where he was going and mocked him, but for once, Thorbjorn did not bite back. Theoda had also become a regular visitor to the camp, bringing food and helping to mend their clothes. At first, the Frankish men protested with her, but they soon stopped after she punched one of them. The Norsemen had cheered, and after that day, they greeted her warmly. She didn't understand what they said to her, but she always smiled back.

After they found the mast, the men went out one more time to find the right tree for the planks they needed for the side of the ship. The Franks refused to go out and after Snorri spoke to Ansovald, they were forced to give their tools to the Norse. This didn't help the already strained relationship between the Norse and the Franks. The people from the town they had attacked avoided them, but the villagers were braver. Especially the children, who would sometimes run towards the Norse warriors, spit at them or throw rocks before running away. The men never retaliated. Snorri had ordered them not to. And besides, they would be on their way home soon. Snorri still would not allow Ulf to go into the forest. But now that they had the trunk for the mast, Ulf could help them prepare it. He was not as skilled as some, but he had spent his youth helping his uncle Olaf build and fix fences, so he knew how to work with wood. They used wood axes to cut off the branches and then spent the next few days stripping the bark off the trunk. The work was hard and would leave Ulf exhausted after each day, but it kept him busy.

Finding the right tree to replace the side planks of the Sae-Ulfr was quicker than the mast and the same day the men had set out to look for it, they came back dragging another large oak tree behind them. Ulf watched as they split the wood for the side planks, using wedges and wood hammers to split the trunk along its grain. He remembered his uncle telling him about this and how it made their ships stronger and more flexible. As with the sailing, Ulf watched carefully, trying to learn as much as he could and even helping when it was possible. The older men in the crew seemed happy to pass on their knowledge, especially Arne. He was one of the few greybeards in the crew, his body and arms covered in scars. The man had known Ulf's father, but was always reluctant to talk about him. Not that Ulf cared much about that. Arne explained to Ulf how to find the right places to put the wedges and even let Ulf split one plank. Ulf was surprised at how many planks they got out of the one trunk. It was more than they needed, but Arne explained it was always good to have extra planks.

When the new side planks were ready, they set about repairing the Sae-Ulfr. The rivets which held them in place were knocked out and the damaged planks were removed. Many of the Frankish men, including Ansovald and Humbert, watched as they worked. The Norsemen paid them no attention, with only Snorri spending time talking to Ansovald through Humbert. Ansovald had asked many questions about the ship and what they were doing, and Snorri happily answered them. Ragnar was not pleased about this, but Snorri did not care. He saw no harm in telling the Franks about their ships, as he believed they wouldn't have the skills to build their own. The woodsmen had watched intently. They were as eager as Ulf to learn about the techniques the Norse used and Ulf often saw them talking to each other and pointing at whatever the Norse were working on, sometimes even miming the actions of the Norse. Ulf helped as they slotted the new planks in place and held them while Arne and a few others knocked new rivets in. All that was required now was for them to caulk the gaps so that water would not seep through while they were sailing. Ansovald had offered as much horsehair as they needed. This they mixed with pine resin and stuffed into any gaps they could find. The job had been frustrating and sticky, but Ulf enjoyed it.

"By Odin, would you look at that!" Snorri said as they finished. "You can't even tell she'd been damaged in the first place."

Ulf frowned as he stood beside Snorri and looked at the Sae-Ulfr while wiping his hands clean on an old cloth. He figured Snorri had to be joking because the new side planks were lighter than the rest of the ship, and even the mast, even though it had not been set in place yet, was a different colour. "Aye, I'm sure Hodr will agree with you."

Snorri laughed and clapped Ulf on the shoulder. Hodr was one of the gods of Asgard, a son of Odin and Frigg. And he was blind. "Perhaps we should get you to build more ships. It seems to do you good." Ulf smiled, but said nothing. Helping fix the Sae-Ulfr had been good for him, but now that it was finished, he had to concentrate on the one thing he'd been avoiding. It had been a few days since he first had the dream of the burning village and he had been having it every night since. He still hadn't told anyone about it, mainly because he didn't want Ragnar and Asbjorn to mock him, but also because he wasn't sure how his friends would react.

"Well, tonight we celebrate." Drumbr wiped the sweat from his face. The weather had been good all week, and the men had all browned a little after spending all day working in the sun.

"Aye," Snorri agreed. "Ansovald has promised us some more ale, and the hunters got us some boar. Tomorrow, we'll take the Sae-Ulfr to the river and set the mast."

"What about them?" Ulf pointed at the three Danes, still tied up near the ship.

"Once the Sae-Ulfr is ready and we get her out to sea, then we'll sacrifice them to Odin and Njörd."

"And what about Griml?" Ulf asked, seeing how the smiles disappeared from the faces of his friends.

"Trust Ulf to ruin the moment," Asbjorn said.

"No, Ulf is right." Snorri looked in the direction of the town they had attacked. "So far, the Norns have been kind to us."

"And our scouts better than his," Ragnar said.

"Aye. We just need to keep them away for one more day. Tomorrow we go home." Snorri smiled, and so did the men.

Ulf kept looking towards the town he could not see. "But how do we know he doesn't know where we are?"

"Because he would have attacked us already," Ragnar sneered. "The man is too dumb to do anything smarter."

Ragnar's response convinced everyone, and even Ulf guessed it could be true.

"Relax, Ulf." Snorri gripped his shoulder. "Tomorrow morning we set sail for Norway and we'll slip past Griml without him knowing about it."

"And what about the villagers?"

Ragnar spat to the ground. "They're not our concern anymore."

"Ragnar's right," Snorri agreed. "We helped them with their neighbours and they helped us fix the Sae-Ulfr. The deal is done. Tomorrow we go home, so forget about them."

"I don't think he'll be forgetting them soon." Drumbr pointed to Thorbjorn, who was slipping away with Theoda again.

Snorri shook his head as the men laughed. "By Freya, that man is worse than a rabbit."

CHAPTER 18

That night, the Norsemen feasted well. As promised, Ansovald had given them a few more barrels of ale, which the men greedily drank. They had built a large fire using some of the leftover wood and a boar was being spit-roasted. The men sang songs, told poems and laughed as the night wore on.

Ansovald was there as well with some of the other senior members of the town, including the trader Humbert. He was enjoying himself as he drank with Snorri and his hirdmen, laughing at the antics of the Norsemen. The same could not be said for the rest of the Franks there. They wore a mixture of fear and disgust on their faces, a few of them covering their noses as if the Norsemen stank. Ulf knew that was not the case. All of them had had a bath in the river that day. Their hair and beards were neatly combed and tied up. Ulf's light-coloured hair had three thick braids, and his beard had a thin braid in the middle. He smiled a small smile of satisfaction as he caught one of the Frankish elders quickly looking away from him while grimacing at Ulf's scars.

Snorri got to his feet, swaying slightly and having to lean on Oddi's shoulder to support himself. He raised his cup into the air and the men fell silent. "Men of Thorgilsstad! Mightiest warriors of Norway!" The men cheered as Snorri continued. "When the king, Halfdan the Black, sent us to Francia, we thought it was a blessing from the All-Father." Ulf watched as Humbert tried to translate the words and all the Franks frowned as they heard this. "We thought this country would make us richer than Fafnir! That we'd go back to Thorgilsstad, our ships filled with plunder and our hearts filled with the tales of our exploits. But the gods had other plans for us." The men went silent, some of them nodding. "We have been betrayed by men we thought were friends, and even the gods seemed to be against us. Two storms we have faced!" Snorri lowered his cup as he spoke. "We have lost many brothers coming to this wretched place." Again, the Franks scowled at each other. "Brak Brakson, Rolf Tree-Foot," Snorri named every man that was lost on this raid. Some of them died in battle, but most were taken by Ran. The men all lowered their heads as Snorri named friends and brothers, sons and fathers. One man started humming a song, careful not to drown out Snorri's voice. A few others joined, including Thorbjorn and Drumbr, while others cuffed tears away.

Snorri remained silent when he finished naming the men he had lost and listened as they hummed the rest of the song. When they had finished, Snorri looked at all of his men, making eye contact with every single one of them. "But now, men of Thorgilsstad, the gods finally smile on us. The Sae-Ulfr is as good as new, thanks to our new friend, Ansovald." Snorri pointed his cup to the old Frank, who smiled at the mention of his name. Ulf doubted the man knew what was being said, as Humbert had stopped translating Snorri's words. "Tomorrow, we make our offering to the gods. We can thank our friends over there for volunteering themselves." The men laughed and cheered as the Danes frowned. "Tomorrow, my men, my friends and my brothers, we go home! Skol!"

"Skol!" the men shouted loud enough to disturb the gods and drank deep.

Ansovald raised his cup. "Skol!" The surrounding Franks scowled, but the Norsemen cheered.

The night wore on and the men drank, ate and danced, while the Franks slipped away when they had had enough. Ulf also caught Thorbjorn sneaking towards the village and heard Snorri and Oddi joke about it. Ulf, though, was not as merry as the rest of the men. He was glad to be leaving Francia, but was concerned about the fact he had not got his vengeance yet. He tried to put it out of his mind as he took another sip of the Frankish ale that was slowly growing on him. But the thought had burrowed deep in his mind like a worm in the trunk of a tree.

Soon the men started falling asleep and even Ulf's eyelids were heavy. Drumbr was on the ground, snoring into the sky, with Asbjorn lying beside him. Snorri and Oddi were exchanging poems as they often did, while Ragnar sat there listening to them. Ulf stared at the fire, which had mostly died down by now as his eyes closed and he fell asleep.

Ulf had the same dream again, as he had done every night. He would stand in the field and watch as the village burnt. People dying engorged in flames and the fire spreading to the Sae-Ulfr. The troll appearing out of nowhere and Ulf trembling as it stood there laughing. The ground shaking as it charged at him while the old cloaked figure laughed. But this time it was different. As the troll neared Ulf, an unfamiliar noise came to him. At first, Ulf thought it was Jörmungandr, and he searched the dark skies of his dream for the giant serpent. But he saw nothing as the noise became louder and then Ulf realised what it was. A trumpet. He stood there confused, forgetting about the troll as he tried to find out where the trumpet was coming from. It seemed to drag him away from the flaming village and the troll. Ulf reached out, trying to grab hold of the old cloaked figure, afraid of where the dream was sending him. The cloaked figure just carried on laughing as it shouted at Ulf.

"This is chaos!"

Ulf woke with a start and found himself lying on the ground near the remains of the large fire from the night before. Shaking his head, he tried to get rid of the images of his dream, but then looked up when the trumpet sounded again. "What in Tyr's name?"

Snorri sat up, blinking rapidly. There was a faint smile on his lips as he remembered the night before, but the smile quickly disappeared when the trumpet sounded again. But the trumpet wasn't what got them to their feet or what really woke the men. "We're under attack!" Snorri roared when they heard the war cry coming from the forest.

Ulf turned to the sound of the war cry as Danes erupted from the trees and charged at the village. "Griml." He could not see the giant, but felt his presence amongst the trees. The Norsemen all jumped to their feet, their hangovers quickly forgotten when they saw the threat. They all looked at Snorri, waiting for his orders.

Snorri was still looking around him, taking stock of the situation. Ulf saw the concern in his friend's eyes and knew what Snorri was going to say even before he said it. And so did the rest of his hirdmen, as they all ran to their tents and grabbed whatever they could carry. Ulf rushed to his chest, yanking it open and grabbing his brynja. He threw it over his head, not bothering with his belt.

"What's going on?" Thorbjorn ran towards them from the village, Theoda in tow.

"The bastard Danes are attacking!" Ragnar pointed at the Danes.

"What?" Thorbjorn stopped, his eyes wide, before turning to Snorri. "Snorri, do we fight?"

Snorri shook his head. "I'm not losing more men." Ulf knew how hard that decision must have been for him, but understood it as well. Their attackers weren't some Frankish farmers with spears and staffs. They were trained warriors with armour and shields, and they outnumbered Snorri's small force. "Grab only what you need!" Snorri's men rushed to their chests and grabbed their armour and weapons. Some also grabbed food and drinking flasks and stuffed them into pouches. Ulf took his helmet and shoved it on his head. Ormstunga was still on his belt, sitting awkwardly because of the brynja, and Ulf took Olaf's axe from his chest. He looked at the axe, the names of his family and friends carved on the handle, and felt the muscles in his throat constrict.

The first screams reached them as the Danes ran through the refugees from the town, cutting down anyone in their path. Theoda shrieked and wanted to run back to the village, but Thorbjorn held her back. She turned to face him and for a moment, it looked like she was going to strike him, but then her expression changed. She looked at the Norse warriors, all of them grabbing what they could and not a single one preparing to fight. Theoda shouted at them while waving her fist in the air, but she did not leave. She just cried as Thorbjorn led her away.

"To the forest!" Snorri ordered.

"And be quick, they're coming!" Ragnar pointed towards the village. The Danes must have realised there were no fighting men amongst the Franks and knew they could send some of their force to confront Snorri's men. They screamed their war cry again as they charged towards the Norse warriors.

"Run!" Snorri shouted, his hirdmen echoing his orders. The men needed no further encouragement as they turned and fled towards the forest which surrounded the village. Ulf grabbed his shield and ran with Olaf's axe in his hand, his loose brynja making it awkward for him. Ragnar had his flung over his shoulder and carried his two-handed axe like it weighed nothing. Thorbjorn was behind them, dragging Theoda along, but she struggled to keep up with them.

"Leave the bitch!" Ragnar shouted over his shoulder.

Thorbjorn glared at Ragnar, but ignored him. The Danes were gaining on them, and Ulf knew they would reach Thorbjorn and Theoda before the two of them could reach the safety of the forest. Snorri saw the same and turned.

"Snorri!" Ragnar yelled.

"Get the men to safety!" Snorri ordered his father's champion as he went to help his friend. Ulf stopped as well and caught the angry glance of Ragnar as he ran past. He was not going to lose another friend, and without thinking, he rushed after Snorri.

"Ulf, what, in Odin's name, are you doing? Get to the trees!"

"What? And let you have all the fun."

Snorri shook his head, but Ulf saw the relief in his eyes. *Tyr, help me save my friend,* Ulf prayed as the rest of Snorri's hirdmen showed up.

"What are you bast—" Snorri started, but Oddi cut him off.

"We're not losing another one, Snorri. By Odin, not if we can help it."

"Fucking bastards." Snorri smiled at his hirdmen and even looked surprised to see Magni there. Magni only shrugged and then looked towards the oncoming Danes. Ulf adjusted his brynja, making it more comfortable, which was difficult because Ormstunga's hilt was in the way. But Ulf could not draw his family sword, as the sun was glowing in the morning sky. Thorbjorn and Theoda had almost reached them, but a group of Danes was gaining on them fast.

"They're not going to make it." Asbjorn unsheathed his sword and looked at Snorri.

Snorri grit his teeth and glanced at the rest of his men as most of them reached the forest. "Fucking bastard," he muttered as he ran towards Thorbjorn. Ulf and others ran after him, all of them knowing they had to get to Thorbjorn before the Danes did.

Thorbjorn saw them coming and was waving them away until Theoda screamed as she tripped, her hand slipping from his grip. He stopped and when he realised how close the Danes were, turned to his friends. "Hurry, you fucking bastards!"

But the Danes were faster and the first one reached Thorbjorn before Snorri and his hirdmen could. Thorbjorn stepped forward, putting himself between Theoda and the Dane. He dodged the first cut while pulling his sword, Blood-Thirst, from her scabbard and stabbed the Dane through the back as the man rushed past. Another Dane reached Thorbjorn, who just freed his sword in time to block the blow. Snorri got there and shoulder barged the Danish warrior, sending the man flying to the ground. He buried his sword in the Dane's chest before he could get up and was then forced to dodge the attack from another. Thorbjorn killed this Dane, but neither could do anything about the warrior who had rushed past them and was about to attack Theoda, still cowering on the ground. Ulf and Magni reached her at the same time and Ulf used his shield to block the Dane's sword while Magni hacked into the man's neck. Blood sprayed through the air, covering all three of them. Theoda looked up, her eyes wide with terror as Ulf took his sax-knife from his belt under his brynja and handed it to her. He wasn't sure why, but he had seen how this woman could fight and decided she was better off having a weapon.

"Get to the trees!" Snorri shouted as the rest of his hirdmen arrived and crashed into the few Danes, who reached them.

Drumbr swung his axe in a wide arc, killing two Danes and sending the rest diving out of the way. "This is for Brak, you goat fuckers!" He stomped on one Dane as he tried to crawl away, the man's head exploding like a pumpkin.

Ulf heard the scream and turned in time to see the axe coming for him. He twisted out of the way and punched the Dane in the side of the head with the rim of his shield. As the man's head snapped to the side, Ulf buried his axe into his chest. He grimaced as blood sprayed over him and was glad that Olaf's axe was still in one piece when he freed her. He sensed the movement behind him and glanced over his shoulder as another Dane came for him. Ulf's heart stopped because he knew he could not turn in time to block the blow or get out of the way. But before the man reached him, Theoda, blood-drenched and hair wild, barged into the Dane and caused both of them to fall to the ground. She rolled on top of the warrior and stabbed him through the eye with the sax-knife Ulf had given her. Ulf stepped around her to block the strike from another Dane and then kicked the man hard in the groin. The young Dane's eyes bulged out of his head as he dropped to his knees. But his suffering didn't last long as Oddi stabbed him through the neck.

"Snorri! There are too many of them!" Oddi danced out of the way of a spear. Magni appeared behind the Dane and stabbed him through the back. Oddi nodded at his brother, who smiled back but didn't see the Dane coming from the side. "Magni!"

Magni tried to twist out of the way, but wasn't fast enough and took a cut to the leg. He cried out as he fell to the ground. The Dane smiled with glee as he prepared to stab Magni, but Oddi's roar made him look up. The last thing the Danish man saw was the tall warrior's vicious face before he took his head clean off.

Ulf twisted out of another attack, his foot almost slipping on the gore. He lifted his shield to block a Dane's sword and turned it away before chopping into the warrior's neck. Ulf winced as he thought he could hear the handle crack and kicked the Dane away to free his axe. Warm blood sprayed into his eyes, blinding him. Panic gripped Ulf as he struggled to wipe the blood out of his eyes by sticking his fingers through his eye guard, but it was no use.

"Die, you Norse pig." Ulf's heart stopped as he thought of his dream and the troll charging at him. But as Ulf stepped back, he tripped over a body and felt the wind of the sword as it cut through the empty air where his head had been. As Ulf hit the ground, the voices of his ancestors came to life in his ears, drowning out all other sounds. He ripped his helmet off and wiped the blood from his eyes as the Dane stood there, ready to kill him. The heat of Ulf's anger tore through his body and he jumped to his feet. Before the Dane was able to react, Ulf punched him in the jaw with the rim of his shield. There was an ugly crack as the Dane fell to the ground, his jaw sitting at an unnatural angle. Time seemed to slow for Ulf, but as he looked around, he realised the futility of their situation. Snorri and Thorbjorn were hacking and stabbing at any Dane who came too close, Theoda the Frank stood near her lover, finishing off any man they did not kill. Oddi stood over his brother and used his long arms to keep the Danes at bay while Drumbr and Asbjorn protected him. But the rest of the Danes were catching up to those they were fighting and, as magnificent as Snorri and his hirdmen were, they could not fight so many Danes. Ulf looked towards the village and what he saw chased the voices of his ancestors away. The village was burning, just like in his dreams. He looked at the Sae-Ulfr and felt the pain in his chest as the hungry flames tore through Snorri's beautiful ship. What made it even worse was the fact they had just repaired the damage from the storm. The villagers were running around, screaming for their lives, many of them on fire while the rest were being slaughtered by the Danes.

And then Ulf saw him. Just like in his dream. The giant troll standing in front of the burning village and glaring at him. Ulf looked to his right, almost expecting the old cloaked figure to be standing there, but all he saw were his friends fighting for their lives. He looked back at Griml, feeling the man's dead eyes on him. But he did not feel the usual fear from his dreams. Instead, it was the flames of his fury as they came to life, ignited by the hatred for the man who had taken everything from him. "Tyr!" he roared as the voices of his ancestors rushed into his ears and charged at the Danes trying to kill his sword-brothers. Ulf punched the first one he came to in the face with his shield. The man's head snapped back and Asbjorn sliced his stomach open. The Dane fell to the ground, his intestines slithering out of his gut like serpents. Ulf turned and sliced another's neck open with the blade of his axe. The man staring at Ulf in shock as his blood squirted from his neck.

But there were still too many Danes and Ulf knew they could never fight all of them and hope to live. He knew then they would die and was furious he that would not get his vengeance. "Odin, I promised I will kill the bastard. Do not abandon me now." Ulf said through clenched teeth. Asbjorn glanced at him, but Ulf did not care. All his focus was on the man he wanted to kill. The man who was out of reach as death was coming for him.

CHAPTER 19

Snorri attacked the Dane facing him, but the man expected it and got his shield up to block the blow. Thorbjorn darted in, using his shorter frame to get under the Dane's shield and stabbed him in the side. The man grunted and as he dropped his shield, Snorri rammed Tyr's Fury through his mouth. Behind him, Theoda shrieked as she pounced on a Dane Asbjorn had thrown to the ground and stabbed the man repeatedly, oblivious to the blood spraying over her. Snorri wondered where she had gotten the sax-knife from, but had no time to think about it as another warrior charged at him.

The Dane feinted to the right, and Snorri almost bought it. He was tired and just managed to twist out of the cut, feeling the man's sword grating against his brynja. Another Dane appeared to his left and lunged at him. Snorri lifted his shield to deflect the sword point, but wasn't quite fast enough. He grit his teeth as the sword cut into his arm, but then had to deal with the first Dane who had raised his axe to cut him down. Ulf appeared by his side and buried his axe into the man's armpit. The Dane twisted, his face creased in agony before Ulf caved his head in with the rim of his shield. Thorbjorn dealt with the other Dane, stabbing the man through the chest and shoulder barging him to the ground where Theoda finished him off.

Snorri used the brief respite to see what was going on. All his hirdmen were fighting hard, all of them panting heavily and drenched in blood. Magni was on the ground, his leg bleeding heavily, and using his shield to protect himself as Oddi kept the Danes at bay. Drumbr also stood with them, using his enormous axe to slaughter anyone looking for an easy kill. Asbjorn and Thorbjorn stood on either side of him, their shields lower than they should be, but even Snorri was struggling to hold his up. And not just because of the cut to his arm. Ulf stood behind him, next to Theoda, with that feral look in his eyes that Snorri had mixed feelings about. Ulf's focus was not on him, though. Snorri followed Ulf's gaze and saw Griml. The large troll was standing between them and the burning village, berating the Danes, who were now hesitant to fight Snorri and his hirdmen. It was then that Snorri also saw his beloved ship in flames. His legs went weak, and it took all his self-will not to fall to his knees. The pain he felt in his chest was indescribable as his eyes stung from the tears that ran down his cheeks. Snorri forced himself to look away, to focus on the battle. The ground around them was littered with the bloody corpses of the warriors who had reached them first, with Snorri and his men fighting like rabid wolves to protect Thorbjorn. All because the bastard wanted to take Theoda with him. Snorri wanted to resent the Frankish woman for putting them in this position, but he couldn't. She had fought well and Snorri always respected fighting men... and women.

"Come on, you swine! Fight me!" Thorbjorn beat his chest as the Danes were backing off.

Drumbr gripped his axe in both hands and shook it at the Danes. "Run, you cowards! You can't beat the warriors of Thorgilsstad!"

Snorri watched the Danes and saw the wary glances they gave each other, but knew the attack wasn't finished. He and his hirdmen were still heavily outnumbered. They might kill a few more, but eventually, the numbers would go against them and the Danes would slaughter them all.

"Kill them, you whoresons! Or I'll kill every one of you!" Griml's' voice echoed over them. Snorri glanced at Ulf, as his friend was trembling with rage. It was good to see him like that again. He was concerned at how subdued Ulf had been recently and worried that his friend had lost his fire. Snorri glanced at his burning ship again and felt his own fire burning inside of him. They had only just repaired her.

"Skjaldborg!" The call came from the Danes. It seemed that they realised a shield wall would be a better way to kill them than coming at them one by one. The Danes slotted their shields together, the sound of it ripping through the air like thunder.

Snorri looked at each of his men, proud that none of them showed fear. Even Theoda looked vicious with her face and dress covered in blood as she stood with them, glaring at the men who were destroying her home. Oddi had helped Magni to his feet, and the Cockerel stood on one leg, his face grim. "In Valhalla, my brothers." Snorri didn't bother with the entire expression. He doubted there would be an 'after the battle' for them. Snorri just hoped that Ragnar would get the rest of his men home and tell his father what had happened here today.

"In Valhalla," all his men echoed.

Snorri smiled at Theoda, wondering where she would go when the Danes killed her. He knew that women who had fought courageously in battle went to Valhalla. Odin did not care about gender, he only wanted the best for his Einherjar. But would the All-Father accept a Christian? Snorri hoped he would. Theoda deserved to be amongst the best warriors that ever lived. She smiled back at him and then looked at the Danes, her eyes widening. Snorri turned and saw them coming, moving slowly to keep their shield wall together. He smiled as he gripped his sword. *Odin, hear me now. Today I will earn my place by your right-hand side in Valhalla.* He was about to charge at the Danes when he heard an unexpected noise from behind.

"Odin! Thorgilsstad!" The roar came, causing the Danish shield wall to stop.

"What in the gods' names?" Asbjorn said, as all of them turned to see what was happening.

"Bastards," Snorri muttered as his men charged at the Danes in a spear formation, with Ragnar at the front. His face fierce as he swung his two-handed axe above his head. "Fucking bastard," Snorri said again, but he smiled as he turned back to the Danes. They were going to pay for burning his ship.

The Danes wavered. Their shield wall had stopped moving, and they were unsure of what to do. At least half the Danish warriors were still in the village, plundering and raping as it burnt around them, and the ones sent to deal with the Norse warriors had fought a hard fight against the eight of them. Now they had another twelve men charging at them with Ragnar Nine-Finger in the lead. And they all knew of Ragnar Nine-

Finger. They had all heard the sagas of his exploits. And not just that. They were facing the wolves of Thorgilsstad. They had already seen how these men could fight, not just here, but also in Rouen and across Francia. So they wavered and Snorri spotted the chance. "Odin!" he roared as his men reached him and charged with them. His warriors made space and Snorri ran beside Ragnar, with Drumbr on the other side. Ulf fell into his right, his feral grin enough to make any man shit himself. And shit themselves the Danes did. They held their ground, their fear of Griml still gripping them, but as soon as Snorri, Ragnar and Drumbr reached them, the Danish shield wall collapsed. Both Ragnar and Drumbr swung their huge axes in wide arcs, killing five men and maiming a few more.

Snorri stabbed one Dane, who tried to turn and run, through the back of the neck with Tyr's Fury, pulling the sword free and slicing another across the chest. Beside him, Ulf roared in anger as he dented another's helmet and crushed the man's skull with the rim of his shield. Most of the Danes turned and ran, with only a few brave enough to stand and fight. Perhaps they wanted to earn their places in Valhalla. One of these Danes, a man almost as tall and broad as Ragnar, lifted his shield to block Ragnar's axe. But the man either overestimated his shield or underestimated Ragnar's strength. Ragnar's axe cut through shield and arm, the large Dane hollering as blood sprayed through the air from the stump where his arm had been. Drumbr silenced him by cutting his head off. Another Dane stabbed at Snorri, who twisted out of the way and sliced the man's leg. As the Dane fell to his knees, one of Snorri's men buried his axe in his head. The man sat there for a few heartbeats and stared at the axe embedded in his skull before Snorri's man kicked him over and freed his axe. Snorri clapped the man on the shoulder and looked around him. The remaining few Danes had been killed, but the rest had retreated to the village, where they were forming another shield wall. Snorri had no idea how many men Griml had with him, but he knew it was more than his men could face.

"Skjaldborg!" he shouted, and his men fell in beside him. The shield wall was only one man deep because there were not enough of them, but there was nothing he could do about it. All he needed to do now was get his men to safety.

"We fighting them?" Ragnar glanced at him. Even the famous nine-fingered warrior wasn't sure.

Snorri shook his head. "Not today. Thorbjorn, keep your woman on her feet this time. We're not coming back for you again."

"Didn't ask you to come back the first time. Could have handled the bastard Danes myself."

"Aye, it helps that you are too short for them to notice you," Drumbr joked, and Snorri smiled. He knew his men were putting on a brave face, but that was what the young warriors needed to see.

"Right, you bastards, back to the trees. Keep the shield wall tight!" Snorri glanced to his right and saw Ulf was there, his eyes fixed on Griml, but keeping pace with the shield wall as it moved back. Snorri followed his friend's gaze and saw the giant warrior berating the Danes again. He smiled. "Look men, the Danes are afraid of the wolves of Thorgilsstad! They don't want to fight us!" His men cheered and shouted insults at the Danes, while still moving back towards the forest. Two of the men grabbed Magni and carried him so that he wouldn't be left behind.

"Keep moving, boys. But don't show them you're afraid," Ragnar said in a quiet voice.

"Who said we're afraid?" Thorbjorn asked. "I'm just tired of killing the Danes. It's been too much of that recently." The men laughed, while Theoda frowned at Thorbjorn. Snorri wondered why she came along, as she walked behind the shield wall, making sure not to stray too far from Thorbjorn.

Griml roared, drawing their attention, and the men stopped. He grabbed one of the Danes out of their shield wall and pushed the man towards them. The Dane staggered to a stop and turned to face his companions, but none of them moved. Griml pointed towards the Norse wall and shouted at the Dane, his voice carrying towards them, but Snorri could not make out the words. When the Dane still refused to move, Griml stepped forward and pulled his axe from his back. In one swift movement, he chopped the Dane in half. Theoda stifled a scream from behind the Norse shield wall as Griml faced the Danes and shook his enormous axe at them.

"The troll's got balls, you've got to give him that," Asbjorn said, which earned him a glare from Ulf.

"Aye, facing the Danes like that after just killing one of their own. He's not worried they might attack him?" Thorbjorn added.

Snorri shook his head. "They fear him and he knows that." As if to prove his point, the Danes roared and charged at them. "Move!" Snorri's men needed no more encouragement and were already moving before Snorri finished the word. Snorri glanced to his right, half expecting Ulf to break away from the shield wall and charge at Griml, but to his surprise, Ulf stayed where he was and kept his pace with the rest of them. "That's it, men! We're almost there!"

Theoda said something behind them, but none of the men understood what.

"You gonna have to learn her tongue, or teach her ours," Oddi said to Thorbjorn. Snorri glanced over his shoulder and saw her pointing at the trees, telling them they were almost there. He smiled until he turned to the Danes again and saw they were closing the gap between them fast. The Danes called to the gods as they waved their weapons in the air.

"Hold the wall!" Snorri glanced behind him again. The trees were getting closer, but so were the Danes. Snorri knew they could not fight the Danes. They had been lucky not to lose any men today, but if the Danes reached them before they got to the forest, then that would not be the case. He just hoped the forest would provide them with the safety they needed. "When I give the command, we charge at the Danes, make as much noise as we can. You two get Magni into the forest." The two men carrying Oddi's brother nodded.

Snorri felt his men looking at them. "Has Loki stolen your wits?" Ragnar asked.

"No, but this is a plan he would be proud of." They were getting closer to the forest, and the Danes were almost on them. Snorri didn't have the time to explain properly, so he rushed the words out. "We run five paces, no more and then we turn and sprint into the trees."

His men murmured around him, now understanding what he was thinking.

"I pray to Odin this works," Ragnar said.

"Aye, me too," Snorri muttered under his breath. He waited until the Danes were about ten paces away. "Now!" His men responded instantly, roaring loud enough to chase the gods out of Asgard as they charged at the unexpecting Danes. The Danes were surprised by this sudden charge and stopped in their tracks.

"Skjaldborg!" one of the Danes shouted, and they brought their shields together to form a wall.

Snorri counted the steps as his men charged at the Danes and when he got to five, he shouted, "Now!" Again, his men responded instantly as they all turned and sprinted towards the trees, leaving the Danes confused. Theoda watched them first charge at the Danes and then run away, her face completely bewildered. Thorbjorn grabbed her hand as he rushed past her and dragged her into the trees. As Snorri had hoped, the Danes just stood there behind their shield wall, too stunned to react.

"Ulf! Come on, you bastard!" Drumbr shouted and when Snorri looked back, he saw Ulf had stopped at the tree line. For a moment, Snorri worried Ulf might try to get to Griml, but then his young friend turned and followed them as they ran through the trees. Snorri was relieved that they had got away without losing any of his men, but he felt the tears running down his cheeks as the image of his prized ship in flames came to his mind. The Sae-Ulfr deserved better than that.

They ran for a short while before Snorri finally called for them to stop. Most of his men dropped to the ground, while others bent over and rested with their hands on their knees, all of them panting. Snorri looked back in the direction they had just come from, but there was no sign of the Danes. "We can rest here, but not too long." Those with water flasks started passing them around, while others checked for injuries. Torsten, one of his young warriors, walked up to Ulf, who was leaning against a tree, his face dark. Snorri was about to stop him, but then he spotted what Torsten had in his hands.

"You dropped this." Torsten offered Ulf's helmet to him. Ulf looked up, and it took him a moment to understand what Torsten was saying. Snorri wondered where his friend had gone in his mind.

"Thank you." Ulf took the helmet from Torsten and stared at it while he rubbed his thumb on the blood that covered it. Torsten stood there for a few heartbeats, uncertain of what to do, and was about to turn and walk away when Ulf said, "You fought well today." Torsten smiled and nodded before walking away.

"The fierce wolf is going soft." Thorbjorn appeared beside Snorri.

"No, but he's learning." Snorri looked at his men, glad that none of them had any serious injuries. A few had some minor cuts, but then so did he. Snorri glanced at his arm. The cut was not deep, and the bleeding was already slowing, so he was not concerned about that now.

"What I don't understand is why the troll fucker didn't fight himself?" Thorbjorn picked at the drying blood in his beard. Theoda sat on the ground, her face pale as she hugged her knees.

"Only the gods know that, but I am glad he didn't." Snorri looked at his men again. "I doubt we would be sitting here if he did."

*

"Fucking Danes," Griml growled as he watched Snorri and his men slip into the woods. His men outnumbered them. They should have easily beaten them and Griml should have been standing here with Snorri and Ulf in front of him, both men with their hands tied behind their backs. Griml smiled as he imagined hacking their heads off and taking that pretty sword from Ulf's dead body. "If she'd let me fight them, then it'd be over by now." Griml glanced to the sky and around him, half expecting her to appear and admonish him. But the only thing he saw and heard was the village burning and the people screaming. Griml smiled.

"Griml."

He turned towards the burning village. The brown-bearded Dane was walking towards him and Griml glowered at the man. Behind the Dane, a few of his men were dragging three men, all of them old.

"Found these two hiding in the church with the women and children," the Dane said as his men dropped the prisoners by his feet. "This one stood outside, killed a few of the men before we could subdue him. We think the fat one is the village chief and the other one is his guard."

Griml looked at the three Franks by his feet. One of them was badly beaten, but his brown eyes were fierce and his shoulders spoke of a man who had spent years wielding weapons. This Frank tried to get to his feet and Griml noticed how he favoured his left leg before one of the Danes kicked him to the ground again. The other two were pathetic. One was an old man with soft skin, his robe made of expensive materials and his shoes of fine leather. The other looked like he had spent too much time at the feasting table. He had brown eyes like the warrior, but this one had never seen a proper fight. Griml looked at the Danes, his raised eyebrow questioning them.

The brown-bearded Dane cleared his throat. "The fat one wants to speak to you, but he does not speak our language. This one does." He pointed to the old Frank in the fine robe.

The Frank with the fine robe got to his knees and spoke to Griml. "I Humbert, this," he pointed to the fat man next to him, "Theuderic. He want speak you."

Griml looked at the fat man, who tried to look brave, but could not hide the fear in his eyes. Unlike the other Frank, who looked like he was just waiting for a chance to attack them. Griml noticed the fresh bandage on the fat Frank's leg and smiled as he turned his attention back to Humbert. "What does he want?"

Humbert shivered before answering, "He leader of big town. Not far. He want you kill brother and he help you fight others."

"Others?" Griml raised an eyebrow. He glanced at the Theuderic's leg again and wondered if he got that wound defending his town, but dismissed the thought he when saw the fear in the man's eyes. He most likely cut himself falling over as he fled.

Humbert pointed to the forest. "The men who run."

The old warrior jumped to his knees and shouted at Humbert, who cowered while the one he called Theuderic tried to shoulder barge the warrior. But the old warrior twisted out of the way on his knees and the fat man just fell to the ground. The Danes laughed and made no effort to help him up.

"Who is he?" Griml pointed to the warrior. "And what did he say?"

Humbert glanced at the man to his side and cowered from his glare. "He Ansovald. This his village. He say he kill me because I betray village."

Ansovald carried on shouting at Humbert, while Theuderic got up to his knees. He shoved his face in Ansovald's and started shouting at him. One of the Danes wanted to pull them apart, but Griml held up a hand to stop him. He needed some amusement today, especially after the Danes had let Snorri and his men escape. Ansovald pulled his head back and headbutted Theuderic, breaking his nose and sending the fat man to the ground again. The Danes laughed, while Griml grinned.

"They don't like each other," he said to Humbert, who nodded.

"They brothers. Fight many years. That why Ansovald ask Norsemen to fight brother."

"So they helped you?"

Humbert nodded. "But I not want. Many not want. Ansovald say we must." Ansovald glared at Humbert, his eyes like knives as he tried to understand what the soft man was saying.

"How can the fat one help me? He can't even fight his brother."

Humbert looked at Theuderic, who had crawled back to his knees again. His eyes were swollen as blood gushed out of his nose. "His town. Very big, has many warriors. They help you fight and kill others." Humbert's eyes darted away and Griml smiled again.

He knelt down in front of Theuderic, the man taken aback by this. Griml saw the fear in his swollen eyes as he spoke. "Your warriors, they are strong?" Theuderic nodded after Humbert translated Griml's words. Griml pursed his lips. "How many warriors have you got?"

"Many, many," Humbert told Griml what Theuderic had said.

Griml grit his teeth as he scowled at Theuderic. "Then why has your town been burnt to the ground?"

Theuderic paled as Humbert translated the words. Before he could say anything, Griml grabbed him by the neck and lift him off the ground as if he weighed no more than a small child. The fat man squealed, his legs kicking before Griml slammed him to the ground. There was a loud crack as something broke. Theuderic lay on the ground, groaning as blood started seeping out of his mouth.

"You think I am dumb?" Griml roared, grabbing his large two-handed axe and splitting Theuderic's head in two. Blood and brains splattered everyone around, causing Humbert to bend over and vomit. Ansovald just glared at Griml, gritting his teeth, but Griml was sure the man would have thanked him if he could.

"What do we do with these two?" the brown-bearded Dane asked.

"We should throw them into the fire." One of the other Danes thumbed over his shoulder at the burning church. "That'll teach him not to kill one of us."

"Then don't be so easy to kill," Griml growled, still staring at Ansovald. The Dane scowled, but Griml knew he would do nothing. "Free them and give them each a sword."

The brown-bearded Dane looked at Griml, his eyebrows raised. "You sure?"

Griml turned and grabbed the man by his brynja, almost lifting him off his feet. "You remember what happened to the last bastard who questioned me?"

The Dane nodded and told his men to do what Griml asked. The two Franks looked confused as their hands were freed and they were given swords. Humbert turned to Griml.

"What this? What you want us do?"

"I want you to fight," Griml said with a vicious grin.

Humbert paled as he explained to Ansovald what Griml had said. If he had expected the old warrior to refuse, then he was badly mistaken. Ansovald attacked the soft man, hacking at his neck and screaming at him the whole time. Blood sprayed all over the old warrior, and before Humbert's corpse hit the ground, Ansovald turned and charged at Griml. The old man moved fast for his age, his limp barely affecting him. But Griml had expected this. He laughed as he stepped out of the way of Ansovald's sword swing and kicked the old warrior hard on his bad leg. There was a loud crack as Ansovald's leg broke and the old warrior fell to the ground. But there was no fear in the old Frank's eyes, only anger as the man glared at Griml while saying something in Frankish.

"To you too." Griml stomped down on Ansovald's chest, crushing his lungs and heart. But Griml didn't stop. He stomped again and again, roaring as his anger took over him. With the final stomp on what was nothing but mush, he turned to the

Danes watching him, his face red and eyes dark. "Find those fucking Norse bastards and don't come back until they're all dead!"

CHAPTER 20

Ulf clenched his jaw as he stared at the flames of their campfire. Around him, most of the men were sleeping while others sat in silence. Even Snorri's hirdmen, usually full of jokes, were quiet as they sat next to him, their gazes also fixed on the flames. They had gone to sleep the previous night, expecting to board the Sae-Ulfr in the morning and sail home. They had the three Danes that they were going to sacrifice to the gods. Spirits had been high. But the gods were cruel and decided that they had not had enough fun yet.

After they escaped from the Danes, Snorri made them walk for half the day to put more distance between them and the village. He also posted scouts further back to keep an eye out for any pursuit, but there had been none. Right now, they were as safe as they could be, but that still didn't stop the men from sleeping in their armour and with their weapons at hand. This morning they had been caught off guard, and the men of Thorgilsstad, the few of them left, would not be caught out again. The injured were taken care of and luckily for them, there weren't many. Magni's leg was bandaged using someone's tunic, while Snorri had refused to let anyone treat his arm, not until all his men were taken care of first.

Ulf usually found comfort in the flames. Their destructive beauty had always calmed him, but not anymore. As he watched the flames dance, all he saw was the vision from his dreams. The village and the Sae-Ulfr burning while people died in flames and the troll standing there, watching him. But this time, it was not his dream he was seeing. It was the memory of what had happened today.

"He must have been waiting." Oddi broke the silence. The men looked at him, but no one responded. "He must have been watching us, and waited for this moment to strike."

"But we caught all the scouts he had sent." Asbjorn picked at a new scab on his arm.

"Well, we must have missed some." Oddi stared at the flames. "It's the only thing that makes sense."

"None of this makes sense," Thorbjorn retorted, sitting next to Theoda, who was sleeping. Ulf was surprised she was still with them and wondered what would happen to her now. Perhaps Thorbjorn was planning on taking her back to Thorgilsstad. She still had the sax-knife Ulf had given her tucked into her apron. He let her keep it. For all he knew, she might still need it. "We should have been on our way home now."

"Well, the gods decided this would amuse them more." Oddi finally took his eyes off the flames, only to stare at the stars through the trees.

"Oddi's right," Snorri said. He had been lying on his back, searching for the answers in the stars, Ulf was sure of it. "We must have missed some scouts. Which meant Griml knew where we were and what we were doing and was just waiting until the Sae-Ulfr was finished." A tear ran down his cheek. Snorri loved the Sae-Ulfr more than his wife. "He waited until we thought we were safe, and then he attacked."

"And he caught us all sleeping," Ragnar growled. The men fell silent again. Somewhere in the distance, an owl hooted, but apart from that, the only noises were some men snoring and the flames crackling away. Ulf remembered the owl they had seen when they were looking for Geir. He wondered if it was the same one, and then he wondered something else.

"Still doesn't explain what happened to Geir," he said, surprising everyone. He felt some of them staring at him, but didn't want to look up from the flames.

"Only the gods will know what happened to him," Thorbjorn said.

"Think he could have told Griml where we were?" Drumbr asked. Even the flames seemed to stutter in shock.

Snorri sat up and looked at the large warrior. "No, Geir would never betray us like that. Something must have happened to him."

"Perhaps Ulf's new friend took him," Asbjorn said, his voice grating on Ulf's nerves more than the words he had spoken. "She would want us to be afraid."

"Asbjorn could be right." Oddi scratched the side of his face. "Geir had always been loyal. His disappearance must be because of some evil. And Hulda's mother looks evil."

Ulf looked up, knowing that none of them had ever seen her. "Why would she take him?"

"She's a volva. They do crazy things," Thorbjorn said. "There's a reason we avoid them." The men went silent again, all of them thinking about Geir.

"She's not my friend," Ulf said after a while, not sure why, but he felt like he needed to defend himself.

"Well, she keeps coming to you." Asbjorn glared at him. Ulf grit his teeth and was about to say something when Ragnar spoke up.

"Shut up, both of you. It doesn't matter what happened to the idiot. What matters is what we do now."

"Ragnar is right." Snorri lay down again. "Nothing we can do now but rest. Tomorrow we will think of a way to get home."

Most of the men lay down and closed their eyes, but Ulf could not. He was afraid of what he might see when he fell asleep, but knew he could not stay up all night. He was exhausted. The owl hooted again and to Ulf, it sounded like the bird was calling to him. Tired of sitting there and staring at the flames, he decided to relieve himself. Ulf walked past the first few trees and found a spot where the others couldn't see him. The owl was still calling in the distance, and Ulf shook his head at it as he undid his pants and squatted.

He had just finished and was about to pull his trousers up when there was a rustling in the undergrowth. He stared at the trees, trying to find the source of the sound, but saw nothing in the dark. The owl had gone quiet and Ulf sensed someone watching him. He looked back towards the camp, hoping that one of the men was standing there. Snorri had posted some guards, but there was no one there. The tree branches danced in the firelight, their shadows twisting and turning like serpents crawling towards him. Shivers slithered up each vertebra in his spine as he glanced at his weapons on the ground.

"You won't be needing those, young wolf." The quiet voice drifted towards him. Ulf jumped and almost tripped over his trousers still around his ankles. "The mighty Bear-Slayer, descendant of Tyr, caught with his pants around his ankles, much like your friends this morning."

Ulf heard the smile in her voice and knew she was mocking him. He pulled up his trousers and quickly tied the rope, which kept them up, before grabbing the hilt of Ormstunga. "You knew that was going to happen!"

The volva smiled as she stepped out of the shadows. The sight of her killed Ulf's anger, and he had to fight hard not to show his fear. "You should keep your voice down, young wolf. Don't want your friends to catch us talking, do you?"

Ulf frowned at her and then glanced at the men of Thorgilsstad sleeping around the fire. "Did you know he was going to attack today?" He kept his hand on the hilt of Ormstunga, but only to help fight his fear.

"You did well to survive that. Really thought they got you this time." The volva smiled. The light of the fire flickered over her face, making her look like one of the monsters his aunt used to warn him about. Maybe he should have listened to her.

"So you knew Griml was going to attack." Ulf grit his teeth. "Why didn't you warn me?"

"I told you he was coming." The volva yawned and Ulf felt his frustration growing.

"What about Geir? Did you take him?"

She stared at him and smiled. "Why did you not fight him? You had your chance to avenge your family."

The question caught Ulf off guard and he couldn't respond, which only amused the volva.

"Ah, the great Bear-Slayer is frightened of the man who slaughtered his family."

"I'm not." Ulf tried to keep his voice firm, but it felt like Hulda's mother saw right through him. Just like Lady Ingibjorg did.

The volva smiled and then glanced over his shoulder. A twig snapped behind him, and Ulf turned to see Snorri walking towards him. He turned around again to face the volva, but she was gone. Before Snorri reached him, Ulf heard her voice drifting on the rustling leaves.

"Remember, young wolf. Embrace your blood."

The words chilled Ulf to his core. They were first spoken to him in his dreams by the cloaked figure, just before the troll was about to kill him. Then later, Lady Ingibjorg spoke them. Ulf had never really understood what they meant. After the battle at The Giant's Toe, he thought they were telling him to listen to the voices which came during battle. When they started speaking to him, the world around Ulf slowed. He felt stronger and moved faster. Ulf did not enjoy battle. He did not like the thought of killing people and would only do it if they were going to kill him. But when the voices came to him, Ulf felt more alive than ever. The sounds of battle drummed in beat with his heart, the blood of his enemies washed his fears away. Ulf was unbeatable as he danced to the music of war. But he had not heard those words since that battle.

"Ulf?" Snorri shook him by the shoulder. Ulf turned to face his friend, who must have seen the shock in his eyes. "What?"

"N… nothing," Ulf finally managed, looking at the trees but seeing no sign of the volva.

"Who were you talking to?" He heard the suspicion in Snorri's voice.

"To myself."

Snorri frowned, and Ulf wondered if it was true. *Was she really here, or did I imagine it?*

"Did you take another knock on the head?" Snorri asked, his grey eyes fixed on Ulf.

"No, I'm just tired." Ulf turned to go back to the camp. "It's been a long day."

"Aye," Snorri said. "You did well today."

"We all did. It was a hard fight."

Snorri smiled. "I'm not talking about the fight. With Torsten. You might not get it, but the younger men look up to you. The stories they hear make them think you are a legendary warrior."

"You made most of those stories up."

"Aye, but they don't know it." Snorri laughed as Ulf smiled. The two of them walked back to the camp and Snorri lay down on his spot again. "Get some rest, Ulf. Tomorrow's not gonna be any easier. I'm sure the gods have something else planned for us."

Ulf looked at the stars, wondering if Odin was sitting there now, watching him and judging him. What would Odin think of him now that he failed to avenge his family?

*

Ulf found himself in the field again, staring at the burning village. The Sae-Ulfr was nothing more than cinders, but somehow her beast head remained, snarling defiantly at the world. The screaming was gone and Ulf was surrounded by an eerie silence, which only fed the fear in the pit of his stomach. He would have preferred the screams of death, but then he never got what he wanted in these dreams. The troll was still there, although it was not laughing anymore. Instead, it stood there, glaring at him while it waited with its giant fists clenched like enormous boulders.

"Fight me!" Its voice reached him. Ulf wanted to turn and run, but couldn't. His dreams never allowed him to run away from the troll he had to face. Maybe that was the message of his dreams. That he could not run away from his fate. Perhaps Snorri and the others were correct. The Norns controlled the destiny of men and they decided that Ulf and Griml had to fight. But who did they decide would win? The only direction Ulf could move was forward, towards the troll, waiting to kill him. But he could not get himself to take that step.

Ulf sensed a presence beside and turned, expecting to see the old cloaked figure, Odin. But it was not the All-Father. A warrior stood beside him, wearing a dark cloak like the old figure. Ulf saw no armour or weapons, but the man stood tall, taller than him, and had broad shoulders. At first, he thought it might have been Thor, but he could not see the ginger hair of the god of thunder. A sense of calm came over Ulf, one he would not expect to feel around a god as unpredictable as Thor. He looked at the hands, trying to guess who this figure might be, but both hands were hidden in the cloak.

"You must fight him," the cloaked figure said in a calm voice. It was like the violence surrounding them did not bother him. But then if he was the god of war, like Ulf suspected, then he must have been used to seeing such chaos.

"I…" Ulf started, but did not know what to say. He looked at the troll, who was beating his chest with one hand, while it held a monstrous axe in its other hand. Ulf's hand went to his side, to where Ormstunga would normally be, but as always, there was no sword. He tried the other side, where Olaf's axe should be, but he knew he would not find her there either.

"What are you afraid of?"

Ulf looked at the cloaked figure. It had asked him that question before, in another dream that seemed so long ago. The first time, Ulf had refused to admit that he was terrified. But if Tyr was really his ancestor, then surely he would understand.

"I cannot defeat him." Ulf lowered his head and half expected the cloaked figure to admonish him.

"No, you cannot," the cloaked figure said with a smile in his voice, which surprised Ulf.

Ulf's eyes were wide as they darted from the cloaked figure to the troll. "Then how can I avenge my family?" The ground beneath Ulf's feet started trembling and when he looked up, he saw the troll charging at him, its monstrous axe above its head. The familiar fear gripped Ulf, and no matter how hard he tried, he could not turn and run.

The cloaked figure turned and walked away, and just when Ulf thought Tyr was abandoning him, it said, "Does the wolf hunt alone?"

"What?" Ulf said as Tyr vanished. Ulf heard the terrible roar and turned in time to see the troll swing its axe down.

*

Ulf opened his eyes. His heart was trying to beat its way out of his chest, and his tunic was drenched in sweat. He sat up, rubbing the sleep from his eyes and seeing Oddi frown at him. The sun was breaking through the trees, waking the men up.

Thorbjorn sat up with a yawn and a stretch. He looked at Theoda beside him and smiled, but that smile quickly disappeared as his eyes scanned the clearing. "By Odin, for a moment I forgot where we were."

"Aye, well at least you got that moment." Oddi got to his feet and rolled his neck.

"Not my fault Freya hasn't blessed you yet." Thorbjorn looked at Theoda again as she opened her eyes. Thorbjorn smiled at her, but she only scowled at him and muttered something in Frankish.

Oddi laughed. "I'm sure Freya just got bored and is amusing herself."

"You're just jealous," Thorbjorn retorted, but Ulf spotted the concern in his friend's eyes.

"Can there be a morning where I don't wake up to you two bickering?" Snorri asked as he woke up.

"You can always go back to your wife," Thorbjorn said.

Snorri thought about it while running his fingers through his beard. "No, I think I prefer waking up to you two bickering."

Theoda got to her feet while the men laughed. She walked to the fire and got it going again before looking around the small camp.

"Think she's looking for some food," Oddi said.

"You don't say, Oddi Viss." Thorbjorn stood up and scanned the camp as well. "Have we got any food?" The men searched amongst the few belongings they grabbed before fleeing the Danes, but all they found was some bread and a few apples.

"Well, that's a good start to the day," Asbjorn complained. Drumbr's stomach rumbled, startling him. Theoda muttered something in Frankish again, shaking her head. The men did not need to understand her words to know what she was saying. They had all seen their mothers do the same, which only made them laugh.

"I'm glad you are all in a pleasant mood today." Ragnar walked into the clearing with three dead rabbits in his hand. "Only Odin knows how you keep making it back from your raids, Snorri."

Snorri smiled at the red-headed warrior. "Because I trust the gods and the Norns, and they have provided us with breakfast." One of the men took the rabbits from Ragnar and handed them to Theoda, where she and the man started skinning them.

"Neither the gods nor the Norns decided to check on the scouts this morning or set some traps on the way." Ragnar scowled.

"No, but they sent you to do it," Snorri smiled. Ragnar was about to say something, but then must have realised it was pointless.

Ulf never understood why Ragnar was so against the gods. He had been before, but then he had a reason. He had always blamed the gods for the deaths of his parents and for having to live on his uncle's farm, away from everyone. So Ulf wondered what had happened to Ragnar for him to not trust the gods. *Do I trust them?* The question came to him and while the men were brushing their hair and beards, waiting for breakfast, Ulf thought back to the dream he had the night before.

"Does the wolf hunt alone?" he spoke the question out loud without realising.

"What in the gods' names are you talking about now?" Asbjorn asked him.

"Does the wolf hunt alone?" Oddi asked with a frown. They were all staring at Ulf. Not just his friends, but also the rest of the men.

"Even the simplest child knows that wolves always hunt in packs," Ragnar growled at him.

"Aye, that's how they can take down prey much larger than them," Oddi added. "You really didn't know this, Ulf?"

"Ulf's been so focused on his revenge that he doesn't pay attention to anything else anymore." Asbjorn shook his head.

Ulf stared at them, trying to make sense of what they were saying. And not just because of the dream he had the night before. All this talk of wolf packs was pulling his mind towards something. Something he had seen in a dream. Or at least he thought it was a dream. Images flashed in his mind and he had the feeling he was soaring high in the sky. But clouds blocked his view, and he knew the answer to what was bothering him was below them.

"Ulf?" Snorri's voice brought him back to the ground. He shook his head to clear his mind and realised that everyone was still staring at him.

"What?" Ulf felt his cheeks go red.

"You sure you did not take a knock to the head?" Snorri asked.

"He lost his helmet during the fight," Drumbr said, scratching his ear.

The men discussed whether Ulf losing his helmet meant he took a knock to the head, but Ulf wasn't listening anymore. The hair on the back of his neck stood up again, and Ulf felt like he was being watched. He glanced over his shoulder at the trees, but saw nothing. He had learnt by now that didn't mean anything. Hulda's mother understood the way of the forests better than anyone he had ever met, better even than Vidar. If she didn't want to be spotted, then no man would see her. And the fact that she, like the gods, had taken an interest in Ulf made him more afraid than he had ever been. *What do you want?*

Revenge! the voice came to him.

CHAPTER 21

Ulf chewed on the roasted rabbit meat that Theoda had prepared for breakfast. He did not understand how she had made something this good. After she and Amund had finished gutting and cleaning the rabbits, Theoda wandered around the clearing and the nearby trees, picking wild mushrooms and anything else she could find. Drumbr had watched her, constantly licking his lips in anticipation. The meal was worth the wait, and it was much better than the usual porridge they had been eating for the last few days. Ulf savoured the taste of the meat, feeling slightly more relaxed but still unnerved by his dream.

Snorri's hirdmen were making fun of Thorbjorn, telling him he needs to keep a close eye on Theoda, otherwise one of them would take her just for her cooking. Thorbjorn threatened to gut any who tried, but he could not keep the smile off his face. A calmness had descended over the small camp, as if Freya had whispered some magic words over them. But this did not last long, as one of the scouts rushed into the clearing. He opened his mouth to speak, but then smelt the spit-roasted rabbit. His stomach rumbled as the man stared longingly at it.

"There is still some left, Bjarni," Snorri said to the man. "Grab some food and then tell me what sent you running here."

Bjarni walked to the fire where Theoda cut him some meat with the sax-knife Ulf had given her. He nodded his thanks to Theoda, who smiled at him. Ulf thought it was strange how she seemed so comfortable around the men. She had even ignored the priests as they had berated her over the last few days, but then, those priests were now all dead, and Theoda was still alive.

"So, what got you so worked up?" Thorbjorn asked after the man ate a few mouthfuls.

"Danes," Bjarni said, quickly finishing the rest of his meal. "At least half a crew making their way through the forest."

"Looking for us?" Oddi asked.

"Hunting us." Snorri frowned as he looked at his men, weighing up his options. "Are they close?"

Bjarni shook his head. "Sven and Holger are leading them away from us. I rushed here to tell you."

"Good, that should keep them off our tracks," Ragnar said. Bjarni smiled, pleased with the compliment from Ragnar.

"Is Griml with them?" Ulf asked.

Bjarni shook his head. "They're being led by an older warrior, but there was no sign of the troll."

"Why is Griml not with them?" Drumbr looked at Snorri.

"Perhaps he is worried his size will give them away?" Thorbjorn suggested.

"No." Ulf glanced at the surrounding trees. *Are you there?*

"Something strange is going on." Thorbjorn gripped his Mjöllnir pendant. Theoda frowned at this, but no one was paying any attention to her. "First, he didn't fight yesterday, and now he's not even hunting us."

"Could be a second group out there, with him leading them," Asbjorn said. Some men nodded as they agreed with this.

"There was no sign of another group," Bjarni said. "And this group is big. I don't think they have enough men for two large groups. Not from what we saw when they attacked yesterday."

"How are Sven and Holger planning on getting back to us?" Snorri asked suddenly, as if he had not been following their conversation. Bjarni opened his mouth to respond but then closed it again, frowning. "And what happens if the Danes capture them?" Snorri's face darkened.

"I am sorry, Snorri." Bjarni lowered his head.

"No, it is not your fault. You did well. But we cannot run forever. The Danes will realise what is happening and then they will come for us."

"We can march to Denmark, from there try to get a ship home?" Oddi suggested.

"Or find a port and steal a ship," Thorbjorn added.

Snorri did not respond. He looked to the sky again, his eyes scanning the clouds or following the path of a bird. Ragnar shook his head but stayed silent like the rest of them. Ulf looked at the trees, wondering if the volva was there. He pictured her hiding in the shadows, smiling at their predicament. "Does the wolf hunt alone?" Snorri asked, surprising everyone. He looked at Ulf as his wolf grin grew on his lips.

"Snorri?" Asbjorn frowned as he scratched his jaw.

"By Odin, he must have taken a knock to the head as well." Ragnar rolled his eyes.

"No." Snorri smiled. "Ulf, perhaps we should call you Ulf Viss." Oddi looked shocked at this, which only made Thorbjorn laugh.

"But we already talked about this. Wolves hunt in packs." Drumbr scratched his head while frowning.

"Aye, but how else do wolves hunt?"

"They stalk their prey?" Asbjorn tugged at his beard as he thought about it. Snorri said nothing.

"They surround their prey. Come at it from different angles." Oddi adopted his clever voice, obviously wanting to show that he was Viss. "Make sure their prey has no escape."

Snorri smiled his wolf grin. "And are we not the wolves of Thorgilsstad?" The men frowned at him at first, but then Kirsten spoke up.

"We are." He glanced at the men around him, all of them nodding but keeping quiet.

"We are."

The men smiled as they checked their weapons and put their helmets on. They had all slept in their armour, which was not comfortable, but no one wanted to be caught out again. Theoda scowled as she watched them prepare and then said something in her language.

"What are we gonna do with her?" Drumbr asked. "We can't take her with us."

"Why not?" Thorbjorn scowled.

"Because she won't be able to keep up with us." Drumbr looked at the others for support.

"You keep up with us and you're bigger than she is," Thorbjorn retorted, his face going red.

"Drumbr is right," Snorri said. "We need to move fast and she'll struggle."

"But we can't just leave her here."

"And what about Magni?" Thorbjorn pointed at the tall warrior as he sat by a tree, his leg bandaged.

"What about me?" Magni struggled to his feet, his face grim.

"You're injured, you idiot," Thorbjorn said, shaking his head.

Magni grit his teeth and stood tall. "I'm not staying here." He looked at Snorri. "I'll keep up. Don't worry about me." Ulf couldn't help but admire the red-headed warrior. The man had changed much since he first joined their raid as the spoilt oldest son of a jarl.

"Well, I still don't think Theoda should stay here," Thorbjorn added when he saw he lost that argument.

Ragnar shook his head. "Women cause nothing but trouble."

"You're only saying that because they don't like you," Thorbjorn said, smiling. For once, he wasn't the butt of the joke.

"Especially not with a face like that," Snorri added, and clapped Ragnar on the shoulder.

"Aye, well at least I still look better than the pup." Ragnar thumbed at Ulf as the men laughed. Ulf wanted to say something, but no words came to mind, so he stayed quiet.

"So, what's the plan?" Oddi asked Snorri.

"We hunt." Snorri smiled, and when his men were ready, turned to Bjarni. "Lead us to the Danes."

Before Bjarni could say anything, Theoda barged her way through and faced Snorri. She shouted at him while jabbing her finger in his face. The men gasped, all of them shocked she would do this, and most of them anticipating Snorri's reaction.

"What is she saying?" Ragnar asked Thorbjorn.

"How, in Odin's name, should I know? I don't speak Frankish."

"She's your woman," Magni said with a huge grin on his face.

"Aye, well, we don't do much talking."

"No wonder she likes you then," Oddi added. "She doesn't get to hear the rubbish you speak."

Thorbjorn was about to respond when Theoda turned on him and shouted. His eyes were wide as she unleashed her fury at him. It was clear she understood what they were doing.

Snorri stepped in front of Theoda with his hands in the air to calm her. She stopped screaming but glared at him. "You stay here, we come back." He used his hands to help her understand his words. Theoda said something to Snorri, her voice still filled with anger, but at least she wasn't shouting. Snorri repeated his words to her again. This time, Theoda looked around the camp and at the men. She shook her head and then walked back to the fire, waving her hand at them while complaining. Snorri looked at Thorbjorn, who only shrugged.

"I think Thorbjorn should stay with her." Asbjorn glanced at the short warrior, a smile in the corner of his mouth.

"I think you should shut your mouth before I put my boot in it."

The men laughed and then turned to Snorri.

"Let's go," he said and followed Bjarni. As the men left the clearing, Ulf looked at his helmet. It was still covered in the blood from the previous day. Ulf was too tired to clean it after Torsten had given it back to him. He looked at the two snarling wolves that made up the eye guard, again feeling his memory tugging at him.

"We'll be back, I promise." Thorbjorn tried to comfort Theoda. At first she glared at him, but then she surprised Ulf by smiling at Thorbjorn. Thorbjorn turned and saw Ulf standing there. "You tell anyone about that and I'll cut your tongue out."

Ulf smiled and then followed his friend as they rushed after the others.

It didn't take them long to catch up with the rest of the men and soon they were all running towards the spot where Bjarni had last seen the Danes. Ulf gripped both his weapons as he ran so they would not trip him up. The voices of his ancestors were humming in his ears. They were excited by this hunt and Ulf had to admit, so was he. His mind had felt like it was caught in a sea storm, not knowing what to think or what to do. So many conflicting thoughts constantly clashing left him exhausted. But running through the forest and feeling the breeze as they rushed past the trees and branches made him forget about everything. About the troll's face that looked like his, about the nagging memory he could not bring to his mind, and about the volva as she stalked him through these lands.

Snorri held his hand up, and the men stopped, none of them saying a word. Like wolves, they were silent as Bjarni picked up the scent of their prey. The Danes hadn't bothered hiding their trail, and even Ulf could easily pick up their tracks. He glanced at Magni, the tall man's face white with pain, but somehow he had kept up with them. Snorri grinned his wolf grin, his hirdmen all copying him. "Remember, they still outnumber us," he whispered to his men. "But they think we are ahead of them, so they won't be expecting us to attack from behind. We stay silent and vigilant. You all know what to do." The men nodded, and when Snorri was satisfied, he signalled for them to move. Through the voices whispering in his ears, Ulf heard the flap of wings and looked up to see the raven sitting on the branch above them, tilting its head as it watched them.

"What do we do?" Torsten turned to one of the older warriors. Ulf wondered the same, but he did not want to ask.

"Just follow me," Ketil responded. Torsten nodded his gratitude to the older warrior.

Ulf turned away from them and went with Snorri's hirdmen as they followed the trail. They had to run because they did not know how far ahead the Danes were, and Snorri was also worried about his two men leading the Danes away. But at the same time, the men needed to be silent, which was not easy as they all wore armour. As they rushed past the trees, Ulf heard his brynja jingling as well as those of the surrounding men. Bjarni was running ahead of them, passing the trees and jumping over roots like a seasoned wolf. He was one of Snorri's best scouts and would often be used to track game or enemies.

As they followed the trail, Ulf realised that Sven and Holger were leading the Danes in a large circle. This had kept the Danes in the forest, but away from their camp. It felt like they had been running for half a day when Snorri gave the signal for them to stop. They were close. In the sudden silence, Ulf could hear the Danes complaining ahead of them. The Danes were tired and angry, and this had made them careless. Ulf saw the wolf grin on Snorri's face grow. He signalled to his men, who split into two groups. Snorri, Ragnar and Thorbjorn led one group which went to the right of the Danes, while Oddi, Drumbr and Asbjorn led the other group, which went to the left. Magni limped after his brother, the bandage on his leg red with blood, and Ulf decided to go with Snorri. He did not know how many Danes there were, so he rubbed the hilt of Ormstunga, praying to Odin and Tyr that Snorri's plan would work. But the men were confident and as long as they remained silent, then they would catch the Danes by surprise. And Ulf had to admit, the idea of killing the bastards who had been chasing them made his heart beat faster.

They moved silently, like wolves, as they surrounded the unsuspecting Danes while keeping their distance. Through the trees, Ulf saw their prey on a small track. The Danes were two men wide, and standing still. In front of the column were two men, arguing over what they should do.

"We should head back. We're going in circles!" one of them complained. He wore a helmet with an eye guard, so Ulf could not see his face, but he looked like an experienced warrior.

"Are you mad!" another said. "You know what Griml will do if we go back and say we couldn't catch them." This man had a brown beard speckled with grey.

"We don't even know who we've been chasing!" The first Dane waved his arm in the air. "Apart from the tracks, we've not seen any sign of them."

"They're just ahead of us. They must be."

"But how? They should be exhausted. They should not be able to outrun us."

"We could just go back to the ship, sail home, and leave that giant turd here. Let the Franks deal with him." Another man said as he picked at something in his beard.

"No, he might not find us, but she will. And from what I hear, she's not one to cross." The older Dane looked at the trees where they were hiding. Ulf ducked down, as did the men around him.

"Says who?"

"Ubba."

"Ubba's dead."

"Exactly. He had that scarred bastard, and then somehow ended with a sword in his guts. He angered the volva, and she cursed him." The warrior with the grey-speckled beard rubbed the Mjöllnir around his neck. "I am not crossing her. It'll be like pissing in Odin's mead." Ulf saw Snorri glance at him with a smile on his face. The Dane was right. Ubba should have killed him. Ulf had thought he would, but then he had slipped on the gore on the ground and Ubba's sword gouged Ulf's helmet instead of piercing his face. Ulf rubbed his finger across the groove on the side of his helmet. He had believed Odin had helped him, but could it have been her? "I can almost feel her watching us now." The Dane shivered.

The group of men scanned the trees, but Snorri and his men had done this many times before and knew how to hide amongst the undergrowth. Ulf copied what they were doing as he pressed himself lower. As he glanced up, he saw a raven and wondered if it was the same one he had seen before.

"Bah. Ubba got cocky, and the gods punished him for it," one of the Danes said. "He had many chances to kill those Norse scum, but he failed. There's only so many times Odin would accept failure."

The words caught Ulf like a kick to the gut. How many times had he failed to get his vengeance? How many of his sword brothers had died because of it? Were they the price he had to pay for failing to kill Griml? Was Odin punishing him? Ulf could not die until he had gotten his revenge, so perhaps Odin was killing his friends instead. His heart beat faster as the thoughts ran circles in his head. The heat of his anger burnt in his stomach. His friends were dying because of him. The voices of his ancestors started whispering in his ears, drowning out the conversation of the Danes and the sound of him grinding his teeth. It also drowned out the wing flaps of the raven as it moved closer to him.

Snorri looked up and saw the large black bird. He knew what it meant and rubbed the Mjöllnir around his neck, hoping the Raven God was on their side. But Ulf noticed none of this. He sat there, leaning against the tree as the thoughts and memories of the last few weeks tormented him. Was all of this because he could not kill Griml? The voices in his ears sounded like they were arguing with each other, some telling him to fight, while others called him weak. Ulf unsheathed Ormstunga, oblivious to the fact that the sun was shining above them, and pulled Olaf's axe from his belt. Lost in his thoughts and consumed by the flames of his anger, Ulf heard a new noise. It sounded like a wolf howling and at first, Ulf thought it was some spirit sent by Tyr to him. But then he realised the sound was much closer. So close it sounded like it was next to him.

Ulf looked to his side and saw Snorri howling into the trees. Other howls joined his from this side of the path and the other. Ulf knew what it meant and before everyone else reacted to the signal, he jumped to his feet, roaring as he charged at the Danes.

The raven cried as it took to the skies. With its keen eyes, it watched the chaos unfold amongst the trees. Odin's bird knew what was coming, and it called to all of its friends. Today, they were going to feast yet again.

CHAPTER 22

Ulf charged at the Danes, his ancestors roaring in his ears as he gripped Ormstunga and Olaf's axe in his hands. He had left his shield by the tree, but Snorri and his men did not as they spread out on either side of him. From the other side of the path, Oddi led the rest of Snorri's men as they came at the Danes, trapping them like wolves trap their prey.

The Danes were stunned as the men they had been chasing suddenly erupted from the surrounding trees, their faces savage as they roared to the All-Father. Ulf reached the first one before he even understood what was happening and sliced his throat open with Ormstunga as he rushed past. Beside him, Snorri crashed into the shocked Danes, his shield battering one warrior out of the way while he stabbed another in the chest with Tyr's Fury. A Dane turned to face Ulf, the man moving so slowly that Ulf killed him before his face even showed the shock the man must have felt. All around him, it was chaos, and Ulf thought he could hear the gods laugh through the voices screaming in his ears.

They were heavily outnumbered by the Danes, but they had caught their prey unaware. Blood sprayed over Ulf as he hacked into another Dane's chest. He sensed the movement to his side and turned in time for the sword jab to miss him. But before Ulf could retaliate, Oddi stabbed his attacker through the neck.

"Skjaldborg!" one of the Dane's shouted, but it was far too late for that.

The Dane facing Ulf blocked Ormstunga with his shield and swung his sword at Ulf's stomach. Ulf jumped back to avoid the sword and bumped into the man behind him. He turned and saw the grey-speckled brown beard of the warrior who led their pursuers. The man roared at Ulf and slashed at him with his axe. Ulf sidestepped the attack as the voices in his ears screamed louder and was about to cut at the man's face when the other Danish warrior barged into him with his shield. The blow numbed Ulf's shoulder, and he did all he could not to drop Ormstunga. But Ulf could not lift his arm to block the older Dane's axe. He twisted out of the way, but the tip of the blade caught his arm just below the sleeve of his brynja. Ulf grimaced, but the sting of the cut only fed the flames of his anger. Forgetting about his numb arm, he launched himself at the older Dane, hacking and stabbing with his sword and axe. The Dane used his experience to block and avoid Ulf's attacks, while the other stalked them as they fought amongst the chaos, waiting for the right moment to strike. As soon as he spotted it, he stabbed at Ulf's side. Ulf sensed the movement and tried to move out of the way, but the press of the bodies on the narrow track meant there was nowhere for him to go. The sword pierced through his brynja, but only the tip made it past the metal links and into his side as another warrior bumped into the

Dane and threw him off. The man roared in frustration as the older Dane used the distraction to chop at Ulf with his axe. For a heartbeat, the voices in Ulf's ears went silent, and he thought Odin had decided he had failed too many times. Time slowed and there was nothing Ulf could do to avoid his death.

"Danish scum!" The shout came from behind the younger warrior who stabbed at Ulf. Before the Dane could react, Thorbjorn hamstrung him. The man screamed, which distracted the older one. Ulf roared as the voices in his ears rushed to life and stabbed the brown-bearded Dane through the chest. The Dane stared at Ulf, his eyes wide as the two of them stood there in an odd moment of silence, blood leaking out of the corner of his mouth and into his grey-speckled beard.

"I hope you kill the troll." With that, he fell to the ground, still gripping his axe as Ormstunga slipped from his chest.

Ulf's blood lust was suddenly gone as he looked at his sword, her blade red. The screaming around Ulf drew his attention away from the dead Dane, and it was like he had only just noticed the surrounding chaos. Snorri was hacking at one man while blocking the sword of another Dane, his face fierce as he roared at his men to fight. Drumbr's face was red with blood and effort as he chopped his enormous axe down, severing a Dane's arm, while one of Snorri's men stabbed the Dane from the other side. Thorbjorn was pulling his sword free from the throat of the Dane Ulf had fought, his grin savage. Ragnar danced around the Danes, chopping off limbs and heads as none of them could get near him. The jarl's champion looked like he was moving to music only he could hear, his eyes almost closed. All around Ulf, the Norse were fighting like savage bastards. The ravens screamed above the battle song as one

Dane dropped his weapon and begged for mercy, but Torsten laughed as he buried his axe in the man's head. It was chaos. It was carnage, and the Norse were loving every moment. These men were fighting for their lives, but more than that, they were fighting for the love of it. Just like Griml had slaughtered his family for the fun of it. In the middle of the fight, Ulf pictured the troll from his dreams, laughing at him as he stood in front of the burning house. Ulf once again saw his own face on the troll. *You are me*, the voice came to him and Ulf screamed. He launched himself at the Danes as the voices roared in his ears and the flames of his anger tore through his body. He hacked into the back of a Dane fighting Magni and caught the disappointment on Magni's face as he rushed past and stabbed another through the mouth. Ulf roared his anger at any who dared to face him before killing them. He hacked and stabbed while dodging out of the way of swords and axes until there was no one left to fight. The forest air was filled with the sounds of men dying, begging the gods or their mothers. Birds fled from the sounds of swords striking wooden shields, while the small animals shied away from the stench of blood and shit as the Norse brought death to the peaceful forest. The remaining few Danes dropped their weapons and backed off, trying to get clear of the Norse wolves intent on slaughter.

"Enough!" Snorri's voice ripped through the trees, stopping everyone.

Ulf stood next to Thorbjorn, both men covered in Danish blood and both panting heavily. His hands trembling as the voices of his ancestors understood the fight was over and there was no more need for them.

Snorri's men, their eyes still filled with blood lust, surrounded the few Danes left. Ulf glanced at Snorri, still wearing his wolf grin, which only made his eyes look more dangerous.

"What do we do with them?" Oddi pointed his sword at the Danes, her blade red with blood. Ulf knew the question was pointless. Snorri always killed the survivors of the enemy.

But Snorri did not answer Oddi. Instead, he walked up to the Danes and stopped a few paces in front of them. "Where is your ship?" The words grated out of his dry throat. "Answer me, or I swear by Odin, you will never see Valhalla!" Snorri threatened the Danes.

Most of the Danes refused to answer, but Ulf noticed the fear in their eyes. It was not a threat any warrior took lightly. One of the Danes limped forward. He had a deep cut on his leg and was also clutching his side. "You may threaten us as much as you like, but there is nothing you can do which will stop us from reaching Odin's hall." The man spat blood at Snorri's feet. Ulf expected Snorri to kill the man, but Snorri only smiled.

He pointed his sword at Ulf. "You know who he is?"

The Dane glared at Ulf as he took in the scars and his steel-grey eyes. "Aye, that's the bastard who killed Ubba the White."

"And his sister," another of the Danes added. Ulf grit his teeth and had to restrain himself. He had not killed Ubba's sister. He doubted he ever could. The image of her which came to his mind almost drenched the flames of his anger. Ulf forced her long, slender body from his mind. Ubba's sister had been about to marry Griml and Snorri decided that kidnapping her would draw Griml away from his thousand-strong army. The plan had worked and after the battle at The Giant's Toe, they had let her go home with her father's hirdmen. But she never made it home, and Ubba believed they had killed her. That was why he had wanted to kill them.

"Aye, he killed Ubba. He also defeated Griml's army almost single-handedly."

"By Odin," Ragnar muttered, and Ulf understood why. Snorri liked to embellish his stories.

"He is also a descendant of Tyr," Snorri continued. "And can talk to the gods." Ulf saw the Danes' eyes go wide, some of them grabbing the Mjöllnir pendants around their necks and whispering prayers to the gods. Snorri saw the same, and his smile grew. "If you don't tell me what I want to know, then Ulf Bear-Slayer will make sure that none of you worms ever see Valhalla." The Danes paled as Snorri said this.

"You can do that?" Thorbjorn whispered to Ulf, who shrugged.

"Of course he can't," Ragnar hissed. "But those idiots don't need to know that."

"We landed by the beach, across the river." One of the Danes stepped forward. The others hissed at him. "What? I want to go to Valhalla!"

"Near the burnt-out town," another added.

"How did you know where to look for us?" Ragnar asked.

"We didn't." The first Dane who spoke shrugged. "Griml took control of Ubba's ship. We sailed up and down the coast for a few days. He kept watching the shore, said he was waiting for a sign."

Ragnar glared at Snorri. "And then you saw the smoke from the town."

"No," the Dane said, which surprised them all. "A man arrived on the beach."

"What man?" Snorri asked, but Ulf already knew who it was. They all did.

"A warrior. Said he was one of yours. We thought it was a trap, but Griml said it was the sign he was looking for."

"He told Griml where to find you," another Dane added. They were all very talkative now.

"Why would Geir do that?" Thorbjorn asked, but no one responded.

"What happened to him?" Snorri asked the Dane.

"Griml killed him."

"The dumb bastard," Thorbjorn muttered. Ulf felt the same and remembered the argument Geir had with Snorri a few days before about him. *Did he die because of my vengeance?*

"We answered your questions. Now what?"

"Now you go to Valhalla." Snorri launched himself at the nearest Dane and stabbed the man through the neck with Tyr's Fury. Thorbjorn, Oddi and Ragnar attacked the remaining Danes, slaughtering them all before they could defend themselves. As the bodies dropped to the ground, Ulf heard the ravens above his head celebrating their upcoming feast. He looked up and saw one raven sitting on a branch, not far from him. Unlike the rest of the dark birds, this one wasn't screaming or flying. It just sat there, staring at him with its beady eyes.

"You telling your friend to let these bastards into Valhalla?" Thorbjorn joked, but Ulf noticed the way he gripped the Mjöllnir around his neck.

"He's not my friend."

"Well, tell him that, whichever one that is. Because they keep following you and it's making me feel uncomfortable." Thorbjorn was still gripping his Mjöllnir pendant.

"I think that one is Huginn." Oddi stroked his red beard. Magni nodded as he leaned against a tree to take the weight of his injured leg, while Thorbjorn shook his head.

"And how, in Odin's name, would you know that?" he asked the tall warrior.

Oddi shrugged. "It looks more like a Huginn than a Muninn."

Thorbjorn's face turned red. "Thor's bullocks! That's the biggest—"

"Will you two idiots stop fighting!" Ragnar stepped in before Thorbjorn could finish his sentence. "Doesn't matter which of the two bastard birds that one is. The dumb thing only wants to feast on the corpses we leave behind." He jabbed his finger at the raven. The raven screamed at him and then took off, flying away from the other scavenging birds.

"Well, now you've done it," Drumbr said, gripping his Mjöllnir pendant like the rest of the men. "He's gonna tell Odin what you said."

Ragnar was about to say something, but then shook his head and turned to Snorri. "I don't know how you put up with these men."

Snorri smiled. "You're just getting old." Ragnar glared at him, which only made Snorri laugh.

Ulf followed the path of the raven while rubbing the names of his family on the haft of his axe. *Tell Odin what you saw today. Tell the All-Father that I can still avenge my family.*

"Now what?" Oddi asked, drawing Ulf's attention back to the carnage around them. Snorri's plan worked and his smaller force had killed the Danes sent by Griml.

Snorri's smile disappeared. "Did we lose anyone?"

Oddi looked at the men as they cleaned their weapons and searched for loot amongst the bodies. "Not that I can see. A few injuries, but I'll check."

Snorri nodded and turned to his men. "Wolves of Thorgilsstad!" All the men stopped what they were doing and looked at him. "As always, you have fought well and we've filled the hall of the slain with more bastards to fight when we get there." The men cheered, sending the ravens and forest birds back to the skies. "Take anything worth taking, but hurry. We do not know if there are more Danes out there." The men got back to what they were doing.

Ulf knelt down to clean the blood off Ormstunga when the leaves rustled behind him. Everyone else heard it as well as they all turned towards the sound, weapons ready and teeth grit.

"Well, if this is the thanks we get, then next time we just let the bastards find you," one of the two men who stepped out of the undergrowth said.

"Aye, ungrateful bastards," the other added, and the men cheered.

Snorri walked up to the two men while taking off two of his golden arm rings. "Sven and Holger, you two saved us all." He handed each man an arm ring, and even Ulf smiled when their faces went red with embarrassment as the men cheered their names.

"Looks like we missed the fight," Sven said, his eyes running over the dead bodies on the path.

"Aye, you two were probably hiding in the trees, waiting for it to be finished before coming out," Thorbjorn joked.

"Is that so?" Snorri raised an eyebrow. "Well, then give me back those arm rings." The two men looked shocked, but then Snorri laughed.

Ulf shook his head, unable to understand how these men could joke around when they were surrounded by death. Ulf always felt exhausted and even now, he had to fight hard to stop his hands from shaking. Everyone clapped Sven and Holger on the back, congratulating and thanking the two scouts for leading the Danes away from them.

Snorri and Ragnar walked up to Ulf as he was cleaning the blood off Ormstunga.

"So much for the curse," Ragnar retorted. Ulf frowned at him, and then he noticed Ragnar pointing to the sky. "The sun is shining, yet your sword is out of her sheath."

Ulf had not even realised and looked at his sword in shock. He didn't remember unsheathing her. She was just in his hand when he attacked the Danes. "I…"

"The curse says not to draw her in the light of the sun," Snorri said with a confident look on his face. "Ulf was behind a tree when he pulled her out of her scabbard. He was in the shade."

"Does that count?" Thorbjorn scratched his chin under his thick beard. They all looked at Oddi.

"Why are you all looking at me?"

"Because you are the smart one, Oddi Viss," Thorbjorn mocked.

Oddi stroked his beard as he thought about it. "I guess that does count, seeing as Ulf is still alive, and we won this fight without losing a man."

Ulf looked at the blade of Ormstunga, now clean of all the blood. He read the inscription on her hilt guard and remembered when the old Dane was about to kill him. If it hadn't been for Thorbjorn, Ulf would have been dead and the curse would have come true. He shivered when he realised how careless he had been. As his friends kept on discussing the curse of Ormstunga, he felt a light breeze blow over the back of his neck, which made the hairs stand up. He looked over his shoulder and even though he could not see her, he knew the volva was there, watching him. And Ulf knew they were not out of danger yet. Griml was still out there.

CHAPTER 23

It didn't take long for them to loot the bodies of the Danes. Snorri took two golden arm rings to replace the ones he had given to Sven and Holger. He also gave a gold one to Ulf for killing the man they thought was the leader. Ulf put the arm ring in his pouch, not wanting to wear it. His arm stung from the cut he had received even though the bleeding had stopped and he already had two arm rings on his right arm, one gold and one silver. Ulf was surprised, though, to see a groove across both rings. The old Dane's axe must have done that. Weapons were taken and if some men found swords or axes better than the ones they had, they would swap them. They would sell the rest when they get to a market. The only thing that Ulf took was a sax-knife from one of the Danes to replace the one he had given to Theoda. This one had a plain carved bone handle, but the blade was sharp and looked to be of good quality.

"We're wasting time here, Snorri." Ragnar scowled. "Why do we need to take the weapons? It's slowing us down."

Snorri smiled. "The men deserve to be rewarded for what they did. And besides, we still owe King Halfdan a cut and with the Sae-Ulfr gone," Snorri's face darkened, "we lost all the treasure we had taken from the church. You know as well as I do, Halfdan the Black is not a man to upset."

"The men will only take what they can carry, Ragnar. This is not the first time we've done this." Thorbjorn waded in on the conversation. Ragnar raised an eyebrow at him but said nothing.

"Thorbjorn's right. My men know what they are doing." Snorri bent down and looked at the brynja of one of the dead Danes. "Torsten, remove this brynja and put it with my stuff. I don't think he needs it anymore." The young warrior rushed to do Snorri's bidding, and Ulf couldn't help but remember Geir doing that the summer before.

"Stop doing that," Thorbjorn said to Ulf, catching him by surprise.

"Doing what?" Ulf frowned.

"Thinking." Thorbjorn raised an eyebrow. "Told you many times before, it's not good for you."

"Odin knows thinking is best left for Snorri and Oddi." Drumbr stripped one corpse of its belt.

"Why Oddi?" Thorbjorn asked.

Drumbr shrugged. "Because he is clever. Even Odin knows that."

Thorbjorn opened his mouth to say something, but the words struggled to come out as his face turned red.

Drumbr started laughing and walked away. "Calm down, Thorbjorn. I am only teasing."

Ulf smiled. Drumbr was slowly getting back to the man he had been before the death of his brother, but he still missed the way the two Brak brothers would joke together.

"I say we get to their ship. If we hurry, we can get there before Griml realises his men are dead."

"He already knows," Ulf said before he could stop himself.

Ragnar shook his head. "And how, in Odin's name, would he know that?"

Ulf looked at the trees. Her presence was gone now, but he still felt like she was watching him.

"Let me guess, the volva," Asbjorn sneered. Ulf ignored him. He did not want to have this argument again. And neither did Snorri.

"Enough of this." His face hardened. "We all know that Ulf is different. If he says that the volva was here and that Griml knows, then I believe him. If you have a problem with that, then you have a problem with me, Asbjorn." The men stopped what they were doing and watched as Snorri confronted one of his hirdmen.

Asbjorn glared at Ulf and then turned to Snorri. "I have no problem with you, Snorri. But I do not like that we are following his feelings."

"Not this again." Thorbjorn waved his arms in the air. "Has Ulf not proven himself enough yet?"

"I do not doubt him as a warrior. I have no problems standing next to him in a shield wall."

"Then what is your problem?" Thorbjorn pressed. Ulf turned and walked away. He did not want to be part of this. He had never asked to be part of Snorri's hirdmen or for Snorri to believe everything he said. And he did not want to be part of this game being played by the gods.

"No problem." Asbjorn clenched his fists.

"Good," Snorri said to his friend. "I trust Ulf. He saved my life and so you have to deal with it." Asbjorn nodded, but still glared at Ulf. "Now, let's finish up. We need to get to the Dane's ship, before Griml or whoever is watching it decides to leave. That ship is our way home."

"What about Theoda?" Thorbjorn asked.

"What about her?" Ragnar responded. "You weren't really planning on taking her home with us, were you?"

Thorbjorn glared at his jarl's champion. He was half the height of the red-headed warrior, but he showed no fear as he squared up to Ragnar. "And what if I did? She's my woman now."

"You can't even speak to her!" Ragnar's face turned as red as his hair.

"She can learn our language."

"Enough." Snorri shook his head and to Ulf, he looked exhausted. "Thorbjorn, we'll be wasting time if we go back to fetch her, and besides, you don't even know if she wants to go with you."

"I'm not leaving without her." Thorbjorn crossed his arms across his chest and almost looked like a bearded child. A very ugly one.

Snorri rubbed his face. "Thorbjorn."

"No, Snorri. You might not love your wife, but I feel something for that woman." The men looked shocked, some of them glancing at each other and whispering stuff. One man laughed, but then paled as Thorbjorn glared at him. Thorbjorn had a reputation amongst the crew, and being one for emotions was not part of it. The only thing Thorbjorn had only ever shown any love for was his sword and violence.

"By the gods, Snorri. Do something about your men," Ragnar complained, but Snorri only smiled.

"I swear to Odin, if I die because of this woman of yours, Thorbjorn, I will kick your arse every day until Ragnarök."

Thorbjorn smiled and nodded, but Ragnar was not happy.

"Snorri, we don't have time for this. The gods know we need to be quick if we want to take advantage of this."

"And we will." Snorri turned to his father's champion. "You take the men, get to their ship. But do not kill my men unnecessarily. If there are too many Danes, then find a place to hide."

Ragnar shook his head. "And what about you?"

"I'll go with Thorbjorn and fetch his love." Some men laughed at this, and Thorbjorn glared at them.

"I'm coming with." Ulf took a step towards Snorri.

"Aye, take the dreamer with you. I'll probably kill him on the way," Ragnar said.

"Well, you're not going without me. You'd probably die tripping over a root," Oddi said.

"I'm going with my brother," Magni added.

"You're still injured," Oddi protested, frowning at his brother, who was leaning against the tree and holding on to his leg.

"Try and stop me," Magni said through grit teeth.

"You're definitely not going without us," Drumbr said as he and Asbjorn stepped forward.

"We still need to keep your arse alive," Asbjorn agreed. "Your mother will skin us if we let you die because of Thorbjorn's cock."

"I'm touched you care," Thorbjorn muttered, but couldn't hide the smile on his face.

"Fine, Ragnar, you get the ship. I'll take my hirdmen and go get Theoda. There are supplies there we need, anyway."

Ragnar nodded, and the two men gripped forearms. "May Odin keep you safe."

Snorri smiled. "I doubt he would do such a thing, especially if my death amuses him."

They watched as Snorri's men took all the plunder they could carry and followed Ragnar. "Be careful with my men!" Snorri shouted. Ragnar raised a hand in acknowledgement. When his men disappeared among the trees, Snorri turned to his hirdmen. "Right, let's go fetch Thorbjorn's wife."

Ulf rubbed his arm as Snorri's hirdmen laughed and walked off in the opposite direction. His arm was still numb, but he doubted he would need to fight again as he followed his friends. A raven cawed above his head and to Ulf, it sounded like it was laughing. The gods were not done with them yet. Odin still had one more move on his tafl board and it was one none of them would expect.

It was the latter part of the day by the time they reached the campsite where they had left Theoda.

"Next time we take Bjarni with us," Asbjorn complained.

"Why? We found our way back," Snorri said with a smile.

"Aye, could have been here sooner." Asbjorn shook his head. He was right. They were all decent trackers. They had spent a lot of time hunting in the forests around Thorgilsstad. But none of them were as skilled as someone like Bjarni, who understood the forests better than he did his own wife. *Or like Vidar,* Ulf thought. But they had found their way back, the seven of them exhausted from the trek after the fight with the Danes.

"Where is she?" Thorbjorn's smile disappeared. They all stopped and stared at the empty camp. They had expected to find Theoda sitting there waiting for them with a scowl on her face. The fire she had prepared their breakfast over was nothing more than ash. The few things they had left behind just lay there. Cloaks were discarded, water flasks lying on the ground, and even a bowl helmet. "Theoda!" Thorbjorn shouted, but there was no response.

"Perhaps she heard us coming and thought we were Danes. She might just be hiding," Drumbr suggested.

"Or Ulf's friend got to her while we were away," Asbjorn added. Ulf grit his teeth, but even he wondered if that was what had happened.

"No, she left." Oddi knelt down by one tree, prodding the ground as he spoke.

"How do you know?" Thorbjorn rushed towards the tall warrior.

"There is a set of tracks leaving the camp and they look like they could be Theoda's."

"How do you know they're her tracks?" Magni scratched his head.

"The same way I know Drumbr's tracks from the rest of ours." Oddi glanced at the large warrior.

"What are you saying?" Drumbr asked with a raised eyebrow.

"He's saying you are fat! Now shut up." Thorbjorn turned to Oddi. "Where are the tracks headed?"

Oddi stared back at Snorri, who had been quiet as he stood there studying the camp. "Back to her village."

They followed Theoda's tracks, the atmosphere among the trees tense as they walked. Thorbjorn was walking ahead, his fists clenched and grinding his teeth. Ulf could hear him do it in the silence that surrounded them. The rest were working hard to keep up with Thorbjorn. They were all exhausted and hungry, but none of them were prepared to abandon their friend. Even Magni, who before this raid to Francia had been despised by them all, kept quiet as he limped alongside his brother, his face grim with the pain. Ulf's arm was still numb, and he felt the constant need to clench his fist to check the feeling, which only made the cut on his arm sting more. But the pain distracted him from his tiredness and the thoughts raging in his head. He kept glancing around the trees, wondering why they were so silent. It could have been because they were storming through the forest, scaring all the birds and small animals away. But Ulf sensed it was something more sinister. *Are you there? Are you watching us right now?* He resisted the urge to grip the Mjöllnir around his neck as his left hand kept stroking the head of his axe.

"I don't understand why she'd go back there?" Drumbr said, puffing as he tried to keep up. No one responded. They were all too focused on their own thoughts. "There's nothing there for her," Drumbr continued. "The entire village must be burnt down by now."

Thorbjorn turned to Drumbr, his face red. "Would you shut up! Not even the gods know why she went back there!"

"Sorry," Drumbr mumbled, looking at his feet.

"Come on, Thorbjorn. He's only asking what we're all thinking," Snorri said, patting Drumbr on the shoulder.

"Aye, well, like the rest of you, he can keep it to himself." Thorbjorn turned around and stormed towards the village.

"I've never seen our short friend like this," Oddi said, frowning.

"He's never had anybody he cared about before," Snorri said.

"Poor bastard." Drumbr scratched the back of his neck.

"Aye, would not want to be in his shoes right now," Snorri agreed.

Magni looked at him, frowning. "But you're married?"

"What's your point?" Snorri asked the tall warrior.

Magni opened his mouth to speak, but then saw the smile on his brother's face and kept quiet.

"Let's go before we lose the bastard," Snorri said, and they rushed after Thorbjorn.

Not long after, the seven of them reached the edge of the forest. In front of them was the carnage left behind from the day before. The bodies of the Danes they had fought whilst escaping still littered the ground. Ravens, crows and other scavenging birds feasted on them. The stench of death filled the air, while the noise from the birds was deafening. Ulf grimaced as one raven picked at the empty eye socket of a dead Dane. The eyes were long gone, but the raven still found something to eat. A fox stalked around, trying to find an easy meal. It ran towards a corpse where some ravens were head-deep in its stomach. Ulf guessed it must have been a stomach wound which allowed the birds to get to the corpse's innards. One raven screamed at the fox, but it was determined and sent them all flocking to the sky.

"Bastard's got balls," Asbjorn said as they watched the fox burying its head inside the corpse.

Snorri's attention was somewhere else. He stood rigid as he stared at the remains of the Sae-Ulfr. Ulf saw the burnt-out skeleton of Snorri's ship. In his mind was the image from his dream. The Sae-Ulfr burnt to nothing with only the beast head remaining. But the real Sae-Ulfr had no beast head left. There was no snarling wolf defying the gods.

A pack of wolves roamed the far side of the village, which surprised Ulf. They had heard wolves howling deep into the night on a few occasions, but he had never seen them in this land. He wondered if that was an omen from the gods while the question from his dream came to him again. *Does the wolf hunt alone?* He also felt that nagging feeling again that there was something he was supposed to remember, but could not. Something the volva had shown him. Something to do with his father.

"Where is she?" Thorbjorn's voice brought Ulf back, and he looked at the village for the first time.

Most of the houses were burnt to the ground, with only the occasional wooden beam still standing, a dark reminder that there had been a house there. The church was the only building left standing and only because it was made of stone, but its roof was gone and so was the bell. Ansovald's large hall was gone as well, nothing left of it other than scarred earth. A black cloud of ravens and crows circled high above in the sky, with larger birds mixed in; eagles and vultures come to join the feast. There was plenty of food for them all. Not even the livestock had been spared, as Ulf could make out the charred bodies of cows and sheep. But there was no sign of Theoda.

"First time I think we get to see the result of our handy work," Oddi said, his face grim.

"But this wasn't our work. It was the bastard Danes and that ugly troll," Asbjorn responded.

"Aye, but who led them here?"

Oddi's comment wasn't aimed at Ulf, but he still felt the weight of this destruction on his shoulders. More bodies to haunt him in his dreams. Ulf wondered if he would recognise any of the villagers when they came to blame him for what had happened here.

"Let's go, we'll not find Theoda standing here." Snorri walked towards the village, and the rest of them followed.

The ravens and crows took to the sky, screaming at them as they walked past the corpses the birds were feeding on. Only to land on the bodies again and continue their feast once Ulf and his friends were far enough away. The fox looked up from its meal, its head red with blood and a piece of what looked like intestines hanging from its ear. It shook its head, and the intestines flew away before it buried its head back into the corpse.

The stench of death was overpowering, which caused the bile to rise in Ulf's stomach. The only thing that prevented him from vomiting was the fact that he had not eaten anything since the morning. And after watching the scavengers feast on the dead, he was sure he would not want to eat again.

"Breathe through your mouth," Oddi said to Magni, whose face was as green as Ulf's must have been. Ulf did the same.

"But now I can taste the dead on my tongue," Magni complained.

"There's no pleasing some," Drumbr said as he toed one corpse. Ulf stared at it and recognised one of the villagers. His eyes were gone, and so were his cheeks and tongue. It seemed the ravens had lost interest in him after that as the man had been thin and there were better fed corpses lying around for them to feast on.

"Stop talking! We must find Theoda!" Thorbjorn shouted, sending the birds to the skies.

"Well, shouting like that isn't going to help," Drumbr retorted.

"Of course shouting is going to help. That way, she'll hear us." Thorbjorn's face was red again as he waved a fist at Drumbr.

"And so will they and the gods know what other animals decided to feast here." Snorri pointed at the pack of wolves, who had stopped and were looking at them. From here the pack looked bigger than what it had done while they stood by the forest and Ulf hoped the wolves didn't want fresh meat.

"There's no sign of her." Asbjorn ignored the wolves and scanned the area. "Are you sure she came this way?"

"Her tracks did. I guess that means she came as well," Oddi said, stroking his beard.

"Maybe not," Magni said, copying his younger brother. The men looked at him with raised eyebrows. "What? Could be some of that Christian magic. Perhaps their god came and took her away."

Thorbjorn grabbed the tall warrior by his brynja and pulled him down so they were face to face. Magni grimaced. "That means she's dead, you idiot! You telling me my love is dead?" Tears were streaming down his face and Magni paled as he struggled to find the words to calm Thorbjorn.

Snorri pulled them apart and looked at Thorbjorn. "She's not dead. But there are a lot of places she could be, and we need to find her quickly."

Ulf saw what Snorri meant, and so did the others.

"Aye, we don't want to be here when the sun sets." Drumbr gripped the Mjöllnir around his neck. The others did the same. It was not the animals they were afraid of, although none of them wanted to be mistaken for a corpse by a hungry wolf or bear. Ulf especially did not want to meet another bear again. The scars on his cheek tingled at the thought. But they all knew there would be a lot of angry spirits here. The villagers would want revenge for what had been done to them, and the Danes who had not gone to Valhalla would be angry at them.

Ulf scanned the area, trying to find any sign of the woman they were looking for when he spotted something. He walked towards one corpse while the others were discussing where Theoda could have been. When he got to it, he could do nothing about the bile that rose from his stomach, but bend over and vomit.

"What's his problem?" Asbjorn sneered as Ulf straightened and wiped his mouth with the back of his hand.

"I found Ansovald," he said, but wished he hadn't.

"By the gods," Snorri said as he saw the corpse. The others rushed towards them and all of them grimaced when they saw the old warrior. Like Ulf, Magni bent over and vomited, and a few of the others looked green on the face as well. Ansovald's injured leg was broken. The angle it was at was enough to make Ulf queasy, but it was his caved-in chest that made Ulf really nauseous. Ansovald's mouth was open, and like the rest of the corpses, his eyes and tongue were long eaten.

"It looks like a boulder dropped on his chest, over and over again," Thorbjorn said.

"Not a boulder," Ulf said, his voice filled with anger, "but a troll."

"How do you know?" Magni asked, his face pale from vomiting.

"Because he is standing there, waiting for us."

CHAPTER 24

They all looked up, their eyes wide as they saw what Ulf was looking at.

"By Odin," Magni muttered as he took in the giant form of Griml.

"Thought he'd be gone by now." Oddi gripped the hilt of his sword still in her scabbard.

"Bastard," Thorbjorn growled.

But Ulf did not hear any of this as he stared at the man who had been haunting him for the last two winters. A wave of conflicted emotions rushed over him, and he grit his teeth as he tried to make sense of them all. All the while, Griml stood there, grinning as if Ulf had fallen for his trap. Perhaps Ulf had and had led his friends with him. They never should have come back to the village, he knew that, but they had to find Theoda. She had nothing left because of them, and the least they could do was offer her safety.

"What do we do?" Drumbr asked, hefting his two-handed axe in front of him.

"I don't know," Snorri said, unable to hide the uncertainty in his voice. "Ulf?"

Ulf did not respond. He could not, just like he could not take his eyes off Griml. Like in Rouen, Griml wore only trousers and boots. His hair was tied back, the sides of his head freshly shaved. Finger bones, as white as fresh snow, were tied into Griml's thick beard. Ulf wondered if they had belonged to any of the bodies scattered around them. In his right hand, Griml had his axe. It was similar to the two-handed axes that Drumbr and Ragnar used, but in his enormous fist, it seemed a lot smaller. His left hand was relaxed, like he was just taking a peaceful stroll on a nice summer evening. But what caught Ulf's attention was not the way Griml stood or the axe in his hand. It was his face. Griml's face had always been frightening. It was the type of face that would give children nightmares, with his small dark eyes and large nose. His mouth, almost too big for his face and filled with rotten teeth, sent shivers down the spine of the most hardened warrior. Ulf swallowed down the fear that threatened to take over as he took in the red paint covering Griml's face and chest, like war paint. But Ulf knew it was not paint. It was the blood of the people that had been slaughtered here.

"Ulf?" Snorri tried one more time, but again Ulf did not respond.

"Do we attack?" Thorbjorn asked.

"This isn't our fight," Asbjorn sneered.

"Is it not?" A new voice came from behind Griml. Ulf recognised it and wasn't surprised that she was there. The others gasped as she appeared from behind Griml, almost as if she had been born from the ashes of the dead. Ulf had seen her many times before, so her appearance did not affect him as much as it did his friends behind him.

"By Frigg, that's her." Thorbjorn's voice was tinged with fear as he took in the short woman that looked like a child as she stood beside the giant frame of Griml. Her deerskin dress was blackened by the ash from the burnt village. And Ulf wondered if she had done that on purpose as she stood there, her mismatched eyes studying them.

"She's real?" Drumbr sounded surprised, as if all this time he had believed that Ulf had made her up.

"Yes, I'm real." Her soft voice filled with malice. "It's nice to see all of you again. It's been such a long time."

"What does she mean by that?" Drumbr asked. Snorri shrugged as he glanced at Oddi, who could only shake his head.

"You don't remember me?" She feigned a sad expression before her smile appeared again, this time crueller than before. "Especially you."

Ulf thought she was talking about him, but then realised her eyes were not fixed on him. He glanced over his shoulder and saw Asbjorn pale.

"I don't know what you are talking about, you bitch!"

The volva smiled. "If you say so. But the gods know the truth, and soon, so too will your friends."

"Asbjorn, what, in Odin's name, is she talking about?" Snorri asked.

"Nothing. The bitch has lost it," Asbjorn responded, the fear obvious in his voice. The volva also heard it, Ulf saw that from the spark in her eyes.

"Enough talking!" Griml's boulder-like voice interrupted them. "It's time."

"Time for what?" Snorri asked, his hand on the hilt of Tyr's Fury. All of Ulf's friends had their hands on their weapons. But Ulf did not. He was too busy struggling to deal with the thoughts in his mind while smoke slowly drifted towards the sky from the embers of the burnt-down houses. Ravens and crows cried out ominously while the pack of wolves growled as they fought over a carcass. "Ulf?" Snorri called him again.

"Ulf," the volva echoed.

But Ulf could not respond to either of them. His eyes were fixed on Griml.

"He's afraid," Griml sneered. "Pathetic. This is the warrior I am supposed to fight for Odin. I could have killed him a long time ago if you'd let me." Griml's voice was like a thunderstorm in Ulf's head. He clenched his fists as the embers of his anger started burning in the pit of his stomach. The volva saw this as well.

"Just like you killed his uncle," she purred. Griml laughed, and the embers turned into a small flame as Ulf ground his teeth. "And what did you do to his aunt?"

Griml licked his lips. "I made her scream long into the night before I burnt that dump they called a house on top of her."

Ulf gripped the handle of Olaf's axe, feeling the names of his family he had carved into the wood burn the palm of his hand. In his mind, he heard his uncle's voice. *Kill him!* It repeated over and over. But Ulf's fear still held him back. The memories of his last fight with Griml were still too fresh in his mind and they threatened to wash over the flames of his anger like a wave.

"Ulf, we're with you. We can fight him together!" Snorri shouted.

"No, this is his fight!" Asbjorn retorted.

"Asbjorn! What is your problem? Ulf is one of us!" Oddi turned on Asbjorn as the volva smiled at them.

"I'm not dying for him!" Asbjorn sneered. "This is his fight, not mine." Asbjorn took a step away.

"Asbjorn, you bastard. Stop!" Snorri's voice was filled with rage. "You will abandon your sword brothers?" Asbjorn stopped and looked at Snorri. "Remember your oath to me!"

The volva laughed. "Yes, Asbjorn, remember your oath." The men frowned as Asbjorn looked at his feet.

"Enough! Fight me, you coward!" Griml roared at Ulf.

The volva took a step forward. "The young wolf needs some more encouragement." She smiled and, as if by some signal none of them had seen, two Danes came forward.

"Theoda!" Thorbjorn shouted as she was being dragged along by the Danes. She struggled, trying to free herself, and one of the Danes slapped her in the face. Theoda's head dropped and when she looked up again, blood ran down her chin from her bust lip. "Let her go or I swear to Odin, I'll gut you all!"

"So many oaths, so many promises. Don't you men get bored with all the promises you make, but never keep?" The volva's face grew serious for the first time. "Young wolf, you made an oath to the All-Father, and yet you cannot attack the man who killed your family."

Ulf gripped the handle of his axe tighter as he stared at Theoda. The fear in her eyes made him feel sick, because he knew what was going to happen. And he knew he was right when he spotted the cruel smile on the volva's lips. "What do you want?" He finally managed.

"Ah, there you are." The volva smiled. "The same thing I've always wanted, but to get what I want, I have to do something first."

Ulf frowned, and so did his friends. "What?"

She carried on smiling. "You made an oath to Odin, young wolf. It's time to deliver."

"It's time to fight." Griml beat his chest.

"The gods want this." The volva looked to the sky. Ulf followed her gaze and saw the late summer sky darken. A thick cloud had moved in, covering the sun and casting a grey light around them. Theoda squirmed between the two Danes.

"Thorbjorn!" she cried, his name sounding strange in her accent. Thorbjorn moaned behind Ulf. They all knew what was about to happen. Ulf gripped the hilt of Ormstunga, willing his anger to come to him, willing his ancestors to guide him. Thunder rolled over their heads, but the voices remained silent.

"Ulf!" Snorri shouted again. "We fight together. Remember, the wolf does not hunt alone."

As Snorri said this, Ulf's eyes darted towards the pack of wolves. They had given up on their meal and were watching them like spectators. Ulf grit his teeth and clenched his fist around the hilt of Ormstunga, while his other hand still gripped Olaf's axe. But he still could not get himself to attack. His feet would not obey him.

The volva saw all of this as if she was reading his mind. "It's time."

The Danes seemed to understand what she meant and dragged Theoda in front of Griml. She struggled as she tried to free herself, but the Danes were too strong.

"Thorbjorn! No!" Snorri shouted as Thorbjorn charged past Ulf.

"Theoda!" He stormed at the Danes. One of them let go of Theoda and stepped forward to stop Thorbjorn. Ulf's mind was filled with a sudden silence. Not even his heart seemed to beat in his chest as he watched his friend step underneath the Dane's attack and slice the man's side open with Blood-Thirst. The other Dane pushed Theoda to the ground and attacked, but Thorbjorn moved too fast for the man and stabbed him through the chest before freeing his sword and hacking at the man's neck. Theoda screamed as Griml rushed past her. Thorbjorn turned to face him, but before he could do anything, Griml grabbed his head, his huge hand enveloping it. He lifted Thorbjorn off the ground, laughing as Thorbjorn's legs kicked underneath him in thin air. Thorbjorn dropped his sword and used both his hands to try to free himself, but he could not release himself from Griml's grip.

Griml roared as he threw Thorbjorn to the ground, his dark eyes fixed on Ulf. Thorbjorn did not move as Griml's large mouth parted in an ugly grin. Time slowed for Ulf. In his mind, he saw a burning longhouse that reminded him of his uncle's farmhouse. The house rushed closer, stopping just in front of him and Ulf felt the gust of wind blow past him. The stench of death carried on it. The door of the longhouse swung open, and inside, Ulf saw the same vision he had seen earlier this summer. Bodies piled up high. All the men, women and children who had died since Ulf set off on his quest for vengeance. He saw his uncle, aunt and cousins, Hulda, Vidar and the men of the Sae-Ulfr, all of them staring at him, accusing him with their dead eyes. And now there were two new bodies huddled together as if they were embracing each other. Thorbjorn and Theoda.

You could have saved us, Thorbjorn seemed to say, but his lips were not moving. A shadow parted from the pile of bodies and Ulf realised it was the troll. But not Griml. The troll had not been Griml for a long time now as Ulf spotted the scars matching his own. It laughed a vicious laugh that made him shiver and the house tremble. But then Ulf felt a presence behind him. The troll stopped laughing and sneered as it looked over Ulf's shoulder. Ulf turned around and saw the cloaked figure standing there. Not the old one with the gnarled staff, but the one that seemed younger, yet old at the same time.

I cannot fight him. I cannot defeat him, not on my own. The cloaked figure nodded but said nothing. Instead, it stepped to the side to reveal a pack of wolves. Ulf frowned at first, but when he looked at the wolves, he realised they were familiar to him. One wolf was fat, two of them tall. Another looked angry and would not look at him, but the wolf in the middle stared at Ulf, its eyes fierce. *You are not alone. We fight with you,* it seemed to say to Ulf.

And so do we, another voice said, this one sounding like many voices in one. Ulf turned and saw the warrior beside him, dressed in his war glory. He knew who this warrior was; he had seen him before. The first time he had fought Griml in battle. It was his ancestors, his father and uncle. His entire bloodline standing beside him.

Ulf blinked, and before him was Griml again, standing over the body of Thorbjorn. Theoda was behind Griml, screaming as he lifted his enormous axe in the air with his ugly grin on his face.

Thunder ripped through the skies, igniting the flames inside of Ulf. "Tyr!" he roared as the heat of his fury rushed through his veins and the voices of his ancestors exploded in his ears. Ulf freed his weapons and charged at the stunned-looking Griml. The volva smiled and stepped aside as Ulf's friends rushed up behind him, all of them screaming their own war cries.

Griml quickly recovered and smiled. "Finally." He bent down and picked up Blood-Thirst, Thorbjorn's sword, before charging at Ulf and his friends.

Griml swung his enormous axe in a wide arc, but Ulf dropped to his knees and slid underneath the axe. He tried to cut Griml's leg with a backhanded cut of Ormstunga, but Griml got his leg out of the way while chopping at Snorri with Blood-Thirst. Snorri used his sword to deflect the blow, but Griml's strength knocked him off balance. Griml kept on moving, jabbing at Oddi with his two-handed axe, which Oddi just avoided, while twisting out of the way of Asbjorn's sword stab. Drumbr lifted his two-handed axe above his head, but Griml moved too fast and shoulder barged the big warrior in the chest. Drumbr was sent staggering back, with a look of astonishment on his face, before crashing onto his back. Griml kept moving and was about to chop down on Drumbr with his axe when Magni stabbed at his exposed side. Griml sensed the movement and twisted out of the way, at the same time changing the direction of his axe so it now came for Magni. Magni jumped back, almost stumbling over because of his injured leg, as Griml kept coming for him.

Ulf jumped back to his feet and turned in time to see Griml move through his friends as if they were novice fighters and not some of the best warriors in Norway. He roared as he charged at Griml, axe in one hand and sword in another. Snorri was at his side, his wolf grin replaced by a grim stare. The voices in Ulf's ears pushed him on and he was about to stab Griml through his back, but the giant warrior heard them coming. He turned, faster than a man his size should, and brought both weapons around.

"Ulf! Watch out!" Snorri jumped out of the way.

Ulf didn't hear Snorri, he couldn't through the voices of his ancestors screaming in his ears. He ducked under Thorbjorn's sword and moved too fast for Griml to catch him with his two-handed axe. But Ulf still wasn't fast enough as Griml struck him with the haft of his enormous axe. The blow caught Ulf on the shoulder and sent him flying sideways. Ulf hit the ground and looked up as his friends attacked the giant troll.

Griml was laughing as he knocked Snorri's sword stab to the side with his two-handed axe and cut down with the sword. Snorri jumped out of the way as Oddi tried to use his height to jump above Griml's head and chop down with his sword. But Griml stepped back and sliced at Oddi with Blood-Thirst. Oddi twisted out of the way and brought his sword up to deflect the blow. Griml kicked Snorri in the chest as he tried to cut him in the side and Snorri was sent flying through the air.

"Bastard!" Asbjorn screamed as he attacked. He stabbed at Griml, but Griml twisted out of the way. Asbjorn turned his stab into a backhanded cut which Griml blocked with Thorbjorn's sword. Drumbr bellowed as he shoulder barged Griml in the back, and was stunned when Griml only took a few steps forwards and didn't fall over.

"Odin's arse," he said as he used his axe to block the backhanded cut from Griml.

Ulf spotted an opening and charged. "Tyr!" he roared, his eyes focused on nothing but Griml's midriff. Griml turned and smiled as he chopped down with his two-handed axe. Ulf twisted out of the way and was about to stab at Griml's stomach when the voices in his ears seemed to scream louder. He sensed the sword instead of seeing it and ducked into a roll as it cut the air where his head had been. Ulf rolled to his feet just behind Griml and before the troll could turn, Ulf sliced into his back with Ormstunga. Griml roared in anger and smacked Ulf with his large forearm. The blow sent Ulf spiralling to the ground, and Ulf did all he could to hold on to Ormstunga with his hand weakened from the cut to his arm. Dazed from the blow, Ulf looked up and smiled. The cut wasn't deep, but Griml was bleeding and Ulf knew he could get to him. He just needed his friends to keep Griml busy. Like wolves attacking a large deer from different sides.

CHAPTER 25

Odin, who is this bastard? Snorri wondered as he got to his feet after being kicked in the chest by Griml. It was like being struck by a giant horse, and Snorri was sure his ribs were bruised as he struggled to breathe. They were throwing everything at the troll, but he swatted them all away as if they were children. Snorri glanced at Ulf, seeing him lift his head from the ground, but smiling. He frowned, but then he noticed the blood on Ormstunga's blade. Snorri looked at Griml again and saw the cut to the giant man's back and the blood being soaked up by his trousers. But the cut didn't seem to bother Griml as he twisted out of the way of Magni's sword stab. He was about to chop Magni's arm off when Oddi attacked from the other side. Griml turned and jabbed his two-handed axe at Oddi, who was forced to jump back. Before Magni could react, Griml pulled his arm back and caught Magni on the head with the butt of his axe handle. Snorri grimaced as the blow sounded over him and was glad that Oddi's brother wore a helmet. Although with Griml's strength, that probably didn't matter.

"Magni!" Oddi shouted, as his brother collapsed, and jumped forward, slicing his sword at Griml. Griml took a step back, laughing as he dodged Oddi's attack.

Snorri jumped to his feet and ignored the pain in his chest as he rushed at Griml. Drumbr did the same and the two of them reached the troll at the same time, while Oddi's attack distracted him. But Griml had sensed them coming and changed direction, moving towards Oddi instead of away. A move that caught the tall warrior by surprise. Turning towards Snorri, Griml sliced his two-handed axe through the air. Oddi just avoided the axe and Snorri had to drop to his knees, so he didn't lose his head. Griml kept on turning and then stood his ground as Drumbr charged into him. The two collided like mountains crashing into each other, but somehow Griml stayed where he was while Drumbr stumbled back, dazed from the collision. Snorri and his men were stunned by what they had just seen and Griml used the respite to take a few steps back so they were all in front of him.

"Pathetic."

"Aye, I expected more from you." Snorri grimaced at the pain in his chest. Around him, his men got back to their feet and stood beside him. Drumbr shook his head to clear it, while Ulf tightened his grip on Ormstunga. The cut on his arm was bleeding again and Snorri wondered if that would affect Ulf. Magni stayed down and Snorri sensed that Oddi wanted to see to his brother, but the tall warrior knew he did not have time for that now. Not while the troll still stood in front of them.

Griml smiled, revealing his blackened teeth. Sweat ran down his face, creating a white line in the blood paint. "All I heard was how great Snorri and the wolves of Thorgilsstad are.

Yet the," he paused as he counted them, "six of you can't even touch me."

"You're bleeding," Ulf said through clenched teeth.

Griml touched his back and saw the blood on his hand. He licked his fingers clean. "I let you do that."

Snorri knew it wasn't true, but when he glanced at Ulf, he saw the doubt in Ulf's eyes.

"Don't listen to him," Oddi said, but Ulf did not respond. The fire was still in his eyes and Snorri prayed to Odin it stayed there.

"Only Odin knows why he chose you for his games, but I am not impressed. Just like I wasn't impressed with your uncle. If the two of you are anything to go by, then your ancestors were nothing but limp-dicked goat fuckers."

Before any of them could respond, the giant warrior roared and charged. The ground trembled beneath Snorri's feet, and for the first time in his life, he wondered if he could defeat another man.

*

The voices in Ulf's ears exploded, their anger adding fuel to the flames of Ulf's fury. Griml had just insulted them, and he had to pay. The pain in his arm was forgotten as he watched Griml charge, the grip on his sword strong. Olaf's axe seemed to vibrate in his left hand as if his uncle's spirit had possessed the wood and iron of the weapon.

"Olaf!" he roared and while his friends were bracing themselves for Griml's attack, he charged.

"Fuck!" Snorri charged with Ulf. The others stood their ground, waiting for the right moment to attack.

Ulf reached Griml first and easily evaded his two-handed axe as it chopped down. As he rushed past, he cut Griml's arm, just above the scar he had given the troll at The Giant's Toe. Griml ignored the pain and stabbed at Snorri with Thorbjorn's sword. Snorri twisted out of the way and Griml brought the two-handed axe around to bury it in his chest. But Snorri felt the axe coming and dropped to the ground, as Ulf turned and chopped at Griml's shoulder with Olaf's axe. Griml sensed the attack and twisted out of the way. But now his back was towards the other warriors and they knew it was time to attack. Griml smiled as he heard them roar, and for a heartbeat, Ulf was stunned by his lack of concern. The giant man turned as Oddi reached him, dodging his sword stab. He lifted his two-handed axe and blocked Drumbr's axe, his arm barely bending even though Drumbr put all his effort into the blow. Asbjorn spotted a gap and darted in. Griml caught the movement and tried to turn, but wasn't fast enough as the tip of Asbjorn's sword sliced his stomach. Griml didn't react to the cut as he twisted the two-handed axe, which was still holding Drumbr's axe in the air. The movement caused Drumbr to lose his balance and as he stumbled forward, Griml headbutted him. The sound of their skulls clashing vibrated through the air, and Drumbr collapsed to the ground even though he was wearing a helmet and Griml wasn't.

"Drumbr!" Snorri attacked, his anger at seeing another of his men go down pushing him on. He cut at Griml's leg, but

Griml avoided the blow. Snorri twisted his sword and turned the cut into a stab, which Griml deflected with Blood-Thirst. Ulf rushed in and chopped at Griml's side with Olaf's axe. Griml got his two-handed axe up to block the blow, but could do nothing as Ulf stabbed at his chest with Ormstunga. The sword point moved towards Griml's chest, and Ulf knew there was nothing Griml could do. For a heartbeat, he thought it was over. But Griml straightened his arm, which held the two-handed axe, blocking Ulf's. The movement pulled Ulf back, which meant only the tip of Ormstunga broke the skin on his hairy chest. Asbjorn darted in and stabbed Griml's leg. The giant warrior too focused on Ulf to notice him. He grunted as Asbjorn freed his sword and jumped out of the way of Griml's attack. Griml turned to face Ulf, the smile now replaced by a wild-eyed glare which almost killed the voices in Ulf's ears. He roared as he brought his fist around and punched Ulf in the chest. Ulf stumbled back, struggling to breathe as Griml sliced at him with the two-handed axe. Ulf somehow dodged the blow but could do nothing about the backhanded reverse swing which sent him flying backwards. He landed on top of a corpse, the wind knocked out of him as Ormstunga fell from his weakened grip. Ulf struggled to get up as his friends attacked the now furious Griml.

Oddi aimed a cut high, but Griml sidestepped, and Oddi missed. Snorri stabbed at Griml's back, but again, Griml twisted out of the way. He swung his axe at Snorri, who dodged it before slicing Griml's arm. Griml bellowed as he kicked out, catching Snorri with a glancing blow. Asbjorn tried to take advantage and went for Griml's other leg, but this time Griml saw him coming. He chopped down with Blood-Thirst and as

Asbjorn dodged out of the way, punched with his two-handed axe. Asbjorn twisted, so the head of the axe caught him on the shoulder instead of the chest. But it still threw him to the ground.

The voices screamed at Ulf in his ears, telling him to get up, to fight. But Ulf felt the fear creep into his chest. He watched as Oddi attacked again, but Griml moved faster, and there was nothing Oddi could do as the axe came for his head. Snorri roared as he attacked from behind and it was enough to distract Griml. But somehow Griml stopped his axe mid-swing and changed the direction, so it was now coming towards Snorri. Snorri ducked low, and the axe went over his head, but as he rushed past, Griml brought up his knee and caught Snorri in the side. Snorri was thrown into the air and landed hard on the ground. Oddi stabbed at Griml's face and Griml ducked to avoid it. But Oddi had been hoping for that and threw a punch with his free hand. The blow connected, but Griml was barely affected by it as he stood up and threw a punch of his own, while still gripping the axe. Oddi avoided Griml's fist, but not the haft of the axe which caught him on his helmeted head. Ulf watched as Oddi's legs buckled and his tall friend dropped to the ground.

For a moment, there was nothing but silence. Even the voices in Ulf's ears had left as he stared at the giant form of Griml, the only one left standing. All around him lay Snorri and his hirdmen. Ulf tried to sit up, but his body had no strength left. All he managed was to roll off the corpse he had been lying on. Ulf glanced at it and realised it was one of the hunters from the village. The man had barely spoken to them and had refused to give them any of the meat he had caught, so Ulf didn't care much about seeing him dead. But what Ulf did care about was the bow and arrows that lay under the man's body. Ulf looked at Griml as the troll stood there, glaring at him. A thin trail of blood ran down his chest from where Ulf had stabbed him, and his leg was bleeding heavily from Asbjorn's stab. There were a few more cuts on his arms and torso, but none of them seemed to affect the giant warrior.

What's it going to take to kill him? Above him, a raven cried, and to Ulf, it sounded like the bird was laughing. Probably like the gods were laughing at him for thinking he could kill Griml.

Griml smiled. It was like he could sense Ulf doubting himself and smell the fear creeping into his stomach. Snorri lifted his arm, but looked in no state to get to his feet as Griml dropped Thorbjorn's sword and walked towards him, while grinning at Ulf. The message was obvious and Ulf struggled to breathe as his panic gripped him. He knew he had to get up and save his friend. He glanced at the others. Drumbr looked like he was coming to, but from the way he moved it was obvious he was still dazed from the headbutt. Oddi wasn't moving, but Ulf saw his chest rising and falling. Asbjorn was struggling to get to his feet, gripping his shoulder where Griml had struck him. But Ulf knew that none of them were able to save Snorri. Griml stood over him now, his grin wide as he lifted his axe over his head. Ulf had to do something. He grabbed the body of the hunter and rolled it over, groaning at the effort. He picked up the bow, the hunter's weapon awkward in his hand. The cut to his arm stung as Ulf gripped the wood. His hand was slick with blood and Ulf hoped he would be able to hold on to the bow. He had never used one before, but had seen many hunters use them, and it never looked difficult. Griml stopped what he was doing and watched as Ulf fumbled an arrow into place and pulled back on the cord, groaning with effort. It was a lot harder than he thought it would be, and when Ulf pulled it back as far as he could, he aimed the arrow at Griml, who just stood there laughing.

"Fuck you," Ulf muttered through clenched teeth, and let go of the arrow. But instead of flying true and straight and burying itself in Griml's chest, it skewed to the side. "Fuck!" Ulf grabbed another arrow and tried it again, but like before, the arrow skewed off to the side.

"Pathetic." Griml laughed as he lifted his axe up high and brought it down.

"No!" Ulf shouted, bow still in his hand. But Snorri somehow rolled out of the way and Griml's axe buried itself in the dirt. Before Ulf could make sense of it, Asbjorn roared as he launched himself at Griml.

Griml twisted out of the way of the attack and, as Asbjorn's sword missed, he chopped down with his two-handed axe. The axe sliced through Asbjorn's leg, severing it with a spray of blood. Asbjorn fell to the ground, screaming loud enough to wake the giants in Niflheim. "Quiet you!" Griml chopped down with his axe, silencing Asbjorn. Ravens took to the skies, screaming as if they were sending Asbjorn to Valhalla.

The world around Ulf seemed to stop. He felt the thump in his chest as if something exploded inside of him. The heat seared his veins as his anger took hold of him and the voices of his ancestors roared in his ears like waves crashing down in a storm. He forgot about his fears and his exhaustion. Forgot about the pain in his arm as he grabbed Olaf's axe, the weapon of his uncle. The weapon he had sworn his vengeance on. The axe seemed to roar as Ulf gripped it and charged at Griml.

Griml saw Ulf coming and turned to face him, his axe in both hands. His dark eyes fixed on Ulf.

"Tyr!"

Griml twisted out of the way of Ulf's attack and, as Ulf ran past, swung his own axe at him. Ulf sensed the movement and ducked, feeling the two-handed axe slice through the air above his head. He turned and chopped at Griml's leg, but Griml got it out of the way. He grabbed Ulf by his brynja and threw him through the air. Ulf landed hard, but the voices in his head would not let him rest. They screamed at him as he jumped back to his feet and attacked again. Griml expected this and chopped down with his two-handed axe. Ulf dodged and sliced at Griml's shoulder. Somehow, Griml got his axe up in time to block the blow, the motion causing Ulf to spin around. Griml struck him on the shoulder with the handle of his axe, the blow numbing his left arm. Ulf stumbled out of the way of the next attack, Griml's axe missing him by a finger, but it was now Griml's turn to fight. Ulf twisted and dodged, doing everything he could to avoid Griml's axe and fist, the voices of his ancestors shrieking in his ears, refusing to let him give in. But as before, Ulf could not find a way through Griml's defence. Every time he thought he spotted an opening and attacked, Griml moved out of the way or blocked the blow. Griml swung his axe in a wide arc, a blow that would chop Ulf in half, but the voices in Ulf's head screamed and Ulf listened. He ducked under the axe and stepped forward, pulling his sax-knife out of her scabbard. Before Griml could react, Ulf stabbed him in the leg, just above where Asbjorn had stabbed him before. Griml roared and brought his axe around again. This time there was nothing Ulf could do as the flat side of the axe struck him and sent him flying through the air again. As he hit the ground, the voices in his head went silent. Ulf looked up, his head swimming, and saw Griml limping towards him, this time not wanting to give Ulf the time to get up. Ulf was suddenly exhausted. With the voices gone, he felt all the pains in his body. His left shoulder ached and his arm was numb. The cut on his right hand stung, and Ulf struggled to keep hold of Olaf's axe. His head ached as well, but Ulf had no time to wonder about that as Griml reached him.

"Now you die, young wolf." Griml lifted his axe, but as he brought it down, it was like he was struck by a gigantic bear. For a heartbeat, Ulf believed it was the bear he had fought in the forest and thought Tyr had sent it to help him. But when he blinked, he realised it was Drumbr who had shoulder barged Griml. Griml stumbled to the side but brought his axe around and swung it at Drumbr. Drumbr blocked the attack, but the force of the blow sent him a few steps back. Ulf gripped Olaf's axe tight as he struggled to his feet while Drumbr was forced to block another attack from Griml. *Uncle, help me kill him.*

Ulf felt empty as he watched Drumbr fight Griml, the two men like giants bashing each other with their huge axes, but Griml seemed to have the upper hand. The voices of his ancestors had left him, and Ulf's right hand struggled to keep hold of the axe. *I have failed you,* he thought as his friend fought the troll. Drumbr lifted his axe high and grunted as he brought it down hard. Griml twisted out of the way and punched Drumbr on the side of his head. Drumbr's legs wobbled, but the large warrior stayed on his feet. Not that it mattered for Griml.

He grinned as he lifted his axe for the killing blow. The scene reminded Ulf of the last time he had seen his uncle as he stood in front of Griml, his legs weak and face bloody. Griml about to kill him. In his mind, Ulf saw his uncle look at him. *Ulf*, he seemed to say.

Olaf's axe seemed to vibrate in his hand, or perhaps it was Ulf's hand shaking. The flames of his anger burst to life inside of him again. "Olaf!" Ulf charged at Griml.

Griml glanced at Ulf, his eyebrow raised. Drumbr saw his chance and came to life. He swung his two-handed axe and there was a loud thud as it buried itself into Griml's stomach. Time slowed for Ulf as the voices of his ancestors came to him again. The blood droplets flying from Griml's body as he saw the shock in Griml's eyes and the whites of them for the first time. Griml grunted and dropped to one knee, a grimace on his face. Ulf roared his uncle's name as he launched himself into the air, Olaf's axe above his head. All of his anger and pain and all of his fears surged through his arm before he buried the axe deep in Griml's head. The handle of Olaf's axe broke where it had been cut from the fight with Ubba, leaving Ulf with the lower part of it in his hand.

Griml just sat there, axe head embedded in his skull and blood running down his face. He smiled at Ulf. "Your... uncle... squealed... like... pig..."

Ulf grabbed hold of the axe head and thrust the broken axe handle through Griml's neck and into his head. Hot blood sprayed onto his hand as he stared into Griml's dark eyes. He saw Griml's spirit leave them and, with it, the last of Ulf's strength. As Griml's body collapsed, Ulf dropped to his knees. The heat of his anger was gone, the voices of his ancestors as well. All Ulf heard was his own laboured breathing and Drumbr panting nearby.

There was a flap of wings, and when Ulf looked up, he saw the raven land on Olaf's axe. The dark bird stared at him before it cawed.

"What do you want?" Ulf asked the bird. He was aware of Drumbr watching him, but did not care. The raven cawed again as it flapped its wings. "Tell Odin it is done. Griml is dead. I completed my oath." The raven tilted its head, and with one last caw, it took to the sky.

CHAPTER 26

Snorri lay on his back, seeing nothing but the darkening sky. He tried to breathe, but the pain in his chest made it difficult. Rolling onto his front, Snorri groaned as he struggled to his knees. He regretted that instantly as he clutched his ribs, the pain even worse now. He hoped he had not broken a rib and struggled to recall how he hurt himself. It felt like a giant had struck him, not once, but a few times. And then he remembered. It was not a giant, but almost as good as. His heart thudded in his chest, the vibrations sending fresh waves of pain through him as he took in the surrounding scene. Death was everywhere. Death and chaos as countless ravens and crows filled the ground around him, their cries ringing in his ears. Foxes and wolves wandered around looking for corpses not yet ravished by the scavenging birds. Even eagles and vultures got their fill. But none of this drew Snorri's attention.

It was Ulf, sitting on his knees, his head hanging low. Drumbr stood near him. The big man swayed as he took off his helmet, blood running down his face. But it was what was in front of Ulf that really got his heartbeat up, which he wished it hadn't because of the pain.

"It's over?" he muttered as he pulled his helmet off. Strands of light-coloured hair covered his face, but Snorri ignored them as he looked for his sword. He found her lying on the ground beside him, her blade clean. Thorbjorn's sword was there as well, which confused Snorri at first, until he remembered Griml fighting with it. He shook his head, glad he had not been killed by his friend's sword, as he picked both swords up and struggled to his feet, gasping at the pain. As he stumbled towards Ulf and Drumbr, he spotted Oddi lying on the ground, staring into the sky as he did before. Oddi was alive, which brought a smile to Snorri's face, but he looked like a mountain had collapsed on him.

"What you smiling at?" Oddi asked, his voice strained.

Snorri looked up at Ulf again. "I think it's over."

"Who won?"

Snorri laughed, but grimaced straight away and clutched his chest. "Not you."

"Aye, well, Odin knows you don't look much better." Oddi struggled to his feet and stood bent over as he surveyed the scene. "I need to find Magni." Snorri noticed the slight dent in Oddi's helmet and the blood trailing down from underneath it.

"I think he's still where he last was." Snorri pointed to where Magni lay, unmoving.

Oddi nodded and stumbled towards his brother. "Bastard better not be dead. He's supposed to take my father's place."

"You don't want to be jarl?" Snorri frowned, even though he knew the answer.

"Who's going to keep you alive if I'm not there?"

"Aye, doing a great job of it." Snorri smiled at Oddi, and the tall man just nodded before going to his brother. Snorri stood where he was for a moment, breathing slowly so as not to hurt his chest. He looked around, trying to find the rest of his hirdmen. Theoda was near the village, huddling over something. Snorri remembered that something was Thorbjorn. "Odin, let my friends still be alive," he prayed, but knew it would be a miracle if that were the case. He carried on walking towards Ulf, still struggling to make sense of what he was seeing. Drumbr nodded at him, but the large man did not look capable of speaking as he sat down and wiped the blood from his head.

Snorri stood over Ulf and just stared at the body of Griml. The head of Ulf's axe was stuck in Griml's skull; the handle broken off. Under Griml's beard was something that looked like wood sticking out from the troll's neck and he guessed it was the rest of the axe handle. He regretted not seeing how Ulf had killed Griml. That would be the greatest saga ever told. Snorri then spotted the large gash in Griml's stomach and frowned, unsure of what might have caused that. He looked around and saw Drumbr's axe and the blood on the blade. *Looks like I missed a lot.*

"Ulf?" he asked. But Ulf did not move. He just sat there like the statues in the square in Thorgilsstad. "Ulf?" Snorri tried again and for a moment thought his friend was dead. That Odin had taken him after Ulf fulfilled his oath. But then Ulf turned his head.

"He's dead," Ulf said, his voice so soft, Snorri only just caught the words over the sounds of the scavenging birds.

"Aye, he is," was the only thing Snorri could say. He was still struggling to make sense of seeing the troll dead. Snorri had fought in more battles than he could remember, but he had never fought anyone like this before. His hand trembled as the thought came to him. *This was the greatest warrior in all of Midgard.* Of that, Snorri had no doubt. He knew he would never have been able to defeat the man if he had to fight him alone. Snorri looked around at his battered hirdmen. The six of them could barely defeat him.

"I hope we never come across a bastard like him again," Drumbr echoed his thoughts. "Don't think I've ever been in so much pain."

"Aye, still struggling to make sense of it." He breathed in deep and grimaced. "For a moment, I thought he'd kill us all."

"He killed Asbjorn," Ulf said, "and maybe Thorbjorn and Magni."

"No, Thorbjorn is still alive." Snorri could see his friend moving and the smile on Theoda's face. *At least one of them is happy.* And then he saw Asbjorn. "By Odin," he muttered as he stumbled towards his friend.

Asbjorn lay on the ground, not far from where Griml was, his right leg severed. Snorri saw it next to him. There was a large gash in Asbjorn's chest, between his neck and shoulder. Snorri shook his head. Asbjorn had been against Ulf joining them from the beginning, and now his friend lay here, dead. Still clutching his chest, Snorri knelt down, grimacing at the pain. He cupped Asbjorn's face. "I'll see you in Valhalla, my friend." Snorri was about to turn away when Asbjorn opened his eyes.

"Snorri," Asbjorn said, his voice weak. He spat blood and looked at Snorri with pain-filled eyes. "F... for... give m... me."

Tears stung Snorri's eyes. "There's nothing to forgive. You fought like a god and earned your place in Odin's hall."

"N... no." Asbjorn coughed and spat out more blood. Snorri was aware of Drumbr's presence behind him. "I t... told G... Gei... to g... go." He coughed more blood out as Snorri frowned at him.

"You told Geir to go to the beach?"

Asbjorn nodded, tears streaming down his face.

"Why?" Drumbr asked over Snorri's shoulder.

"Sh... she told..." He coughed.

"The volva?" Snorri grimaced at the pain in his chest as he leaned forward. Asbjorn nodded. "What did she say?"

Asbjorn opened his mouth to speak, but then coughed. Blood sprayed over Snorri's face, but he didn't move away. He needed to know. "Fo... forgive m... me." Asbjorn's head dropped to the side as his last breath left him.

Snorri stayed as he was, his hand still cupping Asbjorn's face.

"What did he mean by that?" Drumbr moved around Snorri so he could get a better view of Asbjorn.

Snorri sighed, the weight of what Asbjorn had just said heavy on him. "He sent Geir to the beach. He knew Griml would come, and he sent Geir to tell Griml where to find us." Snorri glanced over his shoulder at Ulf, still on his knees by Griml's body. "To find Ulf."

"But why?" Drumbr frowned as he scratched the back of his head.

Snorri was still looking at Ulf. "You know as well as I do that Asbjorn never liked Ulf, never wanted him to join."

"Aye, but he was still one of us. He was our friend, so why would he do that to us?"

Snorri frowned. He was wondering the same. "Only the gods know that. Perhaps he thought that Griml would only attack Ulf."

"But what about Geir? Why send him?"

"I don't know, Drumbr. And the only people that do are dead." Snorri stood up, clutching his chest against the pain.

"Not all," Drumbr said. "The volva. Asbjorn said she told him to do it."

Snorri looked towards the burnt-out village. That was the last place they saw her, before the fight with Griml. "Aye, but I doubt she hung around to answer our questions." He looked at Drumbr. "Say nothing about this. Not to anyone." Drumbr nodded and the two of them looked up as Oddi walked towards them, his face drawn. "Magni?"

Oddi stopped and looked at Asbjorn's body. "He breathes, but he took a hard blow to the head. Until he wakes up, there's no knowing how he is."

If he wakes up, Snorri thought, but didn't say. He didn't have to. Oddi would be aware of that. They had both seen those kinds of injuries before. Theoda shouted at them and when they looked, they saw her waving at them.

"Looks like she's calling us," Oddi said.

"Aye," Snorri responded and the three of them walked towards Theoda. Towards the burnt-out village. Snorri gripped the hilt of Tyr's Fury. Not because he expected another fight, but because he was worried the volva might still be around.

When they reached Theoda, they saw Thorbjorn's eyes were open. Snorri ran his eyes over his short friend, but there were no signs of any injuries. But then, Griml was huge and had thrown Thorbjorn down hard. "You gonna stop lying around like a lazy ox?"

"Too small for an ox," Drumbr added. "A small dog maybe." The three of them smiled.

"Aye, have your fun now, but as soon as I get up, I'll kick all your arses." Thorbjorn grimaced.

"Can you get up?" Snorri asked, his face serious now.

"I still feel all my limbs, so I guess so."

"Then why are you still lying around?" Oddi asked.

Thorbjorn glanced at Theoda and smiled. "She's not given me a chance." Theoda smiled back, unaware of what they were talking about. Her eyes were red, her cheeks tear-streaked, but she lived, and Snorri was glad for that. "I take it the fight is over and that we won, seeing as you're all standing here looking like a herd of oxen ran you over."

Snorri smiled. "Aye, it's over."

Thorbjorn sat up with a groan and looked around. He spotted his sword in Snorri's hand and frowned before seeing Ulf and the body of Griml. "Ulf killed the troll?"

Snorri nodded, clutching his chest again. Breathing easier now, but it still hurt. "Although Odin knows, at one point it looked like he was going to kill us all."

"Aye, I can see." Thorbjorn looked at the three of them again. "Asbjorn?"

Snorri shook his head.

"Fought like a bastard, Asbjorn. Almost had him," Drumbr said. "I've never seen a man that big move like that."

"Aye," Oddi agreed. "It's like he wasn't human at all."

"Then how did Ulf kill him?" Thorbjorn asked.

"Well, he had some help," Snorri smiled. "Now, if you don't mind, Thorbjorn. We have things to do." Snorri looked to the sky. "It'll be dark soon. There's no point heading to the ship now. And besides, I'm not leaving Asbjorn's body for the scavengers." Snorri caught the glance from Drumbr, but ignored it. Despite what Asbjorn did, he had still been a friend and had always been loyal to Snorri.

They spent the rest of the day searching for wood to build a funeral pyre for Asbjorn. Most of the wood in the village had already been burnt and none of the men had the strength to go to the forest and chop more. Ulf had finally stirred himself from staring at the corpse of Griml, but he was more solemn than ever.

"You'd think he'd be happy now that Griml is dead," Thorbjorn commented as he hobbled beside Snorri, carrying some wood that hadn't been burnt too badly. "I mean, he's not the most cheerful to be around at the best of times, but this?"

"Aye, it's not like he'd spent the last two winters talking about anything else," Drumbr added.

Snorri looked at his young friend, feeling the mix of emotions inside. Ulf walked nearby, his head hanging low and his left arm dangling. Oddi had looked at the arm and said it was just bruised, but Ulf still struggled to move it. But then, they were all nursing injuries, even Thorbjorn, who had not even taken part in the fight. He moved stiffly and, like the rest of them, wore a constant grimace on his face.

"Revenge never satisfies as much as people expect," Snorri said. He took a deep breath and glanced to where Asbjorn's body lay. Oddi was busy preparing him for the funeral, cleaning him as best as he could, and polishing his armour. He needed to look his best when he reached Valhalla. "Especially when the price is so high."

Thorbjorn and Drumbr stayed quiet, both men lost in their thoughts. Snorri struggled with his own feelings for Ulf. He had always felt a strange connection to the scarred warrior. At times, he thought it was because Ulf had saved him from the bear, but sometimes it seemed like it was more than that. That was one reason Snorri wanted to help Ulf get his vengeance. The other reason was because he had thought it would be fun. An adventure worthy of the sagas, and the first time he saw Griml, he knew they would make many sagas from this quest. But now, when he had lost so much himself? Many of his crew perished, his ship gone, and worst of all, the betrayal of not just his brother but also a man he had fought beside for many winters. A man who was one of his best friends. He still didn't understand how Asbjorn could have done that. Not liking Ulf was not reason enough to send Geir to his death and to bring the wrath of the troll onto them. Perhaps one day in Valhalla, Snorri would find out the truth, but until then he had to keep this dark secret to himself. He wanted to remember Asbjorn as the friend and warrior he had been. Snorri glanced at Ulf again, who was staring at the body of Asbjorn, the frown on his face showing his own internal battle. Was Ulf to blame for this? Snorri still didn't think so, but he knew who was and he swore that when he found her, he would cut her head off and feed it to the fish, regardless of her power.

"You're turning into Ulf now," Thorbjorn said. Snorri looked at him, his eyebrow raised. "Too much thinking, you and the big man." He thumbed at Drumbr.

Snorri smiled. "Just tired. These last few days have been nothing but chaos."

"Aye, Odin should be pleased," Drumbr said, rubbing his Mjöllnir around his neck.

"Well, I say we should hurry and get out of here." Thorbjorn glanced at all the corpses, still covered by ravens, crows and vultures. The wolves had left, but there were still a few foxes sniffing around. "There'll be too many unhappy spirits here when the sun disappears."

"Aye, but we need to give Asbjorn a proper funeral. He deserves that much."

"As did Brak." Drumbr cuffed away a tear.

"Aye, so he did."

A short while later, as the sun slipped behind the horizon, the group stood beside the funeral pyre. They had stacked all the wood they could find, which was not much, but Snorri thought it would do. Asbjorn's body lay on top of the stacks of wood, his brynja and helmet shining brightly. On his chest were his sword and sax-knife, as well as a shield they found. His leg was placed by his corpse as if it was still attached. The men thought it would be a good idea, then he would still have his leg when he reached Valhalla. Snorri held a torch in his hand and was trying to think of anything to say, but for once, he could not find the words. He looked at the body of his friend, but also saw the faces of all the men he had lost. Ulf's biggest battle had been fighting Griml. Snorri's would be explaining to his village why so many of their men did not come back.

"Snorri, it's time." Oddi nudged him and Snorri realised the sun was completely gone now. The only light came from the torch in his hand and the half-moon in the sky. Thorbjorn's eyes kept darting around as if expecting the dead to stand up and attack them, but the rest of the men were solemn. Theoda stood beside Thorbjorn, her hand on his shoulder. For a moment, Snorri wondered what she was making of all of this. But then he took a breath, feeling the pain in his chest still, and walked towards the funeral pyre. He stabbed the torch into the grass they had stuffed between the gaps in the wood and watched as the flames took. Most of the wood had already been burnt and Snorri worried it might not burn again, but Odin wanted Asbjorn for his Einherjar and the flames suddenly burst into life.

"See you in Valhalla, my friend and brother."

"In Valhalla," the men echoed behind him.

"It's a pity there's no ale," Drumbr said.

"Aye, the bastard's not gonna be happy that he had a sober funeral," Thorbjorn agreed. "He was one of the best warriors I knew."

Thorbjorn started telling a story of a past battle they had all been in. Snorri remembered the fight. Asbjorn fought like a god that day, as he had every day. The men listened and told their own stories of Asbjorn, as the flames consumed the corpse.

Ulf stepped forward and stood next to Snorri. He held the head of Olaf's axe in his hand, the blade still covered in Griml's blood. Drumbr had pulled it free, and Ulf had not let go of it since. It was like he was not sure what to do with it. "I'm sorry, Snorri."

Snorri sighed, but did not take his eyes off the flames. "Why are you sorry?"

"Asbjorn… and the rest. They all died because of me."

Snorri clenched his fist. They had had this conversation so many times already since the battle at The Giant's Toe. "No, Ulf. Their deaths are not on you." He took a deep breath and ignored the pain in his chest. "Their deaths are all my fault." He felt Ulf stare at him, but did not look. "I'm the one who decided to help you."

CHAPTER 27

Ulf stood in the darkness. He could see nothing, but he knew he was not alone. He sensed his wolf brothers behind him. His hand went to his side, but as expected, there was no Ormstunga or Olaf's axe. He waited, expecting the old cloaked figure with the gnarled staff or the one-handed one to appear, but nothing happened. There was no noise, no breeze. Nothing but dark silence.

"Hello!" he shouted, but silence was the only response he got. Ulf took a few steps forward. The ground under his feet was dry and firm. He sniffed the air. There was no smell of burning houses, but there was the faint smell of salt in the air. The same you would get when you were sailing. "Hello!" He tried again. "Where are you?" Still nothing. Ulf's anger grew inside of him - something else that was different from previous dreams. He clenched his fists as he shouted into the darkness. "I killed him! The troll is dead! It's over!" The ground beneath his feet suddenly moved, causing Ulf to lose his balance. *What was that?*

The silence was interrupted by a laugh. A laugh so cruel it filled him with fear as the familiar cold returned and Ulf heard a whine behind him. *The troll is dead, but it's not over yet.* The voice whispered in his head, sounding serpent-like yet familiar.

"What do you mean?" Something tugged at his memory again. The same feeling he had since he met the volva in the forest. Something his mind wanted him to remember.

Remember, young wolf, the voice whispered in his head again.

"Remember what?" The ground rocked under his feet, the sensation of it so familiar to him. As if in answer, a light appeared on the horizon like the rising sun. Ulf took a step back as he realised he was standing on the deck of the Sae-Ulfr. Behind him stood four wolves, the same ones which were there in his last dream. But one was missing. Ulf knew who it was, but he could not think about that right now. Because in front of him was a giant serpent's head, its eyes as blue as an old glacier with pupils so dark it was like staring into nothing. Black scales covered its head, and as it opened its mouth, Ulf saw fangs as tall as the mast.

Remember, the serpent seemed to say to Ulf as its tongue flicked out, and Ulf saw a part of it was missing. *Jörmungandr.*

Ulf grit his teeth as the wolves behind him growled. "I am not afraid of you." Jörmungandr pulled its head back, laughing at Ulf, but then stared at him with its soulless eyes.

"You do not need to fear the serpent, but it is right, Bjørnson." A different voice said to him. Ulf turned and saw the cloaked figure standing beside him and holding a gnarled staff.

"Odin?" Ulf asked, and the giant serpent laughed again, the sound of it sending waves of fear through him. "What must I remember?"

"Remember," Jörmungandr said in its serpent-like voice.

Ulf looked at the old figure again, frowning, as he turned to Ulf and struck him with the staff. Ulf brought his arms up to protect himself, but just before the staff connected, he heard the cry of an eagle and found himself soaring high above the ship. The wolves ran around the deck, all of them howling at him. He saw Jörmungandr circling the Sae-Ulfr in the water, but before he could take in its true size, he was whisked away. Ulf sped towards the land as distant mountains and trees rushed towards him. This was all so familiar to him, like he had done this before. As he flew over forests and valleys, Ulf started to remember. He stopped over a clearing and hovered in the sky as he watched the two large wolf packs, with one smaller than the other. He watched as they attacked each other and the enormous bear ripped its way through the larger pack. None of the wolves facing it could get near enough to kill it. Next to the bear, a magnificent wolf, the one that looked like the leader of that pack, fell. Ulf understood what was happening. The fight he was watching seemed so familiar to him, but he knew it was not one he had fought.

Remember, the voice said to him as the bear turned to the fallen wolf. It growled at the opposing wolves, keeping them at bay so the pack leader could get up. But it didn't. The wolf remained on the ground and glanced behind the bear, where a young wolf with red-tinted fur was creeping up closer.

Remember, the voice said again, and Ulf screamed as the young wolf bit into the back of the bear. The bear rose on its back legs, its head turned to the sky as it cried in pain.

"Why are you showing me this?" Ulf shouted at the clouds.

Thunder ripped through the sky as the bear dropped to the ground and the wolves finished it off. Ulf wanted to dive down and help the bear, but a strong wind appeared out of nowhere and blew him away. Thunder sounded again as rain lashed down and the world around Ulf went dark.

*

Ulf spluttered awake as the wave washed over him. He spat out seawater as the men on the ship laughed and seabirds cried in the sky above.

"Told you we should move him," Thorbjorn said.

"And where would the fun be in that?" Drumbr laughed.

Ulf stared at them, frowning as he struggled to understand where he was. At first, he thought he was still dreaming and looked at the sea as the waves crashed against the hull of the ship, half expecting Jörmungandr to raise her head from the water.

"Ulf?" Thorbjorn raised an eyebrow. "Did the wave wash your wits away?"

Ulf looked at Thorbjorn again and then at Drumbr with a large bruise on the side of his head and a cut in the middle of it. Theoda sat near them, her face green as she leaned on the side of the ship. Magni was lying on some furs and cloaks by the mast, his head swollen, but his eyes were open and he was smiling. The cut to his leg had been cleaned and re-bandaged. Oddi sat with him, his head also bruised and cut. The two brothers were talking as Oddi gave Magni a cup of water to drink.

"I think the waves did." Drumbr frowned at him. "Or perhaps Griml bashed them away."

At the mention of the troll, Ulf grabbed the axe head on his lap and remembered where he was.

After Asbjorn's funeral, the men were too tired to go anywhere and just fell asleep where they were, in the burnt-out village of Ansovald. Thorbjorn had protested, but then Theoda shouted at him in her language and he kept quiet. Ulf was not sure if any of the spirits had wandered around during the night. He had been too exhausted to be bothered by them, but in the morning, they all woke up and no one was missing. Magni had also woken up, much to the relief of Oddi. His head was sore, but Magni could talk and seemed to be aware of where he was. The morning after the fight, they were all exhausted, in pain and hungry. There was no food, so they just sat there, all of them staring at the remains of Asbjorn's funeral pyre. Not that much was left at that point. Only ash and Asbjorn's armour and sword.

Ulf's arm had still been numb, and moving it sent agonising pain through his shoulder. The cut on his arm had been cleaned and bandaged with some cloth Theoda ripped from her skirt. The only other cloth available was on the dead, and none of the men wanted to use that. Thorbjorn was the least injured of them all, and so they sent him to the river to get some water and when he returned, he had a big smile on his face. At first, everyone was confused, and then Theoda screamed as she saw the ship rowing along the river. Confusion had taken hold of them all until they recognised the red hair of Ragnar by the stern. The men on the ship had cheered and Snorri and others laughed. Ragnar had taken the ship and waited all night for them. When the sun rose the next morning and they had not arrived, he used the high tide to go upriver and find them. That was when he spotted Thorbjorn filling up the water flasks. Soon after, they were all on the Danes' ship and were heading back out to sea. Ulf had fallen asleep as soon as the ship left the burnt-out village.

The ship was bigger than the Sae-Ulfr, which explained how Griml had brought so many men with him. Ragnar had explained that only a handful of Danes had been left to guard the ship and they gave up rather than fight the Norsemen. Ragnar had them stripped of everything, including their clothes, and chased them away. He had not wanted to deal with Danish captives.

"They would have been useful as thralls for the king," Snorri had commented.

"Aye, well maybe next time I'll remember that," Ragnar responded.

Ulf got to his feet, groaning at the pain in his shoulder, and made his way to the stern where Snorri stood with Ragnar. Thorbjorn followed him, leaving Theoda where she was, but she seemed too sick to care. The sky was clouded and the strong wind made the water choppy, but at least the men did not have to row. There weren't enough of them for the size of the ship and rowing would have been hard, especially as the men themselves were still tired. Ulf stopped by Oddi and Magni, both men looking up at him.

"How you feeling?" Oddi looked at him, his left eye shut from the bruise.

"Not sure yet." Ulf surprised himself with his honesty.

"Aye, I know how you feel." Magni gave him a weak smile. "But when we get back home, we will drink until we feel nothing and then drink some more."

Thorbjorn laughed beside Ulf. "For once, Magni, you and I agree."

Ulf smiled and continued towards Snorri, who was watching him with a smile. "The Troll-Slayer is awake."

"Heard you killed the bastard using the skull of a dead Frank," Ragnar said, but there was no mockery in his voice. He glanced at Snorri, who couldn't hide his smile.

"Not sure how I killed him." He looked at Snorri, his face suddenly serious. "But I couldn't have done it without your help."

"Told you, Ulf. You don't fight alone."

"Enough of this, you're going to make me cry," Thorbjorn mocked and then looked at the front of the ship. "So we going home?"

"Aye," Snorri nodded, "but we need to go see Halfdan the Black first."

"Why do we need to go to the king first?" Thorbjorn asked. "He'll not be happy when he sees us."

Snorri looked to the sky, his eyes following the flight of the seabirds before answering. "Aye, but he'll be even less pleased if we don't go to him first. And with Thorgilsstad depleted of warriors, we need to keep him happy."

"Won't be easy. We have nothing to give him." Ragnar turned the tiller slightly, using some cue Ulf couldn't see to know where to go.

"There's some plunder on board the ship. It looks like the Danes were busy loading their share of the loot when Griml took over. That and this ship might be enough to calm him." Snorri frowned, and Ulf could tell that even he wasn't so sure.

"So we go home empty-handed." Thorbjorn crossed his arms.

"At least we go home," Snorri said, and Thorbjorn nodded.

"Can always give that Frank as a thrall. The king likes them big." Ragnar smiled.

Thorbjorn's mouth dropped open and before he could say anything, Snorri responded, "I don't think the king can handle her, so for his safety, we'll hide her away." They laughed and then grew solemn once more.

"Just glad this is over." Thorbjorn rubbed the Mjöllnir around his neck.

"I don't know." Ulf's eyes were fixed on Ragnar. There was something that was drawing Ulf to him, something that suddenly bothered him about Ragnar.

"What do you mean?" Snorri frowned.

Ulf thought back to his dream, seeing the fight between the two wolf packs in his mind. "I feel there is more to come. I don't think the volva or the gods are quite done with us yet."

CHAPTER 28

It took them a few days to reach Yngling Hall, the home of Halfdan the Black, the King of Vestfold. The journey had been quiet and morose as the men knew they would not receive a warm welcome. They had spent most of the time sleeping and recovering from their injuries and sailed through the nights, as Snorri did not want to risk going on land. There was some food on the ship, left behind by the Danes, and a barrel the men filled with fresh water before they left. The other thing there was plenty of was wind, which the men were grateful for, and occasionally, Snorri would throw an arm ring into the sea to ask the gods for more wind. Ran seemed to be pleased with them, but then she had got her lover back, so she left them alone and gave them calm water. It was strange being on a ship and not seeing Rolf Treefoot at the tiller, his eyes closed yet still aware of where they were going.

Ulf stood on the prow of the Danish warship and watched as the town of the king grew bigger in the distance. The cut on his right arm started to heal, and he thanked the gods that it had not festered. Oddi had rinsed it with seawater, which stung so badly it brought tears to Ulf's eyes, but now it was wrapped in a clean bandage. His left shoulder was better as well. It still hurt when he moved his arm, and he had a large purple and black bruise, but at least he could move it and grip things. The only other injury he had was a minor cut on his stomach, but that was barely noticeable considering his other injuries. His friends were slowly recovering as well, although Oddi and Drumbr still had bruised faces. Magni was on his feet again, but he had a large lump on his head and suffered from headaches. Snorri still struggled with his chest. His friend said nothing about it, but Ulf saw the grimaces every time he moved or breathed in deeply.

"Not quite the same anymore, is it?" Thorbjorn stood next to Ulf, both men staring at their destination. Theoda was sitting by Thorbjorn's feet, her face a little less green. The calm waters made her feel better, but she still struggled with the motion.

"It looks smaller." Ulf thought of the larger towns and cities in Francia. When they first came here, Ulf had been amazed by the size of the king's town, but now it was less impressive.

"Aye, that happens. But don't tell the king that." Thorbjorn smiled and then watched as another warship approached them. "We've got company!" he shouted to the back of the ship. Snorri saw the ship and waved. Ragnar changed direction slightly so the other ship could come beside them. "They don't recognise the ship. Come to see who we are," Thorbjorn explained when he noticed Ulf's frown.

That made sense to Ulf, so he nodded. The approaching ship was filled with warriors, most of them rowing because they were going into the wind, but some stood by the prow, shields and weapons ready.

"Now the fun begins," Snorri said as he appeared beside them, his grey eyes fixed on the other ship. It was smaller than the one they were on, but she carried more men than Snorri had. "Trim the sail!" Snorri ordered, and a few men rushed to untie the ropes and pull the sail in. The ship slowed as the other one turned to head them off. "Greetings!" Snorri shouted with his hand cupped to his mouth and a grimace on his face.

The approaching ship came close enough for Ulf to see the warrior standing by the prow. Ulf recognised the man from the king's hall the last time they were here. The warrior was shorter than Ulf, but not by much. He had some grey hair in his beard, but still looked strong as he stood with one foot on the gunwale and his hand on the hilt of his sheathed sword. He wore no helmet, his dark hair lifting in the wind. "By Odin," the man said, his eyes scanning the ship he did not recognise and the men on board. "Snorri Thorgilsson."

"Aye, the very same." Snorri waved at the man.

"This is not your ship?" The man looked at one of the warriors to his side, who shook his head.

"No, the Sae-Ulfr is lost." Ulf heard the sadness in Snorri's voice. "This ship belonged to some Danes."

"Danes?" The man scratched his head. "Surprised she floats then." He ran his eyes over Snorri's crew, most likely seeing how few of them there were. "How was the raid? We heard from some traders that a large city to the east had been taken."

Snorri did not respond straight away. He looked at Ulf, and then back at the warrior. "We bring gifts for the king."

The warrior scrutinised Snorri and his men before nodding. "Follow us and we'll show you where to dock."

Snorri waved to the man and then turned to his small crew. "Those who can grab some oars and follow Sigurd's ship."

"Sigurd's one of Halfdan's best men. He's also as wily as a fox, so be careful what you say around him," Thorbjorn explained to Ulf. Ulf nodded and saw Sigurd watching them as his ship turned and rowed towards the town. Seabirds hovered above them, their cries echoing off the water. When the birds realised there was no food for them here, they left to harass other ships.

Only a handful of the men were well enough to row and they did their best to keep up with Sigurd's ship, but they were soon outpaced. "The bastard's doing it on purpose," Snorri explained. "Wants us to look bad."

Ulf didn't respond as he turned his attention back to the town. Like before, thick smog hung in the air over the houses, and to Ulf, it seemed to show them their fate. Fishing boats rowed nearby, the men less welcoming than they had been before. Ulf wondered if it was because they didn't know the ship, or if word of what had happened had already reached Yngling Hall. He glanced at the wooden palisade that surrounded the town. It had looked so daunting to Ulf before, but now seemed like no obstacle after witnessing the stone walls of Rouen.

"Why does the king not build his town out of stone, like they do in Francia?"

"Do you know how to build with stone?" Thorbjorn scowled at him. Ulf shook his head. "Aye, well, neither do most of the people in our lands. Besides, the forests provide us with more wood than stone." Ulf guessed that made sense.

As they neared the docks, Sigurd's ship slowed enough for them to catch up. A man on Sigurd's ship pointed to an empty spot and Ragnar steered towards it. The smell of fish caught Ulf's nostrils and Theoda's, he guessed, as she leaned over the side again and vomited.

"You'll need to domesticate her, Thorbjorn!" Ragnar shouted, and the men laughed. Ulf looked at Theoda and felt sorry for her. She had tied her fate with a warrior she could not speak to and had come to a land very different from her own. Ulf did not know if she was a firm believer in her god. He knew not everyone was. It was the same for them. Some people believed more than others, and some did not believe at all, but Ulf knew Theoda would not find any sign of her god here.

Many of the fishermen on the docks gave them curious glances as they disembarked. Snorri greeted a few of the men he knew, but many seemed surprised to see him, or perhaps they were surprised at the state of him and his men. The last time many of the people saw Snorri, he had been a warrior of great renown, with a beautiful ship and some of the best fighting men in all of Norway. Now, he arrived on a ship none of them recognised, battered and bruised and with a small crew. It did not take much for the people of Yngling Hall to understand that things had not gone well. Snorri ordered his men to stay with the ship as he and his hirdmen went to face the king. They all wore their war gear, apart from their helmets. They were not here to fight, but still wanted to make a good impression. Snorri struggled with the weight of his brynja, and even Ulf's shoulder protested at the extra weight of the chain mail vest.

As they were about to leave the ship, Thorbjorn turned to the men staying behind. "Look after Theoda while we are gone.

I'll gut you all if anything happens to her." Theoda looked uncertain about what was happening. She wanted to go with Thorbjorn, perhaps feeling more comfortable around him, but somehow Thorbjorn got her to understand that she had to stay with the ship. None of the men minded, though. They liked her, especially as she was the one who cooked for them while they stayed at Ansovald's village, and she helped Oddi tend to their wounds.

Ulf kept looking at the wooden houses of the town as they walked towards the king's hall, surprised at how primitive they seemed after witnessing the stone houses in Francia. Even some of the smallest villages had some stone buildings.

"Why does it feel like everyone already knows what happened?" Ragnar asked as they walked past people gaping at them. Women grabbed their children and dragged them away, while some men pointed at them and whispered something to their companions.

"Aye, even the dogs seem wary of us," Drumbr said as one dog looked at them and ran away. A small boy tried to follow them until his mother shouted at him. The boy gave them one more glance and then trudged back to his house.

"Could Tormod have made it back and told the king?" Thorbjorn rubbed the back of his head.

Snorri scratched his cheek as he glanced at the people who seemed to avoid them. "Sigurd never asked about him."

"And no other ships washed up on the beach where we ended up," Oddi added.

Ulf thought of the king's warrior, remembering how he had once been like a brother to Snorri. But they had drifted apart and the attack on Thorgilsstad before they had left for the raid seemed to break their relationship. "But if he survived, would he not have come looking for us?" Ulf asked. "We were carrying plunder meant for the king."

Snorri glanced at him. "That is a question only the gods can answer. If he survived and is here, then perhaps we might find out. But they could have heard the news from traders as well."

"Aye," Thorbjorn agreed. "Sigurd knew about the attack on Rouen. There's no reason not to think that they have also heard of our fight with the Danes."

"Well, we're about to find out," Ragnar said as they stopped in front of the king's hall. The first time Ulf had seen it, he had been disappointed. It was bigger than Thorgils' hall, but it was plain, apart from the carvings on the doorposts. A line of runes was carved on each of them, one claiming the king was from the Yngling dynasty, which was said to come from Frey, the fertility god. The other placing a curse on any man who would attack the king in his own hall. The same two guards stood by the doors as the last time they were here, but this time they did not greet Snorri and his men as warmly as before.

"Well, well. Odin knows, we did not expect to see you here again," one of them said.

"Aye, Midgard is full of surprises, it seems," the other added.

"It'll take more than a few Franks to kill us." Thorbjorn hawked and spat.

"Looks like they came close, though," one of the guards said, studying all of them. Ragnar was the only one amongst them not injured. "Well, I'm sure the king'll be happy to see you." The smirk on his face said otherwise, and Ulf was apprehensive about having to give his weapons to the guards, but that was the custom of their land. Only the king's men were allowed to carry weapons in the hall.

They entered the hall, and it took Ulf's eyes a few heartbeats to adjust to the gloominess after the bright sunlight outside. Inside, the hall was filled with smoke from the hearth fire, which caused Snorri to cough and grip his chest, his face grimacing in pain. But he forced himself to stand straight as they walked towards Halfdan the Black, sitting on his throne at the far end of the hall. Ulf glanced at the shields and weapons which adorned the walls, a few of them newer than the others. The benches and tables that lined the walls of the hall were filled with men, mostly warriors judging by their broad shoulders and dangerous eyes, but there were some who looked to be traders or bændr. The men fell silent as they watched Snorri and his hirdmen enter, and Ulf felt their eyes judging them. He was certain now that they knew some of what had happened.

King Halfdan stared at them as they approached, but said nothing. His face was set in a scowl, his mouth a thin line between his black moustache and beard.

"Think I'd rather face Griml again," Drumbr whispered as they neared the king. The others ignored him, but Ulf understood what he meant. Despite the hearth fire burning strong and the summer sun blazing outside, the atmosphere inside the hall was cold. It almost reminded Ulf of his dreams. They stopped a few paces away from Halfdan's seat, and out of the corner of his eye, Ulf spotted the old man who was there the last time they saw the king. He was sitting on a chair near the king, close enough to listen but far away enough not to be seen.

"Snorri Thorgilsson," the king said, his voice deep and commanding.

"King Halfdan." Snorri dipped his head.

"And Ragnar Nine-Finger?" The king looked at the jarl's champion as if he was surprised to see him there. Ragnar dipped his head, but said nothing. "Strange to see you here and not by Jarl Thorgils' side."

"The jarl allowed me to join his son on the raid," Ragnar responded.

"Did he now?" The king looked at Ragnar and then at Snorri. "You've been home?"

"No, King Halfdan, I thought it best to come here first."

Halfdan the Black stared at Snorri. "To tell me of your failure?" His face hardened.

"Failure?" Snorri frowned. Ulf saw some men on the benches smiling.

"You arrive on an unknown ship. You and your men look," the king frowned at them, "well, I don't even know how to describe the way you look." A few of the men on the benches laughed as Ulf grit his teeth and told himself to remain silent. The last time he had spoken out in front of the king, it had not ended well for him. He wondered about Egil, the warrior the king had tasked with teaching Ulf a lesson. Egil had beaten him comfortably. The last time Ulf had seen the old warrior was when he was attacked by a group of Danes in the forest by Suðrikaupstefna, and Egil had appeared out of nowhere to help. The man had been badly injured in that fight and Tormod had to leave him behind as they set sail for Francia.

"The raid did not quite go to plan." Snorri tried to be diplomatic, which only made Halfdan the Black smile. Although it was not a friendly smile.

"We had a trader arrive from Denmark not so long ago," Halfdan started.

"Here we go," Thorbjorn muttered, his hand flexing where his sword would be.

"The trader told us an interesting tale. What was the tale again?" Halfdan looked at the old man who sat near him.

The old man cleared his throat and took a sip from the cup he was holding. "He told us that during an attack on Rouen, a mighty city to the east of Francia, a group of Norse warriors turned against the Danes they were fighting alongside with. Killed many of them and fled with much of the plunder." Ulf grit his teeth as he remembered the desperate fight outside Rouen. "The Norse also killed the man leading the raid. A fine young jarl called Ubba the White."

"Ubba was a treacherous bastard who betrayed us," Snorri said, his face creased.

"So you don't deny killing this jarl?" the king asked. "And fighting the men I sent you to fight with?"

"Ubba had no interest in sharing any of the plunder with us. From the beginning, he plotted to have us killed."

"He did?" Halfdan raised an eyebrow.

Snorri nodded. "He set many ambushes, and when none of them succeeded, he attacked us during the raid on Rouen. My men and I only just escaped. Tormod could tell you the same."

"I'm sure he would," the king said, looking at Snorri before launching at him. Before Snorri could react, Halfdan the Black punched him hard in the face. Snorri took a few steps back, but stayed on his feet. Ulf tensed and felt Snorri's hirdmen do the same, but they all knew they could not intervene. Halfdan punched Snorri again, and again Snorri took the blow and stayed on his feet. "I sent you on a raid that was going to make both of us richer than ever before!" His face turned red as he shouted at Snorri. "I gave you the honour, even though you killed one of my jarls! But instead of a ship full of plunder, you bring me a half-empty Danish ship! Lost one of my best men and weakened my forces even more by getting most of your men killed!" Spit was flying out of his mouth and hitting Snorri in the face, but Snorri just stood there and took it all. Ulf grit his teeth, feeling the voices come to life in his ears. "Where is Tormod?" Halfdan punched Snorri again. "Where is my ship?" Another punch. "And where are my men?" Another punch, which finally drove Snorri to his knees. Blood dripped from Snorri's mouth, but he did nothing to wipe it away.

"Forgive me, King Halfdan. The gods were against us." He tried, but the king was not having it.

"I don't care if the gods fucked you up the arse! Where are my ship and my men?"

"There was a storm." Oddi stepped forward and was rewarded with a glare from the king. "It drove us back to the Frankish coast, but we saw no sign of your ship or Tormod after that, king. We thought that perhaps they had survived and made it back here."

King Halfdan glared at Oddi for a few heartbeats before returning to his seat. "Tormod never made it back." He looked at Snorri again. "If you had succeeded on this raid, Snorri Thorgilsson, I would have made you jarl of what remains of

Arnfinni's village. But now I can't decide which is the best way to kill you." Snorri's hirdmen gasped.

Snorri got back to his feet, ignoring the blood dripping from his lip, but grimacing at the pain in his chest. "Do with me as you must, King Halfdan, but I ask you to spare my men. They only followed my orders."

The king smiled suddenly, which got them all by surprise. "You say the gods were against you, but they did do something in your favour." Halfdan signalled to the benches, and Ulf gasped as Egil stood up. The old warrior walked towards the king's seat. "Egil arrived with the trader, who told us the news. But Egil had his own tale to tell me."

Egil nodded and smiled at Ulf. "I heard stories from some of the Danes who were left behind. They told me who Ubba was and after hearing what the trader told the king, I explained that there was more to it than that."

"You wronged the man's family, and he sought to get vengeance. Much like your scarred friend sought vengeance against the man who killed his family." The king sighed. "I am still not happy with how this raid went, but I will not kill you, Snorri Thorgilsson. I will, however, take that Danish ship. My men on the wharf said it's bigger than the one I lost and I will take all the plunder she holds. You and your men can walk home, and perhaps by the time you get there, the gods will have guided me on what to do with you. Now leave my hall before I change my mind."

"Thank you, King Halfdan," Snorri said and turned and walked out of the hall, his men right behind him. Ulf caught Drumbr and Magni glancing at the jugs of ale on the table and had to admit, he would have liked a drink as well. But the king had enough of their presence and they all knew it was better to leave.

"Well, that went better than expected," Thorbjorn commented as they got their weapons back from the guards. Ulf frowned at him as he sheathed Ormstunga.

"What are you talking about? The king is furious. The jarl won't be happy about this." Ragnar took his axe and walked off without waiting for any of them.

"Aye," Thorbjorn agreed, "But we still live and we get to go home now. The gods know things could have turned out very differently."

CHAPTER 29

As they left the king's hall, Egil came out after them and told Snorri and his men to follow him. They were apprehensive at first, expecting it to be some kind of trap, but they still followed. Egil led them to the wharves where Sigurd was waiting on his ship with Snorri's men already on board.

"We have fought many battles with the men of Thorgilsstad," he explained. "We know the quality of your men and of you as a leader, Snorri. Whatever happened in Francia must have been very bad for you to lose so many men and your ships."

"Aye, tell that to the king." Thorbjorn scowled.

Sigurd smiled. "The king knows. He's just angry that he didn't get what he wanted and that you lost one of his ships."

Snorri frowned. He looked back up the main street towards the king's hall. Ulf did the same and saw the king standing there, watching them.

"Go home," Egil said. "Rest, recover and when the king needs you again, he'll send word. Which might be sooner than you think." They all frowned and so Egil explained. "There's trouble up north, and the king sees an opportunity to expand his kingdom."

"Aye, but you better get on my ship before he changes his mind," Sigurd added.

So they got on his ship, and Sigurd sailed them to Thorgilsstad. On the way, he asked many questions about the raid. Ulf suspected he was trying to get more information for the king about what had happened. He remembered Thorbjorn warning him that Sigurd was very sly, and Oddi agreed with Ulf. But they answered his questions and told the tales of what had happened. Sigurd's men enjoyed them and many cheered when Snorri explained how they had beaten the Danes. Ulf even got a few slaps on the back when Drumbr told the story of how he had finally killed Griml. He still wasn't sure how he felt about that. Ulf had spent the last two winters wanting nothing more than to kill the troll, but now that it was done, he felt strange. He felt vulnerable. Despite all that had happened, Ulf never really believed he was going to die because of the oath he made to Odin. He truly believed that Odin had been keeping him alive so he could kill Griml. But now that Griml was dead, Odin did not need to do that anymore. And that frightened Ulf.

When they reached the bay which led to Thorgilsstad, Ragnar took over from the steersman to navigate the ship past the three small islands which protected the entrance to the bay. The islands were called Stórr Vördr, which meant big warden, Smár Vördr, small warden, and Mindri Vördr, smaller warden. Only those who lived in the bay knew how to get around them, as there were many rocks hidden under the surface of the water. That was one of the reasons Thorgils had chosen this bay for his village, so he never had to worry about an enemy attacking by sea.

People gathered on the wharf to watch the ship approach. Ulf imagined they recognised the ship and were curious why one of the king's ships would come to Thorgilsstad. But when they saw Snorri standing by the prow and waving at them, they all cheered. A young boy ran towards the village, no doubt to tell others that Snorri had arrived. The cheers on the wharf soon died down when the people of Thorgilsstad wondered why Snorri was arriving with one of the king's men and not his own ship.

As Sigurd's ship pulled in next to the wharf, Ulf saw the frowns on many of the faces when they realised how few men were on board. The look on Snorri's face must have confirmed what many had been wondering, as more boys were sent running towards the village. Some women started whispering to each other when they did not see their husbands or sons. Snorri had left Thorgilsstad with two ships full of warriors and he was returning with barely enough men to man a small warship. Some rubbed the Mjöllnir pendants around their necks as they tied the ship to the wharf, and Snorri jumped off, wincing at the pain in his chest.

"Not quite the welcome you'd expect," Egil muttered beside Ulf. The entire journey here he had sat there and told Ulf of his journey home after they left him in Suðrikaupstefna. Ulf was beginning to like the old warrior.

"Aye," Thorbjorn agreed. "Odin knows this is not the way we expected to arrive home, either." Theoda was sitting next to him, her eyes wide as she took in the village, which would be her new home. She gripped Thorbjorn's arm and made the sign of the cross on her chest.

Ebbe, one of the jarl's more experienced captains, stepped forward from the crowd. "Snorri, welcome home!" He gripped Snorri's forearm and the two men shared a warm embrace before Ebbe stepped back and watched as the few warriors from Thorgilsstad stepped off the ship. "I take it things did not go so well," he said with a grave face.

Snorri shook his head. "The gods were not with us." He faced the people, mostly women and children, who were searching the survivors for their men. "Many men were lost in Francia. They gave their lives so that the rest of us could make it home." Some women broke down in tears, the young children holding on to their skirts and looking confused. Ulf remembered when he had lost his father. He had only been six winters and was still too young to understand what it meant. He had blamed the gods and his father, feeling that he abandoned Ulf. The thought brought his dream back to him, and Ulf saw the fight between the two wolf packs in his mind. He shook his head to clear the image, confused about what it meant. "They all feast in Valhalla with their ancestors," Snorri continued, "and you can sleep soundly knowing that we have avenged their deaths. The men responsible are all feeding the ravens." A few of the people smiled, but most had their heads down, their shoulders shuddering as they mourned their loss.

"The Franks were tougher than we thought?" Ebbe raised an eyebrow.

"No, our host betrayed us." Snorri sighed. "This is not the place to tell our tale. I must see my parents and tonight in the hall I will tell you all what happened."

Ebbe nodded and stood to the side so that Snorri and his men could pass, and before Snorri left the wharf, he turned to Sigurd. "Come to the hall. Quench your thirst if you have time."

Sigurd nodded, and his crew smiled. "Thank you for the invitation. We accept."

The people on the wharf parted to allow Snorri to pass. A few of the people glanced at Ulf as he walked past them, their eyes accusing him.

They walked into the centre of Thorgilsstad, and Ulf was surprised at how small the village seemed to him. The entire village consisted of Thorgils' hall, the jarl's house and Snorri's house. There were other houses as well which surrounded the square in front of the hall, but not many. These were occupied by Thorgils' captains and their families. Most of the warriors either slept in the hall, like Ulf, or lived on the farms which surrounded Thorgilsstad. Ulf looked at the square as they walked towards the hall, his eyes fixed on the three stone statues in the centre. They were the three gods the people of Thorgilsstad revered the most. Odin, whose tall statue stood in the centre. On one side of him stood Thor with his mighty hammer. And on the other, Tyr proudly displayed his missing hand, which he had sacrificed so the gods could bind Fenrir, the giant wolf. Although, before they left for Francia, Ulf discovered a shrine to Frigg hidden in the forest. Lady Ingibjorg had told Ulf it was only hidden to the men because none of them looked for it, but that all the women in the village knew about it. Ulf only discovered it because he had followed Ingibjorg into the forest.

They stopped in front of the hall, not because any of them were afraid to go in. Ulf was eager just to collapse on his bear fur cloak and sleep the rest of the day away, and the others wanted to drink deep into the night. They stopped because of the two people standing by the entrance. Only one of them seemed happy they were home, the other just glared at them. Lady Ingibjorg stood tall, her slender hands clasped in front of her as she smiled at them. But as always, Ulf could feel her green eyes searching his soul for the truth of what had happened. Many believed that Lady Ingibjorg could speak to the gods, and that she was able to read a person's mind. Ulf was never sure what he believed, but she always knew what he was thinking and what to say to him. She was a beautiful woman with a stern face, although Ulf saw new lines which were not there before. It seemed she had not had a peaceful summer. Beside her stood a man Ulf had not seen since the battle at The Giant's Toe. He was shorter than Ulf and much older. His heavily lined face was severe and his hard eyes enough to make even the bravest warrior waver. Although the man had gained some weight since the last time Ulf saw him. Ulf guessed that was because he had locked himself in his house and spent most of his time drinking and mourning the son who betrayed him.

"Father," Snorri said, the surprise clear in his voice at seeing Jarl Thorgils outside for the first time since the previous summer. "Mother," he greeted Lady Ingibjorg with more warmth.

"Welcome home, my son and the warriors of Thorgilsstad!" Lady Ingibjorg said, and then her smile faded. "We would celebrate, but I fear you have much to tell us." She looked at Ulf, her eyes boring inside his mind and almost making him shiver, before she returned her attention to her son. Ulf wondered if she already knew what had happened and how she had found out. *Did the gods tell her, or did they hear the news from traders?*

"Where are the rest of my men?" Jarl Thorgils asked, his voice rough. It sounded like he wasn't used to speaking anymore.

"It is good to see you outside, father." Snorri tried to deflect, but the jarl was not in the mood.

"Don't give me that bullshit! By Odin, Snorri! Where are my men?" His heavily lined face went red. He turned to his champion. "Ragnar? What did my idiot son do?"

"Your idiot son did what he had to while you were cowering away in your cup!" Snorri responded before Ragnar could say anything. The people of Thorgilsstad, who had followed them, gasped. Snorri had never spoken to his father like that. Ulf spotted Sigurd and Egil glancing at each other and the old warrior shrugged.

"Cowering?" Thorgils stormed down the steps and stood nose to nose with Snorri. Father and son, glaring at each other, both faces red and fists clenched. "You have brought ruin to my village!" Before Snorri could respond, someone at the back of the crowd started clapping hands. Thorgils turned to the crowd, his face so red, Ulf worried the old man might collapse. "Who, in Odin's name, dares mock me?"

The crowd parted and when Ulf realised who it was, his heart stopped in his chest.

"No," Lady Ingibjorg gasped, her hand covering her mouth and her usual calm demeanour gone. Ulf looked at Snorri's mother and was surprised by the fear in her eyes. Even Thorgils paled, his mouth open as he struggled to find the words he needed.

The volva walked towards them, still clapping her hands. Snorri and Thorgils took a few steps backwards to distance themselves from her. Ulf wasn't sure if it was because of fear or because of her stench as she stopped clapping, but held her dirty hands in front of her chest. "Hello, sister dear."

"Sister?" Snorri turned to his mother, her face white with fear as a tear ran down her cheek.

"W… what are you d… doing here?" the jarl said, and Ulf wasn't the only one who noted the fear in his voice. Ragnar gripped his two-handed axe and bared his teeth like a guard dog, but the volva only looked at him, her eyes full of disinterest.

"Well, I was in the area and I thought I'd visit my daughter. It's been such a long time since I have seen her." Her voice was filled with honey, and Ulf almost believed her.

The jarl opened his mouth to speak, but no words came to him as he coughed. He looked at his wife; her face still pale.

"Skadi…" Snorri's mother started.

Skadi? Ulf looked at the volva. He had never thought of her name, but now that he heard it, he couldn't think of a more suitable one. It came from the Norse word skaði, which meant scathe, harm, loss and death. Everything she seemed to represent.

"We did everything to keep her safe," Lady Ingibjorg tried to explain. "What happened to Hulda was an accident."

Skadi, the volva and Hulda's mother, tilted her head as she looked at Lady Ingibjorg, her sister. Ulf was still struggling to understand that, and so was Snorri. "Strange, I never thought someone cutting your throat open was an accident." Loathing replaced the honey in her voice.

"It wasn't our fault." The jarl finally found his voice, though it lacked steel. "It was his fault. She died because of him." He pointed his finger at Ulf. Ulf grit his teeth and glared at Snorri's father.

"You took her from me!" the volva shrieked and jabbed her dirty finger at Thorgils, who shrunk away. Ulf could hear thunder in the sky above him, but there were no clouds. "You tricked me and took my daughter!" Her face turned red as spit flew out of her mouth. "You took my daughter, not to protect her, but to protect yourself!"

"Skadi," Ingibjorg started again, her eyes red and tears streaming down her face. Ulf had never seen Snorri's mother like this before and wondered about the power the volva really wielded.

"Keep quiet, you," Skadi shouted at her. "You knew what your husband did! You let him do it!"

The jarl tried to force some steel into his voice as he straightened his back and glared at the volva. "So, what do you want? To kill my son? One child for another? In Odin's name, he's right there. Kill him if you must!"

The people of Thorgilsstad gasped as Snorri's eyes went wide. "Father?"

The volva laughed, a cruel sound which caught everyone by surprise. "The gods know that if I wanted Snorri dead, then he would have been dead long by now." She turned and smiled at Snorri, who did his best to stand his ground. "I've spent so many nights standing over him and watching him sleep. Got quite boring in the end."

"What do you mean?" Snorri frowned and glanced at Oddi, who only shrugged. Even Ulf struggled to understand that. Snorri had set guards every night.

She smiled at Snorri. "How do you think I tricked your man into betraying you?"

"She talking about Geir?" Thorbjorn frowned. Snorri did not respond, but Ulf saw he was hiding something, and so did Oddi.

"Snorri?"

Still, Snorri said nothing. He just stood there and stared at the volva.

"You didn't tell them?" Her smile was cruel, and Ulf knew whatever she said next would not be good. "He never liked Ulf, did he? Never wanted him to be part of your crew."

Asbjorn? Ulf glanced at Snorri, but Snorri's eyes were fixed on Skadi, almost imploring her not to say anything more. Drumbr started fidgeting, and Ulf wondered if he knew.

"It was so easy to convince him to send one of your men to the beach and wave down Griml's ship. So gullible you men are, he really believed that Griml would only kill Ulf and leave the rest of you alone." She laughed, the sound of it sending shivers down Ulf's spine. "So desperate was he to get rid of the young wolf that he sent a young man to his death and almost killed you all."

"Who is she talking about, Snorri?" Thorbjorn asked, but again Snorri kept quiet.

"Tell them," the volva urged him.

Snorri stood quiet for a while as all eyes were on him, but then his shoulders dropped. "Asbjorn. He sent Geir to tell Griml where we were."

Oddi looked like he was slapped in the face. "How do you know this?"

"He told me just before he died. Asked me to forgive him."

"You mean the bastard betrayed us and you still wanted to give him a proper funeral?" Thorbjorn was red in the face as he glared at Snorri.

Snorri turned angrily to Thorbjorn. "He was my friend!"

"And what about us?" Thorbjorn asked as a sadness took over his eyes. "Are we not your friends? We almost died. You almost died!" The volva smiled, pleased with herself, while Ulf struggled to make sense of this.

"But why would Asbjorn believe that? He knew how dangerous Griml was," Ulf said.

The volva turned to Lady Ingibjorg. "What is it you always liked to say, sister dear? Never underestimate the stupidity of men." She faced Snorri and his men again. "So easy to trick, so easy to play." She ran her finger down Snorri's cheek, which made him recoil. In the crowd, Ulf spotted his wife and was surprised by her smiling at Snorri's discomfort. Perhaps she wanted the volva to kill the man who had killed her father. But then the volva turned around and looked at the jarl again. "But as for your son, if I knew where he was, then he'd be dead by now."

Snorri's eyes widened at this, and even Ulf felt like he was struck by lightning. "Father, what does she mean?"

Thorgils grit his teeth. "He is my son."

The volva laughed. "Oh come now, Thorgils. You know as well as I do that is not true. Otherwise, you never would have had your best friend killed."

Thorgils paled and gave a quick glance to Ragnar, who gripped his axe and, with a roar, launched himself at the volva. But she only smiled as she deftly moved out of the way and Ragnar's axe bit into the dirt. The people gasped, and a few of the women screamed as a baby started crying. Ulf thought he heard more thunder, but still there were no clouds. He did, however, spot the raven sitting on the roof of the hall and wondered when it had arrived.

The volva walked towards Ulf, her smile revealing her blackened gums. "You still don't understand it, do you, young wolf?" Ulf shook his head, unable to speak. "Remember your dream." She walked past him, running a finger across his injured shoulder, the muscle quivering at her touch. "Remember your father, Bjørn Ulfson, the bear of Thorgilsstad." As she said that, Ulf heard an eagle cry, and in his mind, he saw the battle between the two wolf packs and the bear fighting in the centre of it all, slaughtering all wolves who came within reach. *Father?* He then saw the young wolf with the red-tinted fur sneak up behind it, baring its teeth as it was about to kill the bear.

"Bjørn died in battle!" the jarl shouted as the dream played out in Ulf's mind.

"Aye, but did the killing blow come from the front or," she leaned closer to Ulf and whispered in his ear, "behind?"

Ulf saw the young wolf launch itself at the bear, burying its fangs into the bear's back, and noticed it had a toe missing on one of its front paws. His vision cleared as the bear stood on its hind legs and roared into the sky. In front of him stood Ragnar, his axe still buried in the ground, glaring at him.

Ulf grit his teeth as the flames of his anger came to life in the pit of his stomach and forgot about everything else around him. The only thing that mattered now was Ragnar Nine-Finger. "You killed my father?"

CHAPTER 30

Ulf expected Ragnar to deny it. He wanted him to deny it. But the jarl's champion stood up straight and freed his axe from the ground, grinning at Ulf. "I did. Just like I'm about to kill you!" Ragnar launched himself at Ulf, his axe held over his shoulder so he could chop Ulf in half. Women screamed at the sudden violence and men cried out in shock, but Ulf heard none of this as the voices of his ancestors exploded in his ears.

Kill! They demanded, and Ulf roared as he charged at the oncoming Ragnar. Ragnar swung his axe high, aiming for Ulf's chest, but Ulf ducked underneath and punched Ragnar in his brynja-protected stomach. As Ragnar bent over from the force of the blow, Ulf spun on his toes and punched the jarl's champion on the side of the head. Neither warrior was wearing a helmet and Ragnar's head snapped to the side. The voices of Ulf's ancestors pushed him on, his pains forgotten as he kicked Ragnar in the back and charged for the follow up attack. Ragnar quickly rolled back to his feet, bringing his axe around in an upward cut. Ulf dodged the axe, but Ragnar turned it around and brought it down at an angle, forcing Ulf to jump to the side.

They had fought so many times in training sessions in the past, with Ragnar always getting the better of Ulf. But now, with all of Ulf's fury coursing through his veins, Ragnar moved so slowly that Ulf wondered how he had never beaten the man before. Ulf threw an uppercut and as Ragnar's head snapped back, he followed up with a kick to Ragnar's chest, which sent the man onto his back. Before the red-headed warrior could get up, Ulf jumped on top of him and rained down punches on his head.

Ragnar's axe was stuck between them and somehow he pushed the axe up and threw Ulf off him. Ulf crashed into the statue of Tyr as Ragnar rolled onto his feet, ignoring the blood on his face. He glared at Ulf, his teeth bared as he gripped his enormous axe with both hands. Ulf needed a weapon. He knew that, but the sun was shining and he no longer had his axe. Through the voices of his ancestors raging in his ears, Ulf heard something that made him look down. *Do not draw me in the light of the sun*, the words echoed in his head. He smiled his own wolf smile as he gripped the hilt of Ormstunga, not feeling the sting in his arm, and pulled her free in the shadow of the statue of his ancestor. Ragnar faltered, surprised by the sudden change in the situation, and before he could recover, Ulf launched himself at the warrior.

Ragnar swung his axe at Ulf's head, but Ulf ducked under the blade and sliced Ragnar's leg open with Ormstunga. Ragnar cried out, and the people gasped in shock while Thorbjorn cheered, pumping his fist into the air, which earned him a glare from the jarl. But Ulf noticed none of this as he turned and stabbed at Ragnar's back. Ragnar sensed the movement and turned out of the way, at the same time chopping down with his axe. Ulf had to jump back to avoid the blow, and Ragnar, ignoring the pain in his leg, followed up with a kick. Ulf saw it coming though and smiled at how slowly Ragnar moved. He stepped out of the way of Ragnar's boot and kicked at his supporting leg. Ragnar landed hard on his back and Ulf stabbed down with Ormstunga, certain he was about to avenge his father. But Ragnar rolled out of the way, his warrior instinct honed by many years of battle taking over. He bounced to his feet and swung his two-handed axe at Ulf, who almost saw it too late. Ulf jumped back, feeling the axe graze his brynja. He counter-attacked, roaring as he stabbed at Ragnar, who tried to twist out of the way but was too slow as the sharp point of Ormstunga pierced his chain mail vest. Ragnar's movement saved him though, as Ormstunga only managed a slight cut on his waist.

The men parted briefly to catch their breaths, both glaring at each other and ignoring everything around them. Ulf attacked again, not wanting Ragnar to recover too much. He brought his sword up above his head and chopped down hard, forcing Ragnar to use the handle of his axe to block the blow. There was a scream as Ormstunga's blade cut through the wood and bit into Ragnar's shoulder. The voices in Ulf's ears rejoiced, but it was short-lived as Ragnar grit his teeth against the pain and smacked Ulf on the head with the broken axe handle. Sparks flashed in Ulf's eyes as he reeled from the blow, his vision too blurred for him to see anything. He stumbled back and sensed the movement in front of him. The voices in his ears told Ulf to duck, and he dropped to his knees, feeling the air move above his head. As his vision cleared, he saw Ragnar standing above him, his shoulder bleeding and about to bury his axe in Ulf's skull. Ulf deflected the blow with Ormstunga and rolled back onto his feet. But the blow to his head had left him unsteady. Grimacing from the pain in his shoulder, Ragnar pulled his own sword from her scabbard, a weapon he rarely used, but was no less deadly with it. He launched himself at Ulf, a wolf grin on his face as he believed he was about to kill the young warrior. But Ulf, still struggling to deal with the blow to his head, gave himself to the voices of his ancestors as they kept him out of the way of Ragnar's sword and axe. Ulf ducked and dodged, occasionally stabbing out with Ormstunga, but Ragnar now had the upper hand and he did all he could to keep Ulf on the back foot. He sliced with his axe and stabbed with his sword, but Ulf avoided everything Ragnar threw at him. It was like a dance between the gods, both men completely synchronised. Ulf sliced with Ormstunga, but Ragnar deflected with his sword and chopped down with his axe. Ulf twisted out of the way and jumped back as Ragnar punched with the head of his axe. Both men groaned and grunted, roared and screamed as they danced in front of the gods. Around the square, women cried out in alarm and men cheered, mostly when they thought Ragnar was about to kill Ulf, but Ulf still had some supporters, as Thorbjorn and Drumbr encouraged him. The jarl stood, grim-faced as he watched his champion fight the boy he had tried to kill before, while the volva smiled gleefully, pleased with what she had caused. Lady Ingibjorg stood still, like the statues of the gods, as she watched the chaos unfold, knowing there was nothing she could do.

But all Ulf saw was Ragnar in front of him. All he heard were the voices of his ancestors in his ears. All he felt were the flames of his anger as he stabbed at Ragnar's exposed stomach.

Ragnar had no time to do anything but to turn to the side and backhand Ulf's weapon out of the way. He caught Ulf on the forearm, the half-handle of his axe striking Ulf on the cut. Ulf cried out as the pain caused his hand to open, and Ormstunga fell to the ground. The voices in his ears went silent, and Ulf heard the people around them gasp. He looked up in time to see Ragnar punch him in the face with the pommel of his sword. The blow caught Ulf on the cheek, splitting it open, as his head snapped back. Ragnar kicked Ulf hard in the chest and Ulf groaned as he fell on his back. All his pains rushed over him like a wave and washed his strength away. Ragnar smiled when he thought the fight was over and stood back, allowing Ulf to struggle to his knees. The people of Thorgilsstad were quiet as Ulf tried to get to his feet, but then collapsed to his knees again.

"Stay down, pup," Ragnar sneered.

"Never," Ulf struggled to say through grit teeth.

Ragnar glanced at the jarl, seeing the smile on his wrinkled face. He looked at Ulf again and held up his left hand with the little finger missing and covered in the blood from his shoulder. "You want to know how I lost my finger?" He didn't wait for a response. "Your father, the mighty Bjørn, cut it off while we were training. He chopped at my spear and cut off my finger, laughing at me while blood poured from the wound. I cried, of course I did. It hurt a lot, and it was my finger. But your father only laughed and called me weak." He glared at Ulf. "So when the jarl asked me to kill him in the battle, I was more than happy to stick my sword in his back. I still dream about the day your father died like the pathetic swine he was. Just like you are about to die." He took a step towards Ulf, throwing down the broken axe and gripping his sword in his right hand.

Ulf sat on his knees, stunned, as the words sunk in slowly, like water on wet soil. But when they did, he screamed as the flames of his anger, and not just his, but the anger of his father, erupted inside of him. The voices of his ancestors roared in his ears and Ulf launched himself at Ragnar, catching the warrior completely off guard. Ragnar tried to cut at Ulf with his sword, but Ulf ducked underneath the blade and punched Ragnar on the chin. Ragnar's head snapped back and Ulf followed by punching the cut on his leg. The red-headed warrior's leg gave way, and he fell to the ground, only to be kicked in the face by Ulf, still roaring at him. Ulf jumped on top of Ragnar and grabbed him by his brynja, lifting his head up and roaring in his face before headbutting him. As Ragnar's head hit the ground again, Ulf punched him, again and again. But somehow Ragnar got his arms under Ulf and, using his bigger size and strength, threw Ulf off. Ragnar's head swam, but he wasted no time when he noticed where they were. He grabbed a fistful of Ulf's light-coloured hair and bashed his head against the statue of Odin. Ulf's rage was short-lived as sparks flashed once more in his head before he collapsed onto his back, the voices and flames gone. Ragnar struggled to get on top of Ulf while shaking his head to clear it from the punches. He gripped Ulf's throat with both his hands and squeezed as hard as he could.

"Now you die."

Ulf's eyes bulged as he fought to loosen Ragnar's grip, desperate for air as his vision blurred. But the larger warrior was too strong. Through his distorted vision, he saw the statue of Odin smiling at him and, for the first time, Ulf thought he was really going to die. He had completed his oath to Odin, so the All-Father had no reason to keep him alive. Ulf's hands weakened around Ragnar's as his lungs burnt for air. His vision darkened, and he pictured a warrior standing on a hill, tall and proud, and beckoning Ulf to join him. Ulf's hand dropped away from Ragnar's and landed on something. With his mind starved of oxygen, it took him a few heartbeats to realise what it was. Ragnar's sax-knife. As his hand gripped the handle of the knife, the warrior on the hill turned and walked away, a single voice whispering in his ear. Ulf listened to it and pulled the sax-knife out of her scabbard. He stabbed up but did not have enough strength to drive the blade through Ragnar's brynja. Ulf tried again and again, but could not get the knife through as his world darkened around him. Ragnar grunted with each attempt, but kept squeezing Ulf's throat, now even more determined to kill him.

Again, the voice whispered, and again, Ulf stabbed. This time, the knife found a weak link in Ragnar's brynja as it broke through and the blade pierced Ragnar under his ribs. Ragnar's eyes bulged and Ulf felt hot blood leaking over his hand, making it harder to hold on to the sax-knife. But Ulf gripped it tightly as he partly pulled it out and stabbed again, this time twisting the blade to cause as much damage to Ragnar's insides as possible. Ragnar's face paled as it became a race of who would die first. He kept on squeezing, but just before Ulf's world turned completely black, Ragnar's grip weakened. Ulf twisted the knife one more time, feeling Ragnar's blood drenching him and his grip completely losing strength and releasing his neck. Ulf sucked in the fresh air as Ragnar shuddered above him and collapsed, the sax-knife still buried in his side. Groaning, Ulf rolled Ragnar's body off him, his vision still blurred and hearing only the sound of waves in his ears. He coughed as he sucked in air through his sore throat, savouring each lungful.

As Ulf struggled to his knees, he sensed a movement above him.

"Ulf!" Snorri shouted.

Ulf acted instinctively as he pulled the sax-knife from Ragnar's body and stabbed the shadow looming over him. The sharp blade pierced flesh as noise suddenly erupted around Ulf. Women shrieked, the volva laughed and men cried as Ulf's vision cleared and he saw the jarl standing over him, a sword in his hand and Ragnar's sax-knife buried in his side. Ulf let go of the knife and scrambled backwards as Thorgils collapsed beside Ragnar's body. He glared at Ulf, his teeth grit against the pain.

"I... I kn... knew I sh... should have kill... d you."

Men rushed around their jarl, a few of them kicking Ulf as they ran past. Thorbjorn and Drumbr appeared by his side and pulled Ulf out of the way. They stood over him, protecting him from the other warriors who'd want to avenge their jarl. Snorri stood rooted to the spot, his face pale as he struggled to understand what was happening. Women and children wailed as Ulf looked at Lady Ingibjorg. To his surprise, she was staring at him, but her eyes were not filled with anger or hatred. All he saw was a sorrow that almost brought tears to his eyes. He turned his head away and searched the crowd for the volva, but she was gone. And so was the raven which had been sitting on the roof of the hall.

Snorri realised he had to do something. Sigurd, the king's man, stood amongst the crowd and watched, no doubt, to tell the king how Snorri reacted to this. He looked at the jarl, who was moving as his men crowded around him.

"Get my father to his house, now!" Snorri ordered the men. "Oddi, see to my father's wound." Oddi looked conflicted, but nodded and followed the jarl's men as they carried him into his house. Lady Ingibjorg turned to follow them. She gave Ulf one last glance, almost as if she was saying goodbye before she went inside. Snorri walked towards Ulf, his fists clenched by his side. A few men fell in behind him, all of them with their hands on their weapons.

"You should kill the bastard!" one man shouted.

"Aye, Odin knows that's the least he deserves for attacking Ragnar and the jarl," another said. The villagers all crept in closer as Snorri stopped in front of Ulf, his eyes hard.

"Let me do it," Ebbe offered. "I'll gut him, and we can throw him in the bay while he bleeds out. Less chance of him getting into Valhalla." The men around added their voices to Ebbe's, all of them agreeing with the old warrior's plan.

"You touch him and you have to deal with me," Thorbjorn threatened, placing himself between Ulf and the men. Ulf looked at the short warrior, struggling to understand why he was defending him.

"Enough!" Snorri's hard voice stilled the others. He glared at Ulf, but Ulf noticed the pain in his eyes. "Ulf Bjørnson, you attacked and killed a man of this village. You attacked our jarl. What do you have to say for yourself?"

Ulf blinked at the strangeness of the question. Ragnar had attacked him first, and it was Snorri himself who had warned Ulf of the jarl's attack. But then Ulf spotted Sigurd standing behind Snorri's shoulder. He took a deep breath and looked his friend in the eyes. "I avenged my..." he paused and then, "our father." The men behind Ulf murmured at that, although Ulf knew all of them had heard the volva's words.

Snorri ground his teeth. Ulf saw how his jaw muscles worked under his beard. "Bind his hands and feet. Leave him by the gods for the night. Tomorrow I will decide your fate."

"I thought the Norns decide our fate." Ulf couldn't help himself. He was angered by this show Snorri was putting on for the king's men.

Snorri knelt down, so he was eye to eye with Ulf. His mask dropped for a few moments as he said, "Then I pray they look kindly on you." And then Snorri stood and his mask was back on. He turned to the people of his village. "Ulf will spend the night before the gods so they can decide his fate! No one is allowed to go near or touch Ulf until I say otherwise!" The villagers agreed as a warrior brought some rope. Ulf wondered if it was the same rope the jarl had tried to hang him with.

Thorbjorn took the rope from the warrior and knelt down to tie Ulf's hands. "I'm sorry it has come to this, Ulf. Odin knows I always thought you a friend. I will stay outside tonight, make sure no one decides to make the decision for the gods."

Ulf nodded his thanks as Drumbr tied his feet. They picked him up and carried to the statues of the gods, while other warriors took Ragnar's body away. There they dropped him in front of the statue of Odin. Ulf looked at it, trying to see the smile he had seen before, but it was gone. He looked at the statue of Tyr, not sure why, and then at Thor, wondering how the gods would judge him as he sat in the blood of the man he had killed.

CHAPTER 31

The night was warm, the sky cloudless as the moon looked down on Ulf, sitting in front of the statues of the gods, not once taking his eyes off of them. Ulf sensed some of Snorri's men outside the hall. They were there to protect him from the others he also felt lurking nearby, waiting for a chance to stick a knife in his back. But apart from one small boy who ran in and spat on Ulf, it was an uneventful night.

The sun rose to Ulf, still sitting as he was before, his knees stiff while his shoulder ached and arm stung. The blood from the cut on his face had dried, and Ulf could feel it cracking every time he moved his mouth. His headache had disappeared at some point, although Ulf wasn't exactly sure when, as he must have fallen asleep. He looked up at the gods one more time when he heard the footsteps behind him. Rough hands grabbed him and dragged him into the hall, but Ulf kept his eyes on the three statues. Women and children gathered outside the hall, all of them glaring at Ulf while some of the older boys spat on him before he was taken inside.

Inside the hall were most of Thorgilsstad's warriors, all of them, apart from Snorri's men, glaring at him. But Ulf paid them no attention as he stared straight ahead at Snorri sitting in his father's seat. Or perhaps it was his seat now.

"Untie him," Snorri said, his lip cut from when the king had punched him, as Thorbjorn and Drumbr put Ulf down in front of him. Oddi pulled his knife out and cut the ropes binding his ankles and hands, and Ulf struggled to his feet, his knees sore from sitting on them all night. There was a bundle by Snorri's feet, which looked like the bearskin they had given him when he first arrived. It was from the bear he had killed. Ulf saw Ormstunga's hilt sticking out of the bundle and frowned. The men were all silent, the only noise coming from the hearth fire, the flames snapping as they danced away, and the birds outside greeting the new day. They sounded cheerful, and Ulf guessed they had more reason to be happy than him.

Sigurd sat on a bench near Snorri with Egil next to him, the old warrior glancing away when Ulf looked at him. There was no sign of Snorri's mother, and Ulf found that saddened him. He wanted to apologise, but then wondered if she would even let him.

"The jarl still lives," Snorri said, wearing the same mask he wore the day before. "But for how long we don't know. So it is up to me to decide what to do with you. I have prayed to the gods, asking them for guidance, and asked for counsel from those older than me. Many believe that you should be put to death, as that is the punishment for attacking a jarl." Snorri stopped and sighed, while Ulf only stared at him. He knew there was no point in saying anything. Whatever they had agreed, that was what the Norns had planned for him, and Ulf had finally decided to leave his fate up to them. He had avenged his family, even those he never knew he needed to, so Ulf was sure they would welcome him to Valhalla with open arms. He almost looked forward to it. And he was exhausted. For the last two winters, all Ulf cared about was his vengeance. All his energy was used to accomplish that and now that it was done, he had nothing left. Snorri continued, "But I cannot put you to death. You saved my life, so I owe you a debt. On top of that, the jarl attacked you and you defended yourself." There was a murmur from the men, as some of them were unhappy with what Snorri was saying. "So, the gods have decided I will not hang you. But you cannot stay here." Snorri stood and addressed the hall. "Ulf Bear-Slayer Bjørnson, you are banished from Vestfold and Norway for ten winters!" There was another murmur from the men in the hall, louder this time.

"Odin's arse," Thorbjorn whispered beside Ulf.

Snorri held his hand up and waited for the men to go silent. "Sigurd has agreed to take the news to the king, who should, by Odin's will, agree with the punishment and at the next Thing we will make it official." He stared at Ulf, his mask now gone, and Ulf saw the heartbreak in Snorri's eyes. "You have three days to leave Vestfold and until the new moon to leave Norway. If you are found in these lands after that, then your life will be forfeited. Ulf, do you understand your punishment?"

Ulf looked at his friend, his brother, and said, "I do."

Snorri nodded and picked up the bundle at his feet before walking towards Ulf and handing it to him. "You have earned these things and they will stay yours. I will give you until sunset to leave Thorgilsstad, but I'd advise you to leave as quickly as possible. There are many who would rather see you dead." Ulf nodded and took the bundle from Snorri. "Your uncle's axe is in there. Thought you might need that," Snorri whispered to him. When that was done, Snorri turned and walked back to the jarl's seat. He looked at it and took a deep breath before sitting down again. "Show him out."

Thorbjorn nodded and escorted Ulf from the hall. Outside, many of the villagers, the women and children, waited. Some only stared, while others shouted at him, cursing him and spitting at him. One woman threw dung at him, but her aim was off and it hit the hall instead. Thorbjorn did nothing to stop any of it, but then Ulf guessed he couldn't. He spotted Theoda standing to one side, confused by what was happening.

"What's your plan with Theoda?"

Thorbjorn shrugged as he walked Ulf to the edge of the village. "Marry her, teach her our ways. If the gods smile on me, hopefully, have some little ones running around soon."

Ulf nodded and as they got to the edge, he saw Drumbr and Oddi standing there, both men with stuff in their hands. Drumbr handed Ulf a small bag and a flask.

"Some food and ale for the road. Should be enough for a few days."

Ulf nodded his thanks and looked at Oddi, confused by what he was holding in his hands. Ragnar's axe, the broken handle replaced by a new one.

"Snorri told me to give this to you. It belonged to your father and was given to Ragnar after that battle."

Ulf took the axe, Skull-Splitter, from Oddi, surprised at how heavy it was. Or perhaps because he was still weak from the fight. He wanted to say something but struggled to find the words.

"What will you do now?" Drumbr asked.

Ulf looked at the path ahead of him and took a deep breath. "There is one thing I need to do, and then..." He looked towards the bay and saw Snorri standing outside the hall, staring at him. "And then I don't know." He smiled, feeling oddly calmed by that.

The others smiled back. "Take care, Ulf, may the gods protect you on your journey," Oddi said.

"Aye, one day we'll see each other in Valhalla and we'll share our tales, but until then, farewell, my friend." Thorbjorn cuffed away a tear.

Drumbr had no words and just grabbed Ulf in a bear hug. When he let go, Ulf saw the tears in his eyes. Without a further word, the three of them turned and walked back to the hall. Ulf watched them go before he turned and went on his way. He had one more place to visit.

*

It took Ulf a day to get to his destination, and when he finally arrived, he just stood there. He wasn't sure what he expected, but thought he would feel something as he stared at the remains of his uncle's farm. Ulf had not been here since Griml's attack and was surprised at how little remained of the longhouse they had lived in. He remembered the old forest godi had told him they found the house burnt, his and his uncle's bodies outside.

In his mind, Ulf pictured the place as he remembered it. The house standing small and proud. Olaf had built it himself. Ulf had been small, but he still tried to help. Beside the house was their small field where they had grown all the things they needed. Barley, oats and some vegetables. On the other side had been a pen for their few cows and sheep. Ulf saw his uncle Olaf working in the field, as he had done most days before teaching him to fight. His aunt Brynhild standing in the doorway, her arms crossed and smiling as she watched her daughters running around with their large hound.

Ulf took a deep breath, feeling the knot in his throat. All that was gone. All that remained were a few of the timber posts which had supported the roof and the small fence they had built around the farm. Plants and grass sprouted from the ashes of the longhouse, and Ulf imagined that in a few winters there would be no sign that a farm had been here once. He had hated being here as he grew up, but now he would give anything to have it all back. A small burial mound sat beside the remnants of the house. The old godi had told him that Vidar buried the bodies of his uncle and cousins. Brynhild's body had been burnt with the house. He made his way to the mound, feeling the heaviness in his chest. When he reached it, he dropped to his knees and stared at it. Not knowing what else to do, Ulf dug a hole in the mound with his hands. He opened the bundle Snorri had given him and took out the axe head, still covered in Griml's blood. He was glad no one had cleaned it as he placed the axe head in the hole and covered it up again.

"It's done, uncle. I have avenged your deaths. I killed Griml with your axe and now I have no need for it, so you can have it back. May it serve you well in Valhalla." A small breeze picked up and blew over him. Ulf smiled as he thought it was his family thanking him. He sat for a while longer, lost in the memories of his family, before deciding it was time to go. As he stood up, Ulf sensed a presence behind him. He grabbed Skull-Splitter and turned to face the threat, but who he saw took the breath from his lungs.

"I knew I'd find you here, although I thought you'd come sooner," Skadi said, smiling at him.

Ulf held the axe in front of him with both hands. "What do you want?"

The volva smiled, a warm smile he had never seen from her before, but it reminded him of her daughter, Hulda. Because of that, he lowered the axe and stood straight. "Not to kill you."

"How did you know I'd be here? I only knew I was coming here this morning." Ulf frowned.

The volva, still smiling, looked to the sky. "The gods told me."

Ulf sighed and guessed he shouldn't have expected a different answer. "So, you got what you wanted?"

"And what did I want?"

"To avenge your daughter?"

Skadi shrugged. "The boy who killed her still lives, but Thorgilsstad is ruined." She looked up again. "Sometimes the gods don't give you what you want, or what you need."

Ulf frowned at her. "So you're not satisfied?"

"I am. Thorvald still lives, but Thorgils won't for much longer. The one who killed her still lives, but the man who took her will be dead soon."

Ulf thought about it and nodded. He realised he didn't really care if Thorgils lived or died. He looked at the volva again. Her face was cleaner and her hair tidier, although it was still covered in twigs and small bones. Even her smell was less repugnant. "So, now what?"

Skadi smiled, revealing her blackened gums. "I don't know, young wolf. I go where the gods tell me." She studied him with her mismatched eyes. "What about you? Where will you go now?"

Ulf looked to the sky, trying to find the answer there like Snorri had done so many times in Francia. "I think I'll also leave that up to the gods. They brought me my vengeance, so why not trust them with my fate?"

"Wise choice, young wolf. I pray you will not regret that. Until we meet again." She turned to walk away, but there was something Ulf needed to know.

"Wait."

The volva stopped and looked at Ulf.

"Is Snorri really my brother?"

The volva nodded. "He is." But she said no more.

"Is Lady Ingibjorg really your sister?"

This time the smile disappeared from Skadi's face. "She is, but that is not a story I want to tell."

Ulf nodded. He understood. "One more thing," he said as Skadi started walking away again. She turned and looked at him. "How do you keep appearing everywhere?"

The volva laughed. "It's simple, Ulf. I walk."

Ulf frowned, not expecting an answer so simple, and watched as Skadi walked off, laughing. He shook his head and looked at the sky again as a raven flew overhead, heading south towards the sea. Ulf watched it and shrugged.

"Then I'll do the same." He smiled. "I'll just walk." Ulf collected his things and followed the raven as it guided him towards his next journey.

The end

Glossary of Terms

Asgard: the home of the Norse Gods

Bóndi (pl. Bændr): a farmer, a husband

Brynja: a coat of chainmail worn by warriors

Drumbr: a byname meaning thick, fat or podgy

Einherjar: Odin's army of fallen warriors who live in Valhalla, they will fight for him during Ragnarök

Fafnir: legendary dragon that guards a great treasure

Fenrir: giant wolf and offspring of Loki

Gjallarhorn: the horn of Heimdall which he sounds to warn the gods of the coming of Ragnarök

Gleipnir: the magical chain forged by the dwarves of Svartalfheim and used to bind Fenrir

Godi (pl. Godar): a chieftain, a priest

Gunwale: the top edge of the hull of a ship or boat

Heidrun: a goat in Valhalla which produces the mead the Einherjar drink

Hel: the underworld where most of the dead dwell, also the name of the ruler of Hel and offspring of Loki

Hirdmen: a retinue of household warriors

Holmgang: a duel between two men

Hrafnagud: Raven-god, a byname for Odin

Huginn and Muninn: Odin's ravens, they inform him of events in Midgard

Jarl: an earl, a Norse or Danish chief

Jerkin: a thick leather vest worn by warriors

Jól: a winter solstice festival

Jörmungandr: giant serpent that encircles the world's oceans while biting its own tall and offspring of Loki

Knörr: a cargo ship, shorter and wider with a deeper hull than snekkjas

Midgard: the world inhabited by humans

Mjöllnir: Thor's hammer

Niflheim: the world of primordial darkness, cold, mist, and ice

Norns: the three sisters who control the fate of men and women

Olgr: a hawk, a byname for Odin

Ormstunga: means serpent's tongue, from *orm* (serpent) and *stunga* (tongue)

Prow: the front end of a ship or boat

Ragi: a byname meaning craven or cowardly, from the old Norse *ragr*

Sax-knife: a large single-edged knife

Skald: a poet, a storyteller

Skjaldborg: a shield wall

Snekkja: a viking longship used for battle

Stern: the back end of a ship or boat

Suðrikaupstefna: Southern Market, from the words *suðr* (south) and *kaupstefna* (market)

Surtr: a fire giant who leads his kin into battle against the gods of Asgard during Ragnarök

Svartalfheim: the world inhabited by the dwarves

Tafl: a strategy board game

Thrall: a slave

Valhalla: Odin's hall where those who died in battle reside

Valknut: a symbol made of three interlocked triangles, also known as Odin's Knot. It is thought to represent the transition from life to death, Odin, and the power to bind and unbind

Valkyrie: Odin's female warriors, they choose who goes to Valhalla

Viss: wise

The Gods

Æsir: the most prominent of the two tribes of gods

Odin: chieftain of the gods, also the god of war, poetry, wisdom and magic

Frigg: Odin's wife

Thor: god of thunder and fertility

Tyr: god of war, law and justice

Vidar: god of vengeance, also known as the silent god, will avenge Odin at Ragnarök

Vali: god of vengeance, avenged his brother Baldr's death

Baldr: son of Odin and Frigg, god of the summer sun and light

Loki: the trickster god

Heimdall: the ever-vigilant guardian of Asgard

Ran: mother of waves, those who die at sea reside in her hall

Vanir: the second tribe of gods

Njörd: god of wealth, fertility and the sea

Frey: god of ecological fertility, wealth and peace, son of Njörd

Freya: goddess of love, fertility

Ullr: god of hunting and winter

Hodr: son of Odin and blind. Is mainly known for killing Baldr

Author's note

When I first sat down to write Son of Anger, I had no idea where this journey was going to take me. Writing was something that had always been a dream of mine, but one I thought I would never accomplish. But this has not been a journey that I made on my own. My incredible wife, Anna, has been by my side every step of the way, helping where she could, even if it was to criticise my characters. And my family, who although are scattered all over the globe, have been immensely supportive as well, even my young nephews who keep asking me to write books they can actually read. Also, my amazing editor Victoria Hughes-Williams who helped me grow as a writer with her advice and feedback. But most important of all are you, the readers. This is, without a doubt, not something I could have done without you. You have been the strong shield wall behind me that gave me the courage to push forward with this journey, and for that, I thank you enormously.

As for Ulf Bear-Slayer Bjørnson. He has finally avenged his family, but his journey is far from complete. I am, however, going to take a short break from his story as I work on a new series, something I hope you will all enjoy. But Ulf will return to continue his tale and spread his name throughout the Viking world and beyond.

To my wife, my family, and friends. And to you, readers. Skol!

BY DONOVAN COOK

Ormstunga Saga
Son of Anger
Raid of the Wolves
Chaos of the Gods

Printed in Great Britain
by Amazon